THE AUTHOR: Naoya Shiga was born in 1883, the son of a success-ful businessman, and received his early education at the Peers' School. In 1906 he entered the University of Tokyo, first studying English, then Japanese literature, but he was never a dedicated student and withdrew in 1910. With a group of friends, many of whom were destined to become famous, he started a journal called *Shirakaba*, which did much to familiarize educated Japanese with contemporary Western art, and through the publication of short pieces in this magazine he established a reputation as a promising new writer. Most of his one full-length novel, *A Dark Night's Passing* (*Anya kōro*), was published in the early 1920s, but it was not completed until 1937. From then until his death in 1971 he wrote very little; despite his small output, however, Shiga remains to this day one of the most revered of modern Japanese writers.

Naoya Shiga

A Dark Night's Passing

Translated by
EDWIN McCLELLAN

KODANSHA INTERNATIONAL
Tokyo • New York • London

UNESCO COLLECTION OF REPRESENTATIVE WORKS
JAPANESE SERIES
*This book
has been accepted
in the Japanese Series
of the Translations Collection
of the United Nations
Educational, Scientific and Cultural Organization*
(UNESCO)

Published by
Kodansha International Ltd.,
17-14, Otowa 1-chome, Bunkyo-ku, Tokyo 112
and
Kodansha America, Inc.,
114 Fifth Avenue, New York, New York 10011.
English translation © UNESCO 1976.
All rights reserved. Printed in Japan.
LCC 76-9351
ISBN 0-87011-362-3
ISBN 4-7700-0691-8 (in Japan)
First edition, 1976
First paperback edition, 1979
97 98 99 00 12 11 10 9

*This translation is
for my friend Jun Etō*

TRANSLATOR'S PREFACE

Shiga Naoya—from here on I shall observe the Japanese custom of putting the surname first—was born in 1883 in the provincial town of Ishinomaki in Miyagi Prefecture, where his father, then an employee of the Dai-ichi Bank, had been posted. Both his father's and mother's families were of the *shizoku* class, i.e., ex-samurai. This fact in itself is of little significance, however, for after the Restoration of 1868, membership in that class simply meant that one was of gentle birth, more or less, and it did not necessarily guarantee one a place in the modern middle class. What is of more interest to us is that both Shiga's grandfather and father happened to be very capable businessmen, and that by the time he was ten, his family were unquestionably of the upper bourgeoisie.

Shiga received his early education at Gakushūin, or the Peers' School, which was a school reserved for sons of the nobility and of the more successful bureaucrats and businessmen. He was there from 1889 until 1906, when he entered the University of Tokyo. He remained an officially registered student at the university until 1910, at first in the English literature department, then later in the Japanese literature department. He was never a dedicated student, and it would seem that his formal withdrawal from that illustrious institution in 1910 was long overdue.

Shiga had by then become an aspiring writer. In the year that he withdrew from the university, he and a group of friends who had also been at Gakushūin began a journal called *Shirakaba* ("white birch"), which was to continue until 1923, although Shiga's active participation in the group lasted only a couple of years. This coterie—it was not entirely literary—included a number of people besides Shiga who were to become famous, such as Mushakōji Saneatsu, Arishima Takeo, Arishima Ikuma, and Satomi Ton. They could not have constituted a "school" in any meaningful sense, for in looking at the works of Shiga, Mushakōji, and Arishima Takeo, for example, one

7

would be hard put to it to find much that they had in common as writers. What they shared was little more than their upper-class background, an intelligent interest in the arts (their journal did much to familiarize the literate Japanese with the works of Cézanne, Matisse, Gauguin, van Gogh, Rodin, etc.), and a more optimistic regard for their own individuality than might have been possible for their fellow countrymen born some years before them or into less well-placed families. At any rate, it was through the publication of shorter pieces in *Shirakaba* that Shiga quickly established his reputation as a young writer of promise; and by 1913 his standing was such that Natsume Sōseki (1867–1916), then the literary editor of *Asahi Newspaper* and a writer of the utmost distinction, asked him if he would care to write a novel for the newspaper, to be published serially. It was to follow Sōseki's own *Kokoro* ("the heart") which was then being serialized. Shiga had started on an autobiographical novel, tentatively entitled *Tokitō Kensaku*, in the previous year, and thinking that he would give that to Sōseki when he finished it, he accepted the invitation. But for whatever reason he was unable to progress very far with it, and in 1914 he reluctantly told Sōseki he could not keep his promise. "Tokitō Kensaku" was the name he would later give to the hero of *A Dark Night's Passing (Anya kōro* in the original).

In 1914 Shiga married Kadenokōji Sadako. She was of an old and aristocratic family, and a cousin of Shiga's friend, Mushakōji. Theirs was a lasting marriage, and on the whole a harmonious one. Of the seven children that were born to them, two died shortly after birth: their first child, a daughter, in 1916, and their first son in 1919.

Shiga's marriage to Sadako was opposed by his father, with whom he had been on very bad terms for some years. Their quarrel over the marriage led Shiga to renounce his right of inheritance; and later, when his first child died, his father retaliated by refusing to allow her to be buried in the family plot. They were reconciled in 1917, however, and the reconciliation lasted until the father's death in 1929.

Shiga's mother had died when he was twelve, and his father had remarried very soon after her death. In a short autobiographical piece he published in 1912, *Haha no shi to atarashii haha* ("mother's death and the new mother"), Shiga writes, "Two months after mother died, they started looking for her successor." But he was very fond of his stepmother, and it is as likely as not that the estrangement between father and son began later, when it became clear that Shiga was not going to be the son and heir that a successful businessman father would have wished for.

The first half of *A Dark Night's Passing* appeared in 1921. A substantial part of the second half then appeared in 1922 and 1923. It was left unfinished until 1937, when at last the concluding chapters were published. From then until his death in 1971, Shiga wrote surprisingly little. Indeed, he was never prolific (between 1914 and 1917, for example, he published nothing), and for a Japanese writer who lived so long, his output was remarkably small. Yet he remains to this day one of the most revered of modern Japanese writers.

Even if Shiga had not written his one full-length novel, he would have been remembered for his short stories, the best of which are considered minor classics,[1] his earlier autobiographical pieces such as *Haha no shi to atarashii haha* and *Wakai* ("reconciliation," 1917), and his lyrical, contemplative near-essays such as *Kinosaki ni te* ("at Kinosaki," 1917)[2] and *Takibi* ("bonfire," 1920), which again have become minor classics. But it is after all his novel that has been responsible for his immense reputation in Japan. *A Dark Night's Passing* of course has its detractors, who are sometimes offended by the extravagant praise it has received from its less restrained admirers. But whatever may be our opinion of the justice of its reputation, the fact remains that its stature among modern Japanese novels is virtually unequalled.

A Dark Night's Passing belongs, somewhat uncertainly, to that genre known in Japan as the *watakushi shōsetsu*—the "I", or the "private," or more loosely, the "autobiographical" novel—which reached the height of its popularity in the 1920's. I say "uncertainly" because

---

[1]See, for example, "Han's Crime," translated by Ivan Morris, in *Modern Japanese Literature: An Anthology*, edited by Donald Keene, New York, 1956; "Seibei's Gourds," translated by Ivan Morris, in *Modern Japanese Stories: An Anthology*, edited by Ivan Morris, Rutland, Vermont, and Tokyo, 1962; and "The Razor," translated by Francis Mathy, in *Monumenta Nipponica*, vol. XIII, no. 3–4.

[2]See Edward Seidensticker's translation in *Modern Japanese Literature*, *op. cit.*

A Dark Night's Passing contains a far greater element of fiction than other, more typical examples of the genre. Shiga's paternity was never in question (except perhaps in his own imagination), and there never seems to have been a family skeleton of the sort he describes in the novel. There was an older son, but he died before Shiga was born. There was no counterpart in real life to Oei, the woman who brings Tokitō Kensaku up. Indeed, most of the pivotal events in the novel are of Shiga's imagining, and if it is autobiographical, it is so in the sense that it is a fictional realization of the author's fantasies, fears, and aspirations.

But whether we call it a *watakushi shōsetsu* or not, it is certainly an intensely private and self-centered novel. The larger concerns of society have no place in it. The secondary characters exist only so long as they touch the hero's life. The identification of the author with his hero is complete, and the predilections of one are those of the other. And though Shiga drops the use of "I" after the prefatory chapter, its implied presence is obvious throughout.

For those Japanese critics who assume that the "larger," less self-centered world is the proper material for fiction, the "privacy" of *A Dark Night's Passing* has always been the major source of irritation. What they often seem to overlook, however, is that self-centered or not, it is an extraordinarily bold novel for the time and place in which it was written. For against the reality of family and the order and conventions that it represents, Shiga affirms the greater reality of his own sexuality, his own search for love, his own communion with nature and participation in myth, his own fantasies and dreams.

No modern Japanese prose writer before him used the language quite as he did. For him it was a means of expressing what I can only call a profound trust in what he saw and heard and intuitively sensed. In this respect, his is the language of the traditional Japanese poet translated into modern prose. It is not a language that is precise in any intellectual, analytical sense. (He did not have a particularly articulate intelligence, and the weakest passages in the novel are where he tries to describe explicitly his ideas concerning the future of mankind, etc.) Rather, its precision lies in the author's ability to convey with clarity and without adornment his sensuous awareness of the immediacy of nature, of voices and gestures, of his own intuitive responses to them. His prose is not as flowing or as rich as Tanizaki's. It is simpler and tauter, dependent on a much simpler vocabulary, and less explicit; but it is wrought with great care, and its direction is always sure. And if sometimes his sentences, or even paragraphs, seem to stand in austere isolation, it is because he is less concerned with unity and rational transition than with the cumulative effect of separate impressions or memories which are felt by him to have some deep, emotional bond between them.

Despite his fastidiousness and good manners, then, despite the control of his prose, there is something unmistakably primitive about Shiga. His perceptions, it seems to me, were largely those of a superstitious man. Fears concerning one's own paternity, obsessive childhood memories of one's mother, dreams peopled by hobgoblins of sexual desire, the longing for reconciliation with nature—all these had a certainty for him not because he had any academic understanding of their significance (he was not learned enough for that), but because they were very real ghosts that haunted him.

There are three people I should like to thank in particular for their help and encouragement while I worked on this translation: Rachel McClellan, Thomas J. Harper, and Jun Etō.

Edwin McClellan

A Dark Night's
Passing

PROLOGUE
THE HERO'S REMINISCENCES

It was about two months after my mother died in childbirth that I first laid eyes on my grandfather. I was six years old at the time. Until that sudden encounter, I had not even known of his existence.

It was evening, and I was sitting idly outside our front gate. A strange old man came and stood over me. He stooped a little, his eyes were sunken, and there was about him a general air of seediness. I took an instant dislike to him.

Smiling unnaturally he made as if to talk to me. In spite I refused to meet his eyes, and stared at the ground. The turned up mouth, the deeply creased skin around it—everything about him was common. "Go away," I wanted to tell him. I refused to look up. But the old man continued to stand in front of me, until I could not bear his presence any longer. I got up and ran through the gate. The old man called out from behind, "Hey, are you Kensaku?"

I felt as though the words had struck me a blow. I stopped and turned around. I was as wary as before, but from habit perhaps, my head nodded obediently.

"Is your dad home?" he asked. I shook my head. The familiarity of his tone filled me with foreboding.

He walked up to me and put his hand on my head. "You've grown."

I had no idea who this old man was; but already I had the premonition that here was someone closely tied to me by blood. I stood there rigidly, almost suffocating.

The old man said no more, and left.

He appeared again two or three days later, and this time my father introduced him to me as my grandfather.

Then, ten days after that, I was sent off to live with him. His was a small, old house, hidden deep in a side street near Ogyōmatsu in Negishi. And here with my grandfather lived a woman in her early twenties named Oei.

My new surroundings were quite different from what I had been used to. Now everything smelled of poverty and vulgarity. And I could not but wonder resentfully why of the children in my family I alone should have been made to come and live with this common old man. But it did not occur to me to ask anyone why I had been so unfairly treated, for since my infancy I had come to expect injustice. Of course there were times when I would become vaguely aware that for the rest of my life I would continue to encounter such unfairness; and then I would feel forlorn, and miss my mother who had died two months before.

One could not say that in the years I lived with my parents, my father was ever positively, openly cruel to me. But always, always he was cold. I suppose I had come to take his coldness so much for granted that any other kind of relationship between father and son was inconceivable to me. I did not think to ask myself whether his behavior toward his other children was in any way different; and I felt no particular sadness that he should treat me as he did.

My mother was inclined to be harsh with me, and scolded me at every turn. True, I was a willful and disobedient child. But often, it would seem, she would punish only me for doing exactly what my brother, too, was doing. I loved my mother deeply, nevertheless.

* * *

I must have been four or five at the time. It was an autumn evening. Seeing that everyone was busy preparing dinner, I crept out of the house, and using a ladder that had been left leaning against the servants' lavatory, I climbed to the top of the main roof. I crawled along the ridge to the large end tile and straddled it. I felt suddenly joyful, and began to sing at the top of my voice. Never had I sat in such a high place. The persimmon tree, so much taller than I before, now was beneath me.

The western sky glowed with the setting sun. And there were crows, flying about restlessly . . .

"Kensaku . . . Kensaku . . ." It was my mother, calling me in a voice that was eerily soft and caressing. "Stay where you are, understand? Don't move, please. Yamamoto will be with you in a minute. Please listen to me, and be absolutely still."

The skin around her eyes seemed taut as she looked at me. And from the unnatural gentleness of her manner I knew that something quite out of the ordinary was happening. I decided that I would try to go down before Yamamoto could get to me. Slowly I pushed myself back a little along the ridge. "Oh, no!" My mother looked as though she was about to cry. "Don't move, please, Kensaku. Be a good boy and listen to me!"

It was her eyes, staring with a strange intentness into mine, that forced me to be still.

In a little while Yamamoto and another manservant reached me, and guided me down gingerly.

Of course my mother gave me a severe beating. Then from the strain she burst out crying.

My memory of this incident gained new clarity when she was gone. For years after, my eyes would fill with tears whenever I remembered it. And I have thought to myself: whatever else, my mother at least loved me very much.

* * *

I am certain this happened at about the same time, though what came before or after, I cannot remember.

I was lying alone on the floor of the morning room, daydreaming. The door opened, and my father walked in. He must have just come home. Saying nothing he walked past me to the cupboard and took out of his sleeve pocket a small package which he placed on top of it. I lay still as he walked out of the room, my eyes fixed on the package. I knew it had come from a cake shop.

A moment later he was back. This time he opened the cupboard door and carefully put away the package. Again without a word he left the room.

Darkness seemed suddenly to fall around me as I lay there brooding over the slight. And by the time my mother came into the adjoining room to put away my father's street clothes, I was in a very black mood, desperately needing an outlet for the intense resentment that had built up inside me.

"Mama, I want some cake!"

"What are you saying!" she said angrily. Indeed, I had only a few minutes before been given my afternoon snack.

"Come on, give me some."

She refused to listen to me. She put away the clothes in the wardrobe, then turned to leave. I got up and stood in front of her. "Please, mama!" Still saying nothing she reached for my cheek and gave it a quick, hard pinch. In fury I slapped her offending hand.

"You've already had your snack, haven't you?" she said, glaring at me.

Now more blatant, I began pleading for the cake my father had brought home.

"Certainly not!" she said. "Stop this nonsense at once!" "I want some," I said stubbornly, as though I was demanding only what was rightfully mine.

I really did not want the cake. What I wanted was to cry my heart out, or to be shouted at, or to be beaten—it didn't matter which, so long as something was done to soothe my nerves, to get rid of the terrible feeling of oppression.

My mother pushed me aside and began to walk away. I grabbed her sash from behind and pulled her hard toward me. She lost her balance and would have fallen if the sliding door had not been within her reach. The door came out of the groove.

She was now truly furious. She grabbed my wrist and dragged me to the cupboard. She got out a large chunk of bean cake, and with her free arm holding my head tight against her side, began to force the jellylike cake into my mouth. I could feel against my tongue thin strips of the sweet stuff oozing through the gaps in my clenched baby teeth. I was so frightened I could not even cry. The excitement was too much for my mother, and she burst into tears. I, too, after a while, began to cry.

* * *

Everything was slovenly in my grandfather's house in Negishi. Every morning, when he got up, he would amble over to the neighborhood public bath with a toothpick dangling out of the corner of his mouth; and on returning would go straight to the breakfast table still in his night clothes.

People of all sorts dropped in. Those who came on card-playing nights were particularly odd. There was a university student amongst the group, I remember; and a secondhand dealer, and a novelist (was he really?), and a woman in her fifties with what I thought was a widowlike air about her, whom everyone called Mrs. Yamakami. This woman always brought along a small, black leather bag, like a doctor's, which contained without fail, I was told, a lot of small change, a new pack of cards, and a pair of gold-rimmed glasses. I learned later that this woman was indeed not a widow at the time but the wife of some aged professor of history. Her nephew had apparently once lived with Oei, and through this connection she had come to know my grandfather. She loved her hobby, which she kept a secret from her husband. Some twenty years afterward Oei told me that this woman's nephew drank a great deal, was always smoking cigars, and was, in fact, an unmitigated debauchee. Three years before my move to the house in Negishi he had, for no clear reason, put an end to his dissolute life.

Mrs. Yamakami usually departed at about ten o'clock, and in her place would appear a young vaudeville entertainer. This fellow never spoke anything but the Osaka dialect, though it was obvious he was a Tokyo man born and bred.

Oei never took part in the game, but was for practical reasons interested in how my grandfather was doing, and would sometimes get very irritated at the way he was playing and make comments. Whenever she did this, the entertainer would say something amusing at her expense in his vulgar way and make the others laugh.

I have often wondered since why my grandfather lived the way he did. He was getting a regular allowance from my father, enough to keep him in modest comfort. Yet he would allow a secondhand dealer to hold auctions at his house for a commission, or buy and sell bric-a-brac himself. Perhaps he simply liked doing such things, profit or no profit.

Oei was not at all a pretty person normally. But sometimes, such as when she put on heavy make-up after her evening bath, she seemed very beautiful to me. And when she was feeling particularly gay, she would start singing popular songs quietly after she had had a drink or two with my grandfather. Then suddenly she would pick me up and put me on her knees and hold me tight in her strong, thick arms. I would feel such ecstasy then, I hardly cared that I could not breathe.

I never did manage to become fond of my grandfather. Indeed, my dislike for him grew as the days went by. But Oei was different—I came to like her more and more.

* * *

One Sunday—or it might have been some national holiday—half a year or so after my move to Negishi, my grandfather and I visited my father's house in Hongō. My elder brother was out on a picnic with one of the servants, and only my father and my baby sister Sakiko, not yet a year old, were at home.

My father seemed in an unusually friendly mood as he received us in his study. He spoke to me kindly. I think now that something good must have happened that day to make him so cheerful, and that he was being charming to me out of mere caprice. But I was quite unsuspecting then. I felt myself drawn to him, and when my grandfather left for the morning room, I remained.

He said suddenly, "Would you like to wrestle with me, Kensaku?"

I merely nodded. But my excitement and pleasure must have been pitifully apparent.

He remained seated. "Come on, then," he said, and held out his hands.

I jumped up and rushed at him. He pushed me away easily. "Say, you're not bad."

I was elated. I braced myself, lowered my head, then charged again.

All I wanted was to hear him say what a brave and strong boy I was. I don't think I cared very much whether I won or lost.

I had never played like this with him before. I was taut with excitement. It was as though my entire body had gained a new strength from such unexpected pleasure, and no matter how often he pushed me away, I kept on hurling myself at him. But not once did he let down his defence for me.

Once more I charged. "How about this," he said, and shoved me back hard. Surprised, I fell backward on the floor with a big thump. I lay still for a moment, stunned breathless. Then I felt a touch of anger. I jumped up and faced him, readying myself for another charge. But the man I now saw seemed suddenly to have changed.

"It's all over," he said, smiling in a strange, tight way.

"Not yet," I said.

"So you won't give up, eh?"

"Of course not."

Very quickly I found myself on the floor again, this time pinned down under his knee. "Now will you give up?" he said. I said nothing. "All right, then." He undid his sash, then with one end tied my hands behind my back and with the other tied my ankles. I couldn't move at all. "Say you've had enough and I'll untie you."

I looked at him coldly. The warmth that I had felt toward him only moments before was now all gone.

The activity had exhausted him, and his face was pale and strained. He was breathing heavily. As he turned away to face his desk, I stared at his heaving shoulders with hate. Soon the outline of his back became blurred; then I burst out crying.

He turned around quickly in surprise. "All right, all right. Silly fellow, all you had to do was ask me to untie you."

But even when my hands and legs were free, I continued to lie there on the floor, crying. "It doesn't take much to make you cry, does it?" he said, and pulled me up onto my feet. "All right, that's enough, go and get something nice to eat."

I began to be ashamed of having shown such open animosity. Yet I could not bring myself to trust him entirely.

My grandfather and one of the maids came in to see what was going on. My father gave an embarrassed laugh and started to explain. When the explanation was over my grandfather laughed loudest of all. He gave my head a light, playful smack and said, "Silly boy."

PART I

1

Tokitō Kensaku had felt a mounting dislike for Sakaguchi for some time now; and this story of his that he had just finished reading proved conclusively that he had been right. Sakaguchi's story had left a nasty taste in his mouth, true; but at the same time there was some satisfaction, a sense of completion, in being able to feel so definite about the fellow. He threw the magazine toward the foot of his bed—he somehow didn't want it near his pillow—and put out the light. It was close to three o'clock in the morning.

Despite the deep fatigue he felt both in his mind and body, sleep would not come readily. He was too tense, he supposed, and thought he would read something light to unwind. But, alas, books of the sort he had in mind were all in Oei's room. Dare he wake Oei at this time of the night? Well, why not, he told himself, and putting the light on again he went downstairs. He opened her door slightly. "I've come to borrow one of your books," he said tentatively, then with more assurance, "Is *Tsukahara Bokuden* in the cupboard?"

Oei put on the light. "It's either in the alcove or on top of the tea cabinet. Can't you go to sleep?"

"No. I thought the book might help."

He found the historical romance—it was a small paperback—on the cabinet. "See you tomorrow," he said. The room went dark again as he was closing the door. "Sleep well," he heard her say.

Kensaku continued to read the harmless little book until he could hear the sparrows singing cheerfully outside. There was a softness in their song, as if it had been moistened by the morning dew.

The next day was a still autumn day, dark with overhanging clouds. It was about one in the afternoon when Oei awakened him. "Mr. Tatsuoka and Mr. Sakaguchi are here." He said nothing. The thought of having to see Sakaguchi was too much for his befuddled mind. Even a less unwelcome prospect, indeed, would hardly have elicited a response from him at that moment.

"Do get up. I'll show them to the living room in the meantime."

She was leaving the room when he said, "I'll see Tatsuoka but not Sakaguchi. Tell Sakaguchi I can't see him."

She looked around quickly, her hand on the door. "Do you really mean that?"

"All right. Show them both in. I'll be down in a minute."

The story by Sakaguchi that Kensaku had found so unpleasant was about a man who has an affair with his fifteen-year-old housemaid; the housemaid becomes pregnant and is sent to an abortionist. Kensaku thought it most likely that it was based on the author's own experience. The facts described were in themselves unpleasant enough; but what he really disliked was the obvious flippancy of the author. He could have forgiven the facts if he had been allowed to feel some sympathy for the protagonist; but the flippancy, the superciliousness of the protagonist (and of Sakaguchi) left no room for such sympathy.

He was angered, too, by the way the protagonist's friend, who he was certain had been modeled on himself, was described.

The protagonist knows that the girl is too childlike to be thought of as a likely mistress for him. Taking advantage of this, he amuses himself by treating her rather shabbily in the presence of his unsuspecting friend. The friend, a naive and trusting sort, secretly pities the girl. His sympathy is perceived by the shrewd and sardonic protagonist, who finds himself resenting it somewhat; and he would then taunt her till she cried, much to his friend's discomfort.

In truth Kensaku had been fond of the maid. She was an innocent and good-hearted girl, and at times he had felt quite drawn to her. But he had suspected, too, that there was something going on between her and Sakaguchi. And so to see the friend described as an unknowing observer, harboring what amounted to a secret longing for the girl, galled him.

The friend's feelings are wholly transparent to the protagonist, who watches him with scorn, hardly able to suppress the inclination to laugh out loud. What smugness, Kensaku thought, what vanity!

He wondered why Sakaguchi had come to his house that day. A week had passed since the appearance of the magazine. Had he expected to get an angry letter from Kensaku, and when it didn't come, become uneasy and begun to feel threatened by the uncanny silence? Or had he come to play the stage villain, gloating over his own nastiness? He had better be careful, Kensaku thought, or I'll give him a piece of my mind. Thus his fancies about Sakaguchi became less and less restrained; and by the time he had finished washing his face, he was in a state of considerable agitation.

As he dressed in the morning room he could hear the two men talking. Their voices sounded remarkably relaxed. His own state of mind now began to seem a little incongruous; and he could not help resenting the indignity of being so belligerent when everyone else was so full of cheer.

Tatsuoka looked at him apologetically as he entered the living room. "I hear you were up until very late last night."

"I was about to get up when you came anyway."

Sakaguchi was nonchalantly reading the newspaper that Oei had brought in. Kensaku knew immediately that he had not come with any ulterior purpose. The man led a rather disorganized life, and no doubt he had allowed himself to be dragged along by Tatsuoka for lack of anything better to do. Even so Kensaku had to make sure. "Where did you two get together?" he asked.

"Oh, I picked him up at his house," Tatsuoka said. "By the way, did you see that thing this fellow published recently?" There was contempt, and a touch of the familiarity of friends, in the way he looked at Sakaguchi. Kensaku did not answer. "It's an unpleasant piece of work. Mind you, I could have forgiven that. But do you know, there's a fellow in it who isn't very bright, and I'm the model for this character! I read it yesterday, and I was so mad I went over to his place this morning to give him a good talking-to."

Sakaguchi sat smirking, his eyes still fixed on the newspaper. Tatsuoka went on: "He says most of the story is imagined, but I doubt it. He's just the sort of fellow who'll write about his friends behind their backs."

Even these remarks seemed to have no effect on Sakaguchi. Kensaku wondered what he was really thinking. One thing at least was clear—he was enjoying himself. Why else would he have that smirk on his face? In his characteristic fashion, he was flaunting his superiority.

Tatsuoka had just received his degree in engineering that year, and was hoping to go to France soon to study engine design. Remarks on literary matters from such a man, Sakaguchi probably felt, he could ignore.

"I told him that what I found most irritating of all was his knowingness about other people's feelings. Of course he can be perceptive enough at times. But he doesn't seem to understand that people do change their minds about things from one minute to the next, that they can have conflicting feelings about something at one and the same time. The trouble with Sakaguchi when he writes is that he only sees what he wants to see in others. Anything he doesn't want to see simply doesn't exist for him."

Sakaguchi at last showed annoyance. "All right, that's enough. You're beginning to repeat yourself."

Tatsuoka looked at Kensaku, and tried to hide his tension behind a smile. "I've been going at him like this ever since this morning."

"What a bore he can be," Sakaguchi muttered, as though to himself.

"What did you say?" Tatsuoka said angrily. "So you don't like what I've been saying, eh? Well, let me tell you, you haven't heard half of what you really deserve. I can be a lot more annoying, you know, if I so choose. You like to think you're a pretty naughty fellow, don't you? What a joke! A shoddy little cardboard villain, that's what you really are, however you may think you appear in your stories. Abortion indeed! Tell me, what's so world-shaking about an abortion?"

Tatsuoka had discarded all pretense at friendly banter. Against such vehemence, brought on by his own smugness, Sakaguchi was quite defenseless. Besides, he was no match for Tatsuoka physically, who was not only twice as large but a third-grade black belt in judo. Further resistance was out of the question.

Kensaku, who had earlier wondered how he was going to deal with Sakaguchi, was a little nonplussed to find himself in the role of neutral bystander. What was there left for him to do, when his intended victim had been quite so thoroughly demolished by someone else?

The awkward silence that followed was at last broken by Kensaku.

"Have you booked your passage yet?"

"Yes. The boat leaves on the twelfth of December."

"Have you made all the necessary preparations?"

"Well, there really isn't all that much to do. By the way, I am thinking of buying some ukiyo prints to take with me. Would you mind coming to look at some with me? I couldn't afford anything expensive, but I thought they would make nice presents for all those people who are going to take care of me over there."

"I don't know much about them myself, but of course I'll be glad to come anytime. I'm told they're frightfully expensive these days, and anyone who remembers what they used to cost can hardly bear to pay today's prices. You know, they may be cheaper in Paris."

"That's bad news, I must say. Perhaps I should think of something else."

"Why not something like that nice decorated paper you can get at Haibara's? It's very pretty stuff, the sort of thing you can't find anywhere else, and people with children will most likely prefer that to some mediocre ukiyo prints."

Kensaku looked at the deflated and silent Sakaguchi, and felt a little sorry for him. But he was far from forgiving him. He was by no means convinced that the friend described in the story was Tatsuoka. True, none of the scenes in which the friend appeared were familiar to him. But this did not mean that the friend himself had not been modeled on him. He had the gnawing suspicion that if Sakaguchi could, he would say something like this to Tatsuoka: "I admit that some of the things that the friend witnesses, you yourself witnessed too. But surely you can see how different his character is from yours?"

No doubt about it, Sakaguchi was a slippery customer. If Kensaku were to complain that he had been used as the model for the friend, he would simply be admitting that he and this rather feeble creature had much in common. Indeed, it would have been much easier for him had he been able to claim, as Tatsuoka could, that the scenes described were familiar to him. The friend in the story, alas, was so unadmirable that to complain merely on the basis of similarity of character would leave Kensaku utterly exposed. To Tatsuoka, Sakaguchi would only need to say, "But who in the world would imagine that you had anything in common with him?" But to Kensaku, he might very easily say, "Do you really have such a low opinion of your own character that you should see yourself in him?"

That's why the fellow thinks he can afford to smirk, Kensaku thought, and became more angry than ever. He was being far too suspicious of Sakaguchi. But it was also true that had he not trusted Sakaguchi so much before, he would not have been so extremely bitter.

Ever since his experience with Aiko, he had found it increasingly difficult to trust people. He did not like this tendency in himself, but there was not much he could do about it. And so now he began to doubt even the sincerity of Tatsuoka's anger.

For Tatsuoka was an old-fashioned sort, and had a deep sense of the sanctity of established human relationships. Had he perhaps known all the time that Kensaku was indeed the model for the friend in the story, and pretending otherwise, given Sakaguchi a severe scolding in his presence in the hope that Kensaku, mollified, might continue his association with Sakaguchi? It was like him not to want to see a friendship broken just before he left for France. Why else would he have gone out of his way to bring Sakaguchi to his house that morning, and then have attacked him with such uncharacteristic vehemence? Tatsuoka admittedly had his share of impulsiveness. But he was a proper man too, and Kensaku found it difficult to believe that he would so blatantly air personal grievances in the presence of a third person unless he had some ulterior reason for doing so.

2

The street was muddy and reminded one of a shanty town. Even the bright lights suggested cheapness rather than gaiety. From both sides of the street women, decked out in brilliantly colored clothes which the more sensitive among the visitors might have found sickeningly gaudy, shouted to the men as they passed by. There was an uncertain shrillness in these women's cries, as if they themselves did not know whether they were begging for mercy or hurling insults.

Tatsuoka and Kensaku walked quickly side by side down the middle of the street, overcome by the oppressive atmosphere. Yet Tatsuoka was appreciative enough. "There are plenty of good-looking ones around, aren't there?" he once said in an undertone.

They and Sakaguchi had come out of Kensaku's house in Akasaka at about four that afternoon. Sakaguchi, still resentful, had wanted to leave them, but Tatsuoka would not let him go. He thought, no doubt, that he had been too harsh with Sakaguchi, and wanted a chance to make amends before they parted. And so the three had gone together to Haibara's in Nihonbashi and from there to a restaurant in Kiharadana. Kensaku drank little, for he was not much of a drinker; but by the time they had finished, the other two were fairly drunk.

It was just as they were coming out of the restaurant that Tatsuoka had suddenly suggested visiting the Yoshiwara quarter. All he wanted to do, he said, was to see it before he went abroad. "It's all right, isn't it?" he had said to Kensaku in a very tentative tone. "After all, it's only to look at the place, nothing more." Kensaku had tried to appear off-hand and noncommittal. The truth of the matter was that he himself had never set foot in such a place, and Tatsuoka's suggestion confused him. It was not that he was against the idea; indeed, he found it quite intriguing. He had simply been caught unawares, and his instinctive response had been to feign indifference.

Kensaku and Tatsuoka now found themselves on Nakanochō, the street with the many telegraph poles. They stood and waited for Sakaguchi, whom they could see coming toward them at a snail's pace, swaying like a stage drunk. He kept very close to the houses, and at regular intervals would lean against a doorway to engage in witty repartee with some female.

"Hurry up, can't you!" Tatsuoka shouted. "It's going to rain any minute!"

Sakaguchi showed no visible sign of having heard. Kensaku looked up at the sky and saw black clouds hanging heavily over the high rooftops. When at last Sakaguchi joined them, Tatsuoka said, "We're going home now. Do you want to hang around here, or do you want to come with us?" Sakaguchi, muttering discontentedly, walked with them in the direction of the gateway.

Before they were out of the quarter, large drops of rain began to fall. Feeling rather tired, the three agreed to stop and rest at one of the teahouses that lined the street on either side. Each had a large paper lantern hanging outside the door, with the name of the establishment written in bold strokes. They chose one at random, one that called itself Nishimidori. The madam, a skinny woman in her forties with sparse eyebrows, was standing outside, examining the sky. She must have been cold, for her large kimono sleeves were folded close over her chest. "Do come in," she said, and led the three up some Western-style stairs which still smelled strongly of varnish, and into the main upstairs room. The woodwork in the room was brand new, almost white, and reflected with unbearable harshness the garish light of the gas lamp. Incongruously a soiled horizontal landscape, claiming to be by Bunchō, hung in the shallow alcove. The Western-style stairs smelling of varnish, and now this tastelessly appointed room shouting with newness—how different, Kensaku thought, from the Nakanochō always depicted on the kabuki stage. Hardly in the mood to relax, Kensaku leaned back against the pillar by the alcove, drew up his legs that ached to the bone from all the walking, and clasped his hands around them.

The madam left and in her place appeared the maid with the tea things. Very large she was, with small eyes, not at all unlike an elephant.

"Do you happen to know if Koine is free?" said Sakaguchi with an accustomed air.

"I'll call her and see, if you like. But it is a bit late. Do you know her?"

"No," said Sakaguchi with perfect aplomb.

The maid, an honest and simple woman by the look of her, was a little disconcerted. Was the gentleman pulling her leg or not? "I'll go and see," she said finally and went downstairs.

Try as they might, neither Kensaku nor Tatsuoka could feel at ease in the strange surroundings. As if to shake off his own uneasiness, Tatsuoka took a cigarette from the tea table, quickly lit it, and stood up with a determined air. He opened the door on the street side and stepped out onto the verandah. There he opened noisily the ill-fitting outer glass door and gazed at the street scene below. Kensaku could now hear the rain falling steadily and footsteps hurrying along the puddly street. "They do run daintily, don't they?" said Tatsuoka.

The maid came in to report that the geisha Sakaguchi had asked for was busy but that another would be coming in her place.

She turned out to be a very young geisha; and not very blasé, for she blushed in consternation at the sight of three boorish-looking fellows sitting glumly in the room. But she collected herself quickly enough and bowed gravely, showing the back of her elegant neck. Kensaku thought she was a rather beautiful woman, and wondered why Sakaguchi was looking at her with such marked indifference. After all, he was presumably more at home in these situations than either of his two companions, in whom a certain amount of ungraciousness could be excused. But it was Sakaguchi who in the end broke the uncomfortable silence by asking her the standard questions. What geisha house was she from? What was her name? Her name, she said, was Tokiko.

They were soon joined by an apprentice dancer, a cheerful but slightly common girl with a flat, round nose. Her name, Yutaka, struck Kensaku as appropriately mannish. The two women retired together to the end of the room and began to tune their instruments— Yutaka her hand drum, Tokiko her samisen.

Tokiko was a tall, thin woman. Even when she was seated, she somehow suggested a straight line. Her movements, her gestures, almost everything about her was linear. Yet for all that she had her own peculiar kind of nimbleness and femininity.

"Let's do something else," Sakaguchi said unceremoniously as Yutaka's first dance came to an end. Kensaku looked at Yutaka: her dancing had been quite awful, but surely there was no reason to be quite so unkind about it, to be so blatantly anxious to see no more of it. But to his surprise Yutaka seemed to welcome Sakaguchi's suggestion, and rushed downstairs to fetch some cards.

It was past eleven o'clock. Kensaku said, "Well, are we staying or aren't we?" He went to the glass door and looked out. Tatsuoka joined him. "What should we do?" he asked uncertainly. The rain was now pouring down. The street was much quieter than it had been earlier. A car passed by, its strong headlights momentarily turning the rain into glittering streaks of silver.

With some show of hesitation they sat down again to join the others in a game of vingt-et-un. As he dealt the cards, Kensaku turned to Tatsuoka beside him and said, "She looks exactly like Ishimoto's wife sometimes, don't you think?" Tatsuoka scrutinized Tokiko's face. "You're absolutely right," he said.

Tokiko was saying something to Yutaka at the time. She suddenly stopped, looked at Kensaku with an air approaching defiance and said, "You know, you look exactly like someone I took a fancy to years ago."

The retort took Kensaku by surprise, and he fell into a confused silence. Perhaps to save him from further embarrassment she turned to Sakaguchi and said brightly, "And you look exactly like my older brother."

"Trying to please us all, eh?" said Sakaguchi, not at all flattered.

She blushed, then gave a nervous laugh. "But it's true!"

Tatsuoka broke in loudly: "Come on, let's get on with the betting!"

After vingt-et-un they played a game called "secret strategy." This required two equal opposing sides, so they asked the maid with the small eyes to join. The three teammates on either side sat close to one another, their shoulders touching, facing the other three. They would put their hands behind their backs, and communicate the strategy for the next showdown by holding the next person's hand in some particular way. On the word "go" each would adopt one of three postures—"the village headman" or "the fox" or "the hunter." The headman beat the hunter, the hunter beat the fox, and the fox the headman. They changed places from time to time, so that on occasion Kensaku would sit next to Tokiko, his hand touching hers. Once, when the other side was slow to make up their minds, she brought her face close to his and repeated the sign he had already given her. "You did mean this, didn't you?" she said, squeezing his hand.

Throughout the game Kensaku was acutely sensitive to her touch. Whenever she held his hand, he would find himself trying to gauge the pressure with extraordinary wariness. He was equally apprehensive when it was his turn to hold her hand, lest by unwittingly exerting undue pressure he should be thought at all suggestive. Yet for all the apprehension, one part of him wished for some little meaningful sign from her. He was being inconsistent, of course; but given his tenseness at the time and his habitual fastidiousness, the contradiction within him was inevitable.

The next game they played was "passing the coin." The sides were chosen by lot: Tatsuoka, Sakaguchi and the maid on one side, Kensaku, Tokiko and Yutaka on the other.

The leader of one side sat between his two teammates. His hands, both closed, were placed, one on top of the other, on his knees. In one hand was a five sen coin. Several times he would slip the coin from one hand to the other (or pretend to do so), then change the position of his hands, top to bottom, bottom to top, until he thought the other side was sufficiently confused as to which hand held it. He would then place his hands over his companions', and go through the motion of transferring the coin. It was now up to the other side to guess which hands were empty. The object of the game was to point to as many empty hands as possible before you got to the one with the coin in it.

Under the blinding light of the gas lamp Kensaku and the two women sat side by side, their fists placed neatly on their knees—Yutaka's, plump and small like a child's, on gay-colored silk, and Tokiko's, rather large for a woman but shapely and white nonetheless, on austere black silk. Against such a background her hands seemed more beautiful than ever. Kensaku sat rigidly in the middle, providing a sharp contrast with his bony, hairy hands, clenched so tight that they looked all knuckles, and his kimono limp from the day's wear.

Tatsuoka pointed to Tokiko's hands and said to Sakaguchi, "I'm sure she hasn't got it."

"Quite right," Sakaguchi said, and looked steadily at Yutaka. "She has it." Yutaka looked back at him with half-closed eyes, then stuck out her chin.

"Then let's start with the other one," Tatsuoka said.

"Your right hand, please!" said Sakaguchi to Tokiko with mock heartiness. "Now your left! See, we already have two points." He turned to Kensaku. "He hasn't got it either—you agree?" Tatsuoka and the maid nodded. "All right then, open up your hairy bear's paws, if you please!" Yutaka laughed loudly. Silent and angry, Kensaku looked at his clumsy hands perched on his knees and unclenched them, palms up.

Ever since they began playing "strategy" Kensaku had felt self-conscious about his uncouth hands. They had made him feel somehow incongruous, no matter how hard he tried to ignore them. Sakaguchi had sensed Kensaku's discomfort, and was now crudely taking advantage of it. That he had been so easily seen through was annoying enough to Kensaku. But what really angered him was the shoddiness of this man, who should have wanted to taunt him in this way.

It was about four in the morning. The rain had turned into a soft drizzle. Through the quietness outside they could hear with sharp clarity the night watchman striking his iron pole on the ground as he made his rounds.

Sakaguchi's eyes were sunken, his eyelids creased. He looked as though his body and spirit were eroding to the core; and surrendering himself to the process, it seemed, he continued his aimless, mechanical chatter.

Dawn began to break. Tatsuoka and Sakaguchi, having at last given in to fatigue and intoxication, lay on the floor, dozing fitfully. Yutaka stood on the verandah and gazed tiredly at the odd visitor or two walking homeward in the autumn rain. Her kimono was loose and disheveled from all the merrymaking, the skirt on the verge of gaping open at the front. In the light of the dawn the gas lamp began to look feeble and purposeless. Bits of left-over food on the plates, cigarettes fallen out of their packs, playing cards and *go* pieces strewn on the floor—everything in the room suggested the end of an episode.

Kensaku, too, was tired—all the more so for not having slept well the previous night. But rest was beyond him. He felt a tautness within, which even such fatigue would not dispel. He sat on a pile of cushions that they had used earlier in a game called "take a seat," and looked at the grubby faces of his companions. He knew he looked no better than they. Filled with distaste for this sordid scene of which he was a part, he wished he could dissociate himself from it that very minute. He took a very deep breath, then glanced down at his own body as if in an attempt to recapture some sense of familiarity with his old self.

He suddenly thought of Nobuyuki, his elder brother. He had always been deeply attached to him, was fonder of him than of any other man. And now the mere thought of him seemed to revive his spirits somewhat. Wondering whether he would be up already, he looked at his pocket watch. It was six-thirty.

He went downstairs. In the dark rear annex hardly made lighter by the flickering taper on the miniature family shrine, the madam was busily engaged in her morning devotions. She was offering a hundred prayers—walking back and forth, to and from the shrine, a hundred times. "Good morning," she said cheerfully with a little bow as she caught sight of him on one of her trips away from the shrine. He was about to ask her where the telephone was when she turned on her heel and headed toward the shrine again. He found the maid in the kitchen, and asked her. On the telephone he was told that Nobuyuki was still asleep. What he wanted to say to him was not very important. All the same, he put down the receiver with reluctance.

Yutaka was fast asleep, still in a sitting position but bent forward, her head on one of the small tea tables. Beside her sat Tokiko, quietly picking the strings of her samisen. Gradually the street got busier. The men were going home, and Kensaku wished he was too. But if he could not leave soon, then he wished at least that the two women would go.

Tatsuoka and Sakaguchi were snoring lightly. Tokiko went downstairs, came back with a pair of coverlets, and put them over the two men. She bowed to Kensaku, then shook Yutaka gently by the shoulder. In a stupor Yutaka stood up, bowed, and tottered toward the door.

"Don't forget your present," Tokiko said, and handed her the thick package of Haibara's decorated paper. Sometime in the course of the night Tatsuoka had given it to Yutaka.

It was nine when the three men, sharing the two oil-paper umbrellas given them by the establishment, at last walked out into the gently falling autumn rain.

3

Kensaku reached home at noon, thoroughly tired. He was about to enter the front gate when he heard the kid that he had started keeping about a week before bleating at the back of the house. It sounded like a child crying. Instead of going in he went around to the little enclosure next to the storage shed. The kid was delighted to see him and began stamping its dainty feet. Its legs, Kensaku thought, were like a little boy's in long trousers. It came over and put its front feet up high on the wire fence.

Kensaku picked up a few of the leaves, wet and flat from the night's rain, that had fallen beside the wall from his neighbor's cherry tree. "Hello, silly fellow," he said, and walked into the enclosure. With light, busy steps the kid followed him from corner to corner, waiting to be given the leaves, and nuzzled at his chest when he squatted down. "Here you are, silly fellow," he said, and gave it a leaf. Contentedly the kid worked its lower jaw from side to side, and the leaf gradually disappeared behind the lips. Kensaku gave it another leaf, and when that disappeared, yet another. There was utter satisfaction in the way the kid stood still, just munching. And as Kensaku watched, that part of him which he thought had deserted him the night before seemed slowly to return. "It's all finished," he said cheerfully, and holding the kid's head with both hands, pulled it toward him. Suprised, the kid at first tried to resist; but soon it became docile and allowed itself to be fondled. On its head where eventually the horns would grow, there were already lumps. Only a couple of days before, Kensaku remembered, when a neighbor's puppy was being much too playful, the kid had struck the puppy's side hard with its head.

"So it was you," Oei said from the back door. "I wondered who it was talking back here."

"Have you given it any bean curd yet?"

"No. I've just sent the maid out for some."

Together they went into the morning room. "Have you had breakfast?"

"Yes, thanks."

"Would you like a cup of coffee then? Or tea?"

"I really don't feel like any right now."

"Were you at Mr. Tatsuoka's last night?"

"No. We went to a rather funny place, as a matter of fact. We spent the night at one of those teahouses in Yoshiwara."

"Did you now. I suppose it was Mr. Sakaguchi who took you there."

Kensaku told her simply what they had done since they left the house. "It was the first time I ever went to such a place," he added, "but somehow it didn't feel like it."

"That's because it wasn't the first time. We once went with your grandfather, don't you remember? Wasn't it when we went to see the procession of the geisha, the year the National Assembly was established?"

"It couldn't have been. I was only three or four when the assembly got started."

"Really? Then perhaps it was one of those times we went cherry-viewing in Yoshiwara. Do you remember those comic plays they used to put on then?"

Kensaku thought he could dimly remember seeing something of the kind as a child.

He asked Oei to lay out his bed for him in his room upstairs. Very soon he was fast asleep.

He was still asleep when Nobuyuki dropped in that evening. Kensaku quickly went downstairs to receive him, and found him standing in the entryway. He must have come straight from the office, for he was carrying a large, brown leather briefcase.

"Asleep, were you?"

"Yes."

"Come out and have dinner with me somewhere."

"All right. But come in for a minute."

"No thanks, I can't be bothered to take my shoes off. I hear you telephoned this morning."

"It wasn't about anything in particular."

Oei then appeared and tried to persuade Nobuyuki to come in, but he wouldn't listen. Instead he tried a little persuasion of his own. "Why don't you come out with us?" he said. "It'll do you good."

He took Kensaku to a rather neat little restaurant in Nihonbashi specializing in Osaka cuisine. There Kensaku told him about his visit to Yoshiwara.

"So you met Tokiko, eh? She's a fine geisha. I met her a couple of times, you know, when she was still an apprentice. Now, that one you can take anywhere with you without feeling in the least bit ashamed." He paused, then suddenly said: "You aren't by any chance thinking of having an affair with her, are you?"

Kensaku wasn't quite prepared for the question. Blushing, he said, "I haven't the slightest idea of how to go about such a thing."

Nobuyuki burst into laughter. "It'll cost you a lot of money, you know," he said.

Ever since his student days Nobuyuki had been a connoisseur of such matters. And there was a time, Kensaku remembered, when it used to be rumored that he was keeping a geisha. He was even now a bachelor, with expensive tastes that were a constant strain on his finances.

As they were about to part outside the restaurant, Nobuyuki said he had a message for Kensaku from their sister Sakiko: could he please take her and their other sister, Taeko, to the matinee performance at the Imperial Theatre the next day? The play was to have actresses in it, so it would not be pure kabuki.

At noon the next day the two young girls—Sakiko was sixteen, Taeko twelve—duly appeared at Kensaku's house. It was an unpleasant day, with a nasty wind blowing.

At the theatre Kensaku found himself being ceaselessly distracted by jejune thoughts of Tokiko and utterly unable to keep his mind on what was happening on the stage. It was tempting to think she might even be there watching the play, and at each intermission he dragged his sisters out into the lobby and the corridors, and wandered about in the hope of seeing her. The search was in vain of course; all he saw were three or four male acquaintances.

In the tearoom during one of the intermissions he came across Ishimoto. "There's something I want to talk to you about," Ishimoto said. "If you are taking your sisters home, we could perhaps meet later this evening."

He was Nobuyuki's friend rather than Kensaku's. When Nobuyuki was about to go away to college in Sendai, he had asked Ishimoto to take care of Kensaku. Kensaku was then in his third year at high school, which, in Nobuyuki's opinion, was a crucial period for a boy. While the others in Kensaku's immediate family had been indifferent, Nobuyuki for some reason had always shown deep concern for his welfare. Ishimoto for his part was at that age when such responsibilities were a welcome challenge; besides, he was genuinely well-disposed toward Kensaku; so that all in all he took very good care of him. Once, when he discovered that Kensaku was not sufficiently prepared for a coming examination in algebra, he had stayed up all night coaching him, putting aside his own studying for the examinations.

Their relationship had continued ever since, quite unchanged—Ishimoto forever the senior, keeping a watchful eye on his ward. The fact of his having still to acknowledge Ishimoto's seniority, Kensaku did not particularly mind; but it was true that he was finding Ishimoto's hovering about like a grandmother increasingly tiresome. Unlike Nobuyuki, who was at once more easygoing and more generally sensitive, Ishimoto was constantly trying to teach him something. He meant well, of course; but knowing this did not prevent Kensaku from getting quite angry sometimes. He had until recently been a cabinet minister's private secretary, but the change in the cabinet had left him temporarily without a job and with rather a lot of time on his hands.

The girls insisted they could go home by themselves, so Kensaku and Ishimoto accompanied them as far as the streetcar stop. When they had gone, Ishimoto said, "Let's not go to a restaurant. We can be more relaxed in a teahouse, don't you think?"

They walked through Ginza to Tsukiji, and there Ishimoto led Kensaku into a large house. "We've come here to talk," he said to the maid, "so just give us something to eat, and don't bother to call anyone."

They were shown into a secluded eight-mat room. It was somber-colored, without a touch of fussiness, and overlooked a tasteful little garden. It was altogether a pleasant room, quite unlike the one in Yoshiwara. On the wall in the alcove hung a picture of Mount Inari, done by a certain Kyoto painter whom Kensaku had always disliked heartily. But in the present surroundings the picture looked not at all bad. The mountain paths depicted on it, Kensaku thought, went rather well with the autumn flowers in the vase below.

What Ishimoto wanted to talk about was finding a wife for Kensaku. "It's really Nobuyuki's idea," he said, "but being a bachelor himself, he didn't think he would be quite the right person to bring the subject up. At any rate, if you are interested, we'll do whatever we can to help you find someone nice. Would you like us to start looking?"

"I think not, but thanks all the same."

"Why not?"

"I simply don't want that sort of help."

"But why?"

"I just don't, that's all."

Kensaku turned his face away from Ishimoto's gaze and looked at the garden. He knew he had been unnecessarily abrupt, and wondered why he always behaved like a spoiled child when he was with Ishimoto. "You do behave like an old granny, you know," he added.

"Well, if that's the way you feel, I won't say any more," Ishimoto said in a frosty tone. Silence fell, but only for a little while, for soon Ishimoto was talking again. This time he droned on and on, and when Kensaku tried to interrupt, he said, "Just wait a minute and let me finish," and continued his monologue. Impatiently Kensaku sat and listened until he could bear it no longer. "Please stop," he implored, "I really have had enough." In the look he gave Ishimoto, there was now open antagonism.

Ishimoto suddenly started laughing; and in a moment Kensaku found himself laughing with him.

His nerves were in a rather bad state, Kensaku explained; he had of late become very suspicious of other people, and it was no time for him to be thinking of getting married, especially to someone who had been found for him.

Though he had no desire to, he talked also about Aiko, for he felt sure that had it not been for the Aiko affair, Nobuyuki and Ishimoto would not have been so anxious to bring up the subject of marriage. "You know," he said, "I am now trying to write something about what happened to Aiko and me. But the fact of the matter is I really don't understand her."

Kensaku then thanked Ishimoto for his concern; but, he added, his private life was his own to take care of, and he didn't want others to interfere.

Ishimoto looked a little disheartened, and said nothing. At that point the maid came in with the food. As they ate, they talked of less solemn matters; and in time the mood seemed to become lighter.

Kensaku said, "Would you be interested in meeting someone who looks like your wife?" This was a question he had been waiting to ask for some time. Partly, he wanted simply to talk about Tokiko; and partly, he hoped to use Ishimoto as an excuse for visiting her again.

"Not particularly," Ishimoto answered. "Who is she, anyway?"

Kensaku told him all about Tokiko. Then he said again, "She really looks very much like your wife."

"You must introduce us sometime," Ishimoto said, but he was only being polite.

Kensaku walked home. On the way he remembered something Ishimoto had said—he claimed he was quoting someone—before they parted: "To think that love between two young people will last throughout their lives is like thinking that a candle will burn forever." Skeptic that he had become, Kensaku at the time had thought the remark not at all unreasonable. But as he now thought of the way his maternal grandparents had lived together, he began to wonder whether it was indeed true. From the time they married until the very end, they had loved each other. Of them at least, something like this would have been much truer: "The first candle will, of course, burn out in time. But before this happens, the light from it will be passed on to another candle, and then to another, so that though the candles may change, the light will burn forever, like the light on a Buddhist altar. As the candles change, so will the way in which two people love each other; yet their love, like the light, need never go out." Yes, he decided, he rather liked that; and he wished he had said it to Ishimoto. Then his imagination took a nonsensical turn. "But don't you see," he heard Ishimoto saying, "I'm speaking of European

candles. With those, you can't pass the light on from one to the next."
To which he quickly replied, "But the people I'm talking about were
pure Japanese candles!"

He smiled to himself, amused by the ludicrous exchange of his own
imagining. And he walked on, his mind now filled with nostalgic
memories of his dead grandparents.

4

Three days had passed since that unpleasant night in Yoshiwara.
Kensaku still thought constantly of Tokiko, and he would recall with
a strange sense of disquiet those moments when she sat near him.
Once he went so far as to hold one of his fingers, in a vain attempt to
gauge the sensation first of holding a finger and then of having one's
finger held. All the time, however, he was suspicious of his own state
of mind. That he truly wanted to start a serious affair with her, he
could not bring himself to believe. Perhaps his desire to see her
amounted to little more than a reluctance to allow his present mood
to dissipate. But if he indeed had no intention of becoming involved,
would it not be very callous of him to go and see her, even if she were
only a geisha?

At any rate, if he was to pay her another visit he would have to
have some ostensible reason for doing so. And as far as he could see,
only Ishimoto could provide that.

He sat down immediately to write him a postcard. He knew he was
trying to use his friend, and this made him self-conscious. Somehow
he seemed unable to find quite the right words. He wasted several
postcards, rewriting his message this way and that to hit just the right
note of nonchalance. Finally he gave up trying and went out to telephone.

"I'm thinking of going to see her tomorrow. Would you like to
come?" At last he had got it off his chest.

"All right," said Ishimoto simply, to Kensaku's relief. "When you
are ready to go tomorrow, give me a ring again."

Now he had to raise some money. The regular allowance he received from his father was sufficient to take care of his basic daily needs; indeed, it enabled him to buy what books he needed and to travel occasionally. But this did not mean that he had much in the way of pocket money. Whenever he wanted some he would go to Oei, just as he had done as a boy, and be given some such modest sum as three or four yen. To go to her for the kind of money he needed now was clearly out of the question.

He sat down once more to write a postcard, this time to a bookseller of his acquaintance in Kanda, asking him to drop in before noon the following day.

Besides books he had a fair collection of ukiyo prints. He might as well sell all those too, he decided. There were some of Hiroshige's "Fifty-three Stations of the Tōkaidō," Shikitei Sanba's compilations of portraits by the first Toyokuni and Kunimasa, scrolls by Utamaro, Koryūsai and Shunchō—all these, together with some worthless pieces he had, made up a sizeable bundle. Carrying it under his arm he walked over to an antique shop nearby.

"I was at two hotels this morning, seeing customers," said the dealer before Kensaku could say anything. "And do you know what one of those damned foreigners said to me when I showed him a Shonzui? 'That's a fake,' that's what he said."

Taken aback by the crudeness of this shopkeeper who was obviously no connoisseur, Kensaku felt a sudden reluctance to show him his collection. Here was the sort of dealer who relied entirely on his own brazenness, who bought things indiscriminately and then went about trying to palm them off on foreigners. Nevertheless when the man said, "What do you have there," and put out his hand, Kensaku docilely handed over the bundle.

With a knowing air and deliberate casualness the dealer looked at each print, making meaningless, noncommittal sounds all the while. By his silly antics the man was trying to convey the impression that he thought very little of the collection. What a fool, Kensaku thought, as he watched him in silence. When the inspection was over, Kensaku had him wrap up the prints again and without another word walked out of the shop.

Back in the house he found Tatsuoka waiting for him. "Here's a going-away present for you," Kensaku said and put the prints, still in the wrapping, in front of Tatsuoka.

"But this is your entire collection, isn't it? Thanks very much, but I couldn't possibly accept such a present. At least keep the good ones. After all, I'm only going to give them away to strangers."

"No, I'd rather you took them all."

They began discussing their recent visit to Yoshiwara. "Now, that woman Tokiko," Tatsuoka said, "there's a handsome geisha for you."

With a touch of hesitation Kensaku said, "I wonder?" He was not being untruthful. For he had always associated the word "handsome" with a sort of large-scale quality, with an air of confidence, which seemed to him absent in Tokiko. Good-looking perhaps, but not handsome. But he was not being entirely candid, either. He had hesitated, he had given that rather lukewarm reply, because it had suddenly occurred to him that Tatsuoka, too, might be interested in Tokiko. "I don't know that I would call her handsome," he added, hoping to sound less negative. "Let's say she's good-looking."

"That's all right with me."

"Do you like Tokiko?" Kensaku asked, taking the bull by the horns.

"I'm not sure I want to answer that. How about you?"

Kensaku was not prepared for the counter-question, and he felt his face go red. "All right, to be honest, I do like her. But if you do too, then I'm quite ready to step aside. I'm not all that fond of her,"

Tatsuoka's large body shook as he laughed. "There's no need for you to be so retiring, you know. I'm going abroad in two months, remember."

"That's true."

"I'm glad," said Tatsuoka, still smiling. "You looked so gloomy the other night, I was beginning to feel guilty about having taken you to such a place."

"But it *was* unpleasant."

"Why?"

"Well, didn't you find Sakaguchi a little on the nasty side?"

"But he's always like that these days."

Kensaku said nothing.

"I take it you won't object to going there again?" Tatsuoka said.

"As a matter of fact, I've arranged to go there with Ishimoto tomorrow."

"In that case, let's go tonight."

At about nine that evening the two paid their second visit to Nishimidori. But, alas, Tokiko could not join them. She had gone to the theatre, they were told, and would probably not return before eleven. The maid had remembered Sakaguchi's mentioning the geisha called Koine during their last visit, and she had tried to get her, but she, too, was not available. Of the geisha affiliated with this teahouse, only Yutaka was free. And so for a second one they were forced to call a geisha sponsored by the teahouse next door. This one turned out to be a rather shabby specimen, hardly the sort to liven up a party. After an hour or so, the two men decided to go home.

As they were about to leave, the maid—her name was Otsuta—said, "If you are thinking of visiting us again tomorrow, do please telephone us first, perhaps in the early evening."

"But I know I'm coming tomorrow," said Kensaku. "Surely I don't have to call beforehand?"

Otsuta was distinctly uncomfortable. "But you see, if you don't . . . "

Kensaku woke up the next morning at about eight. It was raining heavily outside. The water spilled out of the gutter along the eaves and fell directly onto the ground below. Kensaku listened to the incessant noise and thought, what a nuisance. The rain itself didn't bother him, but in this downpour it would surely be difficult to maintain the pretext that he was taking Ishimoto to Yoshiwara merely for the sake of having him meet someone who looked like his wife. And what if Ishimoto refused to brave the rain for something so inconsequential? And what if after he had seen her Ishimoto were to turn to him and say, "So you think she looks like my wife, eh?"

All morning he fretted about the rain. But luckily it began to let up, and by early afternoon it had turned into a drizzle. At last the bookseller, whom he had asked to come during the morning, appeared. "I know I was supposed to come earlier," he said, "but it was raining far too hard."

Kensaku showed him the books that he had piled up in the next room. Fifty yen was what he was offered for them. He then produced an unusually large silver hunter that had belonged to his maternal grandfather. Attached to it was a heavy, cumbersome gold chain. "Could you sell this for me?"

"Certainly."

Kensaku had no idea whether the chain was solid gold or not. He decided he might as well warn the man. "Of course, that may be just gold plate."

The bookseller weighed the chain thoughtfully in his hand and said, "I'm sure it's not. In any case they'll test it with nitric acid before they buy it. If it's the real stuff, you'll get a lot for it." He put his hand on the pile of books beside him and added, "At least twice what you got for these." He stopped and looked expectantly at Kensaku. If he was hoping for some sign of enthusiasm from Kensaku, he was disappointed. He now turned his attention to the old-fashioned watch. "This, too, won't be hard to sell. This sort of watch is particularly popular among sailors. In the tropics, you see, a small watch is no good at all; it just goes haywire in the heat. Anyway, I'll write as soon as I've seen this fellow I know."

He wrapped a large square of cloth around the books; then carrying the heavy bundle on his back he left.

Evening came, and the rain stopped completely. Feeling refreshed after a hot bath Kensaku went out. The sky was beautifully clear. The surface soil on the street had been washed away by the heavy rain, and small pebbles had appeared, clean and shiny. The people he saw walking about all had wet umbrellas in their hands.

He stopped at a magazine shop that he knew and telephoned Nishimidori. Then he telephoned Ishimoto.

"I have a guest right now, but I expect him to leave shortly," Ishimoto said. "If he does, I'll join you there, I promise." He then asked how far one had to go after entering the quarter, on which side of the street the house was, and even what characters were used to write "Nishimidori."

Kensaku got off the streetcar at Minowa, and walked quickly and determinedly along the embankment, like a man headed for a business meeting. He could see to his right, on the other side of the moat, the bright lights of the houses of the quarter.

The streams of people coming from three directions—from San'ya, from Dōtetsu, and like Kensaku from Minowa—converged in front of the Nihonzutsumi police station, then poured into the stone-paved street that led to the gateway. Kensaku was one of this crowd.

The street suddenly deteriorated when one entered the quarter. So as to avoid the mud Kensaku walked along the edge, carefully making his way past one teahouse after another until he reached Nishimidori. There he found Tokiko and the maid Otsuta seated in the entryway, viewing the passing scene and talking casually to each other. They got up when they saw Kensaku, with what seemed to him an air of weary resignation.

"By yourself today?" Tokiko asked as she followed Kensaku up the stairs.

"Someone else will be joining us soon."

"Mr. Tatsuoka?"

"No, it's the husband of the person who I said looked rather like you."

"What did you say?"

Showing some irritation Kensaku said quickly, "His wife looks like you."

Tokiko began to laugh. "Oh, I see. It was the word 'husband' that threw me off."

Three cushions had been placed around the tea table. As Kensaku sat down Tokiko said, "Where are your friends?"

"I was here with Tatsuoka last night."

"Yes, I know. They told me when I stopped by last night. And how is the other gentleman, Mr. Sakaguchi?"

"I haven't seen him since that night we were all here."

Otsuta came into the room, and she too asked, "Where are your friends?"

Somehow Kensaku felt he was being censured. He was already feeling a little guilty about having come to such a place all alone. For one so inexperienced as himself, it was all rather out of character. How had he had the gall even to telephone here, as if he were some regular patron of the establishment? No doubt, if he had not had Ishimoto to use as an excuse, he would never have come.

Tokiko was still amused by her own confusion at Kensaku's involved remark about the "husband," and laughingly told Otsuta about it.

Otsuta looked blank. "I haven't the slightest idea what you're talking about."

"Oh, don't be so dumb. The man's wife looks just like me, don't you see?" She pulled herself up in mock imitation of an arrogant lady. "Aren't you impressed?"

"Not at all," said Otsuta.

Tokiko seemed to Kensaku not quite the same woman that he had met the last time; she was as beautiful as before, however.

"Next time, do come with the others. The more the merrier, as they say. With all of you here, I can have a bit of fun too. There are guests, you know, who sit and say nothing and expect me to do nothing but play the samisen. If they were all like that, I suppose I could be a really good performer, but there are times when I could just break down and cry."

Kensaku remembered what Nobuyuki had said about her. "I hear you dance well."

"Who told you that?"

"Someone I know. He said he saw you do a kabuki number once."

"Really? Oh, I know, he must have seen me do 'Kaheiji of the Crescent Moon.'" She was blushing a little.

They started talking about the other night. "That Mr. Sakaguchi," she said, "he's really good at games, isn't he?" She closed her white, long-fingered hands, then put one fist over the other, and moved them up and down. "You remember how cleverly he played 'passing the coin'? What a tease he was! He fooled me every time, I can tell you."

Kensaku had no reason to share her enthusiasm for either the game or Sakaguchi's mastery of it.

"What's become of this friend of yours who's supposed to be coming?"

"We'll wait a bit, then I'll give him a ring."

"I hope he'll appear soon. We can't do much by ourselves."

"The geisha named Koine, I wonder if she's free?"

"It's still early, I'm sure she will be," Tokiko said hopefully.

But he showed no further interest in Koine.

He thought of all the fearfulness and the worrying of the last few days, the careful preparation that had gone into this visit, and wondered what all of that had to do with the banal conversation he was now trying so hard to sustain. Of course he had not come here with the faintest expectation of having a serious tête-à-tête with her. But what they were saying to each other now was so superficial, so flat.

He told himself that such perhaps was how it should be under the circumstances; that he had been playing his little game all by himself, wrestling with his own little fantasies. Besides, Tokiko was after all trying to be friendly today, however frivolously; she was being more informal, one might say, than she had been on the previous occasion. What more could he expect of her? He had no right to be dissatisfied.

Tokiko was looking at Kensaku, wondering if he was going to mention Koine again. Seeing that he was not, she said, "I hear that the first time you came, one of you asked for Koine. And then last night, too, you apparently asked for her. Tell me, why are you all so devoted to her?" She looked at him slyly with her expressive eyes, and smiled. She seemed particularly beautiful then.

"The people here suggested last night that we call her. It was their idea, not mine."

"Anyway, let's call Koine. We can have more fun if there are three of us," she said, and hurried out of the room. For some reason, Kensaku felt immensely relieved.

Whatever she was doing downstairs, Tokiko was taking a long time over it. As if suddenly remembering that he had cigarettes on him, Kensaku took one out and began to smoke it casually. He was not a regular smoker, and did not care whether he smoked or not. On the pack was the face of a black native girl: "Samoa," the brand was called.

Tokiko came back at last. "Koine can come," she said as she sat down. She picked up the pack of cigarettes, then holding it out toward Kensaku said playfully, "Is she supposed to be pretty?"

"What do you think?"

"Well now, I don't know. She's awfully black."

"Are you saying being so black, she can't be pretty?"

She didn't answer the question. "Anyway, I like the other girl better—you know, the one with a rose or some such flower stuck in her hair. What was the brand called—was it 'Alma'? I think she's very pretty."

"I see."

"That reminds me, they have Almas downstairs. I'll go and get a pack."

"Wait a minute," said Kensaku, "I'll come with you. I want to use the telephone."

It was Ishimoto that he called. "The guest just left," said Ishimoto when he came to the telephone. "I'm afraid it's a bit too late for me to be going out now. Will you ask me again?"

Kensaku had by then come to half-expect such an answer, and was not particularly disappointed.

Ten minutes later Koine appeared. What a beautiful woman, Kensaku thought when he saw her. Her figure was good, and she had a manner that was restrained and exceedingly feminine. She knelt down briefly by the doorway and bowed. "Good evening, Tokiko," she said with a smile as she stood up. She walked over to the tea table and sat down beside Tokiko.

"Look at these," Tokiko said immediately, pushing the two packs of cigarettes toward Koine, "and tell me who you think is the pretty one."

Koine peered at the pictures, then shrieked, "You're joking!" Her laugh was high-pitched, quite incongruous in a woman with her soft, pliant figure and controlled movements.

To Kensaku she seemed in every way the very opposite of Tokiko. They held themselves so differently, their gestures were so different. And whereas Koine's skin was rough-grained and appeared thick, Tokiko's was so fine that when one got close to her, one could see around her temples and her chin the delicate blue lines of her veins.

Kensaku gradually began to feel less and less tense. With five or six drinks of saké inside him he found himself in a rather cheerful and receptive mood.

They began playing their first parlor game. This was seeing who could smoke an Alma cigarette up to the gold tip without dropping the ash.

"You've reached the 'l' in 'Alma,'" Kensaku told Koine.

Holding a fan—it had a picture of a dayflower painted on it—under the cigarette, Koine smoked a little more. Then gingerly she held the cigarette out to him and said, "Where am I now?"

"You are about to reach the 'A.' "

She giggled. "But even after I've finished the letters, there will still be a quarter of an inch to go before I get to the gold tip. I don't see how I can make it."

Tokiko, who was competing with her, said nothing and continued to puff away nonchalantly.

At last the ash on Koine's cigarette fell off. "Oh!" she cried, jerking her body as if to avoid the ash. At that moment the ash on Tokiko's cigarette also dropped and landed squarely on the tea table. "Really, Koine!" she said, giving Koine an irritated sidelong glance. "I'm sorry," said Koine. Tokiko said nothing. "Do forgive me," Koine said, laughing. Tokiko threw what was left of her cigarette in the ashtray. "You'll clean up the mess, won't you?" She looked with distaste at the cloud of smoke drifting about above her head, then stood up abruptly and walked out of the room. Koine brought out a couple of sheets of tissue paper, folded them neatly, and with solemn care swept the ashes off the table onto her fan.

After a while Tokiko came back. She stopped briefly at the doorway, posed as though for a photograph. "Quick, let's hear it," she said to Kensaku. She was referring to a remark he had made earlier, that a woman is at her most beautiful just as she steps into a room.

"I managed to persuade the madam and Otsuta to join us," she said as she sat down beside Koine. She helped herself to a cigarette, then eyed Koine thoughtfully. "No, I'd better not," she said and moved to the other side of the table. She then calmly proceeded to light her cigarette. Koine was incredulous. "What cheek!" she finally managed to say, then burst into high-pitched laughter.

When the madam and Otsuta appeared they immediately began playing vingt-et-un.

It was one in the morning when Kensaku left in a rickshaw. The ride to Akasaka seemed to him almost interminable. Yet it was a fine moonlit night, washed clean by the earlier rain. And when he saw the double bridge bathed in moonlight as they sped beside the Imperial Palace moat, he felt tranquil and refreshed.

There was a letter from the bookseller when he got home. The chain was indeed not gold plate, it said, but it contained rather a lot of copper, and so fetched less money than one might have wished. Alas, the watch, too, turned out to be of little value, and all the bookseller could get for it was what the metal would fetch melted down.

5

Kensaku's feelings toward Tokiko underwent a remarkable change after his second meeting with her. He still thought her beautiful, he still liked her. But now there was none of that oppressiveness, that disquiet which before had accompanied his thoughts of her; instead there was a sense of lightheartedness, a sense of comfort at last. And he would remember with a touch of disbelief how anxiously and with what effort he had arranged the second meeting. Had he lost all sense of proportion then?

Of course, this change of mood in him had been in part brought about by Tokiko's own attitude. But perhaps there was a more important cause. Perhaps this new sense of comfort he now enjoyed had come into being mostly because he had needed it and sought it. It was perhaps his way of regaining some of the confidence he had lost through the Aiko affair.

A part of him now wanted to push the relationship with Tokiko further; another part of him wanted to draw back, fearful lest he be hurt again. No wonder, for that earlier experience had left scars on him that still felt very raw at times.

Aiko's father had been from the Mito domain, a practitioner of Chinese medicine. Why, Kensaku did not know, but Aiko's mother had been given to this doctor in marriage as an adopted daughter of Kensaku's maternal grandparents. At any rate, this lady and Kensaku's mother had been very close friends from childhood. And after Kensaku's mother died, this lady would often talk to him about her. "Your mother was a good person," she would say. "Terribly emotional she was, easily moved, and very kind." As girls they had been madly fond of the theatre; once they were caught impersonating actors by Kensaku's grandmother, and were roundly scolded.

Kensaku, who could not believe that anyone truly loved him, cherished all such memories of his dead mother, for they tied him, no matter how tenuously, to the one person who he was sure had loved him. She had not been exactly a kind mother; yet her love for him he had never doubted. Oei, of course, had shown him fondness; and so had his brother Nobuyuki. But what he could call real love, he had known only from his mother. And with the passing of the years since her death, this love he had known became more and more dear to him. How real it might have seemed to him had she lived, he could not say.

It was in Aiko's mother, then, that Kensaku had sought and found reminders of his own dead mother. Once, at a gathering in his father's house in Hongō—the occasion was probably the thirteenth anniversary of his mother's death—Kensaku had seen Aiko's mother sitting on the other side of the room, dressed in a severe, fine-patterned kimono, quite out of style, with a black satin sash. Somehow the sight of her dressed thus had filled him with a sense of longing; and from time to time he had caught himself gazing at her. Later in the ceremony, when by chance they were seated next to each other, she said, "You know, this dress was your mother's." Kensaku was very moved—what the emotion was, he did not know—and could not think of anything to say. After a while she smiled and said, "See how short the sleeves are?" Then she pulled her arms up inside the sleeves. "There's no material left to let down, which means I've got to shorten my arms, right?"

Aiko had an elder brother by the name of Keitarō. He was the same age as Nobuyuki, two years older than Kensaku, and though they went to different schools, the three of them played together a great deal. Yet neither Nobuyuki nor Kensaku liked Keitarō much. There was something in his nature that kept him apart from them. Of the two brothers, Kensaku saw Keitarō more; for he visited Keitarō's house constantly, in the hope of finding Keitarō's mother in.

Aiko was younger than Kensaku by five years. As a boy he was wont to regard her as a nuisance. Whenever she found Kensaku and Keitarō playing she would want to join in, though of course she could never keep up with them. Or when she found Kensaku having a chat with her mother she would try to drag her away, saying, "Time for beddy-bies, time for beddy-bies." Having known her through childhood, then, he was not particularly conscious of her sex when she reached puberty.

She was fifteen or sixteen when her father died. And it was at the funeral, when he saw her dressed in funeral white and crying, that he was first drawn to her.

There were many occasions after that when they were alone together, such as when he helped her prepare for the English examination, and at such times he was particularly careful not to show his newly awakened feelings toward her. Timidity was one reason, but another was that what he felt was not yet exactly a passion. Besides, she seemed to him still so innocent, hardly a fit object for whatever it was that he felt. Here he was perhaps mistaken, for she was no more immature than other girls her age. If indeed she behaved at times childishly in his presence, that was probably because having known him for so long, she felt no need to put on airs.

As her graduation from high school approached, he began to hear talk of marriage plans for her. He believed that were he to propose, he could not be turned down. Yet there were times when he would not be so sure, when he would be assailed by an inexplicable uneasiness. He would then tell himself that the fear was groundless, that he was simply being timid.

He wondered to whom he should declare his intentions: was it to be Aiko's mother, or Keitarō? He was loath to go to Aiko's mother; it would be too much like taking advantage of her past goodwill. But he was no less reluctant to approach Keitarō first. Their life ambitions, their views on everything, were so markedly different that naturally a mutual contempt had developed between them. Keitarō was then employed by a certain company in Osaka, and was engaged to the company president's daughter. It was quite clearly to be a marriage of convenience for Keitarō, and he had more than once said as much to Kensaku, seemingly without shame. To tell such a man that he wished to marry his sister was something Kensaku could hardly relish, certain though he was that he would be accepted.

There was no other way, he reluctantly concluded, than to inform his father of his wish and ask him to approach Aiko's family.

It has been his habit since childhood not to speak to his father unless he absolutely had to. This had come to be accepted as a matter of course by both sides, and neither minded it very much. Yet, despite the absence of open resentment between them, it was still a difficult thing for Kensaku to have to talk to his father about so personal a matter.

At last one evening he visited his father and made his request. "I have no objection at all to the marriage," said his father, "if they haven't. But you are now the head of your own household, so I should think it would be more proper if you, rather than I, were to approach them. Don't you agree?"

Kensaku had not gone to his father expecting much in the way of spontaneous support. But of course he was hurt. For however prepared he might have thought he was for any lack of enthusiasm on his father's part, he had harbored in some corner of his mind the hope that he would be friendlier. Besides, the response was even more negative than he had reasonably anticipated. There was in his father's manner not only coldness but something strangely menacing. Why must he trip me up like this, he wondered, just as I am about to take a step forward? Why?

He thought of going to Nobuyuki to ask if he would act as intermediary. He remembered how happy his brother had seemed when he had first told him of his desire to marry Aiko. "What a wonderful idea," he had said. "Let's hope that they'll give their consent. She's a fine girl." But could he go to Nobuyuki now, after being told by his father that the proposal should come from himself? No, he decided, he had better leave Nobuyuki out of it. What difference did it make anyway? It was his business, and he might as well take care of it himself. Besides, it would be simpler that way.

Thus resolved he had gone one day to Aiko's house to speak to her mother. She was at first shocked, then became pitifully nervous as Kensaku proceeded to explain the purpose of his visit. In the unbearably tense atmosphere Kensaku, too, lost what little assurance he had had earlier, and began seriously to wonder if Aiko had already been promised to some other man.

Aiko's mother said at last, "Of course I can't give you an answer now. I have to consult Keitarō and the other members of the family. We'll then get in touch with your family in Hongō."

Kensaku explained that though his father knew about it, his proposal had nothing to do with Hongō, and that indeed it was his father's wish that it should come from him directly. "How strange," Aiko's mother had replied unhappily.

With a heavy heart Kensaku went home. His father's response had not been entirely unexpected—at least he could tell himself that. But he had really hoped for more from Aiko's mother. On the surface there was nothing untoward in what she had said; but it was the coldness that lay under the surface that bewildered him.

He refused to lose hope. He would now wait until Keitarō next came up to Tokyo, and get a firm answer from him. Surely there was something not quite right about Aiko's mother.

Ten days later he learned from Nobuyuki that Keitarō was in town. He waited for four or five days to hear from Keitarō, not wanting to take the initiative and so appear forward. But there was no word from him. It was irritating, not to say insulting. Unable to wait any longer Kensaku decided to telephone him.

With his usual adroitness Keitarō said, "I wanted to come and see you right away, but I came up this time specifically to take care of some business at the branch office here, and I've been so busy I haven't been able to see anyone."

Suppressing his anger, Kensaku said, "Will you be at home tonight?"

"I'm afraid not. I've been asked to a dinner party."

"How about tomorrow then?"

"Tomorrow night? Let's see—yes, that will be all right. Come to dinner if you like." His tone was light and friendly, but Kensaku didn't have to see his face to know he was being blatantly insincere.

Kensaku had resolved from the start not to mention his desire to marry her directly to Aiko and not to involve her personally in any of the discussions. This was in keeping with custom, and custom was very important to Aiko's mother; besides, he wanted to save Aiko any embarrassment, for it took very little, he well knew, to throw her into a state of confusion. But now he began to regret his resolve, and to realize that had he not been so confident of the outcome, he would surely have involved her. He had never thought it possible that he could receive such treatment from her family. Could it be that his father was in some way being obstructive behind his back?

He had told Oei, before telling anyone else, of his wish to marry Aiko. She had been very glad for him, yet, he remembered, a look of sadness had momentarily crossed her face. Had she known something then? No, he quickly told himself, he was being silly. After all, if he were to get married, she would have to leave him. Why shouldn't she have been saddened by the prospect?

When he visited Keitarō the next evening he found two other guests already there. He knew neither of them. They had been fellow students at the commercial college, Keitarō said. "I was supposed to meet them earlier in the day, but I couldn't because of unexpected business, so I asked them to come over this evening. In two or three days' time I shall be quite free, so I'll come over to your place then for a nice, long chat. Anyway, stick around tonight if you can stand to listen to the inanities of Philistines like us. Who knows, we may even provide you with material you can use later in your work." He laughed merrily.

Kensaku could barely hide his anger. Had the man no shame? How dare he lie like this, with not a hint of embarrassment? And together with the anger came the realization that all this lying and evasion by Keitarō could only mean that his suit was not likely to succeed. "How long are you staying in Tokyo?" he said at last.

"I'm not sure," Keitarō said. "I'm needed back in Osaka, of course, and I should leave as soon as I've finished my work here. But no matter what, I'll visit you the day after tomorrow, sometime in the evening. Is that all right with you?"

"Yes."

Kensaku stayed for an hour, then left. Aiko and her mother had gone out for the evening; they were visiting relatives, he was told. That their absence had been deliberately arranged, he had no doubt.

His own house at that moment seemed too bleak a place to return to. Besides, he could not bear to be questioned by Oei. Had she been tied to him by blood, he might have rushed home like a dejected boy and sought consolation from her. Aimlessly, then, he walked about the deserted streets, not caring what he saw or where he was.

When finally he returned to his house, it was past eleven o'clock. His brother Nobuyuki was waiting for him. He said as soon as Kensaku sat down, "Tell me, must it be Aiko? Is she the only one that will do?"

"Well, no, not exactly."

"Do you really mean that?"

Kensaku said nothing.

"Look, if you really want her, I'll be willing to talk to her mother and Keitarō—quarrel with them, if I must. I don't know if they'll listen to anything I have to say, but I'll do all I can. Mind you, I'm willing only if you are absolutely bent on marrying her and no one else. If, on the other hand, she doesn't mean all that much to you, then my advice is give up the idea. Which is it to be?"

"All right then, I'll simply forget about it."

"Good," said Nobuyuki, nodding his head. The nod was almost a bow. There was a brief silence, then he spoke again: "Yes, that's the best thing to do. I know how unpleasant the whole thing has been for you. And I know it wasn't just once that you had cause to feel insulted. But you know what sort of a fellow Keitarō is. True, Aiko's mother likes you, but a woman is pretty helpless at a time like this."

"It's Keitarō's way of doing things that I don't like. If he wants to say no, why doesn't he say no and be done with it? Why must he be so evasive and so devious? By being unpleasant, he hopes that I'll get the hint and stop bothering him."

Kobuyuki was silent. "He has no shame," Kensaku said.

"But he has always been like that," was Nobuyuki's answer. Little more was said before he left.

Kensaku thought it most unlikely that Keitarō would come as he had promised. He wished nevertheless that Keitarō would keep his promise, if only because a blunt rejection, with reasons given, would be better at least than this quagmire of uncertainty and indirect insults. He was sure that Keitarō intended to arrange a marriage for Aiko that would benefit himself. The man would of course never tell him to his face that such was his intention; but if only he would!

As expected Keitarō failed to appear two evenings later. Instead a letter from him, sent by express mail, arrived. It was written hurriedly. "I have just received a telegram from Osaka," it said, "requesting my immediate return. I intend to come to Tokyo again in about two weeks. I have heard all about your proposal from mother, and I shall write to you about it in detail from Osaka. You must think me very unreliable. Do forgive me."

A week later a much longer letter arrived from Osaka. This was the gist of it: "The fact of the matter is, about a month before I came to Tokyo, Mr. Nagata [Keitarō's immediate superior and a protégé of Kensaku's father] came to me on behalf of a fellow employee of the company, suggesting that I give Aiko to this man in marriage. I agreed, though of course only tentatively. And I must admit that part of my purpose in coming to Tokyo this last time was to talk about the proposal with my family. So imagine my surprise when mother told me of your proposal. Of course I was at fault for not having got in touch with mother immediately after my conversation with Mr. Nagata. But as you know, I hardly ever write home. Besides, I was rather busy, and I knew that I would be in Tokyo soon. Anyway, when I heard about your proposal from mother, I simply didn't know what to do. True, I had only given a tentative promise, without consulting anyone in the family. But a commitment is a commitment, no matter how much I might wish to see my sister get married to an old friend of mine like you. Before I could say anything to you, I owed the other party at least the courtesy of an explanation. There was no other way, I felt, than to approach Mr. Nagata after I got back to Osaka, try to make him understand the situation and get his consent, then proceed to present your case to Aiko and the rest of the family. Well, Mr. Nagata was agreeable enough; but his candidate, alas, was another matter. The fellow simply refused to back down. His relatives and friends had already been informed of the engagement, he said, and he was not about to make a fool of himself by telling them that the other party had decided to cancel it. If I still insisted on going back on my word, he said, there was nothing he could do about it; but it was unconscionable of me to try to do so without his express consent. He was, in short, outraged—with some justification, I think. You see, Aiko had always said she would leave all marriage negotiations up to me. I should not have taken her quite so literally and been so rash as to more or less promise her to someone without consulting her and others. But what's done is done, and I am forced to keep my promise. I expect that I gave you much cause for displeasure just before I left Tokyo, and all I can do now is to ask you to understand my position and to continue to regard me with goodwill."

Many times as Kensaku read the letter he muttered, "Liar! Liar!" And he wondered how any man could write such stuff with so little shame.

Three months or so later, Aiko went down to Osaka as a bride. But the man she married was not Keitarō's fellow employee, whoever that might have been. He was some rich man's younger son.

The episode left a wound in Kensaku deeper than he would have thought possible. It was more than mere disappointment in love; rather, it was the sudden awareness brutally forced on him of his own capacity for disappointment in people. Aiko had been hardly more than a pawn in the entire affair. Her part in it, he could learn to view with resigned acceptance. Even Keitarō's behavior, unforgivable as it had struck him at the time, ceased to gnaw at him, for the fellow had never been any different. What hurt him most, then, was the attitude of Aiko's mother.

He had been so certain of her affection for him. But what could that "affection" have been? What could it have meant to her? If, before the rejection of his suit, she had shown him some sign of fondness or concern, he would have found some consolation in it. But what puzzled him was that she had pushed him away as though no bond had ever existed between them.

It was beyond him to resign himself to some simple, cynical generality about life. Had he been able to do so, he would have been more comfortable. But because he could not, the heaviness in his heart persisted.

He thought that perhaps if he were to write about the affair, some things might become clearer to him. But as he began to put down on paper all that had happened, the narrative could not get past the inevitable question, why had he been treated thus?

He realized with distaste that gradually a vulgar, unpleasant suspicion of all people's motives was taking root in his mind. His recent experiences with Sakaguchi, besides, had only intensified his suspicious mood. He tried to resist this growing suspicion in himself, not wanting it to color his view of everything around him. He told himself, this is a temporary sickness. Yet he was very careful to avoid any situation that might again betray him. Indeed, his present state of mind went beyond mere cautiousness; it was more akin to fear.

And so, unwilling though he was to crush the new emotion he had come to feel toward Tokiko, he could not bring himself to nurture it, not even when he had come to enjoy a certain sense of comfort in his relationship with her. That the new emotion, thus untended, should immediately begin to wither was inevitable.

6

The third day after Kensaku's second meeting with Tokiko was the anniversary of the death of a boyhood friend of his. This friend had died fourteen, fifteen years before. With others who had also known him well Kensaku went out that day to visit his grave in Somei.

It was evening when they got back to Sugamo Station from the graveyard. The understanding had been that the group would, after visiting the grave, all go to some cheerful part of the town and have dinner together. Now opinion was divided as to where in the city they should go: one half of the group wanted to catch the train there and go to Ueno, and the other half wanted to catch a streetcar outside and go straight to Ginza. Kensaku, for reasons not entirely clear to himself, was strongly in favor of going to Ueno. That it would be easier to visit Tokiko from there was not exactly his motive. Ueno seemed more attractive to him at the time, that was all.

In the end those who preferred Ginza prevailed. But once there, there was again disagreement: this time, it was over choice of cuisine. They had all been boyhood friends, and now they felt free to act like willful boys again. There was an innocence about the argument, a pleasant sense of the irresponsibility of youth recaptured. Some wanted to go to a European restaurant recently opened by a Frenchman, and some wanted to go to a Japanese restaurant known for its tasty beef. Neither side would give in. One of them, a fellow by the name of Ogata, went so far as to say, "Don't go to that French place. You'll find bits of glass in their hors d'oeuvres, I know."

They finally agreed to split up for dinner. The group favoring Japanese-style beef would later join the others at the French restaurant for a cup of tea.

It was about nine when the entire party, now together again, came out of the French restaurant. They ambled past the night stalls that were lined up along one side of the street. It was time they went home, some started saying.

It was then that Kensaku decided to pay Tokiko a visit. "Come with me," he said to Ogata.

"No, I can't. My elder brother and his wife are in town, and I should see them tonight."

But Kensaku, once having decided to see Tokiko that night, was not about to change his mind.

"How can you be sure she'll be available?" Ogata said. "It's rather late, you know."

"But if she is free, will you come with me?"

"You *are* anxious, I must say. All right, let's at least find out if she can join us."

They walked into a nearby cafe and from there Kensaku telephoned Nishimidori. It was Otsuta who answered. "Tokiko has gone to the theatre," she said, sounding quite sorry. "And Koine is away on a trip. She left yesterday and hasn't come back yet."

"But I take it Tokiko will be coming back as soon as the theatre closes?"

"I think so, but let me make sure. Give me your number, and I'll call you back."

A few minutes later she telephoned. "Apparently Tokiko and the customer left before the end of the performance. She's having dinner with him now at a restaurant, but thinks she'll be free afterward."

"All right, we'll come."

Ogata liked to drink. "I might as well get started here and now," he said, and immediately ordered a whiskey and soda. By the time they left the cafe, he had had two more.

"It's a funny thing," Otsuta said as she greeted them, "but right after I spoke to you I found out that Koine had just returned from her trip." She had another maid show the men to their room upstairs while she herself went to the telephone to call the two geisha.

Koine soon appeared on the scene, then a little while later, Tokiko.

Tokiko seemed a little stiff. This Kensaku attributed to the presence of Ogata, whom she had never met. She must also have been tired, for she showed little gaiety that evening. From time to time she would look nervously at Koine, then fuss with the collar of her kimono. Kensaku realized with amusement that she felt disheveled in comparison, having come directly from an outing.

That night again they played childish games. Kensaku could not help wondering if indeed this was quite what was expected of him as a patron. He himself would have liked nothing better than to pack up and go home after a few games, but at four in the morning going home was easier said than done. And he wasn't sure if asking the establishment to put out a bed for him was quite the right thing to do.

Outside a quiet, autumn rain was falling. Half-listening to the lulling sound, Kensaku and Ogata dozed off, and the women got up and left.

The two men slept until ten in the morning. It was only after they had had a hot bath that they began to feel more or less awake. They asked for the same two geisha, but only Koine came. Tokiko had already been engaged for the day by another customer of Nishimidori, who had reserved the front room, across the corridor from theirs.

Ogata fought off sobriety by continuing to drink at regular intervals. They played no more games; and no one seemed to have anything to say. Koine had given in to the pervasive languor; she sat still and gazed with empty, sad eyes at Ogata who was stretched out on the floor, seemingly asleep for the moment.

He suddenly opened his eyes, and became aware of Koine's gaze. He must have felt awkward, for he said, though without much conviction, "Haven't you any interesting stories to tell?"

"Let me see," said Koine, the sadness still in her smile. "Did you hear about the geisha from the Shitaya quarter? She was being taken somewhere in a car, and she happened to turn around and what do you think she saw through the rear window? A white fox pushing the car!"

"No, I can't say I've heard the story. Where did this happen?"

"I think it was in Ōmiya. On the way there, maybe. Anyway, it happened recently." Koine looked quite solemn as she continued. "You can imagine how frightened she was. Of course she could have told the man she was with, but you know how vindictive foxes are."

Kensaku was appalled by the banality of the story. If Koine had really believed it, he wouldn't have minded so much. But she clearly didn't. Why then tell it with such solemnity? "I don't find the story at all interesting," he said.

Koine readily agreed. "It isn't very good, you're quite right."

"You know very well it never happened."

Koine was agreeable. "When you think about it, it is a bit fishy," she said, and laughed.

She was in fact being accused of disingenuousness. But she was quite cheerful about it, only too ready to agree with Kensaku. Such malleability toward her customers he found both irritating and touching. He said, "It sounds like some third-rate comedian's story that didn't quite come off."

"You're absolutely right," Koine said happily, and laughed. Her laugh was as usual high-pitched. "An apprentice geisha from our house heard it in some restaurant or other. I really did think it was meant to be a true story. But of course you're right!"

"Tell us another one," Ogata said wearily, his eyes still closed.

"But I can't think of one," Koine said uncomfortably. "There simply aren't that many interesting stories."

There was silence for a while. Then suddenly, to the surprise of the two men whose minds had wandered elsewhere, she started giggling to herself. "All right, I'll tell you a true story!"

It was about a man who had survived an attempt at love suicide with a geisha from the Yoshiwara quarter. In the course of being examined by the magistrate he had used some slang word current in Yoshiwara, which referred to closing time in the quarter but which sounded like "discount." The magistrate, by no means a connoisseur, had angrily shouted, "Discount? Discount? What do you mean you got her at a discount!"

Koine seemed greatly amused by her own story. Alas, Ogata, like the magistrate, had never heard the slang word (though Kensaku had), so that the point of the story was somewhat lost on him.

Very soon Ogata was snoring gently. Despite his fatigue Kensaku felt wide awake. For lack of a better idea he had a *go* board brought in, and started playing a simple game with Koine.

He could occasionally hear Tokiko talking in the room opposite. He had by now ceased to have illusions about his relationship with her. Nevertheless it gave him a forlorn feeling not to have her in the room with him when she was so near, to hear her talking to some other man in another room. He was constantly aware of her presence in the same house; he would surely have felt better if she had not been there at all.

Tokiko always looked in whenever she had occasion to pass their room, and once or twice even came in for a short chat. It was surprising how much more lively he would feel when she came in.

When at sundown the rain finally stopped, Ogata and Kensaku left the house. Tokiko's customer was still there. They stopped at a European restaurant just outside the quarter, and there Ogata drank more whiskey. His capacity for alcohol was apparently limitless. Though Kensaku was still very tired, it had been a great relief for him to come out of the oppressive atmosphere and be touched by the air outside, so clean and fresh after the rain; and very quickly his spirits had lifted.

Having decided to go in the direction of Nihonbashi, the two walked to Minowa and there boarded a streetcar bound for Ningyōchō.

Ogata immediately leaned his head back against the window without bothering to take off his hat, folded his arms over his chest, and closed his eyes. The hat was dark green felt, uncannily resembling thick leather.

Many of the passengers got off at Kurumazaka Junction and equally many came on. One of the new passengers was a pretty young woman with her eyebrows shaved off, holding a baby hardly a year old. She was followed by a docile-seeming teenage maid carrying something in a cloth wrapper. They sat down opposite Kensaku.

The baby was fat and active. He was prettily got up in a fine muslin kimono and a padded waistcoat. But he was perhaps too small for the kimono, for the collar hung rather loosely around his neck, and his plump, soft shoulders, shining pink, were visible. He bubbled and gurgled without cease, his head, hands and feet jerking all the time. The young woman was perhaps in her early twenties. But Kensaku, to whom all married women somehow seemed older than himself, wasn't sure. With light, friendly familiarity she was talking to the maid.

Two seats away from this young mother sat another woman carrying a girl, perhaps four years old, on her back. The woman was clearly a maid, and the girl presumably her mistress's daughter. The girl had for some time been staring silently at the active baby, her big eyes filled with curiosity. The baby, now seeing her for the first time and sensing her interest, began to struggle, making little screechy noises and reaching his tiny hands out toward her. The girl made no response, and continued to stare—almost angrily, Kensaku thought.

The young mother, who had been engrossed in conversation with the maid, at last became aware of the fuss her baby was making. She turned toward the girl. How lightly her head moved, Kensaku thought, and how lively her eyes were. She smiled and said, "He wants very much to come to you, doesn't he." The girl remained silent, as solemn as ever. The maid who was carrying her said something in reply, with obvious reluctance.

The young mother, suddenly oblivious of her surroundings, began kissing—it was more like pecking—her baby all over his face. It was as though momentarily she had lost all control of herself. The baby jerked about happily, loving the ticklish sensation. The woman bent her head lower, showing the back of her pretty neck, and started kissing the baby's throat. It was too much of a display for Kensaku; it was like having something sickly sweet in one's mouth, and instinctively he turned away and looked out of the window. What a coquette she is, he thought; ah well, when the baby gets a bit older he will have his own little tricks.

Somehow the whole scene looked to him like an unconscious re-enactment of the love play that went on between her and her young husband. The suggestion of such intimacy made him uncomfortable; yet the woman was so full of life, so assured, there was such a feeling of harmony about her, that he could not but think her very beautiful.

Tentatively, almost fearfully, he began to imagine himself having a wife like her. No doubt about it, it was a happy thought; indeed, for a moment, he wondered if with such a wife he would want anything else.

As the streetcar approached the next stop the young woman put the baby gently on the maid's back. "Off we go," she said to the baby, "Kimiya is going to give you a nice ride now."

Kensaku watched the three get off, feeling strangely happy. And later, whenever he remembered the woman, he would remember his own happiness at the time.

The two men got off at Kodenmachō and proceeded on foot toward Nihonbashi. The city lights shone prettily on the pavement still wet from the rain. They crossed the temporary bridge at Nihonbashi, walked on a little farther until they came to a small side street, and there they went into a neat, unpretentious restaurant.

"They give you good saké here," said Ogata, and started drinking again. Drinking seemed to clear his mind and make him more communicative. He began by comparing geisha of the Nakanochō district, whom he had never seen until the day before, with geisha that worked around Shinbashi and Akasaka, then went on to tell Kensaku about an affair he was having with an Akasaka geisha. It had become a rather messy business, he said. Her employer was doing everything he could to prevent the two from seeing each other.

Kensaku, who normally disliked being told such things, listened to Ogata's story with sympathy and interest. For in the way his friend talked about his affair and his determination to continue to see the girl despite the complication, there was not a trace of exhibitionism or pomposity.

The two left the restaurant at about nine o'clock. Not yet ready to part ways, they strolled aimlessly down the main street.

"I have a bottle of whiskey at Seihintei," Ogata said. "Shall we go there?"

"Do you still want to drink?"

"Yes, I do." Ogata had inherited his fondness and extraordinary capacity for alcohol from his father, and could drink endlessly without ever behaving like a drunk. "They have a girl there who used to be a geisha in Yokohama."

"Does this bar specialize in ex-geisha, then?"

"Oh, no. She's the only one. I suppose she finds it easier than being a geisha. A bar girl's life is much more informal, after all. Besides, she doesn't have to spend so much on clothes."

At Seihintei they went up the stairs to the second floor, then down a step on the other side of the landing to a mirrored door. This door opened into a gaudily decorated room that looked to Kensaku like the inside of a cinema. Waitresses rushed past, carrying bottles and glasses. Several stopped as Ogata entered and greeted him enthusiastically: "Good evening, O-san!" "Good to see you, O-san!" The two found a small private room and sat down. Now and then a burst of loud laughter reached them from another room nearby.

Kensaku had bought some eye lotion on the way, and now he put a few drops of it into his eyes, bloodshot from lack of sleep and too much smoking. He put his elbows on the table and rested his head in his hands. He kept his smarting eyes closed for a while, thinking how tired he was. Finally he sat up and said to Ogata who seemed equally exhausted, "They're a lively lot here, I must say. Of course, anyone would seem so compared to us."

A woman in a waitress's kimono walked in carrying a bottle of whiskey in one hand and two bottles of soda water in the other. There was something like a tease in her smile as she said to Ogata, "This is yours, isn't it?" She walked up to the table and bowed politely to Kensaku. "How do you do." Then she bowed to Ogata silently, as though words of formal greeting were unnecessary between such friends.

"Did you write this?" said Ogata, pointing to the thick, black "O" drawn uncertainly on the whiskey label. "What a clumsy hand."

"Who cares, so long as one can read it," she said, reaching for the bottle opener stuck in her sash. She poured the whiskey and soda into the glasses, then rushed out with the empty soda bottles.

"That wasn't the ex-geisha, was it?" asked Kensaku.

"No. She'll be here soon, I expect."

A moment later another waitress came in quietly, her manner made tentative by the presence of a new customer. She was a big woman, quite beautiful. Kensaku was sure this was the ex-geisha. She went to Ogata's side and said, "Nice to see you again so soon."

Her eyes, with lids that looked a little swollen, suggested a kind of sleepy seductivity. Her lips were a brilliant color, with a touch of befitting cruelty about them.

Ogata gulped down his drink, then poured more whiskey and soda into the glass and pushed it toward her. "Here, you drink this."

She sat down, picked up the glass and looked at it thoughtfully. "It's too strong," she said, and put it back in front of Ogata.

"No, you've got to drink it." As he was about to pick it up again she put out her hand to stop him. "I don't like it that strong, I tell you."

"All right, then, we'll share it fifty-fifty." In the ensuing struggle some of the yellow liquid spilled over onto the thick tablecloth.

"All right," she said, picking up the glass resignedly, "but you've got to drink first," and put it down in front of Ogata as though it were something dirty.

"Promise?"

"Yes, yes, I promise."

Ogata sat up straight, then gulped down about a half, perhaps a little less, of the drink. The woman, now quite docile, picked up the glass and brought it gingerly to her red lips. With an exaggerated grimace she took a few sips, saying, "It's terribly strong."

The waitress who had come in first now returned with more bottles of soda. She stood over her companion and said seriously, "What do you think you're doing, Okayo? You know you shouldn't be drinking that strong stuff."

Okayo looked a trifle angry. She said impatiently, "All I did was drink a part of what was left."

The other woman, ignoring her, turned to Ogata. "You're a naughty man, O-san. Please don't get her drunk."

"That's the trouble with chief waitresses," said Ogata. "They're all tyrants."

The waitress, saying nothing, poured some soda into Ogata's glass. She then looked at Kensaku's glass and said with a smile, "This gentleman hasn't touched his drink at all."

"That's why I asked Okayo to have one with me. I can't be expected to drink alone, can I? If you won't let her, then you join me, Osuzu."

"No thanks, I'm not that tough," said the one called Osuzu and sat down beside Okayo.

Okayo suddenly turned on Osuzu and said in a low, angry voice, "Maybe you're getting on in years, but that doesn't give you the right to be so righteous."

There was distaste on Osuzu's face. "That really was a mean thing to say."

At this point Ogata interceded: "It's no fun fighting when you're sober, so have a drink before you get started again."

The two women looked at each other in embarrassment, then burst out laughing. They put up no more resistance to Ogata's cajoling, and began drinking a little to keep him company. Occasionally Osuzu would grumble, but only halfheartedly.

Okayo was called away several times to attend to customers downstairs, but whenever she could she would come back upstairs and join them.

Kensaku, feeling awkward and inexperienced, said very little. There was a bowl of grapes in front of him. He huddled over it, almost hugging it, and with an air of concentration popped one grape after another into his mouth.

Okayo came running back into the room after one of her trips downstairs. "It's terribly warm," she said, and stretching out one of her kimono sleeves with both hands began fanning herself busily. She was clearly drunk. Her eyes, moist from the drinking, glowed beautifully in the electric light.

"Be careful, Okayo," said Osuzu. "You really must stop, otherwise you'll collapse again."

"Collapse indeed!" said Okayo crossly, glaring at Osuzu. "You know very well I'll never do a thing like that!"

Kensaku bent his head back and put a few more drops of lotion in his eyes.

"I think I could use some of that," Ogata said. Kensaku, his eyes shut, held out the bottle.

"Let me put the drops in for you," Okayo said.

"Can you really do it?"

"Of course I can." Okayo took the bottle and went around to the back of Ogata's chair. "Put your head back further."

"Like this?"

"No, further."

In the meantime Osuzu had quickly lined up four chairs together. "Lie down here, it will be easier," she said.

Okayo sat down on one end and said, "Here, O-san, put your head in my lap." And when Osuzu picked up a clean napkin and gave it to her, she said, "Well, well, we *are* being formal tonight," and spread it over her lap.

Ogata obediently lay down. Okayo said, "Shall I hold your eyes open for you?"

"No, thanks, I'll do it myself." He stuck out his elbows and with his hands pulled open both eyes. Okayo missed on her first attempt, and the lotion trickled down toward Ogata's ear. She laughed. "Open it again." Osuzu, standing over Okayo, said, "But Okayo, can you see what you're doing in this light?" Osuzu looked up at her. "Of course I can. You watch." She took careful aim and squeezed the rubber cap on the dropper. But, alas, there was so little lotion left in it that nothing came out. Ogata, who had had the whites of his eyes turned up in readiness for the drop, now brought them down a little to see what was going on. Okayo let out a screech and jumped up, knocking down her chair. Ogata, taken aback, jumped up too.

In a frightened voice Osuzu said, "What's the matter, what's the matter?"

Okayo stood still, clutching the bottle of lotion. Finally she said hoarsely, "Don't you understand, there his eyes were, all turned up, looking at nothing in particular, then suddenly those black pupils appeared, staring at me!"

With a touch of disgust Osuzu said, "Oh, have some sense, Okayo." Okayo just stood there, her face ashen, saying nothing.

At about midnight the two went back to Nishimidori. It seemed to require less effort to do that than to go home. And once at Nishimidori, they began to feel more alert, less in need of sleep. But this revival of energy was only temporary. By three o'clock Kensaku was done for. Nothing now seemed so inviting as his own bed. He made Ogata promise to drop in on his way home the next day; and, wearing a padded kimono borrowed from the establishment, left by himself.

Night was about to end outside. As he watched from the rickshaw, the early morning sun, so beautiful after the rain, rose gradually in the east, and he remembered a boat trip he once took about ten years before along the Japan Sea. It was autumn. He was standing on deck, waiting for the dawn to break. And there, behind Mt. Tsurugi already lightly covered with snow, the sun had slowly begun to rise.

7

It was already noon when he awakened. The first thing that occurred to him was that it would be a little embarrassing to have to face Oei after having stayed away for two whole days. Outside a shrike was crying noisily. He might have stayed in bed a while longer, but he bestirred himself and got up. As he slid open the wooden storm window, the shrike, perched on top of the neighbor's parasol tree, flew away with a shrill parting cry.

It was a fine day. There was no wind, and in the gentle autumn sunlight the parasol tree cast its shadow diagonally over the wet ground beside his house. A thin trail of smoke rose from his bath-house chimney. He now remembered telling the sleepy maid as she let him into the house that he would want a hot bath when he woke up.

"You're up at last," said a loud voice from downstairs. It was Nobuyuki. Then Oei came up. "He's been waiting for over an hour," she said.

Kensaku hurried downstairs and found Nobuyuki seated by the brazier in the morning room, smoking a cigarette. Without bothering to sit down Kensaku exchanged a few words with his brother, then said, "You don't want a bath, do you, Nobu?" "No, but you go ahead." "All right then, I won't be long."

Kensaku enjoyed the hot bath as though he hadn't had one for a long time. The sunlight poured through the glass window, reaching the bottom of the tub; and the vapor, turning into minute particles in the stream of light, played above his eyes. Had his brother not been waiting, he would have stayed much, much longer, enjoying to the full his own tranquil mood.

When Kensaku returned Nobuyuki said with a friendly smile, "You really mustn't go out so much. It worries Oei." Kensaku mumbled meaninglessly in reply. Nobuyuki then said, "I bumped into Yamaguchi yesterday. He wanted to know if you had a story he might publish in his magazine."

"In which issue?"

"He mentioned next month's issue, as a matter of fact. But I don't suppose he has any real deadline in mind."

"Well, if he's willing to wait, I'll send him something sometime."

"Haven't you got a piece all ready to go?"

"I did get started on a story recently, but I couldn't finish it."

Nobuyuki nodded, apparently knowing what Kensaku was referring to.

"When I write something, I'll send it to him," Kensaku repeated.

"But you must have all kinds of things you could send if you wanted to."

"True, but I don't much care to see them in print."

"All right. I'll just tell Yamaguchi he'll have to wait. He seems awfully anxious to publish your stuff, I must say."

This Yamaguchi had been a classmate of Nobuyuki's at high school. For some reason he had never finished college, and was now working as an editor for a serious journal.

"But why is he so anxious?" asked Kensaku.

"Well, it was Tatsuoka apparently who first mentioned you to him. He then went to Sakaguchi to ask what he thought, and from what I gather Sakaguchi said all kinds of nice things about your work."

"He did, did he?" said Kensaku, feeling a little queasy. "And when was this?"

"The night before last, I think."

"I see. Well, I'm not going to make any promises, but maybe someday I'll take advantage of Yamaguchi's offer."

Lunch was served, and for once Oei sat down and ate with them. Curious to know what Ogata was doing, Kensaku excused himself immediately after the meal was over and went to the neighborhood bookstore to telephone Nishimidori. Otsuta answered. "He left a little while ago," she said, "but just wait a second . . ." Then another voice said, "Hello . . . do you know who this is?" It was Tokiko.

"Of course," Kensaku said in a tone that sounded stiff and boorish even to himself. He might have tried sounding more friendly if it hadn't been for all the people in the bookstore, who seemed to him to be listening intently.

"Is something the matter with you?" Tokiko asked. Then Kensaku heard her say to Otsuta, "Something's the matter with him." Kensaku waited. "Is Mr. Ogata coming to your house? If he does, would you please say I'm sorry I got angry during vingt-et-un? He's so lucky, I'm afraid I lost my temper a little."

A trifle bored, Kensaku ended the conversation as quickly as he could and went back to his house. Ogata arrived shortly thereafter. He had already had a few drinks. "Tokiko is all right," he said jocularly, "but she can be pretty nasty at times."

"I suppose you're talking about that card game we had. I just spoke to her on the telephone, and she asked me to apologize for her."

The incident had occurred early that morning just before Kensaku decided to leave. They were playing vingt-et-un. It was uncanny how all the good cards seemed to go to Ogata; he simply couldn't lose. Time and again the others would replenish their dwindling supply of chips, only to have them quickly taken away by Ogata. Eventually Tokiko's resentment at Ogata's luck became apparent, and she even made a few pointed remarks. What it was that she said was not clear to Kensaku, for he was not paying much attention; but soon afterward Ogata suddenly said, "I'm going to quit . . . it's no fun winning all the time," and lay down. Kensaku had continued to play with the other two, seeing nothing significant in Ogata's action.

But as he thought about Tokiko's apology on the telephone and Ogata's remark about her just now, he began to understand that the little incident, which he had hardly noticed at the time, had not been dismissed quite so lightly by these two. And he was reminded that at the same place, a week ago, Tatsuoka had remained more or less oblivious of Sakaguchi's misbehavior and his own annoyance. Perhaps he ought not to have been so surprised at Tatsuoka's seeming insensibility; after all, when placed in the same situation, he himself had been no more observant. But be that as it may, why had Sakaguchi of all people commended him to Yamaguchi, if indeed it was true that he had? What could he have had in mind?

Nobuyuki soon left. As the afternoon wore on Ogata began to complain that he was cold. Clearly, his body was in need of alcoholic reinforcement. There was some sherry in the house that Oei sometimes drank before going to bed. Ogata eyed the bottle suspiciously as Oei brought it out, then with a look of distaste began to drink the sickly sweet wine.

At about four o'clock Kensaku and Ogata left the house and went to Shiba to see Tatsuoka. With him in tow they walked around Hikagechō briefly, then went to Seihintei. But for some reason Okayo was not there that evening.

The next morning Kensaku woke up feeling decidedly under the weather. He got up nevertheless, for there was some business he had to take care of at the Maruzen Bookstore. Overcome occasionally by violent fits of sneezing he made his way to the bookstore, then rushed back to bed. Run-down by his recent irregular life, he succumbed to the cold with little resistance. All next day he stayed in bed. He said to himself, I really must try to live a little differently. Yet the self-admonition was halfhearted at best, and left him as restless as ever. The next day he still felt weak, but the fever was gone. That afternoon he decided he was well enough to have a bath; and once in the tub, he could not bear the thought of returning to bed. By early evening he was at Nishimidori, having picked up Tatsuoka on the way. Both Tokiko and Koine came, but the gathering lacked cheer somehow, and as time passed it became increasingly tedious for Kensaku.

He had felt closest to Tokiko on their second meeting, he thought, when ironically he had decided he had no more illusions about her. Since then their relationship had been like an old piece of elastic, limp and unresilient. He knew—and he was saddened by the knowledge—that he would never feel more than a mild fondness for her. It's all that business over Aiko that has made me like this, he wanted to tell himself; but this was not true. With a renewed sense of loneliness he had to admit that in the end he had not felt any greater love for Aiko.

And what am I doing in a place like this, he wondered, when I know I don't fit in? What is the point? He looked at himself then, and what he saw did not please him. Patiently he waited for the night to end, haunted by thoughts of his own worthlessness.

At about noon the next day Ogata came to Kensaku's house. He had come, he said, partly to ask a favor. A relation of his was thinking of marrying a girl whose brother had been a classmate of Nobuyuki's. Could Kensaku ask Nobuyuki if he knew anything about the family?

Then he said, "By the way, didn't you come home at all the day before yesterday?"

"Why do you ask?"

"You remember that girl called Okayo at Seihintei? Well, she wanted me to ask you to join us, so I sent a rickshaw over to pick you up, but you weren't in. It was about ten o'clock. Weren't you told about it?"

Kensaku blushed. Why would Okayo show such interest in him? Or was she just being whimsical? He simply had no way of guessing. His own feelings about her were somewhat ambivalent. He had found her attractive enough the first time he saw her, but she had a rough, almost coarse way about her that repelled him, though it had its attraction too. And he could sense that if he were to get involved with her, their affair would not be a particularly pleasant one.

All in all, then, he had been mildly intrigued by the very thought that she would be more than he could hope to handle—and that had been the extent of his interest. Besides, he had been quite sure that he had made no more of an impression on her than numerous other casual customers.

But all such reservations notwithstanding, there was of course pleasure in being told that he had found favor in her eyes. And he suddenly caught himself falling into an incongruously romantic frame of mind. He looked at Ogata quickly, hoping that his face showed none of the sweetness he was feeling.

The pleasurable mood soon turned into annoyance, however, when he remembered that Oei and the maid had said nothing about the rickshaw that had been sent to fetch him. Such an occurrence could hardly have been forgotten by Oei, whose daily life was after all routine and uneventful. Obviously, she had omitted to tell him on purpose; and she must have instructed the maid to say nothing about it either.

Ogata said, "Look here, I've got to go to Tōkaiji Temple today at four—there's to be a family memorial service—but I'm free until then, so how about going out somewhere for a meal?"

They chose a restaurant in Sannōshita, not far away, where they were shown to a room that faced a small, cleanly swept garden. It was a quiet time of day for the restaurant. They decided to sit out on the verandah under the eaves, and there they talked pleasantly, enjoying the peaceful scene.

"In a few days' time I'll be going to Kyoto," Ogata said. "I've been put in charge of a group of women relatives who want to visit Momoyama. I told them I wouldn't mind being with them during the day so long as I was left alone at night, free to do as I pleased."

A neatly dressed maid came in to change the flowers in the alcove. Presumably because the two customers were far enough away not to be disturbed, she spent an inordinately long time arranging and rearranging the flowers until she was quite satisfied.

"Call that old lady, will you?" said Ogata to the maid. "You know the one I mean. And what was the other one's name—Chiyo-ko, was it?"

The maid went out to the corridor, put the old flowers down on the floor, then came back in and sat down to await further orders. "Just call those two," said Ogata. The maid bowed and left.

In a short while the geisha referred to as "the old lady" came. She was in her forties, small and skinny and rather pale. She had the look of a very heavy drinker; and she loved to talk.

"We'll be leaving as soon as we've finished eating," said Ogata to the maid as she brought in the first course, "so tell Chiyoko to hurry."

The old geisha said to Ogata, "And when are you going to take me there?"

Instead of answering her, Ogata turned to Kensaku and said, "I promised granny here I would take her to Yoshiwara. She was terribly impressed when I told her about our visit there."

"I certainly was," said the geisha with an ingratiating laugh.

"Those Nakanochō geisha won't associate with boys, you know."

She and Ogata then began gossiping about people Kensaku had never heard of. She talked incessantly, and laughed rather too often. It was a cheap, brassy laugh, highly irritating.

"And is Fukiko around?" Ogata asked suddenly. A look of wary anxiety came over the old geisha's face. She was for once at a loss for words. Ogata was trying to appear casual, but one could tell he was tense. Kensaku guessed that Fukiko was the geisha Ogata had recently told him about.

The old geisha at last said, "She's away on a trip." That she was lying was obvious even to Kensaku.

"Where?" Ogata asked.

"I have an idea it's Shiobara," she said, then quickly and not very naturally began to talk about maple-viewing in Shiobara and Nikkō, whether it was too late or too early for it, and so on. Ogata maintained his bland expression and said no more about Fukiko, as though she were now totally forgotten. It amused Kensaku to see how uncomfortable Ogata's two innocent-seeming questions had made this pretentiously worldly-wise woman.

Kensaku remembered an anecdote about Fukiko recounted to him by Ogata four or five days before. She already had a regular patron—so his story went—some rich merchant. He knew all about her relationship with Ogata, but, apparently choosing to ignore it, continued to be generous to her and her mother. An employee of his, angered by her conduct, went to her house and accused her of being a wanton and an ingrate. In fury she brought out the kimono the patron had given her that spring and in the employee's presence tore it to shreds. Then she rushed out of the house, found a taxi, and went to Ogata's house. Not daring to go into the house, she stood outside helplessly, still weeping. By chance Ogata's younger brother was late coming home that night—it was about one in the morning—and he found this pathetic figure standing by the gate. She begged him to let her see Ogata.

This was the way Ogata had ended his anecdote: "I was of course in bed when my brother came to me with the message. I had heard the taxi outside the house, and I was wondering if it might be her. But once you're in bed, it's not that easy to get up and rush outside.

So I decided to stay where I was and do nothing. She went away before long. I haven't seen her for two months."

Just as they were about to finish their meal the geisha called Chiyoko arrived. Unlike the old geisha she was large, supple-bodied and beautiful, altogether a magnificent woman. In physique she reminded one a little of Koine. But what caught Kensaku's attention most were her eyes. They had a strength and quiet beauty which made one feel strangely restful.

The two men left the restaurant soon afterward, and parted company at the bottom of Akasakamitsuke. With no particular destination in mind Kensaku slowly walked up the hill toward Hibiya, thinking not of the beautiful Chiyoko whom he had just met, but of Okayo, the waitress at Seihintei, and repeating to himself Ogata's remark that she had wanted to see him.

The truth was he was drawn to almost every woman he saw— Tokiko, say, or the young mother on the streetcar, or Chiyoko; and for the present at least, to Okayo most of all. And before he could stop himself, he was asking himself the unwelcome question: "What is it that I want?" He knew the answer; but it was so unpleasant, he wanted to hide from it.

8

A younger friend named Miyamoto dropped in to see Kensaku, carrying a basketful of mushrooms. He had been away for a while in the Kyoto area. The two friends were upstairs in Kensaku's room chatting when a messenger came from the neighborhood caterer's to say there was a telephone call for Kensaku. It was early evening.

The caller turned out to be Okayo. "Come and join us," she said.

"Is Ogata there?" Kensaku asked.

"Yes, he is."

"Then please tell him to come here right away and have dinner with us. Say it won't be much of a meal, but we do have Kyoto mushrooms."

In her characteristically quick-tempered way Okayo said, "I certainly will not!"

"But why not? It will be all right if we come over to your place after dinner, surely."

"It's far too complicated, and a nuisance for O-san too."

After a few more exchanges of this sort Kensaku finally gave in. "All right, my friend and I will be there after dinner."

Two hours later Kensaku and Miyamoto went to Seihintei. They found Ogata in a small private room, drinking whiskey with Osuzu and Okayo. Okayo was sitting beside him. "She's got a lot of cheek, this one," he said, grabbing her by the shoulder and shaking her. "How dare she turn down your invitation without asking me first."

"You're absolutely right," Osuzu said. "You probably missed a very good dinner."

"But Mr. Tokitō himself said there wasn't going to be anything special," said Okayo.

"What did you expect him to say!" exclaimed Osuzu. "Do you expect a host to praise his own dinner?"

"Oh, don't be so dense," Okayo said, glaring at Osuzu. "I managed to get them all here, didn't I?"

"Osuzu," Ogata broke in, "how about all of us going to Hashizen for some tempura and saké?"

"I don't know that I even want to look at tempura," said Miyamoto quietly.

"You don't want to go?" said Ogata. "All right, then, we won't."

"Quite right," Osuzu said. "This isn't the best time of year for tempura. It's always wise not to take chances between seasons."

In the manner of an actor addressing the audience in an aside, Okayo said, "There is much wisdom in this old lady."

Miyamoto could hold his drink. He was having peppermint liqueur, and it appeared he could drink any amount of the sweet stuff and remain sober. Indeed, he seemed unusually withdrawn. He hadn't slept on the train last night, he had told Kensaku earlier that day, and perhaps that was the reason.

"What's the matter with you?" Okayo said to Miyamoto who sat opposite her, peering into his downcast face. "Do cheer up. You can't sulk all by yourself when everyone else is trying to have fun." She turned to Kensaku. "What is the matter with him?" She sat up, and as she did so, Kensaku's hand, innocently resting on the back of her chair, got caught between it and her back. "He didn't get enough sleep last night," he said, trying gently to extricate his hand.

"I wonder who kept him up," Okayo said, looking at Kensaku coquettishly and ever so slightly increasing the pressure on his hand.

"Nothing of the sort," Kensaku said shortly, yanking his hand free. "He was on the night train." He wondered if his abruptness might have annoyed her, but her face was perfectly nonchalant.

He had acted ungraciously, mostly out of distaste for her kind of flirtation. Now a part of him regretted his action. What was he being such a prig about anyway? Besides, an opportunity had been presented to him right under his nose, and he had rejected it. The trouble with him, he decided, was that he was too sober. He pointed at the bottle of peppermint liqueur which he had earlier refused to touch. "Pour me some of that," he said.

Okayo watched him drink down the liqueur in a gulp. "See, there's more to him than you might think," she said. She herself was quite drunk now. Her eyes shone seductively, her lips had become a brilliant red. And her manner was gradually getting rougher.

Some of the liqueur had spilled on the thick, starched tablecloth, and under the gaslight the green stains looked rather pretty. "What a lovely color," Osuzu said, bringing her head closer to the table.

"In that case, I'll make you some more," Okayo said, and with the salt spoon started sprinkling the liqueur all over the cloth.

"What do you think you're doing!" Osuzu said.

Okayo glared back at her. "I thought you said you liked the spots."

"They are pretty, I must say," said Kensaku.

"Aren't they," Okayo said, bringing her face close to his and then nodding meaningfully.

He was not sure what the nod meant, but anxious to do the right thing this time, nodded back. But somehow the nod wasn't timed quite right, and succeeded only in making him feel very foolish. Miyamoto, who hadn't spoken a word for some time, suddenly said in a coy, effeminate Kyoto voice, "My, what good friends you two have become."

Kensaku thought that Miyamoto was laughing at his awkwardness. His pride was now at stake. He sidled up to Okayo and whispered loudly into her ear, "You know, I like you." It was all done very badly.

Surprised by Kensaku's unexpected behavior, Okayo seemed for a moment to lose her composure. But she rallied quickly, and with uncharacteristic simplicity and sweetness said, "Thank you."

Much bolder now, Kensaku pressed his shoulder against hers and said, "What are we going to do about it?"

Okayo was her old self again. "Oh, let's do something about it," she said in a girlish, wheedling tone, then rested her head on his shoulder. Kensaku sat still, conscious of her hair brushing against his cheek.

"What a scene!" said Osuzu, and laughed loudly.

Putting his arm around her, Kensaku brought his mouth close to hers and made as if to kiss her. Their foreheads touched, but their lips were two or three inches apart. They stayed in this position for a while. Their faces, made hot by the drinking, seemed to heat the very air between them. The sensation Kensaku experienced then was so pleasurable he almost fell into a trance.

Sensing at last the silence around him, he looked up. The heavy curtain had been drawn discreetly across the entrance. Their companions had all disappeared somewhere.

Okayo sat up, her face moist with sweat. Feeling suddenly sober and awkward, they couldn't even manage a nervous joke.

"I bet they're in the next room," she said.

"Let's go and see."

There was no one there. But they found Ogata and Miyamoto in the large room beyond, listening helplessly to a loud-mouthed drunk. The latter turned out to be Yamazaki, who had been three years ahead of Kensaku at school and was now a practicing lawyer. Beside him sat a waitress named Okiyo, a small, pretty girl with thin eyebrows.

Kensaku had never liked this Yamazaki, and had invariably found himself becoming pugnacious in his presence. But suppressing his aversion this time, he sat down with them.

Yamazaki, the bore that he was, kept on pressing Okiyo to drink more. Holding down one of her hands, he would push the glass up to her lips. She would insist she didn't want any more, but would then take a drink, seemingly without a qualm.

Okayo, presumably still drunk, sat quietly beside Okiyo.

Kensaku was beginning to feel restless. He turned to Ogata and Miyamoto and asked them in an undertone if they would like to go to Nishimidori. Miyamoto refused to commit himself. "I'll telephone them," Kensaku said. He stood up, then stumbled on a chair leg and fell to the floor. He picked himself up and started to walk slowly away from the table. Okayo followed him, saying, "I'd better come with you." "I'd rather you didn't," he said. She punched him hard on the back. "You brute!" Looking straight ahead he walked away in what he imagined was dignified silence; but he discovered that uncontrollably a fatuous grin had spread over his face. First he got rid of it, as though it were a mask, then turned around. "Come along then," he said. "No thank you," she replied.

Carefully he made his way down the stairs. He stood still before the telephone for a moment, waiting for the sick feeling in his chest to go away.

"Tokiko is miles away, and won't be available this evening," the maid said on the telephone. "But I'm sure Koine will be free, so please come."

Thinking that the wrong person was available, he put the receiver down. As he went slowly up the stairs he could hear only Yamazaki's loud voice.

He found him wrapped around Okiyo, trying to kiss her on the mouth. Stubbornly Okiyo kept her face averted. In the end he had to be content with kissing her somewhere on the back of her heavily powdered neck, his face half-hidden behind her kimono collar. "Oh lord, it tickles," she said, making a face at Okayo who was standing behind them. "Have mercy!"

Okayo, biting her lower lip in anger, began to shake her fist above Yamazaki's head.

Shortly afterward Kensaku, Ogata and Miyamoto left Seihintei. They decided not to go to Nishimidori after all.

9

Early in the morning two days later Nobuyuki dropped in. Kensaku was still in bed. His brother was on his way to the office, he was told, so would he please come down immediately? He found Nobuyuki in the entryway, his face ruddy and healthy-looking from exposure to the cold air outside. Kensaku greeted him sleepily. "I can't come in," said Nobuyuki. "But here's a letter that someone sent Sakiko." He casually pulled out of his overcoat pocket a green, Western-type envelope and handed it to Kensaku.

The handwriting was in red ink, and looked weak and cheap. Written on the back was a girl's name, Shizuko. The sender's address was given as a dormitory in a certain women's college. And over the sealed edge of the flap this person had written pretentiously, "As yet unopened."

"This is the letter I forwarded to Sakiko yesterday," said Kensaku.

"That's right. The fellow knows she's your sister, and must have assumed she lived here."

Expecting to find the content as cheap as the handwriting, Kensaku began reading the letter. Perhaps because he had expected the worst, he decided it wasn't half so bad as such a letter could be. It was written in an incongruously formal style, and this was the gist of it: he was of the opinion, the writer said, that there was nothing wrong in a man and a woman seeing each other, so long as the relationship was kept pure; he therefore would request a meeting with her on the following day, on her way home from school, in the grounds of Hikawa Shrine, at two or three o'clock; he would not take up more than a few minutes of her time. He had recently graduated from a certain private university, he added, and was now lodging at the home of Viscount X (he named this nobleman) in Kōjimachi. Repeatedly he asked Sakiko to keep the letter confidential; and he ended by saying that if she thought that such a meeting might affect her good name—he understood that a girl of her age had to be careful—she was not to hesitate to say no.

"A tentative sort of fellow, isn't he?" said Kensaku, amused.

"True, he doesn't seem as bad as the last fellow who wrote her. Anyway, will you go and speak to him? Scare him a bit, if need be."

"I suppose I can try to see him, if you really want me to . . ."

"I could go myself, but I don't like to leave the office on an errand like this."

"All right, I'll go. Incidentally, this viscount he mentions happens to be Matsuyama's grandfather. But I don't think there's any need to speak to Matsuyama about the fellow, do you?"

"I shouldn't think so," Nobuyuki said as he prepared to leave. "He's probably quite harmless. Of course, it mightn't do any harm to tell him you know Matsuyama."

It was a cold day, with rain falling intermittently as if it couldn't quite make up its mind. Kensaku went to his room upstairs, had a fire put in the brazier, then for a change sat down before his desk and started writing in his long-neglected diary.

I feel, he wrote, as if some heavy object were pressing down on me. My head is covered with something black and fearful. Above, there is no sky, only layer upon layer of some dark and oppressive matter. Where does this feeling come from?

At times I feel like a lamp over the gate of a house, lit before sundown. The dim, orange light burns helplessly behind the blue frosted glass, waiting for the dark to give it brightness. Wait passively, that is all it can do. But this light wants desperately to burst into flame and burn everything around it. It does not want to remain so feeble, a prisoner behind the frosted glass. If only a storm would come and smash the glass, and let the flame reach up to the wooden eaves and envelop all in its fiery arms.

I must start working seriously. I live and work as though I were in a tight box, I feel so constrained. I must learn to feel free, free to do what I want with a sense of purpose and comfort and generosity. I want to walk with a firm step, swinging my arms, not with such timidity and purposelessness as I do now. I mustn't hurry, but I mustn't stop. And I can't be like the feeble light, wishfully waiting for the coming of the storm.

I must not seek peace in resignation. I must not throw away anything, I must not give in, I must find peace and satisfaction in having always tried. There is no death for anyone who has done something that is immortal. I do not mean only those in the arts—not any more—but scientists as well. I don't know much about the Curies. But I am sure that no matter what fate befalls them, what they have done for mankind will always give them the strength to survive, a peace of mind and satisfaction that no accident can touch. I want to have that peace of mind, that comfort. I want to see what no one else has seen, I want to hear what no one else has heard, I want to feel as no one else has felt.

I do not want to think that the fate that awaits this planet will necessarily determine the fate of mankind. The other animals do not know what fate will befall our planet. Only man knows, and only man fights against it. And behind his instinctive, insatiable ambition is this blind will to resist his fate. The conscious part of man acknowledges the inevitability of his end. But this blind will in him completely refuses to do so.

Man progressed as earth's condition improved, as it became more congenial to him. And when earth's condition at last begins gradually to worsen, as earth becomes colder and drier, so will man begin to decline; and then, with the death of the very last, solitary human being on earth, our race will come to its end. Not only man, but all other species, too, will become extinct one by one, and all our remains will lie buried under the ice. This is no wild fancy. All living things will as a matter of course meet this dreadful, inescapable fate. But will man—this nervous, struggling creature so committed to progress almost without purpose—ever learn to accept such a fate obediently? Perhaps he will. Perhaps when the condition of this planet has deteriorated and man himself has become a lesser creature, when our descendants gaze without sympathy or understanding upon the strange, useless things that their ancestors had built—at what cost these creatures will never know—perhaps then, man, now without mind or hope, will passively accept his end. But until such time, he will continue his search, perhaps in the name of progress, for a way to forestall his doom.

Women bear children and men do their chosen work. This constitutes human life. In primitive times, all that a man had to do was work for the happiness of his own immediate family or of his village. Then gradually the notion of the tribe was extended until in Japan it came to be the feudal domain. And later this was replaced by the nation, which in turn was extended to include the race, then finally to mankind at large.

Our notion of immortality, too, undergoes a similar process of extension. As children we care only about our own individual, bodily immortality; that is the only kind that has any emotional meaning for us then. (And even now, I dread death.) But as we grow, our own personal immortality comes to have less and less meaning. We come to have no faith in it. Instead we seek satisfaction in the work we do, hoping that that at least will remain, hoping that though we as individuals will die, our own species will continue forever. Perhaps we may eventually reach a point when we are delivered from this hope. There are indeed faiths in which such deliverance is offered. Be that as it may, men instinctively strive for progress no matter what they do. Often, this strife becomes a blind obsession, the end becomes forgotten, and what is reaped in the name of progress is unhappiness for mankind. But no matter what the result may be, the driving force behind this strife is the desire for immortality for the human race, the terrible need to deny the inevitability of its fate. I remember the day when for the first time in Japan an airplane was flown. The pilot's name was Marse. As I watched the plane taxiing along the ground, then suddenly rise into the air, I found myself moved almost to tears. Where did this emotion come from? I suppose the excitement of the crowd around me was partly responsible. But there was something besides that. After all, have I not been equally moved when all alone I have read accounts in the newspaper of great scientific discoveries? And I think that at such times, it is the human will within me, hidden from my consciousness, that is responding.

We all know that mankind will eventually disappear. But this knowledge does not bring despair to our daily lives. Sometimes, it is true, when we contemplate the destiny of the human race, we may feel unbearably forlorn. But this forlornness is of the kind we feel when we think about infinity. The strange thing is that while we recognize the inevitability of man's extinction, we ignore it emotionally. And the desperate struggle for progress continues. Is this not because somewhere in us is the hope that man may somehow escape the destiny of this very planet? And is there not some great subconscious will at work in all of us, the will that this hope shall be realized?

10

Such, then, was what Kensaku wrote in his diary, neglected this past fortnight or so. These thoughts had of late been haunting him, though in a form less articulated. For some time now, he had felt that people around him were chasing after shadows, working toward some objective whose nature was undefined in their minds, as though propelled by a great will which too was unknown. In art, in religion, or in science it was all the same, he thought. And he himself was no exception. Too often, when in a nervous state, he would feel as if he was being pursued by this unknown thing.

Excitedly he started to walk around the room.

"Kensaku! Kensaku!" It was Oei calling from the bottom of the stairs. "Do you want lunch?"

He stopped, like a man awakening from a dream. It was his habit to get up late and eat a meal which was a combination of breakfast and lunch. But this morning he had been forced out of bed early by Nobuyuki and had eaten a proper breakfast.

"I suppose so," he said, a little ungraciously. "I'm not hungry, but I'll come down."

During the meal Oei said worriedly, "I hear you're going to see this young hooligan. Are you sure it's safe going alone? Don't you think you should ask Mr. Tatsuoka to come with you?"

Kensaku now remembered his promise to Nobuyuki. "There's no need to worry," he said. "I'm sure he'll turn out to be quite harmless." But he felt a twinge of uneasiness, not so much about what the other fellow might do as about what he, so prone to fly into a temper, might do.

Deciding he had perhaps eaten too much, he took some digestive aid, then went upstairs. He pulled out the wastepaper basket from under his desk, and using this as a pillow, lay down on the floor. The earlier excitement had passed, and he was left with a certain sense of emptiness. Not long after, Miyamoto came.

"Where should we have the farewell dinner for Tatsuoka?" he asked. "We must decide pretty soon."

"You mean to say you haven't decided yet? We've got only a week left, you know. Just pick a place, it doesn't matter where, then ask Tatsuoka when he'll be free."

Chastised, Miyamoto said hesitantly, "But I've already made sure when he'll be free. It's just that I'm not sure what sort of place we should pick. I mean, we oughtn't to go to a place like Seihintei or Nishimidori, ought we?"

"Of course not."

"I'm glad you agree," Miyamoto said and began to laugh. "You see, I wasn't sure. I mean, those places are all right, but I didn't think they were quite appropriate for a farewell dinner. On the other hand, I didn't know how all of you would feel, and I had to make sure."

Kensaku began to laugh too. Miyamoto continued: "I'm inclined to choose Fujimiken or San'entei. I don't know what sort of food we'll get there, but they're pleasantly old-fashioned, don't you think? It would be just like the old days, when they used to give all those send-off parties for people going abroad. And we should get our photographer from some well-established shop, like Takebayashi, for example." When it came to such matters, everyone in their circle deferred to Miyamoto's experience.

Kensaku told Miyamoto about the young man who had written to his younger sister. "I'm about to go and talk to him if I find him. Do you want to come along?"

"No, thanks. He might produce a pistol, you know. 'Hands up!' as they say." This last remark was accompanied by the appropriate gesture.

"All right. Wait for me here."

It was two o'clock. Carrying his umbrella though it had stopped raining, Kensaku walked to Hikawa Shrine, no more than a quarter of a mile from his house. It was normally a popular gathering place for the neighborhood children, but because of the rain it was quite deserted. Kensaku walked about the grounds in search of his sister's admirer. Behind the hall of sacred music he came upon a pale, undernourished young man sitting on a stone. He was a pitiful sight. On this chilly day he wore only a thin, summer kimono, slightly soiled. No wonder he looked shriveled. There was fear in his eyes as he watched Kensaku approaching. "It can't be him," Kensaku said to himself, and walked past the young man nonchalantly. At the teashop beside one of the small chapels the owner was putting away the benches. There was no one else, except for an occasional passerby, clearly innocent, who would walk quickly through the grounds.

Then Kensaku suddenly remembered Seigen, the lovesick priest, as he was portrayed on the kabuki stage. It was a passing fancy, nothing that he himself could take seriously, but the association was enough to make him wonder if the shabby young man wasn't perhaps the culprit after all. The young man was still sitting in the same place; it was possible that he was indeed waiting for someone. Kensaku went toward him. Yellow leaves lay on the wet ground, fallen from the large gingko tree above. Spearing a leaf here and a leaf there with the point of his umbrella, Kensaku walked past him and back again. Moving only his eyes, the young man watched Kensaku uneasily. At last Kensaku stopped in front of him and said, "Are you waiting for someone?"

The young man, too frightened to speak, could only fidget guiltily. Kensaku began to think that perhaps he had found his man. "What are you doing here?"

"I'm not . . . , I'm not . . . " Unable to complete the sentence, he began to shake his head frantically. Then at last he added, panting, " . . . waiting for anyone." He was shaking uncontrollably, and his eyes were like a beaten dog's. His thin hair, lackluster from undernourishment, was about two inches long all over. The skin on his hands and feet was dry and scaly. Looking up at Kensaku's cross face he said, still panting, "I have a home. It's in Tansumachi." Unconsciously he began picking at a hangnail until it bled. Still he continued to pick at it, seemingly unaware of the pain. He was not a vagrant, he was saying. He had clearly mistaken Kensaku for a detective.

"I beg your pardon," Kensaku said, with a slight bow. He did not know it, but his face still looked cross.

He walked over to the main gate and stood there. He saw the young man, still seated on the stone, periodically throwing surreptitious glances in his direction.

Another young man—this one was a little younger than the other, eighteen or nineteen—approached the gateway. Though not in uniform, he looked to Kensaku like a student. He carried an open book which he would briefly look at from time to time. Kensaku guessed that he was trying to memorize something. Or was he pretending to be doing so, just in case he was being watched? The young man, realizing that he was being stared at, became visibly embarrassed.

There was no other way than to confront him, Kensaku decided. He walked up to him and said, "Excuse me, but are you by any chance waiting for someone?" Having learned his lesson from the last encounter, he was considerably more polite this time.

The young man was very controlled. He looked Kensaku straight in the eye and said, "No, sir." His manner was simple, without a touch of insolence. No doubt about it, this was a well-bred young man.

"I see," Kensaku said and stepped aside with a bow.

He might as well hang around until three, Kensaku decided, and went into the teashop. He found one bare bench, without so much as a cloth on it, that had not yet been put away. As he sat down the owner called out, "Welcome." But he seemed in no mood to serve his solitary customer, and continued to sweep away the dead leaves in his little rock garden. Kensaku didn't mind. He lit a cigarette, enjoying the quiet, autumnal mood and thinking it was not a bad way to wait for the writer of the letter. He glanced at his watch now and then, determined to leave at three o'clock. The shabby young man was still there. Kensaku remembered the bleeding hangnail, and thought how it must be hurting now. He wanted very much to go over to him and say something comforting. But what was he doing there, clad in that thin kimono, sitting forever all by himself? He was not ill surely, and he was not a beggar. What kind of life did he lead? Kensaku could not begin to guess.

Seeing that his tenacious customer was not about to leave, the man in the shop resignedly brought out some tea and cookies. A few minutes later Kensaku was ready to go home, having given up any hope of catching the culprit. As he put some coins down on the bench and stood up, he caught sight of Oei coming up the stone steps toward the main gate. Their eyes met, and instinctively they exchanged smiles.

"This way is quicker," he said, and together the two walked toward one of the side gates. As they passed the young man on the stone, Kensaku stopped and made as if to speak to him. The young man suddenly stiffened and looked away. Silently Kensaku walked on.

Once out on the street Oei said, "You know where he lives, so just write to him."

"Yes, I will."

When they got home, Kensaku asked Miyamoto to wait a little and went upstairs to write his letter. In it he mentioned threateningly that Matsuyama, the viscount's grandson, had been a friend of his since boyhood.

Miyamoto's first comment as Kensaku rejoined him was, "You know, it might be fun being a young hooligan like this fellow." He laughed, and Kensaku laughed with him. But he felt a certain discomfort; for he could not help feeling that Miyamoto was in fact giving expression to a desire they all shared.

Again the mistlike rain began to fall. The two decided to play chess. They played until it got almost too dark to see the board, until the pleasure of the game wore off. The electric lights came on, and Kensaku, who had been staring at the board for some time in a vain effort to concentrate, finally said, "Let's stop, shall we?" "Yes, by all means," Miyamoto said, and threw his pieces down on the board. Then he collapsed on the floor and closed his eyes.

Immediately after dinner they went out. Afraid of catching another cold, Kensaku took his Inverness cape with him. From Tameike they went by streetcar to Shinbashi, and from there walked toward Ginza. There was a breeze, and the delicate branches of the willow trees that stood side by side with the street lamps swayed prettily in the light.

Miyamoto was interested in pouches, and whenever he saw a shop that specialized in them he would go up to the window and intently scrutinize the display. "You're still interested in such things, are you?" Kensaku asked. "Of course I am," Miyamoto replied. Then he proceeded to give a discourse on the subject. The intricate ones, he said, the sort made by true artisans, were necessarily old and thus weren't very clean. After all, you had no idea who might have had them before. But there was a lot to be said for the kind made for common use by the less pretentious peasant craftsmen. You could buy them new, they were therefore clean, they were also cheap, and there was something appealing about their honest simplicity. Besides, you could always throw them away without compunction. "I bought quite a few of them around Kyoto this time," he said. "I'm thinking of visiting Korea soon, you know. They've got very nice ones there."

As they passed by the Formosan Cafe, Kensaku had a feeling Ogata might be inside. He looked in, and sure enough Ogata was there, wearing a raincoat and a felt hat with the front of the brim pulled down. "Hey, Ogata's inside," Kensaku said to Miyamoto who was a few steps ahead. Miyamoto came back and peered shortsightedly through the doorway.

"Shall we go in?" Kensaku said.

"No, let's not. The 'Spider Monkey' is there. Let's tell Ogata to come out." Miyamoto then called a waitress over and asked her to give Ogata their message. Ogata came out, then went back inside to fetch his walking stick.

As the three walked toward Kyōbashi Ogata pointed to a cafe on the other side of the street. "How about going in there?"

"No, I don't think so," Miyamoto said. "We'll find even worse bores than the 'Spider Monkey' in a place like that."

"What's the matter with you tonight? Don't you want to drink?"

"Oh, I have nothing against drinking," said Miyamoto, grinning. "It's people that I'm worried about."

"Well, I'm sorry, but I can't suggest a place that provides drink and guarantees there'll be no people around."

In the end they agreed to retrace their steps and go to Seihintei.

The three sat down in a little room upstairs with Okayo and another waitress, not very attractive, named Omaki. Osuzu was busy with customers downstairs.

Kensaku was in a relatively settled mood that evening and did not feel like drinking. Okayo, too, refused to drink despite pressure from Ogata.

"There's a reason," she said bitterly. "I got into a lot of trouble with the management recently."

"That's right," said Omaki. "She got drunk and made a fool of herself again."

"What do you mean 'again'!" Okayo said, allowing a certain coarseness to creep into her voice, and gave Omaki's shoulder a shove. Then she added thoughtfully, "Someone with ambitions like me has to be careful, I can't afford to get drunk."

Kensaku remembered that the day before, he had written a postcard to Ogata in which he wondered if Okayo had double or single eyelids. As if reading his mind, Ogata now suddenly mentioned the postcard: "Okayo, it might interest you to know that Tokitō here was trying to remember if you had double eyelids or not. Why don't you show him."

Okayo, who had until then appeared to be in a bad temper, cheered up and looked coyly at Kensaku. "They're both. What I mean is, one is single and the other is double. This one here is single, and this one is double."

"It's the other way round," said Kensaku.

"Really?" she said. She rubbed her eyes gently with her fingertips, then blinked them. "You're right."

Once more she looked at Kensaku coyly, then gave him a strange smile. Kensaku began to feel a trifle uncomfortable. In writing that postcard he hadn't quite expected such overwhelming results.

But all in all it proved to be a rather dull evening. Kensaku toyed with the idea of telling them about his visit to Hikawa Shrine, but decided against it. It wouldn't do to have the waitresses repeat the story to their other customers. The two women, seeing that the men had little to say for themselves, were having a private conversation of their own.

"You know the alley. It's where the movers have their shop."

"You mean the shop where Mr. Handsome works?"

"That's it."

Ogata was listening without interest, but he felt obliged to say something. "I don't think I like this Mr. Handsome."

"We aren't talking about him," she said, almost in rebuke. "We are talking about the alley where he hangs out."

"I like alleys even less." Ogata made the joke with an air of defeat. He grinned weakly.

Omaki said, "This neighborhood is full of good-looking men, you know."

"Let's hope they admire you as much as you admire them," Ogata said.

"That reminds me, O-san," said Okayo, giggling. "Okiyo—you know Okiyo, she's one of the girls here—well, she told us recently that there was a stunning-looking barber somewhere in Rogetsuchō. So Omaki here and I went for a walk to see if we could catch a glimpse of this man. The trouble was we hadn't bothered to ask Okiyo where exactly the barbershop was, so we ended up walking around for miles, peeking into every barbershop we happened to see." The two women exchanged sidelong glances, then blushed and burst out laughing. At that moment Okayo's face appeared particularly vulgar to Kensaku. He looked uneasily at Miyamoto and found his friend smiling at him. The smile was almost a sneer, but there was a touch of sympathy in it too.

Okayo and Omaki, now in their element, began an endless discussion of the various good-looking fellows in the neighborhood. There was the chief clerk at the movers (Mr. Handsome), there was the grocer's son, and what about the taxi driver, and so on. And all the while, Miyamoto stared at them with open disgust.

It was her custom, Okayo said, to go to the public bath at about ten o'clock every morning. And if the place was empty she would swim about in the bath, holding a wooden bucket in each arm. "She's awfully good," Omaki interjected.

Kensaku imagined this fleshy woman swimming about in the hot bath with the aid of two buckets. It couldn't be a very dignified spectacle, he thought. But in the very indignity of the image there was something unbearably erotic.

Okayo then described with great animation the time a man from the gas company had come into the bathhouse to fix the light. She was in the bath. He had a large stepladder with him. Long after the light had been fixed he had remained on top of the ladder, refusing to move. She had had to stay in the water an interminable length of time.

Kensaku had never credited her with much grace or dignity. It was her air of lively abandon and her peculiar coquettishness that had initially attracted him. But such an exhibition of vulgarity as he had witnessed tonight was too disenchanting; and he was sure that the longer he knew her, the more conspicuously cheap she would become. How much more attractive she seemed, Kensaku thought, the first time he had met her.

The three friends left shortly thereafter, and immediately parted company.

The next morning Kensaku received a letter in answer to his own of the previous day. The writer was abject in his apology. He had once seen a photograph of Kensaku's younger sister, that was all. He had had no intention of writing to her, but had been persuaded to do so by a nurse at "T" Hospital. (He mentioned the nurse's name.) If the Matsuyama family should ever come to know of his misdeed, he would be in serious trouble. Would Kensaku please take pity on him, and accept his most heartfelt apology?

"T" Hospital was where Sakiko had stayed for a time last year. And Kensaku remembered the nurse. She wasn't such a bad-looking woman. He wrote a letter to Nobuyuki, simply describing the events of the day before, and enclosed with it the letter from Sakiko's admirer. He next wrote to the pathetic young man, assuring him that he would say nothing about the incident to his friend Matsuyama.

11

It was not long afterward that Kensaku on his own initiative visited a brothel. Late one morning, on a cloudy, chilly day, as though he were about to accomplish an act which he had coolly and carefully deliberated upon, he left his house and set out for Fukagawa.

About two years before he had once gone there from Kiba, and then on through Sunamura to the Nakagawa River. He therefore had some idea of the local geography. He got off the streetcar a little past Eitaibashi, and with a look of utter cheerlessness proceeded along the road past Hachiman Shrine. He was very conscious of how ugly the expression on his face must be. And toward everyone he passed on the road he felt a touch of enmity, sure that they all knew where he was going. His mouth dry from tension, he marched on.

He crossed several small bridges, then turned right, and there at last, across the muddy moat, were the houses. Anxiety in him mounted. It was not at all like going to see Tokiko in Nishimidori; there, his purpose had been so different. Yet, for all the unpleasant sensation he was suffering now, he did not feel like going back.

A rickshaw came toward him. It had merely a hood on top, and no curtain in front. The rider was therefore quite visible. It was his dark glasses that first caught Kensaku's attention. Immediately he recognized Tajima, a fellow who had been a couple of years ahead of him at college. The shock of seeing someone he knew, especially someone so respectable, was such that Kensaku was unable to take his eyes off him until he had walked several more paces. Tajima seemed to be staring too, though because of his dark glasses Kensaku wasn't sure.

The only other place Tajima could be coming from was the fish hatchery. Obviously, that was not where he had been. Kensaku might have been less sure, perhaps, if his acquaintance hadn't been wearing those glasses. What a dreadful place to meet each other, Kensaku thought angrily. But, he quickly reminded himself, he had not quite reached his destination; he could after all go past the hatchery, then to Sunamura, and go home or even stop by at Nishimidori or somewhere. But to do that just because he had seen Tajima would be an abject thing to do. Besides, if he didn't go today, he was sure to come back again very soon.

Two hours later he came out of the district in quite a different frame of mind. He felt remarkably at ease with himself, quite free of remorse.

The woman had been an ugly creature. With a pallid, flat face, she looked like a slatternly housewife from the slums. She was dull-witted, and very good-natured. He had no intention of ever seeing her again, but somehow he came away feeling he would like to do her a nice turn. Should he perhaps send her a money order? She did say that for every customer she received only five sen from the management.

It was after he had thus begun visiting brothels that he became newly aware of Oei. True, he had not been unaware of her sexuality before; indeed, he had often indulged in erotic fantasies about her. In these she had invariably been the temptress and he the upright virgin. He would always be lecturing at her in an appallingly priggish fashion. What a terrible sin it would be, he would say to her, what a mess they would make of their lives if they were to give in to temptation, etc., etc. Oei had in reality never given any cause for such fantasies; but Kensaku had indulged in them all the same.

Now, however, Oei had come to be a more immediate object of Kensaku's desires. At night in bed, when erotic thoughts would run rampant in his mind and the printed words in the book he was holding would become a meaningless blur, it was always the figure of Oei sleeping downstairs that would dominate his lewd imaginings. He would try to chase the figure away, but to no avail; it was always there in his consciousness. He would then in desperation get out of bed, and in forlorn but excited anticipation go downstairs, walk past the bedroom toward the toilet. What he hoped for in his near-delirious state was that the door would suddenly slide open, and he would be gently led into the room. But this never happened. And in angry frustration he would return upstairs. Later there were times when he would stop hopelessly in the middle of the stairs on his way down, not knowing whether to proceed or go back to his room; and he would sit down in the darkness, confused and despairing.

His visits to brothels became more and more frequent. Yet he could never feel like a debauchee. If he could, he would have found more pleasure in his own debauchery. He searched constantly for a woman who would infatuate him, but without success. Occasionally something akin to passion would touch him, only to disappear quickly. It was as much their fault as his, he would then tell himself.

He did not see Tokiko or Okayo as frequently as he used to. But whenever in the company of Ogata or Miyamoto—which was often enough—he would visit them. He had reached an impasse with Tokiko. But if he had been given the choice of either getting closer to her or moving away, he would have found the latter alternative less difficult.

It was always so. It did not matter how attractive he might at first find a woman, his initial passion—if it could be called that—would soon leave him. Surely, he would ask himself, it could not be true that the women he had met were all superficial, that there were not some who might in time have deserved a deeper commitment from him? Why was it that every time he thought he might become involved with some woman he would draw back, certain that he was not emotionally prepared for such involvement? To push his relationship with a woman even then, when he knew full well that she would never mean very much to him, struck him as callous and unnatural. If he was to have an affair, he had to be pushed into it by an emotion beyond his control. Sometimes, when he thought such emotion was beyond him, he would begin to hate himself. But his self-hatred seemed to have little to do with what he did with his body. With every passing day, his self-indulgence became more intense.

As his life grew more anarchic, so did his mind, and his lewd fantasies about Oei became more and more uncontrolled. He wondered fearfully what would happen to them if his present condition were to persist. This woman, who had been his grandfather's mistress, was almost twenty years older than he. He imagined their future together. What he saw—and he shrank before the prospect—was his own destruction. His obsession with her was like a prolonged nightmare. During the day, when he felt more relaxed, he would look at her and wonder at the thoughts he had had of her the night before. Surely he must have dreamed them? But when night came, the lewd thoughts would again assail him, with greater urgency than before.

One night he had a dream. In the dream he was asleep. Miyamoto came in, wearing an eerie smile. "Sakaguchi died," he said. Kensaku, still asleep, thought, "So he won't be coming back to Tokyo after all." He knew that Sakaguchi had gone on a long journey without telling anyone. And he had sensed all along that Sakaguchi might never return, might meet with a certain kind of death. He remained silent. Miyamoto, still with that strange smile, added, "Apparently he tried *harima*. Yes, he finally did it." Kensaku thought, "So I was right."

He did not know what exactly *harima* was. All he knew was *harima* was an extremely dangerous method, and that Sakaguchi had learned about it previously in Osaka. He knew too that Sakaguchi had passed on the information to Miyamoto.

In his depravity Sakaguchi had constantly sought new ways of deriving sexual pleasure. How jaded he must have been, Kensaku thought with a shiver, to have gone so far as to try *harima*. His depravity must have become like some outside force, pushing him toward his own destruction. Knowing as he did the terrible risk, how could he have done it of his own free will?

"What does one do in *harima*?" Kensaku was about to ask, then checked himself. For he realized with sudden, overwhelming fear that if he knew, he would try it. True, he might come out of it alive; but the chances were he would not. Yet, so long as there was one chance in a hundred of his surviving it, even one chance in a thousand, he would be impelled by that evil force to try it. In ignorance lay his protection.

Miyamoto was smiling sardonically, in anticipation of the fatal question from Kensaku. But Kensaku never asked the question. Then he awoke from his dream within the dream. A nasty, eerie sensation remained inside him. He felt as though he had been visited by a ghost, a ghost in the guise of Miyamoto. He got up to go to the toilet. The window of the toilet was open. It was a still, moonlit night. Not a leaf moved. On the ground of the large garden (it was much larger than his own garden) the roof above cast a shadow like a dark mountain. Something in the shadow seemed to move. It was moving on the ridge of the roof. Then he remembered that upstairs he had heard a thud, as though something had jumped down onto the roof.

The dancing creature was the size of a child seven or eight years old. It had a large head, but the body was incongruously tiny. The devil was more comical than frightening. Not making the slightest sound it danced about grotesquely like a badly made puppet, unaware that its shadow was being watched. The absolute silence of the night was undisturbed; and all that moved was this dancing shadow. So long as this creature danced, Kensaku thought, those under the roof would continue to be tortured by the spirit of lewd desire. Yet it was a great relief to know that the shape of the spirit was so insignificant and cheap.

Then he really woke up.

12

In the space of only two or three months the kid had become a young goat with three-inch horns and a pretentious little beard.

"The goat's beginning to stink," Oei said at the dinner table one day, pulling a face. "How about giving him a bath?"

"That won't do any good."

"He not only stinks, he's become so fierce Yoshi is too frightened to go into the pen. He's always knocking the feed box over or bumping his head angrily against something."

"Shall we give him away?"

"How about a pet shop? If we pay them something, they'll take him."

"But they're sure to sell him to a medical laboratory," Kensaku said. "It'll be like sending him to the executioner."

"That won't do, then. Perhaps we should get him a wife."

"No, it would be best if we could find somebody to take him. For one thing, I'm thinking of going away on a trip."

Oei showed some surprise. "Where?"

"I haven't decided, but I thought I'd like to go away for six months or even a year and live somewhere in the provinces."

"But what has made you want to do such a thing all of a sudden?"

"Nothing in particular, really. But you know, I've got to do something about the way I'm living right now."

"Am I coming with you?"

"No."

Kensaku looked at Oei's unhappy face, wishing he could offer some explanation. She said at last, "Have you told Nobuyuki?"

"Not yet."

"But why do you want to go away? Is it that you can't do enough work here?"

"I'm sorry, I really can't explain. Let's say I need to change my ways."

"Well, if you have to go, you have to go. But you will come back afterward?"

"Of course. This is my home."

"I should have thought a month would be enough if all you wanted was a change of air."

"I'm taking some work with me that will take a long time to finish. I'm going to stay away until it's finished."

There was a brief silence. Then she said, "What are we to do about this house? There's no need to go on renting a large house like this just for me."

"Of course we'll keep it. It's only a year, after all."

"Are you sure there isn't a special reason?"

"But I've already told you."

"You're being terribly vague." She smiled at him accusingly. Perhaps she imagined that Kensaku was taking some woman with him.

"I want to be absolutely alone, if you must know. I want to get away from my friends, from my family, from everybody."

Kensaku had purposely referred to her indirectly as "family." It pleased her, and she was somewhat mollified. She said pleasantly, "Won't you be lonely?"

"I suppose I shall be. But I'll get a lot of work done."

"I certainly shall miss you. If I get too lonely I'll just close the house down and come and join you."

Kensaku gave a noncommittal smile. Then he began telling her about his plans: he thought he might pick a place along the Inland Sea, rent a small house perhaps, and manage on his own.

"It sounds terribly pleasant." Oei gave Kensaku a thoughtful, kindly smile, as if to say, "What a carefree person you can be!"

That evening he telephoned Nobuyuki to make sure he would be at home, then set out for the house in Hongō.

"I envy you," Nobuyuki said. "Go to Onomichi. That's a fine place."

"Is it? I don't mind where, so long as it's nice. I suppose I can go there by ship?"

"Yes, you can. You hate trains, I remember. Yes, that should be pleasant. Why don't you sail from Yokohama?"

The suggestion appealed to Kensaku immediately. He asked Nobuyuki to check the sailing schedule and book a berth for him. He then arranged to meet Nobuyuki again the following day, and left.

A few minutes before four on the following afternoon Kensaku stood at the corner of Mitsukoshi Department Store, waiting for Nobuyuki to come out of a nearby building that housed his fire insurance company. The year was nearing its end and it was a busy time of day; one streetcar after another coming from the north and the south along Muromachidōri would stop in front of Mitsukoshi, then as the conductor said his piece would move on again. Mingled with the rickshaws, automobiles, carts and bicycles were the pedestrians, hurriedly weaving through the traffic in all directions. There were even dogs. Men rushed past him, almost grazing the tip of his nose and leaving a cold draft in their wake. I shall soon leave all this, he thought with a mixture of pleasure and regret, and live in a quiet, distant place overlooking the sea.

He began to walk slowly toward the Bank of Japan. Just as he was passing the small post office he heard a clock strike four. Soon, countless human beings were pouring out of the Mitsui Building that formed three sides of an open square. Some paused to light a cigarette, some trotted after colleagues that were ahead of them. Very quickly the square was full of bustling figures. Other buildings too—the Bank of Japan, the Specie Bank—were spewing out people, who marched past Kensaku in little groups. He soon spied Nobuyuki coming toward him. He had a companion, an ordinary-looking, fat man in his fifties. Nobuyuki was doing all the talking. He held a rolled-up magazine in one hand, and he would occasionally slap his other hand with it to emphasize a point, and the fat man would nod in agreement. He quickened his pace as soon as he saw Kensaku.

"Have you been waiting long?"

"No."

From behind Nobuyuki the fat man said, "I'll say good-bye here."

He touched the brim of his felt hat—he didn't take it off—and bowed quickly.

"Aren't you coming this way?" Nobuyuki said.

"No, it so happens I'm going the other way today."

"All right, then. Remember, don't worry about me—the amount is too small to make a fuss about. I'd be grateful if you would try not to let the whole thing become too unpleasant."

"I understand," said the fat man. He bowed once more and walked away in the direction of the outer moat.

When the two reached the main thoroughfare Nobuyuki said, "Let's go over to the other side," and nudged Kensaku all the way across the street, over the streetcar rails, with his overcoat-covered shoulder. "What do you want to eat?" he said once they had reached the other side.

"Anything you say."

"Fowl?"

"All right."

They reached the temporary bridge at Nihonbashi. There was an enclosure down below, where the foundations for the new bridge were being built. A gasoline-powered pump was hard at work getting out the water that had seeped inside. From the strangely warped galvanized roof two chimneys protruded, one narrow and one wide. The narrow one was more active, vibrating energetically as it emitted steam. The wide one was rusty, and at much longer intervals tiredly coughed out insignificant amounts of smoke.

Laborers carried down from the bank straw baskets filled with cement and gravel which a formidable, bearded fellow would then work over with a shovel. Near him two men, having placed a straw mat over poured cement, were pounding it with a heavy wooden pounder that they held between them.

A man wearing a suit and Japanese gaiters was busy with a surveying instrument. Beyond him a man was bracing two poles, stuck in the ground some feet apart, by nailing planks on them diagonally in the shape of an "X." Just below him a woman laborer squatted beside a puddle of water streaked with oil and washed her face.

The two brothers pulled themselves away from the bridge railing. Nobuyuki said as they walked, "It's a hand-to-mouth existence they lead. They work today so that they can eat today. But you know, I envy them their sense of immediate necessity. It's something that's completely lacking in my kind of work." After a short pause he said, "Sometimes I can't help feeling very uneasy about what I'm doing."

Kensaku looked at his brother in surprise. This was a side to Nobuyuki he had never thought existed. "Are you thinking of leaving the company?"

Nobuyuki nodded. "Yes, I am. I intend to resign as soon as I have a clear idea of what I want to do with myself."

"There's no need to wait, surely?"

"I suppose not," Nobuyuki said and looked away, slightly offended.

Kensaku realized he had been tactless. In his relationship with his father and stepmother, Nobuyuki was peculiarly timid. Despite his earlier dissolute life, which had naturally caused them much unhappiness, he had somehow always retained an incongruous sense of filial responsibility. And he was still inordinately fearful of doing anything that might hurt or disappoint his father. Of course his father loved him in return. "What sort of thing do you want to do?" Kensaku asked, but his brother would not give a clear answer.

They soon found the restaurant they were looking for. It was a small place specializing in fowl.

After they were seated Nobuyuki said, "That fellow I came out of the office with, he's one of our salesmen. He told me something that really shocked me. A couple of months ago a rather elderly salesman named Kawai came up to me and asked me if I would lend fifty yen to a younger colleague of his, a fellow by the name of Noguchi. Kawai told me that there had been illnesses in Noguchi's family, and that he was badly in need of money. Well, I never did like this old fellow Kawai, but I've always liked Noguchi, who's really much too nice to be a salesman. Besides, I myself had heard that Noguchi's kids were ill. So I handed over fifty yen to Kawai to give to Noguchi. Kawai then asked what interest I wanted to charge, so I said I didn't want any interest. He then offered to make Noguchi write out a formal receipt. Again I said no. Being the sort of man Noguchi is, I said, he'd probably be too ashamed to show his face in the office if he couldn't pay me back, so why not tell him that it's your money.

Don't mention my name at all, I said. And what do you think I found out today? Kawai apparently went over to poor Noguchi and lent him my fifty yen *minus* twelve yen in advance interest. Of course Noguchi spent the money a long time ago, but Kawai still has the note he made Noguchi sign. That fat man you just saw me with was furious, and kept on saying he was going to knock Kawai down. I had to tell him that knocking him down wouldn't do any good. Don't make a fuss, I said, just go and get the note and the twelve yen from him. Kawai unfortunately is a very successful salesman, as you might guess, so firing him would be out of the question."

What a tolerant fellow Nobuyuki is, Kensaku thought. If he had been Nobuyuki he would probably have lost his temper, called the nasty old man into his office and given him a dressing down he would never forget.

"Why let him get away with it?" he said. "At least tell him what you think of him."

"But what good will that do? He'll just hate me for it. He'll never think he did anything wrong, you know."

"How can you be so tolerant? Didn't you get angry when this other man told you the story?"

"Yes, I did. But when one realizes the pointlessness of trying to punish the other fellow, one soon stops being angry."

"Maybe so, maybe you're right. But I simply couldn't make myself think like that."

"You only make matters worse for yourself when you start arguing with a fellow like Kawai."

"But that wouldn't be enough to make me want to forgive such a man."

"Well, let's say that unlike you, I was born easygoing."

An hour later they left the restaurant and walked to Ginza. In a shop there Nobuyuki bought a camel's hair scarf and gave it to Kensaku. A going-away present, he said.

PART II

1

It was a remarkably gentle winter day. The ship had already cast off its moorings. Below on the pier, standing among a host of others who had come to see the passengers off, were Oei and Miyamoto. Kensaku had asked Oei not to come, saying that after all he was going to get off at Kobe and he wanted no fuss made over such a short trip. But Oei had insisted. She wanted to see the ship, she said, and had come along to Yokohama with Miyamoto in tow. "Please take good care of yourself, and please write regularly," she had said to Kensaku on the ship as the bells started ringing. Kensaku had momentarily felt quite emotional.

The propellers were churning; gradually the ship moved farther and farther away from the pier. The three continued to wave at each other, smiling occasionally, until Kensaku became embarrassed by the protracted ceremony. When at last the ship's course was set and there was a distance of some fifty yards between the stern and the pier, Kensaku bowed, muttered his final farewell and walked away, not without some feeling of guilt.

His was a small, four-berth cabin, but luckily there were few passengers aboard and he was its only occupant. He sat on one of the stools—there were no proper chairs—wondering what he might do. Restlessly he got up and pulled out his suitcase from under the bunk. With the key attached to his watch chain he opened it and aimlessly examined the contents. Then he began to worry about the two he had deserted. Very soon he was back on deck.

The ship was farther out than he would have guessed. The faces of those still standing on the pier were no longer recognizable. But there were two figures standing apart from the rest, and he was fairly certain they were Oei and Miyamoto. Indeed, the one holding a half-closed parasol at a slant was unmistakably Oei. He waved his hand, and the two figures responded immediately, Miyamoto enthusiastically with his hat and Oei more restrainedly with her parasol.

Much more comfortable now that he couldn't see their faces, Kensaku pulled out his handkerchief and started waving it. When the ship reached the opening in the breakwater, Kensaku could not see them at all. A thin mist (or was it smoke?) spread over the harbor, and the shore became vaguer and vaguer behind the gradually thickening veil. It was a strain now to locate the pier that they had just left. They passed an English warship lying with stately calm on the surface as though rooted to the bottom of the sea. On her stern was painted the name "Minotaur." By then even the large buildings standing along the pier had become invisible.

Kensaku leaned against the railing and watched the water being churned by the propellers. The colors created by the agitation were strikingly beautiful. At the back of his mind was the picture of Oei and Miyamoto leaving the pier, walking across the stone-paved yard with its cobweb of rails and out into the streets. From below deck a gong sounded, announcing lunch.

There were not many people at his table—a young, English-speaking foreigner, a nanny in the employ of one of the first-class passengers, and a ship's officer. The officer and the foreigner were conversing. Kensaku sat in silence, trying to eat the tasteless beef. The foreigner, who was sitting next to him, turned to him and said in English, "Can you speak English?" He answered in English, "No, I can't." Then thinking that a foreigner living in Yokohama could hardly not know any Japanese, he asked in Japanese, "But can't you speak Japanese?" The young foreigner, uncomprehending, cocked his head and blushed in embarrassment.

The nanny soon left the table, presumably to go to her ward. (She was never seen again.) Then the officer excused himself. Kensaku, left alone with the foreigner in the large, deserted hall, had no choice but to talk to his sole companion in his inadequate English. After lunch, when Kensaku was sitting alone in the smoking lounge on the upper deck, the young foreigner came in with a deck of cards and asked him to play. Kensaku declined, being in no mood to learn the rules of some new game the foreigner might introduce. The foreigner resignedly played solitaire, periodically gathering the cards and shuffling them loudly.

His home was in Australia, he said. He had been transferred to

Yokohama from the United States only three weeks before. Then he had received a telegram saying his mother was ill, and was now on his way home to Sydney. He wanted so much to catch a view of Mt. Fuji; did Kensaku think it was too cloudy for that? He had good cause to wonder, Kensaku thought: for the misty and unseasonably gentle weather earlier had been a forewarning of worse weather to come. There was now a wintry chill in the air, and the sky was a bleak, dull grey.

As the ship was rounding the coast of Misaki Kensaku changed into a kimono and lay down in his bunk. He was soon fast asleep. When he awoke it was already past four o'clock. He threw on his overcoat and went up on deck. Mt. Fuji was clearly etched against the clouded, evening sky. Immediately beneath were the mountains of Izu in attendance on the giant, and in the foreground, the sea. It was all a little too neat, and reminded Kensaku of a Hokusai print.

In the smoking lounge someone was playing the piano badly. The playing stopped, and the young foreigner came out. "So that's Mt. Fuji," he said with evident satisfaction.

It was too cold to be standing outside, so Kensaku went into the lounge to look at the view from there. Ōshima, the first of the Seven Islands of Izu, was already behind them. One by one the other islands made their appearance. The young foreigner had returned to the lounge, and alas was again at the piano. With his briar pipe stuck in the corner of his mouth, he sang in a low voice as he played. Occasionally he would stop and address a remark to Kensaku: he had once heard Paderewski play; he had a sister who was a very good violinist, etc.

Kensaku was still sleepy. He had slept little these last four or five nights, and the two-hour nap he had just had was far from enough. He went back to his bunk. But this time he lay wide awake. The ship was rolling quite badly. Besides, the cabin was near the stern, and he was assailed by the most outlandish noises—the ceaseless grinding of the rudder chain, the rhythmic pounding of the engine, the chop-chop-swish-swish of the propeller blades cutting the water.

He began to feel a little seasick. He noticed that his hands were an unpleasant pink color, just as though he had drunk too much. On the wall opposite the bunk was a mirror. His face, half-buried in the pillow, looked back at him, nicely framed. It, too, was pink. He was wont to fall sick whenever he traveled. Was he now catching a cold? He was half-dozing when the dinner gong sounded.

The young foreigner complained that he had forgotten to bring a book with him. It was just as well, he said, that the ship's library would be open the next day. Kensaku had brought with him an English translation of the works of Garshin, the Russian writer. He lent this to the foreigner.

It was a cold night. From habit he became wide awake now that it was late. He sat alone in the large, chilly dining hall writing postcards. He wrote to Nobuyuki, Sakiko, Ogata—they had come to see him off at Shinbashi Station—and to Oei and Miyamoto. Then he wrote to Tatsuoka, who would be somewhere around Penang by now. He addressed the card to the Japanese embassy in Paris.

Tatsuoka's departure for France was a sad event for Kensaku. Tatsuoka showed little interest in the arts—his indifference sometimes seemed to Kensaku almost an affectation—but he was passionately devoted to his own work. And when he talked about the designing of aircraft engines and his own hopes as a designer, he could move even Kensaku, who knew nothing about such things. Kensaku missed him very much.

His feet, in cotton socks and hemp-soled sandals, felt thoroughly chilled. Above him hung a large fan, which he would look at suspiciously from time to time. It would presumably start working when this ship, bound for Australia, reached some such place as Manila.

The postcards were all written. He decided he would go up on deck once more before turning in and look at the view. But the night was pitch-black, and there was nothing to see. A tiny light shone high up on the mast. At first Kensaku thought it was a distant star. There was not a soul in sight. There was the sharp cry of the wind, and the sound of the wave crests breaking as the wind hit them—that was all. Neither the engine nor the rudder chain was audible. The ship, like some enormous, silent monster, pushed her way through the wind, farther and farther into the dark.

He stood huddled in his overcoat, his legs spread apart in a steadying stance. Even then he almost lost his balance several times, for besides the strong wind there was the rolling of the ship to contend with. The wind beat against his bare head until he felt his scalp going numb. His eyes itched, irritated by the eyelashes bent down by the wind. Above and below, to his right and left, the darkness stretched without limit. And here he was, standing in the very middle of this enormous thing. Everyone else was asleep in his house. He alone stood face to face with nature, as mankind's chosen representative. But together with this exaggerated sense of self-importance came the helpless feeling that he was about to be swallowed up by the great darkness around him. It was not altogether unpleasant. He fought against it nevertheless. As if to prove to himself his own presence, he tightened the muscles in his lower abdomen and breathed deeply. As soon as he stopped doing so, however, he again felt in danger of being swallowed up.

A black shape approached him. It was the cabin steward. The wind carried away his words, and Kensaku had no idea what he was saying. He retreated into the darkness. Kensaku, too, finally left the deck to return to his cabin. His body was thoroughly chilled.

He was tired. But from force of habit he took a magazine with him to bed. Within ten minutes he was struggling to keep his eyes open, to catch the elusive printed words that kept on running away from him. And when temporarily he would succeed in recapturing his consciousness, the print would become clear, but the meaning would be a plaything of his dreams. Finally he let his eyes close and submitted happily to sleep's onslaught. And as he fell asleep, there was this thought in his mind: the dreadful, hectic life of these last three months is at last over, and now this deep, peaceful sleep has come.

He opened his eyes and saw the silvery light of an overcast day filtering through the thick glass of the porthole. He lifted his head to take a look outside. The sea was still rough, the waves rising and breaking under the cold, leaden sky. It was eight o'clock. He got up and went to the dining hall. He had breakfast alone, for the young foreigner had already had his. After breakfast he went back to his cabin to fetch his overcoat, then went up on deck. The wind had abated a little. He could see in the distance the coastline of Kishū.

He found the young foreigner aft, marching vigorously back and forth, back and forth. He was out of breath but somehow was able to continue humming a tune. "Good morning!" he called out to Kensaku. "Join me, it will make you warm!" Kensaku was dressed informally in kimono with long woollen drawers underneath, hardly a suitable outfit for marching. He declined and went into the smoking lounge. A few moments later the young foreigner came in, holding the book Kensaku had lent him. He was much impressed by the short story "Four Days," he said, using words like "terrible" and "morbid" to describe its quality.

The steward came in. Kensaku asked him, "When are we arriving in Kobe?" He had a train schedule with him, and he wanted to see which west-bound train he could hope to catch.

"We are a little behind because of the weather last night," the steward answered. "But we are going full speed now, and we ought to reach Kobe by about three."

He was right. Even before the ship had completely stopped, launches from the various hotels began circling round, in a manner reminiscent of predatory rickshaw men. The last to come was a large launch of the Japan Mail Lines. Kensaku boarded this and went ashore. In a few minutes he was on a rickshaw speeding toward Sannomiya Station, his suitcase, bearing the custom officer's chalk marks, perched between his legs.

2

In the soft glow of the sunset the becalmed sea along Shioya and Maiko was beautiful. On a small boat swaying gently near the shore a fisherman sat crosslegged, mending his net. From a pine tree growing in the white sand a rope stretched to a larger fishing boat, already moored for the night. Kensaku sat by the train window, happily gazing at the scene. As night approached he became sleepy again. It seemed that after the irregular life he had been leading, his body was starved for sleep. He went into the dining car and had a simple meal. Back in his coach he changed into a kimono and lay down on the seat. At about eleven the porter awakened him to tell him that they would be in Onomichi soon.

Both the inns listed in the guidebook were right in front of the station. He chose one and went in. It was a surprisingly dignified-looking establishment. He could hear someone playing the samisen, however, so he said to the head clerk, "Give me a quiet room." He was shown to a back room upstairs. He crossed the room immediately upon entering and slid open the door. The outer storm door had not yet been closed, and the light from the room illuminated the pickets along the top of the garden wall. Beyond the wall was a modest path, and beyond that a narrow strip of sea hemmed in by a large island. Moored here were dozens of small fishing boats and cargo boats, their reddish yellow lights shining prettily on the water. The gaiety of the scene reminded him of a busy Tokyo street at night.

A maid brought in a brazier and said to Kensaku, who was standing on the verandah, "Do come in and get warm." Kensaku came in, shutting the door behind him, and sat down beside the brazier. The maid pushed the tray of tea and cookies toward him. "Is it too late to call a masseur?" he asked. "Oh no, not for a guest like you," she said rather familiarly, and hurried out. Made uneasy by the friendliness of the maid, Kensaku began to wonder if the inn was quite respectable.

The masseur turned out to be a talkative fellow. He went through an endless list of places Kensaku might visit: in Onomichi itself there were the temples of Saikokuji, Senkōji, Jōdoji, not to mention the one associated with the priest Motsugai, nicknamed "Fisticuff" for his martial skills; not far away was the beautiful island of Sensuitō near Tomonotsu, then there was the statue of Kannon in Abuto; and on the island of Shikoku there were the hot springs of Dōgo, Kotohira Shrine in Sanuki, the castle town of Takamatsu, Yashima, Shidoji Temple of the puppet play, etc., etc. Kensaku began to think that it might not be a bad idea to take a trip for a week or so. After all, it would take that long for the rest of his things to arrive from Tokyo.

The masseur, distracted by his own eloquence, had eased up considerably on his pressure. "Would you mind," said Kensaku, "doing it a bit harder?" Immediately the masseur started grinding his elbow with all his might into Kensaku's shoulder. A rice pounder on a waterwheel would have been no more merciless.

"What school of massage do you belong to?" Kensaku was able to say.

"I belong to the Ogata School, sir."

Kensaku thought of Ogata standing elegantly on the platform at Shinbashi Station, and could not help smiling at the incongruous association of his stylish friend with this shabby masseur.

A lovely sound, like the plover's song reproduced on the kabuki stage, reached them from the sea. Hearing this sound breaking the stillness of the night moved Kensaku deeply. It made him poignantly aware of the loneliness of his own journey; yet in that awareness there was contentment.

"What was that sound?" he asked.

"Oh, that was just a boat's tackle creaking."

Next morning at about ten Kensaku walked out of the inn, intending to go to Senkōji, a temple in the mountains. He was told that the temple was just above the center of Onomichi, and that from there one could see the whole of the town. It would be a suitable vantage point, he thought, for picking a likely place to live.

He crossed the railroad and came to some stone steps leading up to a temple gate. Over the gate hung an enormous paper lantern. On it were written in vigorous calligraphy the words, "the lion roars." He walked through the grounds and came out of a gate on the other side. He followed several small, winding paths at random up the mountain. Finally he paused at one of the forks and sat down, deciding that he was lost. Then he heard a boy's voice singing to a bugle tune, "Kill them all, shoot them down." A boy of twelve or thirteen came rushing down, swinging a thin bamboo stick. Kensaku stopped him and asked, "Is this the right way to Senkōji?" The boy looked up the mountainside in the direction Kensaku was pointing. He thought hard for a while, then gave up. "I don't know how to tell you. Just follow me." Without waiting for an answer he started climbing the steep path he had just come down, his little body bent forward and his arms swinging energetically. They went up the mountain diagonally to the right. Soon a field of barley, grown two or three inches, came into view just above them to their left. Overlooking the field was a row of three houses. The end house on the left had a "for rent" sign on it. Kensaku thanked the boy, and went to have a look at the house. There was a housewife outside one of the other houses, hanging out clothes to dry. She was kind and friendly, and told him about the house for rent.

He climbed on for another hundred yards or so, and saw another row of three houses. This time the one on the right was for rent. The view from here was better. He found an old woman who was also very helpful. How good these people are, Kensaku thought—the boy, the housewife, and now this old woman. And though he knew it would be too simple-minded to allow these few encounters to form his opinion of Onomichi, he could not help feeling already drawn to the place.

He at last reached the stone steps that led up to Senkōji. They were narrow, and went up an extraordinarily long way. Somewhere in the middle of the climb there were a few teashops, all displaying souvenir postcards neatly framed. But their doors were closed. He reached the top of the steps, turned left, then began climbing another flight of somewhat wider stone steps. At the top was a rustic-looking teashop, draped with reed curtains. Beside it was a great pine tree, spreading its branches over the roof. He sat down on the bench in front of the shop.

Over the island right ahead of him, he could see in the distance the snow-capped mountains of Shikoku. Scattered around for miles over the Inland Sea were innumerable islands, large and small. He had rarely seen a view of such magnitude, and he sat happily gazing at it. Against the backdrop of the quiet shores of the near island, a ship with the mark of the Osaka Steamship Company painted white on her chimney was sailing calmly into port. From time to time she would emit some steam, then a deep-throated sound—boh, boh— would reach Kensaku's ears. A small boat, carried by the tide, passed the ship with surprising speed. A clumsy, wide-bottomed ferryboat was moving diagonally against the tide with an undaunted air. But as he watched with fascination this novel scene, he began to wonder if he would not soon tire of such obvious beauty.

Kensaku ordered a boiled egg; and as he ate it the owner of the teashop told him that the island opposite was called Mukaijima, and the strip of sea this side of it, Tamanoura. Years ago, he said, the great rock standing in Senkōji had an enormous, luminous gem embedded in it. It gave off such light that the citizens of Onomichi needed no lanterns when going out at night. One day, a foreigner saw this gem from a ship. He came ashore and asked if he might buy the rock. The citizens, thinking that no man could possibly take such a large rock away with him, agreed. To their chagrin, the foreigner went up the rock and merely cut out the gem, and took that away with him. Ever since then, on moonless nights, the citizens of Onomichi have had to carry lanterns like anyone else. "If you go to the top of the rock," he said to Kensaku, "you'll find a huge hole the size of two soy sauce barrels. I'm told that the gem was a diamond or something like that."

Kensaku liked the story. Normally, natives weren't quite so ready to tell legends in which their ancestors figured as idiots.

The owner told him of an empty house near the temple, built by a retired merchant who had recently died. Kensaku walked along a narrow, damp lane covered with rotting leaves and found a small cottage standing in the shadow of a large rock. It was far too sedate, gloomy in fact, the sort of place where one might hold solemn tea ceremonies. Besides, it was badly in need of repair. He returned to the teashop and from there began climbing the very last flight of stone steps. All around him were large rocks, pine trees that looked as if they had been there for centuries, stones with epitaphs and poems carved on them. He thought of distant temples he had visited long ago, such as Yamadera in Yamagata, Nipponji on Mt. Nokogiri. Senkōji undoubtedly had a different air about it. Having been founded by the Chinese priest K'ai-shan who had come there from Nagasaki, everything about it was more Chinese—the arrangement of the rocks and the trees, the style of the gate, the belfry.

The Jewel Rock stood near the belfry. It was about the size of a small two-storied house, and sure enough, the entire rock did resemble a stylized ball of fire. From the belfry Kensaku could see almost the entire city. Hemmed in by the mountains and the sea, it was disproportionately long and narrow. Housetops were packed together tight, and immediately below him were numerous stubby chimneys of vinegar makers' houses. Toward the end of the town the houses thinned out, and the shore looked more attractive. He wished he could find a house there.

120

He began his long descent down the stone steps firmly and unflaggingly. By the time he reached town, the straps on his new clogs—he had sent someone at the inn out that morning to buy him a pair—were quite loose.

He came out of a shabby alley onto a busy street. The street was narrow, but the general appearance of it was substantial, with a surprising number of prosperous-looking merchants' houses. The people he saw walking about seemed energetic and purposeful, not at all the sort that would let a foreigner trick them out of a giant gem.

He noticed a peculiar smell hovering over the town. At first he was not sure what it was, but when the smell got stronger as he approached a vinegar shop, he knew. Another peculiarity of the town was the dirtiness of the alleys. Then there were the dried gourds. It seemed that every kind of merchant had them hanging outside his shop—antique dealer, grocer, watchmaker, seal engraver, confectioner, ironmonger, foreign goods importer, and, of course, dried gourd seller. When he returned to the inn, one of the maids told him that the innkeeper himself had a trunkful of them.

He went to bed early that night. He was awakened at dawn. Accompanied by the head clerk he walked to the nearby harbor. The street looked as if it had just been swept, and the lamps were still on. It was a cold, frosty morning.

The Inland Sea did not look quite as beautiful as he had expected. The tide was rising, and it was strange to see the water flowing rapidly like a river, making rippling waves, toward the east.

He got off the ship at Takahama, and from there went by train to Dōgo. He spent two days there. Then he returned to Takahama, and sailed to Ujina. From Hiroshima he went to Itsukushima. If he had liked any of these places better than Onomichi, he would have stayed. But in four days he was back in Onomichi.

The journey had been somewhat wearying, and he was ready to settle down. The rest of his luggage had not yet arrived from Tokyo, but the day after his return he arranged to rent one of that second row of houses he had seen on his way up to Senkōji. He got in touch with a mat maker and a paperer, and had them go up to the house to make new floor mats and put new paper on the door screens.

3

Kensaku's new residence was the last of a row of three modest, attached houses. In the middle lived a nice old couple, and the woman agreed to cook and wash for him. In the other end house lived a lazy good-for-nothing named Yamashita, a man in his early forties. He did no work himself and depended for his daily pocket money on his wife, whom he sent out to work as a maid at an inn downtown. What money he could squeeze out of her he spent on saké.

The view from Kensaku's house was pleasing. Lying on the floor of the small front room he could see all kinds of interesting things. On the island opposite—Mukaijima—was a small shipyard. From early morning he could hear the sound of hammering softened by its passing over the water and the town. Halfway up the mountain to the left of the same island was a stone quarry surrounded by pine woods. The singing of the stonecutters as they worked carried over the rooftops of the town and reached Kensaku directly.

On his first evening in the house he sat on the narrow verandah, enjoying the view. On the porch beside the roof of a merchant's house in the distance the tiny figure of a boy faced the setting sun, shaking a stick. Flying around busily over the boy were five or six white pigeons. Their flapping wings shone pink against the red sky.

At six the great bell of Senkōji above him began to strike slowly. With each strike one deep echo, then another would reach him from far away. Beyond Mukaijima was another island, Hyakkanjima. On this island was a lighthouse. During the day Kensaku had seen the top of it showing over a dip between the mountains of Mukaijima. Now the light came on, only to go out again in a moment. At regular, short intervals the light would appear between the mountains and then disappear. From the shipyard, lights the color of molten copper flowed over the darkening sea.

At ten the ferryboat that sailed daily to Tadotsu returned, blowing her whistle. As she sailed slowly into port her various lights—the red and green ones on her bow, the yellow ones on deck—were reflected on the water like flickering colored chains. The town had gone quiet, and he could hear with incredible clarity the raucous voices of the seamen.

His house was very simple—a six-mat front room, a three-mat rear room, and an earthen-floor kitchen. The mats and the paper screens were new, but the walls were full of cracks. He bought pieces of pretty printed cotton in town and with these he covered the worst ones. Over the smaller cracks he pinned satin leaves used in making artificial flowers. It was a cheaply made house, and though because of its smallness one could get it warm enough by lighting both the gas heater and the gas cooker, once they were out it became cold immediately. On cold, windy nights he would hang a double blanket over the screen doors to keep out the draft. Outside the screen doors were wooden storm doors, but even with these shut the draft would blow in with such force that the blanket stirred constantly. The floorboards under the mats were so warped that once when he carelessly put an open jar of pickled scallions down, it fell over. Also, because of the unevenness of the floorboards the mats did not fit, so that there was a bad draft blowing in from below. He crumpled up the pages of a magazine he was reading and shoved these down the gaps between the mats with a poker.

This spartan life, so different from the life he had led in Tokyo, he rather enjoyed. At last he felt relaxed enough to start on a long-range project he had been planning. This was to be a work based on his life from childhood to the present.

He was born while his father was abroad studying. When it was that his father returned, he could not remember, but he could remember the small, slightly decrepit house in Myōgadani where he lived while his father was away. Living with him were his grandmother, mother, elder brother and younger sister.

One went up the narrow, creaky stairs and came to an atticlike room with a low ceiling. His grandmother was often sitting there before a loom. In the evenings she and his mother would sit under a hanging lamp, drawing thread out of silk floss. They would then lay the pieces of thread out neatly on a large bean paste strainer, which they had converted into a tray by covering the bottom with paper.

He remembered how angry they had been when once out of curiosity he touched the threads. And he could remember, too, the deep humming sound of the spinning wheel. These fleeting memories seemed to him to be of another life.

One day he saw a fox—he knew it was a fox only because his grandmother who was sitting with him on the verandah told him so—walk across their garden nonchalantly, giving them an occasional watchful look, and disappear through the hedge. There was that other time when he saw a monster beetle on a branch high up on a persimmon tree and thought it an enormous cicada. He also remembered having an argument with a local boy of about the same age: each had insisted that *he* was called "sonny" by the neighbors. The argument had taken place under a tree. Might it have been that persimmon tree?

It was soon after his father's return that they moved to the house in Tatsuokachō in Hongō. Once when the maid was sent out to Yamashita in Ueno to buy some bread for his father she took him with her, carrying him on her back. On their way home they had stopped by the pond to look at the baby turtles. He was holding the package with the bread in it. A pretty young housewife came by, snatched the package from his hand and walked off with it.

When the family's former domainal lord died, he heard his elders talking about the lord having "hidden himself." He imagined therefore that the farewell ceremony at the lord's mansion was some elaborate, adult version of hide-and-seek. There was a gold screen placed behind the coffin. He had surreptitiously gone behind this screen, certain that the great man was hiding somewhere there. And later, at the funeral service in Denzūin Temple, he had been quite shaken when the priest started hammering the bell. For some reason it struck Kensaku as a cruel, hateful thing to do.

These insignificant, pointless, and fragmented memories kept on emerging from somewhere deep in his mind like bubbles that rise out of the bottom of a marsh. But there was one incident he remembered that was different from these. It happened when they were still living in Myōgadani. He was in bed with his mother. Thinking that she was fast asleep, he crept under the bedding toward the lower part of her body. Suddenly his mother's hand reached down, pinched his hand hard, then dragged him up. She said not a word, and her eyes were closed as if she were asleep. He understood enough to know that what he had just done was shameful. His shame was perhaps no less than an adult's would have been.

He felt shame still as he remembered the incident. He was also puzzled by the memory. What had made him do such a thing? Was it curiosity or was it some kind of urge? If it had been mere curiosity, why would he have felt such shame at the time? And if it was an urge, did it appear in everyone so early in childhood? He did not know. At any rate, one thing was clear, and that was that it was not an entirely innocent act. Yet toward that child who was at most four years old at the time, Kensaku could hardly feel moral indignation. Perhaps, he thought wretchedly, he had inherited such an inclination; perhaps even with such things, one may be cursed by the sins of one's forefathers.

It was with childhood reminiscences like these, then, that he began his writing. Mostly he worked during the night hours until daybreak. For about a month his work progressed at a steady pace, and both his daily life and his health seemed satisfactory. Then gradually everything began to deteriorate.

He deliberately did not write often to Oei. Once reason was that he wanted to rid his mind of all those fantasies about her; another was that he was trying to resist his own growing sense of loneliness. He wrote fairly regularly to Nobuyuki; but out of pride he was careful to explain that he wrote to him only during those hours which in Tokyo he might have spent at home casually chatting with a friend. Oei wrote him long letters. It seemed that Nobuyuki was letting her read most of his letters to him.

As his work faltered he began to suffer from the monotony of his life. Every day was the same. The only thing that changed was the weather. He had made a calendar out of one of his lined writing sheets and had stuck it on the wall. At the end of each day he would cross out the date on his calendar. So long as his work was progressing satisfactorily this daily routine gave him no discomfort. But with the onset of his general feeling of malaise, the act of crossing out the date began to seem too symbolic of another day truly wasted. Having come away to be alone, he was now finding his isolation unbearable.

Below him a Tokyo-bound train goes past, making a great noise. While it is immediately below, he can see only the smoke. Then he can hear it no more, and in the distance he sees the train going around the curve of another mountain like a twisting caterpillar, emitting black smoke and pulling itself along with all its might. It seems to him to move terribly slowly. He looks at it with envy, and wonders how it can reach Tokyo by next morning. To a man leading such an inactive life, next morning does seem very soon. In a while the tail of the train disappears around the corner.

But it never occurred to him to pack up and return to Tokyo. If he were to do so, he would never come to Onomichi again. Besides, returning to Tokyo so soon would be an admission of defeat. He had to finish his work, however good or bad it might prove to be. Often during the day he would go to town and hang around the post office or the railroad station. This was because these places seemed to him closest to Tokyo. The barley, two or three inches tall when he had first arrived, had now grown to about six inches.

He had the feeling that his face muscles around the cheeks had gone slack. He found it difficult to open his eyes wide. And he realized that for weeks, from morning to night, his face had kept the same glum expression, never angry, never amused. He had not even taken a deep breath once.

Early one evening, when a strong north wind was blowing, he decided he would go to some deserted place along the beach and shout as loud as he could. He found a spot just outside town. Nearby stood three tile kilns. The pine oil sizzled loudly as the wind hit the kilns, and the fires glowed brilliantly in the dusk. He stood still for a minute gazing at the almost blinding glow, then walked up to the top of the stone embankment and faced the sea. There was no song for him to sing. He gave a few meaningless shouts, but they sounded to his ears like feeble, miserable cries. The cold north wind beat against his back. The black smoke from the kilns was being blown out over the sea, and would scatter into wisps over the dark silver of the water. In frustration at his own feebleness, he walked back to the house.

There was a cunning little local prostitute he had come to know who would say things like, "Please, boss, take me away somewhere—I'll pay the expenses." She was a peasant girl, plump and pretty.

Made bold by the knowledge that she was attractive to him, she would brazenly feign sadness over her predicament and squeeze an extra yen or two out of him.

One pleasant afternoon he crossed the channel by ferry to see the salt fields on Mukaijima. Afterward he decided he would walk to the other side and take a good look at the other island, Hyakkanjima, only the top of which he had so far managed to see. He was walking up a gently sloping road between two hills when he saw a man and a woman coming toward him. The woman looked like the young prostitute. Instinctively he turned into a narrow path that cut through a bamboo grove, walked a few yards, stopped, turned around and waited for the couple to pass. He was right, it was the prostitute. She was wearing a colorful, long-sleeved outer kimono. The white make-up on her face was so thick, she looked almost grotesque. She was talking gaily to her companion, who wore a felt hat pulled low over his eyes. He was young, and looked like some sort of clerk.

Kensaku came to enjoy his work less and less, and his health and emotional condition continued to deteriorate. His shoulders were now always painfully stiff. His head felt heavy, and when he held the scruff of his neck hard the muscles there made an ominous sound. He lost his appetite and slept badly. Most of the time in bed he would doze rather than sleep and be continually visited by unpleasant dreams.

But at night when working he came to experience more and more frequently protracted periods of abnormal, high-pitched excitement —not that his work necessarily progressed during these periods. Unable to sit still any longer he would stand up and start wandering around excitedly in the small six-mat room, not hearing the clatter of the loose floorboards underneath. At such times he would feel as if he had become a person of immense significance, ready to confront all.

During the day, however, there was no respite from misery. He was nearly a sick man, both spiritually and physically, He was weary, he felt the lack of sleep; his eyes were bloodshot; indeed, there was hardly any life left in him at all.

Once, at the suggestion of the old woman next door, he visited a blind masseur who lived just below the stone steps of Hōdoji Temple.

The masseur called himself Iwabē, and had formerly been a stevedore at the harbor. His technique was punishingly rough, so much so that Kensaku found him almost hateful, but it did no good. Reluctantly Kensaku decided he would stop working temporarily.

4

Late one morning on a pleasant, springlike day, Kensaku sat in the front room with the screen doors wide open, eating his breakfast-lunch. From between the stones of the wall in front a large lizard had dragged its half-dormant body out to bask in the sun. Kensaku too felt more alive. He could see beyond Mukaijima the faint, blue-green outlines of the mountains of Shikoku. Suddenly he wanted to travel again. He brought out a guidebook and was looking at the timetable for ships going to Sanuki when the old woman from next door came and sat down on the verandah. "You never miss a meal, do you?" she said to the two puppies that were always there when Kensaku ate. Only their little black noses showed over the edge of the verandah, twitching as though they had a life of their own.

"Would the ferryboat be best for going to Kotohira Shrine?" he asked.

"I think so. There'll be so many people going there today, the steamer run by the steamship company will be packed."

"The ferryboat leaves at two, doesn't it?"

"That's right. So you're going to Kotohira Shrine, are you?"

"Yes. Don't worry about the house. Please leave everything as it is. There isn't anything here that a burglar would want."

"Oh, I'm sure you have something you wouldn't want to lose," she said, laughing.

"I shall put everything of any value in a bag. May I leave that with you?"

"Of course. The moon should be lovely tonight in Tomonotsu."

"Were you ever there to see it?"

"Oh, no," she said. "We went on a pilgrimage tour of Shikoku last year, and we passed Tomonotsu on a ship, that's all."

"I thought I would view the moon at Tomonotsu tonight, go to Takamatsu the day after and see the castle garden that I hear is now open."

"They say it's a wonderful garden, even better than the one in Okayama."

Kensaku scraped together on a plate what was left of his meal and gave it to the dogs. One of them growled menacingly and kept the other away from the plate. "Stop that!" the old woman said, and pretended to try to kick the dog from where she was sitting. Her swinging foot in the straw sandal looked quite innocuous.

Kensaku saw down below the figure of her husband coming up the steep, narrow path at a slow and steady pace. He was retired, but had a part-time job with the steamship company selling tickets at the harbor. "Your husband's coming back," Kensaku said. She looked down the hill and smiled. "So I see."

Their neighbors' six-year-old girl stood in front of the small gate of her house and shouted, "Hello!" The old man stopped, tried to straighten his back and looked up. He was wearing heavy clothes which hung loosely on his bent back. "Hello, Yoshiko!" he shouted back in a voice that was hoarse yet pleasing to the ear.

"Hello!" the little girl shouted again, and again the old man responded, "Hello, Yoshiko!"

When the exchange between the shrill voice and the hoarse voice had ended, the old man allowed his body to bend to its earlier position and resumed his slow climb. The old woman went back to her house.

Kensaku went down the hill to get some money out of the post office which was in the near end of town. He walked up to the opening at the counter where it said "Savings and Money Orders," and produced a money order. "I'm very sorry," the man behind the counter said, "but we closed at noon. We just handed in our accounting for the day." Kensaku had totally forgotten that it was Sunday. Not wanting to give up too easily he stepped back and looked at the big clock above his head. It was already twenty minutes past noon. He had no choice but to postpone his trip.

The following day was cold and unpleasant, with meager sunlight. The sky looked untrustworthy, and there was a little wind. He hesitated at first but in the end decided to go anyway. At one-thirty that afternoon he was standing on the wharf, waiting for the boat.

The boat arrived half an hour late, so that her departure was equally delayed. He stayed out on deck, wrapped in his grandfather's shabby Inverness cape. The boat sailed eastward alongside the stretched-out town. Halfway up the mountain on which Senkōji stood was his little house, looking smaller than ever. On the bamboo pole under the eaves hung the wadded kimono and the outer kimono he had worn that very morning. From where he stood, they looked tiny. The old woman sat on the verandah, just in front of the hanging clothes. He raised his hand a little. She responded by raising hers awkwardly. She seemed to be smiling.

The boat now sailed past Saikokuji, the temple farthest up the mountains, then another temple, Jōdoji, and finally the edge of town. She began to take a more southerly course, and after rounding Mukaijima sailed straight out to sea. A whole string of islands came into view. Innoshima and Hyakkanjima were the only ones he knew by name. They were so close together that he could see nothing between them; it was rather like sailing along a coastline with a lot of inlets.

The sky was now completely clouded over. A cold wind blew from the west. He thought of going to his cabin but decided that it would be a pity not to see as much of the scenery as possible. He pulled together the upper layer of his cape, buried his chin deep in it, and remained seated on the bench.

The boat wove her way through the islands. Each one of the barley fields on the hillsides was clearly distinguishable from the adjacent field by its shade of green—one would be dark green, the next one would be light. Under the cloudy sky the greens had a lovely, soft sheen like velvet. The lines of the mountains on the islands were etched with greater clarity and forcefulness than if the sun had been out. Kensaku was reminded of the thin cracks on the dried gourds hanging in the shops in Onomichi, and thought how strong and beautiful were such lines made by nature.

The boat passed certain islands far out from their shores and others close in to them. Every beach that showed signs of habitation would be certain to have standing on it one or two old pine trees bent by the winds from the sea. And always underneath the trees there would be an old-fashioned stone beacon with the words "everburning light" carved deep on it. Kensaku remembered the legend so often told: a girl, in love with a young man living on another island, swam every night from her island to his, guided by the beacon; the young man then ceased to love her, and one stormy night blew out the light and let her drown. Every beacon that Kensaku now saw seemed to befit the legend.

The temple of the Abuto Kannon became visible. It was on a headland that stuck out into a narrow channel between the mainland and an island. The outer shrine stood on land and the inner shrine on a ten-foot-high stone platform built on a great rock jutting out of the water. The two buildings were connected by a sloping, covered bridge about ten yards long. There was nothing else man-made in the vicinity, and Kensaku felt as though he were looking at a Chinese painting.

The boat rounded the headland and continued along the coastline. Kensaku saw several pine-covered miniature islands that looked almost small enough to be put in one's garden. Not long after, the boat reached the port of Tomonotsu. Nearby, the island of Sensuitō lay serenely in the water. Kensaku was a little disappointed to find that it pointed in a direction quite different from what he had imagined from postcards. Nevertheless it was a fine island, restful and dignified. The town was too built-up for his taste. There were chimneys sticking out here and there, painted with signs advertising brands of the local specialty, a "life-preserving" medicinal wine.

He had intended to stay the night there to view the moon, but looking at the cloudy sky decided he might as well remain on the boat and continue the journey.

It had become too cold to sit on the bench any longer; reluctantly he stood up and went to the lounge. He was traveling second class, so that there were only a half-dozen other passengers sharing it with him. He followed their example and lay down. The boat was pitching a little, and he could hear the sound of the hull hitting the water every time she came down. He was sleepy, but was afraid that if he went to sleep he would catch cold. He sat up and began reading a novel he had brought with him.

An officer wearing gold braid on his sleeves walked in, followed by an ordinary seaman carrying a phonograph. The officer himself carried a box of records. "You must all be bored," he announced. Seeing that Kensaku was the only passenger sitting up, he walked up to him and put down the box in front of him. "They're all yours, sir," he said, grinning.

Kensaku continued to read for a while; then, since no one else seemed interested, he pulled the box toward him and began looking at the records. They were all folk-type ballads, mostly of the *naniwabushi* variety. But some were *gidayū*, which he liked. He played three of these, one after the other. There were two men lying near him discussing the stock market. One of them stopped talking, listened to the record being played, and said, "She's really special, that Roshō. What a voice she has." He looked around and said to Kensaku, "Excuse me, but are there any 'gay-mood songs'?"

"What?" said Kensaku with deliberate brusqueness. He guessed that "gay-mood songs" meant *naniwabushi*, but decided to pretend he had no idea what the man was talking about. He put on another *gidayū* record. The man thus dismissed fell silent. Kensaku was immediately sorry, and put on next a song called "The Song of Four Seasons" sung by a Yoshiwara geisha, thinking that it was the one that went, "Spring means flowers/ So let's all go and see them/On Mt. Higashiyama." For a few seconds all that came out of the megaphone was the scratchy sound of the needle on the record, then the singer burst into song in a startlingly gay voice, "Spring is here/Oh, how happy/ You and I together." With a cross look on his face he listened to the rest of the banal, cheerful song. Summer followed spring, then came autumn, and the singer was still happy. There was no defense against such cheer; he pictured himself, morose and a little startled, seated beside the blaring megaphone, and the ludicrousness of the scene almost made him smile. Accompanied by the various noises made by the boat—chug, chug, chug, chug (that was the engine), boh, boh (that was the whistle), thump, thump (that was the hull hitting the water)—the singer was at last singing of the couple's happiness in winter, when they could sip saké together as they viewed the snow. When the song ended he got up and went back on deck.

A few passengers were standing there talking to the officer who had brought the records. The boat was already off the Sanuki coast. One of the passengers said to the officer, "Purser, which one of those mountains is the one with Kotohira Shrine on it?"

"It's that one there," said the officer, pointing. "It's supposed to resemble an elephant's head. Lord Kotohira on Elephant Head Mountain—that's how they used to refer to the shrine in the old days, I'm told. You see that black patch on the side of the mountain? It looks pretty small from here, but when you get there you'll find that it's a big forest."

Four or five fishing boats, their sails taut, sped past over the indigo sea. The purser said that they were now just about in the middle of the Inland Sea, where the tides from the east and west met as they came in and parted as they went out. "Next month will be even busier," he said, "when Zentsūji Temple has its festival."

Kensaku moved away from the group and went astern. There he sat down on a bench and looked at the line of mountains in the distance. There was a mountain on this side of the one the purser pointed at which seemed to Kensaku to have a much greater resemblance to an elephant's head.

The elephant, which has until now only shown its head, suddenly rises out of the ground. The people are thrown into a panic. Will this monster destroy all mankind, or will they find a way to destroy it? Soldiers, statesmen and scholars from all over the world gather together and rack their brains. Guns and mines won't do, for the elephant's skin is a hundred yards thick, and they would only scratch its surface. Trying to starve it would be useless, for it eats at fifty-year intervals. The more intelligent men say that so long as it is not annoyed it will do no mischief. Certain men of religion in India say that it is a god. But the great majority of men clamor for its immediate destruction, and are full of foolish ideas as to how this might be accomplished. The elephant begins to get angry.

Before he knew it, Kensaku himself had become the elephant, excitedly preparing for his one-man war against the world at large. He is in a city. Each time he stamps a foot, fifty thousand men are crushed to death. Guns, mines, poison gas, airplanes, airships—all such ingenious devices created by man's intelligence are directed at him. He takes a deep breath, exhales through his long nose, and the airplanes, feebler than mosquitoes, fall to the ground; the airships float away helplessly like balloons. He draws up water into his nose and disgorges it, and there is a flood; he descends into the depths of the ocean and comes up suddenly, causing a tremendous tidal wave . . .

"I hope the trip hasn't been too boring for you, sir. That over there is Tadotsu. We'll be arriving in about ten minutes." It was the purser. Little did he know that at that moment Kensaku was far from being bored.

The boat began sounding her whistle persistently—it was a deep, unpleasant noise that shook one's eardrums—as she approached the harbor of Tadotsu, a town crammed with rooftops.

And so ended Kensaku's absurd fantasy. He himself saw nothing particularly amusing in it. True, when it came to the point where he was about to take on all of mankind, he felt a little odd; but to him whose natural inclination to fantasize had become gradually more pronounced during his recent solitude, the entire fantasy did not seem at all silly.

He went down to the lounge to pick up his umbrella—he had no luggage to worry about—and came up again. The sun, which had not shown itself all day, was now out, a bright red ball hanging over the island of Okinoshima. There were fifteen or so passengers standing about.

"Are you going to Kotohira Shrine?" one of them asked.

"Yes."

"Are you by yourself?"

"Yes, I am."

"It must be lonely, traveling all alone."

"Yes."

"What inn are you staying at?"

"Where would you recommend?"

"Well, the best one is Toraya, then Bitchūya, I suppose. But I doubt they'll give you a room if you're by yourself."

Kensaku simply nodded in reply.

"Why don't you try a place called Yoshikichi? I'm spending the night in Tadotsu myself, and that's where I'm going, so come along with me if you like."

Kensaku looked the man over. He was about twenty-five, common-looking, and probably some kind of salesman. He also had a dirty face and hands. He seemed to take it for granted that Kensaku would be staying at the same inn, and proceeded to explain where it was and so on.

Moored in the harbor were old-fashioned wooden cargo boats of various sizes and shapes, tossing restlessly in the choppy water.

Kensaku was the first to get onto the floating pier. He walked across it quickly, steadying himself against the wind that blew sharply at him from the side. It was low tide, and the bridge that connected the floating pier to the landing was at a sharp incline. As he went up this steep bridge a whole tour group of old ladies, carrying their wooden clogs, came down gingerly in their bare feet to board the boat. A few yards behind him the grubby salesman had separated himself from the rest of the disembarking passengers and was hurrying after him. Not caring if he hurt the pursuer's feelings or not, Kensaku quickened his pace. He had no idea where the railroad station was, but he was afraid that if he were to stop and ask someone for directions the fellow would catch up with him. He walked on quickly toward what looked like the busy part of town.

The fellow had given up the chase. As Kensaku passed by the post office, he saw one of the clerks leaning out of the window, looking bored. He stopped and asked him where the station was. It turned out to be very near.

There was a good fire going in the stove in the waiting room. After about twenty minutes a train, smaller than the standard, came in. He got on it and proceeded to Kotohira.

5

That night in Kotohira he stayed at the inn which he had been told would not be likely to accept a lone guest. On the following morning he went to see the shrine. Its treasures gave him particular delight. He thought quite beautiful the bindings of its ancient copies of such classics as the *Tales of Isé*, the *Tale of Hōgen* and the *Tale of Heiji*.

He normally disliked Kanō Tan'yū's paintings, but he liked the snow scene by him that he saw there, in black and white on a folding screen. Was he so starved for such things, he wondered, that even this painter could move him?

On the way to the main building, too, he had found pleasing examples of man's art. He liked particularly the approach to the steep stone steps leading up to the main building. But the path that one took from the main shrine to the inner shrine seemed new, and was without man-made beauty. All that impressed him there were the great mountain trees, a refreshing change from those pines in Onomichi. But his admiration for these trees was short-lived. For their bark soon struck him as ominous-looking, and his nervous condition was such that they began to frighten him.

In the afternoon he went to Takamatsu as planned. He could not get into the castle garden that he had wanted to see. Instead he visited Ritsurin Park. Afterward he walked around the town. He found on one street corner a shop specializing in imported wines and foods. It was not much of a shop to look at from the outside, but on going in he found that it was not at all badly stocked. There was no such shop in Onomichi, and what he wanted to do was buy a supply of imported tinned meat and take it back with him. He went around the shop slowly, examining the shelves. But all he saw in the way of tinned meat were the standard Japanese brands, cooked in native sauces, which he could easily get in Onomichi.

A young man with heavily pomaded hair came up to him. "Can I help you?" Kensaku could not tell whether he was the proprietor or an employee.

"Yes, please. Do you have any imported tinned meat?"

"Yes, we do," the young man said and went away. He came back immediately holding a large, dark blue can. The label said in English, "Pure English Oats."

"Are you sure this is meat?"

"Of course," said the young man without hesitation.

Kensaku took the can and shook it. It made a dry, rattling sound. He gave it back to the young man, and asked again, "Are you sure it's meat?"

The man looked at the label and said, "Yes, that's what it says," then read out with surprising fluency, " 'Pure English Oats.' "

Kensaku walked out in silence. He felt a little angry, but then remembered that his own appearance was hardly calculated to impress any shopkeeper—a dirty cloth cap, a black twill Inverness cape made twenty years ago, cheap clogs with loose straps, a fat, inelegant umbrella, and on top of all this an unshaven, cheerless face. What customer looking like that would know anything about imported food? All the same, it was difficult to forgive the impudent fellow, and he was almost tempted to return to the shop and force him to open the can in his presence.

He decided to go to Yashima, and went to the streetcar terminal by rickshaw. He got on a streetcar bound for Shidoji Temple. His streetcar was almost empty, but those returning to the terminal were packed. Apparently the city newspaper and the streetcar company had that day held a fair for the public in Yashima, providing such entertainment as treasure hunts, etc. And when he got off at Yashima he faced a whole multitude of returning merrymakers, mostly with flushed faces, leaning on each other as they tottered tiredly toward the station. They were a motley crowd—shop clerks and apprentices wearing identical saffron-colored kerchiefs around their heads or necks, drunkards accompanied by geisha, fathers with their children's balloons tied to the cloth bands of their hats, men being carried on palanquins bizarrely bedecked with flowers, students, railway employees in their uniforms, stallkeepers carrying their wares home. He walked in the opposite direction past them, an alien figure in the midst of this festive crowd. Yet he was not unhappy, for as he walked he remembered with gentle nostalgia the outings he had enjoyed as a child—going to Kameido to view the wisterias or to Ōkubo to view the azaleas, or to the Komaba playing grounds on a field day. They were fleeting yet soothing memories. By the time the road which had been on dusty, level ground began at last to climb, the returning crowd had thinned out considerably. Slowly he walked up the road that cut through pine woods, resting often. The salt fields that stretched all the way from Takamatsu gradually came into view below him. From the chimneys of the huts where the sea water was being boiled, thick, white columns of steam rose, undisturbed in the still, evening air. Far into the distance the white columns lined the landscape. The view did much to ease his melancholy.

There was hardly a soul in sight when he reached the plateau. Scattered all about him were crushed lunch boxes, tangerine peelings and the like. Little shops that sold postcards and dried crab were closing down.

He walked on until he came to an inn nestling in a pine grove and overlooking the sea. There was one group of customers that had not gone home with the rest making a lot of noise in one of the annexes. Aside from serving these, the maids were busy clearing up.

Kensaku was shown to another annex, a sedate little cottage that stood on the top of a cliff. Down below was the sea. To his right was the island of Shōdoshima, wrapped in evening mist. Far and near were other islands whose names he did not know. Immediately below were wooden cargo boats like those he had seen in Tomonotsu harbor, moored for the night with lighted mastheads.

The deepening dusk seemed to rise out of the sea. But even in the gathering darkness he could see the arched outline of the sea as it rolled toward the shore. It was a fine view, though for some reason it gave him no pleasure.

A maid came in with the dinner. He was not hungry, and ate very little. As she cleared the table the maid said, "You'll be sleeping in the main house."

"Let me know when the room's ready."

He felt depressed. What he felt was not the transitory sadness of a lone traveler but something much darker and more oppressive.

The maid returned to show him to his room. It was quite close, just on the other side of the main garden. Above the pine grove behind the cottage hung the moon, large and rose-colored. One entered the garden through a small gate with a roof over it. As Kensaku was about to go through the gate he almost stepped on a man lying face down beside it, apparently quite unconscious. The man had not had a haircut or a shave for months, and looked like a beggar. He must have urinated as he lay there, for his trousers were dark with a spreading stain.

The maid hardly paid any attention to the prone figure. But Kensaku could not dismiss him quite so easily. Once in the room he said to her, "Are you sure the man isn't ill?"

"Oh, no, he's just drunk."

"Is he from these parts?"

"Yes. He's a beggar, without a home or family. He took advantage of today's festivities and had too much to drink."

The fire in the copper brazier was burning nicely. Kensaku sat beside it, wishing that the maid would leave. He knew that she was dutifully waiting to put away the clothes he was wearing; but he was not about to put on the night kimono provided by the inn. The maid remained, impatient but stubborn. Finally he said, "You may go."

"But sir, your clothes have to be folded properly."

"I understand, but really, they're not worth the trouble."

The maid departed, laughing. He stood up immediately and took off only his outer kimono. He turned the sash around so that the knot was in the front, and went to bed in his own clothes.

He opened the book he had brought with him, but it failed to draw his interest. He lay still, as though made immovable by the dark loneliness that assailed him. It was truly a quiet evening, and very cold. Though the fire in the brazier was still going, his face felt cold, and his feet seemed to take forever to warm up.

Outside, the beggar had begun to snore.

Wide awake, Kensaku thought about the beggar's life, with no home to return to and no one to wait for him, and could not help likening that condition to his own. There was no one who would feel truly sorry if he should fail in his work, no one with whom he could share his joy if he should succeed. His father and stepmother, his brother and sisters—he belonged to none of them. If only he had a family that he could call his own. . .

The loneliness that he felt then seemed to reach the very core of his being. He was no less alone, he thought, than the drunken beggar lying beneath the cold night sky.

And then he became aware that of all the people he knew, it was Oei whom he now wanted to see, it was Oei to whom he felt closest.

Why then should she not have been much more involved in his life? What they felt toward each other was almost like blood kinship. His father had long ago determined her role for him: she was a servant, destined to leave the household when Kensaku got married. But why should she and Kensaku have so readily accepted the role imposed on her by his father? Why had it never occurred to either of them to question the reasonableness of his father's dictate?

Of course, to marry a woman who had been his grandfather's mistress would be an odd thing to do. But how much better to marry her than to continue to lust after her secretly as he had done, or worse, to begin an illicit relationship with her. He knew that such a marriage would make him a target of ridicule and abuse. But he would not mind that; indeed, it would make him a better man. Aside from the fact that she had been his grandfather's mistress, then, there was little reason why they should not marry each other. It was the most obvious thing to do. He could then settle down, and she would have security. Why hadn't the idea occurred to him before?

He felt much happier now. He promised himself he would write to her immediately upon returning to Onomichi if he had not changed his mind by then. But would Oei accept his proposal? He decided then and there that if she did not, he would go back to Tokyo at once and try to allay her fears.

6

The next day Kensaku caught the boat for Onomichi. The weather was quite good, and he could have stopped at Tomonotsu this time and viewed the moon. But he was in no mood for such leisurely pastimes and returned to Onomichi directly.

That night he sat down to write his letter. But how was he to begin it? The simplest way of course was to state his intention bluntly. But as the saying went, that would be like pouring water into the ear of someone fast asleep. The person jumps up in shock, hardly in a state to listen intelligently to a proposition, no matter how cogently presented. He decided there was no way but to write to Nobuyuki and have him talk to Oei.

He began by describing honestly how painful had been his secret desire for Oei while he was still in Tokyo, and proceeded to explain how he had come to his decision in Yashima.

He understood, he then said, how unpleasant his proposed marriage would be to their father, stepmother, and the rest of the family in Hongō; but he had no intention of seeking anyone's approval of it, for had not their father told him, when he had gone to talk to him about Aiko, that he, Kensaku, as head of his own household, should handle all such matters himself? Besides, if he were to consult the family in Hongō they might try to interfere and he would not like that. And if, because of this marriage, they should sever all relations with him, he would not complain.

No doubt, he continued, Oei would be surprised. But he would ask Nobuyuki to explain the situation to her so that she would understand. Of course Nobuyuki would have his own reservations about the proposal; but he must ask Nobuyuki to put those aside for the moment, self-centered though such a request might seem; and would he try to explain his younger brother's point of view as only he, who knew him so well, could?

He then wrote a letter to Oei. He was sorry he had not written for so long, he said. He hoped she was well. He was not going to say anything in this letter, for in a letter to Nobuyuki he had written in detail what he had to say. The two letters would be posted at the same time. Nobuyuki was sure to visit her on the day following his receipt of the letter, and he would say all kinds of things that would shock her; but he hoped she would overcome her initial shock and calmly try to understand his feelings. He implored her not to lose courage, for there was nothing to fear.

When he had finished the letters he was overcome by a strange sense of dejection. By these two letters, he thought helplessly, I have committed a large part of my life. But he had no second thoughts. And though it was past midnight he decided he had to post the letters immediately lest he should later be tempted to change his mind. He lit his lantern and walked down the hill to the railroad station to deliver the letters.

He anticipated an uneasy period of waiting until the replies came. Even if they answered immediately, it would be three days before he heard from them. And if they procrastinated at all, it would be at least five days. He could see already how nervous and fearful he was going to be during these next five days. It was disconcerting to find how uncertain he was so soon after exhorting Oei not to lose courage, so soon after displaying his determination in his letter to Nobuyuki.

What angered Kensaku, what made him so pathetic in his own eyes, was the fact that there were even now two utterly conflicting desires at war within himself. One was the desire that his proposal should succeed; and the other was that it should somehow fail. Which of these was true to his innermost feelings, he could not tell. What he was sure about was that whatever happened, he would learn to come to terms with it. But until the decision was made, either way, he would continue to suffer from the conflict within him. Such was his habit, indeed his sickness. And characteristically he soon became a passive actor, willing to allow Oei's decision to shape his fate.

Yet, however confused and tentative his mental state may have been, his body, stimulated beyond bearing by thoughts of Oei after their marriage, suddenly began craving constant satisfaction. During the days of waiting for word from Tokyo, he visited the local brothel several times.

Six days passed, and at last Nobuyuki's letter arrived.

"I was at first taken aback by your letter. To be honest, my immediate response was to wish, for various reasons, that you would change your mind if you could. But there was that unfortunate business over Aiko, and given your character besides, I knew that it would be useless for me to try to dissuade you; and so I decided that I would do as you asked—show Oei your letter and, where needed, explain your point of view. I would then write and report to you on the meeting and express my own thoughts on the matter.

"Today, on my way home from the office, I stopped by at your house and saw Oei. I'll tell you here and now that she will not accept your proposal. She showed me your letter to her. From it she had guessed what you had in mind, so that when I showed her your letter to me she was not very surprised. She read it, then immediately said that it wouldn't do. She spoke with assurance and dignity, and I was impressed. Truly, her attitude was such that I could not argue with her. You might think me feeble, you might even think that I had gone to see her in the hope that she would speak and behave as she did. And to be honest, I had half-hoped that she would. I would nevertheless have spoken on your behalf had she given me the chance.

"We talked about all kinds of things. Incidentally, she'd been in bed with a cold for two or three days and got up today only because I visited her.

"I hate to have to write what I feel I must now write in this letter. You see, I have kept something from you which I should have told you long ago. I was wrong, I know, and I am sorry. Yet even now, I can hardly bring myself to tell you. But I must, for though at first it will be like pushing you off a cliff, that will be better than making you suffer for the rest of your life because of my silence.

"You are the child of our mother and the man you knew as your grandfather, the man you went to live with as a boy after our mother died. I don't know the details. I heard the story for the first time from our aunt in Kobe, when I was about to graduate from high school. I think that father still doesn't know that I know; and because I have not talked about it—why would I want to?—I know very little more than what I learned from our aunt. At any rate, you were born when we were living in Myōgadani, sometime during those three years when father was away in Germany studying. And what I am about to tell you will, I feel, add to your pain; but I will not hide anything from you now. When mother was pregnant, grandfather (your real father) and grandmother wanted her to have an abortion, and keep the whole matter a secret from father. But our grandfather in Shiba apparently was furious when he heard about their plan. 'Is not one crime enough?' he said, and stopped them. Soon after, mother went to live with him in Shiba. He wrote to father in Germany, telling him honestly what his daughter had done. He fully expected father to divorce her. But father wrote back saying that he forgave her. And very soon after this, I have been told, grandfather in Myōgadani went away somewhere.

"When I first heard about the terrible circumstances of your birth, the curse under which you were born, I was shocked and saddened. And the question that had always been dimly present in my mind ever since childhood—why was Kensaku always treated differently from the rest of us?—was at last answered. For many years after that, I was certain that you knew too. I could not imagine that Oei would not have said something about it to you during all those years you were together; besides, even if she hadn't, I thought it likely that you would have sensed something of the sort. It was only during that whole Aiko affair that I realized to my extreme surprise that you knew nothing about it. Today, when talking about this with Oei, I was once again reminded of what a marvelous woman she is. She had promised father never to tell you about it, and she kept the promise. 'I wouldn't have told him anyway,' she said. 'Why should I want to hurt him?' Perhaps she is right, and perhaps I am wrong in telling you about it now. All I know is that she is an extraordinary woman.

"I need not tell you that it was because of your birth that Aiko's family rejected you. Her mother sympathized with you; but her sympathy was not enough to make her your ally. What more can we expect of people like that, to whom convention is everything?

"I watched you suffer, and I felt that it was wrong to let you suffer in ignorance, not to tell you the truth however painful it might be. I was sure, too, that if I did not tell you then, you would later hate me for my silence. But another part of me wanted to believe that silence was best. Perhaps I was running away from my responsibility. But I could not bear to say anything that would increase your suffering. Besides, it was hard for me to tell such a story about our dead mother. Finally, there was the fact that you were a writer. Perhaps it was this consideration that held me back most. I was sure that if you were told the story it would appear somewhere in your writing, especially if it caused you great pain. Such an attitude may seem very limited to you, but I did not want to see father, now about to enjoy at last the peace of old age, being hurt all over again; and he would be very hurt if he were to see his wife's old mistake being aired in public. I don't believe that we could imagine the suffering he must have gone through when he heard about it in Germany and during the years when he tried to forget it. To open up his old wound—the mere thought of doing such a thing horrified me. Perhaps such a fear on my part comes entirely from weakness. It is true that as father gets older, I find myself becoming more and more afraid of causing him any pain.

"At the same time, I felt I was doing you a great wrong. You had the right to know the truth about yourself, if only because in your work it is important; and my witholding it from you was wrong. If you had refused to give up the idea of marrying Aiko, I would have done my best to persuade her family to accept you; and I had resolved to tell you the truth about your birth if my intercession should end in failure. You might as well know that I was greatly relieved when you said you were prepared to forget about Aiko.

"When our aunt in Kobe told me about you, she said sadly that you had been born under a curse. For a long time I felt as she did. But later I began to think that this was a sinister presumption more appropriate in cheap fiction than in real life. What reason had I to believe that your entire future had been damned by your birth? If everything in Kensaku's life were to go smoothly and innocently, I began to tell myself, of what relevance would be the way he was born? Why should I worry about it so much? What is past is past, I told myself; let the past be buried; let Kensaku look to a future that is of his own making, let him shape his own fate. And then that Aiko business happened. Something that you yourself had had nothing to do with was held against you. In that affair, you were indeed under a curse. Yet, though I was shaken by its outcome, I could still tell myself not to exaggerate its significance. But this time, I sense some kind of danger in what you are trying to do. It will be like willfully laying another curse on yourself. It frightens me.

"Whatever her other reasons may be for not wanting to marry you, the main reason why Oei has refused so adamantly is that she shares my fear for you.

"I want to be your ally in the things you do. So far, you have never made it difficult for me to give you whatever moral support I could. But in this instance, I cannot wish you success. There is something dark waiting for you not so far away, and before my very eyes you are heading straight toward it. I must try to stop you. I sympathize with the way you feel about Oei. I see nothing at all immoral about it. But that has nothing to do with the fact that I am very afraid for you. And I am convinced that this fear of mine should not be dismissed lightly.

"I have pretty well said everything I set out to say. I have but one worry: how much of a blow will this letter be to Kensaku?

"Won't you come back to Tokyo immediately? I think it would be best if you did. I could come to see you in Onomichi, but that would be a little more complicated. If you want me there, please send me a telegram. It might be fun going to Kyūshū together. But do try to come back to Tokyo.

"I am confident that you will not be thrown into absolute despair by this letter. But it will hurt you deeply, I know—more deeply perhaps than it would have hurt the rest of us, for you feel more. But please don't let it crush you.

"I do not think that Oei will write a separate reply. For one thing, she has not yet recovered from her cold. But she will be so happy to see you again. I, too, want to see you. I hope you will decide to come back soon."

As Kensaku read the letter he could feel his cheeks going cold. Sometime or other he had stood up, and now with the letter in his hand he began to wander about the tiny room. "What am I to do?" he said. "What am I to do?" In a small voice he kept on repeating the question, hardly aware that he was doing so.

It was all like a dream to him. The being that was himself, the person he had known until now as himself, seemed to be going farther and farther into the distance like a thinning mist.

Why had his mother done such a thing? Because of what she did he was conceived. He understood that he owed his existence to that act alone, that the two things were inseparable. Yet he could not accept what his mother had done. His mother and that shoddy, common, worthless old man—the mere thought of the association was ugly and unclean.

He was then suddenly filled with overwhelming pity for his mother, his mother who had been defiled by that man. "Mama!" he cried out, like a boy about to throw himself into his mother's arms.

7

He was thoroughly exhausted both in mind and body. He could not think any more. He lay down and slept for two hours.

He woke up at about four. By then he had become almost his normal self. He washed his face, went out to the verandah and squatted there, gazing listlessly at the scene. It occurred to him after a while that Oei and Nobuyuki must be worried about him. He decided to write Nobuyuki immediately.

"I have read your letter," he wrote. "Yes, it was somewhat of a blow. For a time I seemed to have lost all sense of my old self. But I had a short sleep, and I am fully recovered. I am grateful to you for having said what must have been difficult for you to say.

"I do not want to say anything about mother. Sadness—that is what I feel most for her. I have no inclination to blame her. At present all I can think is that no one could have been more unfortunate than she.

"As for father, I somehow feel that I shall now in all likelihood learn to acknowledge, more than ever before, my debt of gratitude to him. I know that what he did for me was more than any ordinary man would have done, and I believe that I must thank him for it. I can imagine, too, the suffering he must have gone through all those years. It must have been terrible. The only question I now have concerning him is what our future relationship ought to be. Perhaps it would be best if I could, without causing him discomfort and without being unreasonable, take this opportunity to clarify our relationship once and for all.

"But I should like to see my relationship with you and Sakiko and Taeko kept exactly as it has always been. I want this very much.

"Please don't worry about me. Of course what you told me made me miserable for a time, and perhaps it will again and again in years to come. I don't want to seem to be running away from anything, but I should like not to let the way I was born weigh too heavily on my mind. Perhaps what happened was a dreadful thing. But I had nothing to do with it; I cannot possibly hold myself responsible for it. That is what I think. That is the only way, the only right way, I can think.

"To know how I was born is unpleasant. But what is the point of letting this knowledge make me suffer? It would be both futile and absurd. And I do not think of myself as being under some sort of curse. Surely it would have been much worse if I had inherited tuberculosis. You suggest that in that Aiko affair I was cursed. But what gave me pain was not so much my being turned down as my not knowing why I had been turned down. If I had known, I should not have felt so lost. I do not say this with any thought of blaming you. I understand well why you did not want to tell me. I do not think you were being at all unfair, especially when I consider how concerned you are about father's welfare. And I am deeply grateful that this time you decided to tell me. If you had maintained your silence, I should have had to continue living in ignorance about myself; and it is likely that in spite of my not knowing, I should have felt a heavy, dark cloud hanging over my head. I ask you again not to worry about me. Through my new knowledge about myself I shall be able to do my work with greater determination than before. And in that new determination I shall seek my salvation. There is no other way for me. By that means, I shall be able to accomplish two things at once: do the work I want to do and find myself.

"I shall stay here a while longer. But if at any time I begin to feel helpless, I shall not force myself to stay here out of perverse pride. There are times when I want to see you and Oei very much. I should find it only too easy to play the weakling if I allowed myself. But I must settle down and try to get more work done. I have so far accomplished too little here. When it is time for me to return to Tokyo, I shall do so without reserve.

"I can sympathize with your fear lest the affairs of our family should appear in my writings. I cannot promise that they will not appear in some form or other. But I shall try to be careful not to cause discomfort.

"Please give my best wishes to Sakiko and Taeko. And please tell Oei not to worry.

"I must have a little more time to think about Oei. If she is absolutely determined not to accept my proposal, then of course there is nothing more I can do about it. But in the meantime I shall have to decide for myself whether I should try once more or give up the idea entirely."

When he had finished writing the letter he felt as if he had retrieved the whole of his old self. He stood up and reached for the hand mirror hanging on the pillar. He peered at the face reflected in the glass.

It was a little pale, but otherwise it was as it had been. In fact the recent excitement had given it a look of vitality. He found himself smiling. I am now really alone, he thought; and with the thought came a new, pleasurable feeling of freedom.

He heard the old lady from next door announcing herself. Slowly and tentatively she pulled open the screen door and looked in. She had brought him the rice for his dinner. Seeing that he had not yet prepared any side dishes to go with the rice she said, "I have some dried flatfish. Shall I grill some for you?"

Kensaku had no appetite. "No, thank you. I'll eat later, so please just leave the rice there."

She put the rice tub down and left. Soon she returned with a heaping plateful of parboiled spinach, put it beside the rice and went away again.

Kensaku was beginning to feel restless. He was in no mood to stay cooped up in the house all evening. Remembering that a kabuki troupe from Osaka was performing in the theatre in the pleasure quarter, he went next door to see if the old couple would like to go with him. Unfortunately their granddaughter now living in the nearby town of Mihara was coming to stay the night with them. The old man tried to persuade his wife to go, saying there was no need for both of them to stay at home. But she refused with a smile. She was his second wife, and had no children of her own. The girl coming that night was her step-granddaughter.

"You can't miss an opportunity like this," said the old man feelingly. "After all, how often do you go to the theatre?" But his wife would not listen. Kensaku saw that so long as he remained, the same scene would be repeated endlessly. "I'll ask you again," he said, getting up. Holding the small lantern the old lady lit for him, he went down the hill by himself.

They were doing the Moritsuna scene, where Moritsuna examines the severed head purported to be that of his brother. The setting was makeshift, provided by several gold screens arranged cleverly on a single-level stage. The actor playing Moritsuna danced with surprising skill to the samisen music. His art was so simple, so lacking in introspection that it was a pleasure to watch him. He made no demands on the audience, he danced to please the uncritical eye.

Kensaku stayed for three more acts, then left. He walked slowly along the deserted road by the seashore. Loneliness filled his heart; but it was a quiet loneliness, humble and accepting. He felt as if Oei, Nobuyuki, Sakiko, Taeko—indeed everybody—had moved far, far away from him; he could see their figures, but they were tiny, like figures seen from the wrong end of a telescope. It was a truly lonely feeling, for they seemed dearer to him now than ever before. He then thought of his dead mother. She was the only one, he thought, she was the only one I ever had. Once more his mind wandered back to his childhood. He savored his memories with unabashed emotion; for they were then his sole means of emotional release. As he remembered once more the time he went up on the roof, his eyes clouded over with tears. But when unguardedly he remembered the scene in his mother's bed, he was hit hard by the sudden realization of the sorrow she must have felt at the time. His act must have seemed to her like a cruel reminder of the sin she herself had committed. And he began to wonder whether it was because he was indeed the child of sin that he could have done what he did in her bed.

He knew he had to stop thinking that way. Like a man who consciously brakes his quickening pace as he is going down a hill, he tried to recapture his earlier mood. He made himself think of the vastness of the world around him. There was the earth, there were the stars (unfortunately it was cloudy that evening and he could not see them), there was the universe; and in the midst of this vastness there was this minute particle that was himself, busily weaving a web of misery in the little world of his mind. Such was his customary way of combating his own fits of depression; and this time it seemed to have some effect.

He realized he was a bit hungry. He wondered whether he should go to the European-style restaurant he went to sometimes, but that meant walking all the way back through the pleasure quarter, and he didn't want to do that. He decided to go instead to the oyster boat restaurant that was a short distance behind him along the shore.

The boat—it was really a houseboat—lay beside a pier, and one got onto it by means of a miniature suspension bridge. Inside he was greeted by a lively boy of about fifteen wearing a faded blue workman's jacket. The corridor that led to the rooms was like a small tunnel, and Kensaku had to stoop as he followed the boy. The room he was shown to also had a low ceiling, from which hung a dim electric light.

The dreariness of the room began to affect him as he waited for the food. Deliberately he tried to direct his thoughts toward his work, but with little success. The air around him seemed permeated with a sense of foreboding. Like a heavy, dark cloud it enveloped him, and though he wanted to chase it away, he seemed to have no strength left to do so. His head and breast felt empty, like voids waiting to be filled by it. Let it come in, he thought submissively; it will go away in time.

He stood up, opened the low screen door and looked out. Just above the stone embankment was the road, unlighted and dark. On the other side of it was a row of five or six warehouses, their gables outlined against the night sky. Rickshaws passed by, carrying women who were talking to each other in high-pitched, excited voices. They were probably geisha from the pleasure quarter on their way to some inn to entertain guests.

There must be many others besides himself, he thought, who also had been conceived in sin; and perhaps all of them so conceived had inherited some dreadful congenital trait. Yet, though he was ready at that moment to believe that a bad seed had been planted in him, he did not forget that he was blessed with aspirations too, aspirations which would help him contain its growth. He must learn to be abstinent, he told himself; now that he knew about his own birth, he simply had to try doubly hard to lead a disciplined life. Why should he allow this inherited trait, if it existed, to destroy him? Was he not more fortunate than a child conceived by a man in a drunken stupor and thus maimed for life? Yes, he would in future try to curb his dissolute ways.

The boy marched in carrying a huge tray. He placed this on a small, wobbly table, bowed with charming quickness and marched out.

Kensaku had thought he was hungry, but all he could eat from the tray were the vinegared oysters.

He felt something small and hard on his tongue. He brought it to his lips and placed it gently on the tip of his forefinger. It was a pearl the size of a killifish's eye. Of course, it was of little value; but that such a thing should have got into his mouth struck him as a good omen.

8

Ten days went by. In that time he went through alternating periods of depression and of cheer. When he felt cheerful, he would resolve never to be depressed again. But when the sense of well-being, or excitement, passed, depression would come over him again like a fever. He would then wait patiently for it to run its course and hope that perhaps in time it would stop recurring.

He sent the little pearl that he had found on the oyster boat to Sakiko. A few days later a letter from her arrived thanking him for the present. And in the same post was a letter from Nobuyuki. This was what it said:

"I'm afraid I've done something very stupid, and I hope you will forgive me. I had a terrible fight with father, probably the worst I've ever had with him. It would never have happened if I had not been so thoughtless. I'm afraid I've done you a great disservice.

"You see, I went and told mother about your proposal to Oei. I shouldn't have, I suppose, but at the time it didn't occur to me that I was doing anything indiscreet. At any rate father heard about it immediately. His fury was such that at first I was dumbfounded by it. I had never seen him so angry before. 'Absolutely not!' he said. 'Dismiss Oei at once!'

"I think I can understand now how he must have felt; and when I consider what it was that made him act that way, I am filled with pity for him. His anger is not directed at you or Oei, but at what he calls 'this thoroughly unacceptable, immoral thing.' I should have understood this at the time, but I didn't. I was too taken aback by the violence of his response to think clearly. What was uppermost in my mind then was that I had let you down, and that the least I could do was to say something on your behalf.

"I thought, too, that in insisting on Oei's immediate dismissal, father was overstepping the bounds of his authority. He had no right to give such orders; he had no right to want to treat Oei so arbitrarily. I had of late come to like and respect her very much; besides, she had always been kind and loyal to the family, and we owed her a great deal. And so I'm afraid I got a bit angry. I shouldn't have, but I did. I spoke up for you and for Oei, mostly for Oei, and not with much tact.

" 'So you, too, are like that, are you!' he shouted, and threw the pen box that lay on his desk at me. It hit the floor just in front of me, and as it did a pen nib flew out, landed neatly on its point and stuck in the mat. I remained silent for a while, thinking that it was useless to say more; yet I did finally say, 'Kensaku will not listen to you.'

" 'I won't allow it!' he said. I left him then. Later, when I had calmed down a little, I began to understand father's feelings. For the first time in years, I wept. What a fool I was, I thought. Through carelessness I had brought you and Oei unexpected trouble and caused father to remember afresh that painful, half-forgotten episode in his life. Please try not to reproach me too much. I failed you, but I did so through thoughtlessness, not out of any ill will.

"This is a difficult letter for me to write. There is nothing pleasant I can say in it. I have repeatedly disappointed you. I have done nothing to merit your trust. You have every right to expect more of your elder brother. (I don't care what the facts are, you are still my younger brother as far as I am concerned.)

"On the evening of the same day I saw father again. He was much calmer, as was I. But he had not changed his mind one whit. I could not oppose him anymore, and I promised him my support.

"What he wants may be expressed, for form's sake, as follows. So long as you are in Onomichi, there seems to be no reason why you should maintain a house in Tokyo. Besides, Oei, her situation being what it is, can have no expectation of remaining with you forever. Surely it would be kinder to her to help her become independent now so that she need have no fears for her future.

"Father said it had always been his intention to give her two thousand yen when it came time for her to leave, and was quite prepared to give her that money now. I said that she could hardly be expected to start a shop or whatever with so small an amount, and asked him to give her five thousand. He would not consider that, but in the end he agreed to give her three thousand. No doubt you will find my giving you such details distasteful. But please understand, I had to make sure of father's intentions just in case you should decide to accede to his demand. I realize, of course, that there's only a very slim chance of your doing so.

"Mother is as sorry as I am that she told father about you. But it is just as well for us that she cannot interfere in this matter. At any rate, I went to your house yesterday to tell Oei what had happened— not to relay father's 'command,' you understand, but merely to inform her of what he said to me, for I am aware that this is something that requires the consent of everyone concerned.

"To put it frankly, this is where you and she stand. Father knows that you are free to reject his demand, that he cannot order Oei to leave you. But what he means you two to know is that should you decide to be difficult, Oei might not get any money at all. I told Oei exactly what I have just said, crude as it was. Oei, on her part, refused to give a definite answer. I could understand her dilemma. The money involved is not much, but she is hardly in a position to dismiss it lightly. She has no intention of marrying you; which means that one day, when you marry someone else, she will have to go. The question for her, then, is this: should she stay with you, knowing that one day she will have to go anyway, and thus forfeit the money just for the sake of postponing her inevitable departure? Obviously, she sees the advantage of doing as father says. On the other hand, I could see plainly how extremely painful to her was the thought of having to leave you now. 'I can't say,' she said. 'I'll leave it to you and Kensaku to decide.' Indeed, what else could she have said? And so I left without any clear answer from her. She did say repeatedly, however, that if you were going to stay in Onomichi much longer she would like to move into a smaller house. There was no sense, she said, in continuing to keep up such an expensive house just for her. I agreed with her.

"I got home rather late last night—partly because I didn't want to have to see father—and found your letter, written on the twenty-eighth, waiting for me. How much like you, I thought, to refuse to be completely crushed by what I told you. I was impressed. I can imagine what pain my letter must have caused you. Yet here I am, writing you this unpleasant letter. I feel helpless and depressed. And now that I have read your letter and seen how little inclined you are to change your mind about Oei, I can't help worrying lest this new obstacle put up by father should make you even more determined. I know, it is presumptuous of me to say that I'm worried; but I *am* worried. I am worried for you, of course; but I am more worried for father, who would suffer if you should have your way in this matter. I feel so helpless, I don't know where to turn. If I were a stronger man, perhaps I could do something useful. But caught in the middle of all this, with father on one side and you on the other, I find that I am quite powerless. Father makes his pronouncements; you on your part insist on acting according to your wishes. I sympathize with both, for you're right in your own way and he is right in his. But when I stand back and ask myself what my role is to be, what is the right thing for me to do, I am at a complete loss.

"I am a real coward. A few years ago there was a certain woman. I got her a house and she lived in it for about a year. I had made her a promise, but I broke that promise. I knew that father would never approve, and I didn't want to have a fight with him on her account. I shouldn't have minded a fight, perhaps, but supposing I had won, what would that have done to father? I simply didn't want to force the issue. Luckily the woman was very understanding. I suppose to you what I did would seem unthinkable. I remember that on the day before you left, I told you that I wanted to change my way of life, and you asked me why I didn't resign from my company right away. This is no place for me to go into details, but I really do want another kind of life. But here, too, I seem incapable of doing anything. That I myself at times become tired of my own weakness is, I'm afraid, no consolation to you.

"All I can do is to tell you simply that I wish you would give up the idea of marrying Oei. As I tried to say in my last letter, I don't wish this mainly for father's sake; I feel that such a marriage will darken your entire future. I wish, too, that you would take this opportunity to part from her. I am sure that later all of us concerned will see that it was a good thing to do. You are proud, and you will not be easily persuaded to change your mind. But if you can allow yourself to be persuaded, then all of us will benefit. I, of all people, have no right to ask anything of you. My only defense is that I have honestly said what I should like to see you do. That you had every reason to expect more of me, I know only too well.

"I could have sent this letter much earlier, but I put off doing so as long as I could, for the thought of your having to read it so soon after the other one was no less pleasant than my having to write it. I have not been to see Oei, though I am concerned about her; and I have avoided father since my last meeting with him."

Kensaku was filled with anger as he finished reading the unpleasant letter. He did not necessarily think that his anger was just; but neither did he think that his father's anger was any more just.

He had never forgotten his father's coldness toward him when he had gone to speak to him about Aiko. "You're the head of your own household," he had said. "Go and talk to her family yourself." Kensaku had been hurt by his father's attitude, but had gradually come to find solace in the thought that at least it implied his independence. And so this time, though he had of course expected his father to be displeased, he had never imagined that he would be quite so violent and autocratic. It was his willful inconsistency that angered Kensaku.

He did not feel particularly kindly toward Nobuyuki either. Why should Nobuyuki have mentioned the matter at all to their stepmother when it was still at such a tentative stage? There had been no immediate need to consult her; in other words Nobuyuki had simply gossiped. Another thing that annoyed him about Nobuyuki was that for all his expression of sympathy toward him, he seemed to regard their father's wishes as absolute.

It was not that Kensaku did not sympathize with Nobuyuki's feelings. He even felt that he owed it to him to be understanding. At the same time he had to ask himself, "But where does that leave me?" And there was yet another thing that raised a question in his mind about Nobuyuki. In the letter he had let it seem that in his conversation with their father he had only mentioned Kensaku's proposal to Oei, and so by implication that he had said nothing about his own disclosure to Kensaku of the true circumstances of his birth. But Kensaku was certain that Nobuyuki had mentioned it. How could he not have? Then why not say so in the letter? Presumably because he was afraid to have to confess to yet one more act of weakness on his part. For once having told their father that Kensaku already knew about his own birth, he should then at least have tried to persuade him that Kensaku must be allowed to manage his own affairs. And what was all this talk about three thousand yen? Did he really think that it was an achievement to have raised Oei's prize by one thousand?

He sat down and wrote a reply immediately.

"I have just read your letter. I was annoyed by father's attitude. All this difficulty might have been avoided if the relationship between him and me had been made clear. That you should have told him about Oei before such an understanding between him and me had been reached was a bad mistake. There's no point in my berating you about it now. But I want you to know that I have no choice now but to act as though he and I were both formally aware of our new relationship. In other words, I shall have to act the way I see fit.

"Of course, with regard to the proposed marriage, the decision is not mine alone to make. But that question aside, I should like to insist that whether Oei and I should or should not live apart is for the two of us, and no one else, to decide. (That we may eventually have to separate is at the moment irrelevant.) I shall add this: if I do not marry her, then I am determined to continue to live with her as I have always done, and to be careful not to enter into any other kind of relationship with her; in which case everything will be exactly as it was before, and father should be satisfied. I say I will be careful not because I am concerned about father, but because I know I must guard myself against my own inherent weakness.

"It was good of father to offer Oei the money. Though I know it isn't exactly my place to do so, I must nevertheless reject the offer on Oei's behalf. I have money of my own—albeit money that once belonged to father—and I shall give some of it to her.

"I don't think it is all that necessary for Oei to move, but if she wants to, she can of course do so with my blessing. I am sure she will be able to find the sort of house she likes in one of the suburbs.

"I can understand why father should have been so upset. But I can hardly be expected to accept his authority quite so unquestioningly as you do. And I must say that I feel no less dubious about your willingness to suffer the discomfort of being unsympathetic to both him and me. Perhaps I am being selfish here. All I know is that I should feel quite unnatural if I were to behave as you would have me behave. Don't think ill of me."

9

Kensaku left Onomichi shortly thereafter, before Nobuyuki had had time to answer his letter. The immediate cause of his departure was a mild case of tympanitis. The local doctor who examined him had told him that if he was intending to return to Tokyo in the near future anyway, he might as well leave as quickly as possible and go to a specialist. But even if his ear had not given him trouble, he would probably not have stayed in Onomichi much longer. Of course he left with great uneasiness. The thought of once more living the way he had done those last three months in Tokyo was almost enough to detain him. There was his work too, nowhere near completion. How could he live like that again, he wondered, rushing about frantically yet always with that oppressive feeling of guilt? The effect on him of such a life, he suspected, would be much worse now than it had been before. He had become more vulnerable; and whatever he had imagined was chasing him then would seem even more real now. Yes, he told himself, he would simply have to make up his mind not to lead that sort of life again once he was back in Tokyo. But, he wondered, what did such a resolution amount to? How firm was it, and how long would it last? The truth was that he had little confidence in his own ability to restrain himself. And in view of his past experience, he would have been unrealistic had he trusted himself more.

The sky had been cloudy in the early evening, then sometime during the night it had suddenly cleared, and the humid, warm air had turned chilly by dawn. He had gone to sleep with only a thin coverlet over him, and the cold woke him up. Too lazy to get up and find a heavier covering he had curled up and gone back to sleep. When he woke up again, he had caught a cold. By the following evening one of his ears had begun to hurt. He must have blown his nose too often and too hard. It was a dull, heavy ache, not unbearable but bad enough to wake him up several times during the night and make the morning seem very slow in coming.

He had gone to see the doctor immediately the next morning. Incipient tympanitis, the doctor had said. He gave Kensaku olive oil and some stuff for a poultice, and advised him to see a specialist soon. Kensaku had come away happy that something beyond his control had made his return to Tokyo necessary. And once his mind had been made up for him he set about immediately and with unseemly haste to prepare for his departure.

The old lady helped him pack, and her husband went into town to pay his electricity and gas bills. In less than an hour he was ready to leave.

Though Onomichi was officially a city, the express trains did not stop there. He decided to go as far as Himeji on a slow train and then catch an express there.

He went to the station just before noon, accompanied by the old couple and another neighbor named Matsukawa who carried his rather heavy suitcase for him.

Kensaku got on the train, opened the window and stuck his head out to say his final farewell. His face was wrapped in an incongruously large, white kerchief. The old couple kept on saying awkwardly how sorry they were to see him go. Kensaku, too, was sorry to leave them. But he did not think he would want to see Onomichi again, a good place though it was; for he could not separate it in his mind from the pain he had suffered there. He wanted now to get away from it as quickly as possible.

There were few passengers in his coach. It was a sultry day for spring, but a pleasant, strong breeze was coming in through the window. He pulled the window down a little and leaned his head against the pane. He had not slept well the night before, and very soon he was dozing.

He became aware of busy activity around him. Lazily he opened his eyes, and saw that they had already arrived in Okayama. The three women who were sitting in front of him—were they respectable housewives or something else?—got up and left and were replaced by a young couple with two children. The husband was a tall man in uniform, a lieutenant in the artillery. He put their luggage away neatly on the rack first, then folded a traveling rug, laid it on the seat, and bade his wife, his son, who was about six, and his daughter, who was younger and had a fine head of hair, sit on it. He himself chose to sit at the end of the seat by the aisle, somewhat removed from his family.

Kensaku went to sleep again. He was very tired. He woke up about an hour before the train was due to arrive in Himeji. This time he felt wide awake. He could stay on the train as far as Kyoto and catch the express there. But he wanted to see the castle in Himeji, commonly called the "White Heron"; also, he remembered that Oei had asked him to get some brazier tongs that Himeji artisans were known for.

The boy lay down between the folds of the rug, his head toward his father. Now the little sister wanted to lie down too. The mother, who was sitting by the window, stood up and helped the girl get inside the rug from her end. The air cushion which she had put up against the window for her own use she now put under her daughter's head. The little girl was delighted. The mother sat down, brought out a small towel, rolled it up and rested her head on that. She was a young woman, but she did everything calmly, without fuss.

"Mama, I want my pillow lower," said the girl. The mother lazily reached for the valve and let some air out. "I want it lower." The mother obliged. "But I want it still lower." This time the mother said, "Do you want a pillow or don't you?" The girl became silent; she then closed her eyes and pretended to go to sleep.

The army officer reached into his pocket as if he just remembered something. He pulled out a pocket mirror, then a small tube. He squeezed some greasy substance out of the tube onto the tip of his forefinger, and began twirling the turned-up ends of his short, reddish mustache. He looked into the mirror all the while, seemingly with great satisfaction.

His wife watched him expressionlessly, her head resting on the towel. The man continued to fondle the ends of his moustache with unabated pleasure. A smile slowly spread over his wife's face. Then her shoulders began to shake. She made not a sound, but she was laughing. The officer, choosing not to notice her amusement, twirled on.

The children, still with their eyes closed, began kicking each other. The girl was trying her best not to giggle.

The officer moved his eyes away from the mirror for an instant and ordered them to be still. His wife merely smiled.

The boy, not heeding his father's command, kicked harder. The top fold of the rug fell to the floor, exposing four small legs. Bored with their game, the two sat up.

The boy went to the window beside his mother and opened it. The girl followed his example and opened the window beside Kensaku. There was a strong wind blowing outside. The boy stuck his head out and began singing as loud as he could. The girl, not so intrepid, merely joined in the singing. Their voices were drowned out by the noise of the wind. The boy sang louder, but it was no good. He gave up singing and tried a few crude, guttural shouts, but that was no good either. His singing and shouting became more and more frantic. How much of a male he already is, Kensaku thought, enjoying the spectacle.

"Be quiet!" shouted the officer. The girl, terrified, stopped immediately. The boy took no notice. The wife just kept on smiling.

The train arrived in Himeji at five o'clock, four hours before the next express was due to leave for Tokyo. Kensaku went to an inn opposite the station, and there he changed the poultice and had dinner. Then on a rickshaw he went to see the castle. The white-walled keep, made to seem at once grander and more distant by the mist, stood high above the ancient pines. The rickshaw man, a local patriot, was an eager guide, and was disappointed that Kensaku did not want to go beyond the entrance to the outer grounds. Kensaku allowed himself to be taken next to the shrine commemorating Okiku, the hapless serving girl of the legend. It was quite dark by then. Kensaku walked around the grounds quickly, then climbed back on the rickshaw. In late autumn of every year, the rickshaw man said, Okiku's spirit would return in the form of swallowtail butterflies which would hang from the branches of the trees in the shrine.

On hearing that the inn sold brazier tongs and other local specialties, Kensaku had the rickshaw man take him straight back there. At the inn he bought several pairs of tongs and a swallowtail. The swallowtail, said the manager, represented the figure of Okiku as she hung over a well in the castle, her hands tied behind her back. Even the rouged lips, he said, were on the butterfly.

The departure time of the express was nine o'clock. He had booked a berth, so he lay down immediately upon boarding the train. He woke up just as the train was approaching Shizuoka. It was already light outside. In Shizuoka Station he bought a Tokyo newspaper which he began reading avidly. He had not laid eyes on one ever since he left Tokyo. Mt. Fuji soon came into view, then the mountains of Hakone with their many crevices. He gazed at them with loving familiarity. And the Tokyo speech of the family that came on at Numazu was like music to his ears.

Ōiso, Fujisawa, Ōfuna—these were now behind him. He was filled with such an overwhelming desire to see Tokyo that he could hardly sit still. To keep himself occupied and under control he began to count the loose threads on the ends of the cords of his outer kimono.

He had sent Oei a telegram from Himeji. He was sure she would be waiting for him at Shinbashi Station. He supposed that there would be a moment of embarrassment when they first saw each other. Never mind, he reassured himself, the important thing was that he would be seeing her again in less than half an hour.

The train began slowing down. Before it had reached the platform he stuck his head out to look for her. He saw her immediately. Her head was turned toward him. Thinking that she had seen him, he waved at her. She showed no sign of recognition. With an inane expression on her face she was peering into the windows of another coach. He got off, handed the various small pieces of baggage he had with him to the porter, then hurried toward her.

He was only a few paces away from her when she at last saw him. With a look of relief she rushed up to him. "I was beginning to think you weren't on the train," she said. "But what on earth have you got on your face!"

"I have a little trouble with my ear," he said. "But it doesn't hurt any more." His pleasure at seeing her was as great as he had expected; and there was no awkwardness on either side. If she felt any embarrassment, she was hiding it very well. As far as he could tell, she was the same Oei that he had always known.

As they moved along the platform with the crowd she asked again about his ear; then almost in a congratulatory tone she said, "What a good thing you decided to cut short your stay in Onomichi." She lowered her voice as she added, "You're thinner. Obviously trips like that don't agree with you." Kensaku smiled in reply. "I telephoned your brother at his office," she continued, "and he said he would stop by on his way home."

At the gate the rickshaw man whom Kensaku regularly hired was waiting with a traveling rug folded over his arm. Kensaku gave him the ticket for his suitcase and asked him to take that and the smaller pieces to his house. He and Oei would go home by streetcar.

"You haven't had lunch yet, have you?" said Oei.

"No, I haven't."

"I've got something ready for you at home, but shall we go to a restaurant instead?"

"I don't mind either way."

"How was the food in Onomichi?"

"Well, if you were willing to cook yourself, you could get all kinds of nice fresh fish."

They passed Seihintei. Not wanting to be recognized by Okayo, Osuzu and the rest, Kensaku tried to make himself as inconspicuous as possible. When they came to the streetcar stop, Oei asked again, "Well, what shall we do about lunch?"

"All right, let's go to a restaurant. It would be nice to have decent European food for a change."

They went to Fūgetsudō which was quite near. There Oei kept on asking questions about Kensaku's life in Onomichi. After lunch Kensaku telephoned Nobuyuki from the restaurant.

When they got home, Kensaku immediately went upstairs to his study. The pictures on the walls, the bookshelves, the desk—they were all exactly as he had left them. But the room looked a little different. It was too tidy, and the camellias in the alcove looked a little out of place.

Oei came into the room and said, "There's nothing better than home, is there?"

"I feel like a poor boy who's just moved into a mansion."

"I suppose your house in Onomichi was pretty dirty. Widowers and cockroaches live together, as they say."

"The old lady next door kept it quite clean."

"Your bath is ready, so go and have it now."

10

After his bath Kensaku went immediately to "T" Hospital, not far from his house, which specialized in the nose, ear and throat. It was a small, private hospital where Sakiko had stayed, so that he was fairly certain the doctor would agree to see him even if the visiting hours were over.

Though the actual pain had lasted only that one night, when he rubbed his thumb and forefinger together close to the bad ear he could hear no sound; and he felt generally dull and debilitated.

The doctor appeared immediately in his kimono and examined the ear with a reflector. "Yes, it's congested," he said lightly. "I don't think it's anything serious. I'll just get some of the fluid out." He reached for his white jacket hanging on a hook and put it over his kimono. His manner was extraordinarily casual.

The fat, young nurse picked up a scalpel, pincers and other shiny instruments out of a container with disinfectant in it and arranged them neatly on a piece of gauze.

"Haven't they turned on the electricity yet?" asked the doctor. The nurse played with the switch, then shook her head. "Never mind, we'll do without it," he said. Sunlight was still coming in through the west window. The nurse proceeded to wrap the ends of several short pieces of wire with cotton wool.

The surgery was simple and quick. There was a loud sound as the scalpel touched the eardrum. Simultaneously he felt a sharp prick. The scalpel in his ear felt very large and ominous for a moment, and he wondered briefly if the doctor was about to inflict more pain than he had led him to think. But his fear proved to be groundless.

"There's more fluid than I thought," said the doctor as he cleaned out the ear with the cotton wool tips. Kensaku could see that they came out slightly bloody. The doctor then put some medicine in the ear and applied a poultice. "Come back again tomorrow morning," he said.

In the anteroom, while waiting for his prescription, Kensaku began to wonder what had become of the nurse who had encouraged the young man to write the letter to Sakiko. It was only when he saw the fat nurse that he had remembered her. Was she still working there? He hoped not, for he was not particularly anxious to see her. He had not disliked the woman. She was rather good-looking. She was also bright, and possibly a little too cynical. But toward him she had behaved modestly, almost demurely. She had little of that aggressive, down-to-earth manner so characteristic of nurses. She would smile shyly when he spoke to her and say something noncommittal in reply. He had at about that time published a few short stories in a journal run by a group of old university friends. Hearing about this from Sakiko, this nurse asked her if Kensaku would lend her copies of the journal. He knew of course that she had little interest in the journal itself, and that she was merely curious to see what sort of things the brother of one of her patients wrote. He would not have minded if she had gone and borrowed copies of the journal from someone else; but he was not about to exhibit his own writings to her. At home he picked out a half-dozen issues of the journal which did not contain his stories and took those to the hospital and left them with Sakiko.

On his next visit Sakiko chided him for his perversity. The nurse was standing by her, smiling. Soon after that Sakiko left the hospital. And then about a year later the young man, encouraged by the nurse, had written that ill-advised letter. That so demure-seeming a girl could be capable of such impropriety had come to Kensaku as an unpleasant surprise. It was just as well, he had thought at the time, that he had refused to let her see his stories.

Outside on the street the children were playing noisily. Kensaku thought again about the nurse as he walked toward home. Was she still working in the hospital? Had she seen his letter to the young man? If indeed she had, if she had been told about the outcome of the young man's silly overture, a sudden encounter now between them at the hospital would be embarrassing to them both. The imagined encounter soon led to musings of a much less innocent sort. No doubt about it, the streak of impropriety in her made her a fitting object of Kensaku's low desires.

Nobuyuki was waiting for him at the house. He came out to the front hall and, instead of greeting him in the ordinary way, said, "I hear you're having ear trouble."

"There was some fluid, but the doctor got it all out."

"It wasn't too serious, then?"

"No. I feel fine now."

Kensaku followed Nobuyuki into the morning room. Nobuyuki's dinner was on the table. He sat down and bowed. "Welcome home." Kensaku bowed back, saying nothing.

"Your brother was just about to have dinner," Oei said. "Do you want yours now?"

"I don't know."

"What do you mean, you don't know? It's *your* stomach, after all."

"All right, I'll have it now."

She began serving his dinner with ill-disguised enthusiasm.

"You said he had aged ten years," Nobuyuki said to Oei. "You were exaggerating."

"He certainly has aged. Look at him, he's like an old man."

"He's lost some weight, I admit."

"He doesn't look so bad to me now, but when he first came up to me at the station I thought for a moment it was his grandfather."

The word "grandfather" hit Kensaku like a blow in the stomach. Nobuyuki noticed immediately, but Oei was unaware of what her remark had done to Kensaku. "There he was, his face wrapped up in that huge piece of cloth," she went on blithely. "I suppose he looked more like him then because only his features were showing."

To be told that he resembled that common old man hurt Kensaku deeply. He looked at Oei, scarcely able to hide his anger at her insensitivity. And then he became conscious of a new, complicated emotion arising within himself. From the time he was six, when he had first encountered his grandfather, the nasty first impression of him had remained. Not once had he felt a trace of love for him; always he had felt as though they were strangers, without any bond of kinship. It had not been entirely his fault. For his grandfather had been born with a truly common streak in him. A certain cheapness had hung about him all his life, in everything he did and said. That Kensaku, on first learning about his own illicit birth, should have wished that some other man had fathered him was therefore unavoidable. And what had been most unbearable of all was the thought of this detestable man going to bed with his mother. No wonder, then, that he should now feel so resentful at being told that he resembled him. But what took him by surprise was this other conflicting emotion that emerged side by side with the resentment and the hurt—an emotion whose nature he was for a moment at a loss to understand fully. It was, he sensed vaguely, a kind of love for one's flesh and blood, a kind of longing for that man who was in fact his father. And he realized that behind his resentment at being told that he resembled him, there lurked a strange, secret joy. The sudden, unexpected intrusion of this new emotion threw him into complete confusion.

During dinner Nobuyuki asked questions about Kensaku's experiences in Onomichi. Kensaku answered as pleasantly as he could. When they had finished eating he invited Nobuyuki upstairs.

"Yes, of course," said Nobuyuki, trying his best to sound casual. But as he stood up, he could not hide his resignation. Oh God, he might have said, the time has come to talk of unpleasant things. Kensaku followed his brother up the stairs, feeling both compassion and amusement.

The two brothers sat down with the fireless brazier between them. Nobuyuki broke the long silence. "You didn't get the letter I sent you the day before yesterday, did you?"

"No."

"Well, as I tried to say in the letter, there's nothing I can do about the situation now. You do what you think is best, and let father do what he thinks is best. Given your character and his, that's what would happen anyway, even if I were to try to intervene. Besides, there's really no place for me in all of this. I know that it was my thoughtlessness that caused all the trouble, and I'm sorry. But there's nothing I can do about it now. I've decided to keep my mouth shut and let the two of you work out your own solutions. I said so to father the day before I wrote you my last letter. You may think me irresponsible, but I feel I have no alternative. There will again come a time, I'm sure, when I can be of help; but until then, I shall mind my own business. All right?"

"Certainly. Mind you, I don't know exactly where father and I stand now, but I do think that so long as you continue to involve yourself, nothing definite is likely to happen."

"I suppose you're right."

"You see, the trouble with you is that you want everything to stay the way it was. But now that I know who I am, that's impossible. What has to be broken has to be broken. And if there's something left that can't be broken, then perhaps that can help us establish a new kind of relationship. But if there's nothing worth keeping intact, why bother to pretend there is?"

"If your thinking has reached that point, there's not much I can say." There was a touch of disapproval in Nobuyuki's eyes. "But I had hoped for some kind of compromise. Compromises are not always unsatisfactory, you know."

Kensaku was silent. He did not think that he had said anything wrong; but he did wonder if he should have been quite so blunt. The difficulty was that neither of the two brothers could be expected to share the other's feelings toward this man they both called "father." Nobuyuki was deeply attached to him; Kensaku felt he owed him hardly anything at all.

The maid brought in tea and cake. The two brothers sat in silence while she poured the tea. "Yoshi!" Oei called out from the bottom of the stairs. "I am putting some fruit down here. Please serve it to the two gentlemen."

Kensaku said to the maid as she was about to go downstairs, "It's dark down there, so don't step on the fruit." She was much amused.

"Let me more or less repeat what I said in the letter," Nobuyuki said when the maid had put the fruit down and left. "Father hasn't changed his mind a bit. And he's even more adamant than before that you should make no mention whatsoever of the family in your writings. I told him what you yourself said in your letter, that you would do your best to avoid writing anything that would cause embarrassment. He replied that it was all very well for you to make such promises, but your standards were not necessarily his, and what you might consider harmless he might find very embarrassing. In other words, he wants you to give him a firm assurance that you will never in any way mention the family in your writings. I suppose that once one starts worrying about things like that, nothing short of the kind of guarantee he's demanding will seem satisfactory. Anyway, I thought he was being quite unreasonable, so I said I for one wouldn't want to interfere to that extent with your work, nor could one expect any writer to swear to absolute secrecy about his own private life. His answer was, why couldn't you find something other than your own family to write about? The trouble with him is that he has no sympathy for your profession, and has no idea what writing is all about. I asked him—and the question does seem a little frivolous now—what then was his opinion of the sort of work you were doing. Did he approve of writing as a profession? He said he didn't mind your being a writer at all. Then why not leave Kensaku alone, I said, and wish him success in what he has committed himself to do? And then I said something quite stupid: I reminded him of the time he had tried to build a railway line through a town on ground level instead of overhead. Had he then given much consideration to other people's opinions? He was furious, of course, and started shouting at me."

Kensaku remembered the incident. Their father, on assuming the presidency of a railway company, had immediately tried to put a line through this town, and for reasons of economy had refused to consider building it overhead. To his surprise there was an uproar about it. The irate citizens had demanded to know if he had no concern for their safety. Tens, indeed hundreds, of lives were at stake. Had he no conscience? The opposition became so formidable that finally he had had to give in and build an overhead line.

"Of course he would be furious," Kensaku said, laughing. "Anyway, I'm not exactly trying to build a railway. Needless to say, I am not going to promise him anything. And I'm convinced that this is an opportune time for me to sever formal ties with the house in Hongō. If I don't do it now, there will be no end to the complications that will arise. It's good for neither side to go on looking for compromises just for the sake of appearances."

"Yes, I suppose you're right. But for some reason, father doesn't seem to want to agree to anything that's final. There's something else I ought to tell you. I myself didn't know this until recently, but the money you now have didn't come from father. Officially, you received it from him. But actually it was all left to you by grandfather in Shiba. Not a penny of it was father's."

Kensaku stared at Nobuyuki in disbelief. Then he blushed with embarrassment. For ever since he first learned about his true paternity he had felt uncomfortable about the money he thought he had been given by his father. It seemed a little mercenary on his part to insist on the one hand that he have no further formal ties with Hongō and on the other to keep "their" money. He had been half-inclined to refer to it in his letters to Nobuyuki, but in the end had not done so. The reason was simple: if he returned the money, he would find it very difficult to live. But for all his reluctance to part with the money, what had saved his self-respect was his confidence in his own ability to return it once it became clear he could not keep it without seeming shameless.

The two brothers said nothing for a while. Then Nobuyuki quietly started talking about himself. "You know, I'm still intending to resign from the company. I mentioned this briefly to father, and he was surprisingly understanding."

"I'm glad. And what will you do with yourself?"

"I'm thinking of studying Zen." Kensaku, taken aback, couldn't think of anything to say. Nobuyuki continued: "I've been quite envious of you lately. From the point of view of circumstances, or fate, or whatever one may call it, you're a more unfortunate person than I. But as far as your nature, your personality, is concerned, you're a far more fortunate person. And no doubt about it, your way of being fortunate is far better than mine. You're the really fortunate one of us two."

Nobuyuki was being uncharacteristically pontifical. Showing his annoyance Kensaku answered, "I hardly consider my own nature to be one of my blessings. And I am not so unfortunate by circumstance as you seem to think."

"Perhaps I didn't express myself well. I don't know the proper words for the kind of thing I'm trying to say. But I do envy you. I really can't help feeling that you're a more favored being than I am.

You're strong-willed. You know what you want, and you fight for what you want. I don't say that I'm entirely lacking in assertiveness, but I certainly don't have very much of it. I only recently decided to study Zen, it's true, but I started being dissatisfied with my way of life a long time ago, and I couldn't bring myself to do anything about it. You asked me once why I didn't just leave the company, remember? Well, I simply couldn't."

"But why did you come to dislike the company so much?"

"It never was a pleasant place. But at first I was able to lose myself in the bustle; besides, the novelty of earning my own living was enough to keep me happy. It's the same with all the young fellows that we hire. They're so pleased that at last they're independent of their fathers. They were boys before, and now they're suddenly men —at least, that's the way they feel, and that's the way I felt at first. But the feeling disappears very quickly. Those with families to support can't afford to start asking questions about what they're doing, I suppose; but fellows like me, who aren't working out of sheer necessity, can't help losing interest eventually in our kind of work. After all, we are always someone else's employees, even when we come to be called directors. Inevitably we begin to wonder if this is all that our lives amount to. A man settles down at forty, they say. I don't agree. From what I've seen, it's usually at that age that men begin to wonder about what they're doing. I've started relatively early, I suppose."

"Have you told father about your taking up Zen?"

"Yes, I have. I thought he would never agree to it, but surprisingly he said he would think about it. You know that when he says that, he usually means he won't object. I was reluctant to bring up the subject with him. There was all that business about you, and I didn't want to add to his worries. But even I finally couldn't stand my own indecisiveness, and forced myself to go to him. What I envy about you is that you seem always to be able to focus your attention and energy on one specific objective. My life seems quite without focus. Partly it's because of my feeble character. But most of the trouble is in the way I live and work. And so what I shall have to do is to start building a new way of life from scratch."

How tolerant father can be, Kensaku thought with some bitterness, when it's Nobuyuki he's dealing with. He thought the discrepancy natural, nevertheless, and tried to tell himself that he ought not to be bitter about it. Besides, there was some childish charm in the way Nobuyuki tried to please Kensaku by telling him of the happy outcome of his own conversation with their father.

But Kensaku could hardly share Nobuyuki's confidence in the efficacy of Zen. Zen was becoming awfully fashionable, and Kensaku naturally felt animosity toward it. "Have you decided on the temple yet?" he said.

"Engakuji, I think. The abbot there is the leading authority, as you know."

Kensaku looked at Nobuyuki doubtfully. What little he knew about this abbot, he didn't like. He was the sort that spoke to large audiences at such places as the Mitsui Assembly Hall. For men like him, who went about scattering seed indiscriminately on barren ground, Kensaku had no respect. He could not think of any other Zen priest, however; so he kept his skepticism to himself.

11

About a month passed. Nobuyuki left the company, rented the annex of a farmhouse at a place called Nishimikado in Kamakura, and from there went to Engakuji every day for his lessons. Kensaku visited him once at his new abode. It had only recently been built, and stood at the foot of a jutting cliff. It wasn't a bad place at all. In the alcove were piles of books on Zen that Nobuyuki had lately accumulated.

With Nobuyuki now in Kamakura, the situation between Kensaku and his father became even more uncertain than it had been before. This suited Kensaku well enough. He knew that given their respective natures, any attempt at clarification of their relationship would most likely lead to unpleasantness. Besides, without formal consent from his father, he more or less had what he wanted: he had stopped going to the house in Hongō; and he was still living with Oei. No doubt his father was displeased with the turn of events. Presumably Nobuyuki, on his occasional visit to Tokyo, had to listen to his father's complaints about Kensaku. But if he did, he chose not to report them. Kensaku, seeing no hope for a situation that would satisfy both sides, chose to remain silent also.

What played some part in his willingness to leave things as they were was the change in his thinking about Oei. He was not anxious to find a precise explanation for this change. But of one fact he was sure, and this was that he was haunted by the superstitious notion that if he were to marry Oei, he would somehow be acting out his curse exactly as Nobuyuki had warned; it would be as though he were willfully succumbing to fate. For were not the cruel gods waiting for him, the child of a woman seduced by her father-in-law, to marry the mistress of that very same man? And what would they do to him then?

He was in truth not half so strong as Nobuyuki seemed to imagine. When confronted by opposition he would resist with seeming conviction. But the conviction was never so firm within as it seemed outside; and as soon as the opposition weakened and he was once again free to move, he would lose whatever firmness of purpose he might have had.

He had tried, with some success, to think of his own birth rationally and positively. But as time passed, and as the initial tension within him began to wear off, he became more apt to let it depress him. And he came to feel more and more unsettled.

He thought of moving. Nobuyuki had previously agreed to make use of his business connections and help Oei find a house. This was when Kensaku was still in Onomichi and Oei had shown some inclination to move into a smaller house. Since Kensaku's return, however, no more mention had been made of the possibility of their moving. Perhaps, Kensaku now began to think, new surroundings might revive his spirit and help him get into a more settled mood. Perhaps he would then start working seriously again. And so Nobuyuki was once more asked to help in the search for a house.

One day Nobuyuki appeared, bringing with him Ishimoto whom Kensaku had not seen for some months. "Let's go and have a look at a few houses tomorrow," Nobuyuki said. "There are a couple in the

Gotanda area, and a couple more near our property in Ōi. I'll sleep here tonight, all right?"

That evening the three men had dinner at a certain teahouse in Yanagibashi. With them sat two young geisha and a maid. Another geisha by the name of Momoyakko had been asked for repeatedly, but the answer was always a half-hearted assurance that she would be there soon.

It was Kensaku that had wanted Momoyakko. "I hear that you have a geisha here in Yanagibashi who used to be a ballad singer," he had said. "Her professional name then was Eihana."

"I remember her," Ishimoto had said. "You once took me to hear her. That was a long time ago. A pretty girl, wasn't she? She was the daughter of some confectioner, I think."

One of the geisha present happened to live right opposite her in the same alley, and knew a lot about her. And when even after several telephone calls she still failed to appear, the two geisha and the maid began to gossip about her. None of them seemed to approve of her very much. That they indeed regarded her with positive ill will became clear once they were certain she was not known personally to any of their guests. The men were now regaled with stories of the villainous Momoyakko: she had once picked a quarrel with a senior geisha of the district during a concert given by apprentice geisha; she had taken the ring off a drunken customer's finger while in a taxi; she had smothered to death her own baby—this was some time ago—as soon as it was born, and she was still living with the man who had fathered the baby; a rich, young fellow had recently become utterly infatuated with her, and was always coming in his car to fetch her or, when he couldn't come, would send a gift with a letter attached.

It had become clear to the men at any rate that Momoyakko, the former Eihana, had the unenviable reputation of being the most wicked geisha in town.

From the time he was a boy Kensaku had frequented the vaudeville theatre and other such places of popular entertainment. Initially he had been taken to these places by his grandfather and Oei. But later, when he was about to leave high school, he had begun to visit them by himself. He liked women ballad singers most.

Eihana then was a petite girl of twelve or thirteen. She had the makings of a beautiful woman, but what drew Kensaku to her at the time was her seeming defenselessness. A skinny body and a pale face with very thin eyebrows—she reminded one of a young white fox. Her voice was high-pitched even for a young girl's, yet there was in it a note of sadness. A friend once said to him, "You know, she's the sort that will put all she has into everything she does." Kensaku had thought the remark somehow very true. For behind the sadness and the pain in her still inarticulate singing, there was a quality that suggested great pride and rebelliousness. Later, whenever he thought of Eihana, he would remember his friend's words.

Others from his class began to accompany him to the vaudeville theatre. Once, when Eihana was on the stage, one of these friends—his name was Yamamoto—said to him, "I know that girl."

She was the daughter, he said, of a confectioner specializing in Imagawa cakes. The back of their house was immediately on the other side of the wall of the Yamamotos' garden, though on the street in front there was another house between theirs and the Yamamotos'. This piece of information immediately aroused interest among Yamamoto's friends. But at the time he and Eihana had never even spoken to each other.

In the Yamamotos' grounds there was a well, famous in the district for its fine water. That summer, about six months after Yamamoto had seen Eihana on the stage, the neighbors as usual began coming to the well with their buckets. Eihana was one of these.

The well was near the Yamamotos' bathhouse. One evening when Yamamoto was having a bath he saw Eihana through the reed screen that covered the open window. He thought she could not see him; but when she had filled her bucket she bowed in his direction and thanked him. After two or three more such encounters they began talking to each other. She would lean against the well crib, her hands behind her back, and he would sit on the edge of the tub, and they would talk until the water in her bucket turned tepid. What they talked about mostly was the theatre. Not long after this Kensaku saw placed on Eihana's little table on the stage the mug that Yamamoto had given her.

They remained merely friends. Yamamoto's family were nobility. They had an aged steward, very small and fierce, whom Kensaku and his friends nicknamed "the angry runt." Even if Yamamoto and Eihana had wanted to be more than friends, the old man alone would no doubt have presented a formidable obstacle; but neither seemed much inclined to push their relationship any further.

Eihana grew more and more beautiful, and her body gradually developed into a woman's, though she did not put on much more weight. Her art improved, and her name began to be known.

It was about that time that a famous ballad singer, the second Hayanosuke, announced her intention to retire soon and the choice of Eihana as her prospective successor. Eihana would thus be assured of an honored place in her profession. She would temporarily retire from the stage, study intensively at the studio of the first Hayanosuke, then formally succeed to the name when she was deemed sufficiently accomplished. But at this crucial point in her career she suddenly ran away from home to live with the son of a local bookseller.

Their place of hiding was soon discovered. It turned out to be only a few blocks from Eihana's house. The young man was taken home. But Eihana was immediately disowned by her parents for her offense. They were, it turned out, only her foster parents. She had been born the bastard child of some army sergeant.

Parted from her lover, disowned by her family, her career ruined, she of course must have felt desperate. To make matters worse, she was pregnant. And so to the first man that came along she abandoned herself completely. Perhaps she loved him. But she was a woman about to drown and would have grabbed at anything that came within reach.

She had an abortion. There were those who denied this and claimed that the child was actually born but was immediately smothered to death by her. Whatever it was that was done to the child, all agreed that it destroyed her voice.

Shortly thereafter she apparently went to Niigata with her man, and there became a geisha. Then she went to Hokkaidō. The man—he was simply a pimp—remained with her. The story was that because he knew her guilty secret, she was virtually his prisoner. But since Kensaku had heard about it, it must have been a fairly widely known secret.

Such, then, was Eihana's story as Kensaku knew it. He had heard nothing more about her for these past three or four years. Then one day, as he was glancing through the gossip column in an entertainment magazine, he happened to see Eihana's name. She had returned to Tokyo, it said, and was now a geisha in Yanagibashi. Her new name was Momoyakko.

One of the geisha said, "You have no idea how busy we are now that the *sumō* season has begun."

"Do you go much yourself?" asked Ishimoto.

"We manage to see most of the matches."

"Whereabouts is your box?" Ishimoto himself went fairly regularly.

"On the north side of the ring."

"I see. Is it anywhere near the Ishimoto family's box?" Ishimoto and his *sumō*-loving friends had a box, but he was referring to the one held by the main branch of his family.

"Well, yes—they're not too far from us. We've seen them there a couple of times."

Casually Ishimoto then asked, "Are any of the young men of the family known in these parts?" He had numerous nephews, most of whom were playboys.

The geisha quickly looked at her companions. They all smiled strangely. "We know of one," she said.

"About how old is he?"

"He's a cadet at a military school, I think. He's the young man we were telling you about—you know, the one that likes Momoyakko so much." She suddenly started to giggle.

Kensaku was surprised. He had pictured the son of some wholesale merchant in the role of Momoyakko's infatuated pursuer. That he should have turned out to be one of Ishimoto's nephews struck him as a little incongruous.

After a few more questions Ishimoto said, "I'm not so sure it's such a good thing for this young Mr. Ishimoto to get mixed up with a woman like Momoyakko."

The women all nodded in agreement.

Momoyakko, the former Eihana, never did appear. The maid was very disapproving. "If she doesn't want to come, why can't she say so in the first place," she said. At about nine o'clock the three men left.

"What an interesting coincidence," said Ishimoto as they walked. "I knew something of the sort was going on because my sister-in-law told me. But I had no idea he hung about in Yanagibashi. You know, he had the gall to go up to his parents and ask for a car. If he had a car, he said, he would stop misbehaving. So they gave him fifty thousand yen, and with ten thousand of that he went and bought himself a car. Can you imagine anyone being so gullible? How could my brother have seriously believed that his son meant what he said? Stop misbehaving if he had a car, indeed!"

Nobuyuki and Kensaku both laughed. Ishimoto turned to Kensaku and said, "But this would make a good short story, surely. Not only what we learned today, but there's all that background stuff about Eihana you seem to know so well."

"Quite so," said Kensaku with an obvious lack of enthusiasm. "At least, it's good conversation material." This last remark was ungracious, but he had to make it; for he resented Ishimoto's assumption that the stuff of gossip could immediately be translated into writing.

They walked at a leisurely pace as far as Ginza, and there the two brothers parted from Ishimoto. They returned to Kensaku's house in Fukuyoshichō at about eleven o'clock. With Oei, who had waited up for them, they sat down in the morning room and talked for a while.

Nobuyuki recounted for Oei's benefit the story of Eihana. It was a tale told with little pity and in a spirit of censure about a woman steeped in evil. Kensaku was not pleased. Oei listened attentively, looking appropriately disgusted. "What terrible women there are," she said.

Kensaku was filled with anger. He thought of that little pale-faced girl on the stage, so helpless yet proud, and wanted to tell them, "It's not Eihana that's bad!" But they had never seen the girl, and they would not know what he meant; and as he sat there trying to contain his anger, it suddenly occurred to him that here was something he could write about.

12

It was already past two o'clock in the afternoon when Nobuyuki and Kensaku left the house. They went to Gotanda first. They walked up a hill past a small steel mill, then along a ridge that overlooked a wild field of about a quarter of an acre. They soon found the house. It was a shabby bungalow. It had a fairly large front garden, but Kensaku doubted that it saw much sun. The whole place looked as if it would need a lot of work before it became habitable. Inexperienced as he was in house-hunting, he had no idea how such a house would turn out to be after one had lived in it. All he could say was that as it now stood, it looked dirty and uninviting. The next house they looked at was in such cramped surroundings that Kensaku didn't want to go anywhere near it. Lazily they walked along the highway toward Ōmori. The strong smell of budding oak leaves was everywhere. Nobuyuki talked about Zen with almost an air of smug authority. He also had the enthusiasm of the novice, and recounted one story after another from *The Blue Rock* with obvious delight.

He stopped, looked about him, and said, "Yes, our property is at the end of this lane here. Shall we go and have a look? We had a new hedge put in all around it, and none of us have seen it yet."

"All right."

"Do you remember Kamekichi, the gardener?"

"I think I've seen him at the Hongō house. A small fellow with an enormous head—am I right? Looked like a village idiot, I recall."

"That's him. He's goodness personified, one might say. He's a devout follower of the Tenrikyō sect, you know. 'In all matters I follow the teachings of our Divine Prophet'—have you heard him say that?"

Once when Kensaku was having tea with the family at Hongō this gardener had come in. He bowed so low he was almost bent double. Even his legs seemed to participate in the bow. He was the picture of humility, goodness and, alas, idiocy. Kensaku's sisters began to giggle, but the fellow seemed not to notice. He sat down and received his

179

cup of tea as though it were a gift from heaven. His speech, too, was incredibly polite. The show of meekness in him was so overwhelming that only the most heartless would have refused to entrust him with everything they had.

But Kensaku at the time had wondered to himself if the fellow wasn't really a little too good to be true. There was something about him, he felt, that didn't quite ring true. And later, at home, he had written down his suspicion in his diary.

Kensaku now said to Nobuyuki, "You know, all that goodness may just be on the surface. It's too obvious for my taste." Nobuyuki disagreed.

They came to the property. It was a rectangular area of about two acres which stretched alongside the road. Until recently a cultivated field, it had been changed to a residential site. A rough fence filled in with a cypress hedge had been built around it.

"How do we get in?" muttered Nobuyuki as they looked for an entrance. "I do believe they forgot to put in a gate."

"That's hardly likely."

"But can you see an opening anywhere? Come to think of it, I don't know that I said anything about a gate when I gave Kamekichi the job."

The two laughed as they continued their search. The hedge proved quite impenetrable.

"I'm afraid he must have completely forgotten about it," said Nobuyuki resignedly. The oversight was not without its charm. They went to see the farmer who was nominally managing the property and asked him to tell Kamekichi about the gate. (A couple of months later it was discovered that Kensaku had not been wrong about Kamekichi. For a fee that was too high considering the size of the property he had agreed to keep the grass cut. He had then secretly rented it out as grazing land and let the horses deal with the grass. In this way he had pocketed a double fee for doing no work at all.)

The sun was about to set. They went to look at a two-storied house in the Sannō neighborhood in Ōi. It stood by itself and had a pleasant appearance. "It's new," said Nobuyuki. "That alone makes it attractive. Besides, the rooms seem nicely arranged." Kensaku was too tired to want to look at another house; this one was good enough, he decided. "I'll rent it," he said. They immediately went to see the landlord who lived in the neighborhood, and made the necessary arrangements.

The first train to come in at Ōmori Station was west-bound, going toward Kamakura. It was agreed that Kensaku would go as far as Yokohama with Nobuyuki; they would have a Chinese dinner there together, then part company. Late that evening Kensaku caught the train back to Tokyo.

Five days later he and Oei moved. He had looked at the house hurriedly, and in the evening. Now that he was in it, he found it considerably less pleasant than he had thought. It was unquestionably a house built to rent. If one walked at all heavily upstairs the whole house would shake and the rooms below would be covered with dust let loose from the ceiling. "My hair has been filthy ever since we moved here," complained Oei, who was always downstairs.

Nevertheless Kensaku's mood changed somewhat for the better. It was an opportune time to start working seriously again. There was the long piece that he had worked on in Onomichi and was still unfinished, but he did not want to touch that for the time being. He would write about Eihana, he decided.

He had no idea how he would feel about her if he were to meet her. But was there not something wrong about his uncertainty as to how she would seem to him in person? Who was this woman he wanted to write about? Was it Eihana, or someone he wanted to think of as Eihana? Could there be anything between them, some measure of mutual understanding and sympathy, if they were to meet? He simply didn't know. And it was discomforting to know that what made him want to write about Eihana in the first place was only his anger at Oei's total lack of sympathy for her. It might be a good idea, he said to himself, to try to meet her sometime. The thought was very tentative, however; for he knew that he would find it most difficult to initiate such a meeting.

He tried to imagine what the meeting would be like. How would Eihana behave toward him? Would the awareness that he knew her past revive in her some part of her old self? Or would she, made thoroughly cynical by her experiences, just pretend to be moved by memories of the past? Either way, he thought the very hopelessness of her condition would touch him. Save her from despair—such a thought now occurred to him; and he imagined himself giving succor to this woman who had murdered her own child and committed countless other sins but was now repentant. Eihana thus imagined remained a peculiarly unreal figure, however. It was not pleasing, either, to think that on meeting her he might indeed be tempted to act like a simple-minded Christian proselyte. How truly difficult it must be, he thought, for just one human being to be saved.

He was reminded of a woman calling herself "Omasa the Viper" whom he had seen in Kyoto the year before. She was performing in a small makeshift theatre—it was hardly more than a hut—near Yasaka Shrine in Gion. He happened to pass by the theatre late at night, and had stopped to look at the large, illustrated signboard outside. On it was the picture of a woman, her head shaved clean like a nun's, engaged in a monologue. According to the caption it was Omasa telling the true story of her life—as "an act of confession," it said. Thinking no more of it he was about to walk on when he saw a tall figure, dressed in a long cloak and wearing a kind of lay priest's hat, coming out of the theatre at the head of a group of young women. If Kensaku had not seen the signboard, he would have assumed it was a man. But it was Omasa the Viper. She was, he guessed, in her fifties.

The young man who had come out to take down the signboard bowed to her. She looked at him briefly and gave a slight nod. She was standing directly under an electric light, so that Kensaku was able to have a good look at her. What he saw was an ill-tempered and extraordinarily cheerless face. It was the face of someone whose heart knew no joy.

He knew nothing about Omasa the Viper. But he thought he could surmise this much: she had been in prison, and probably had been given an early pardon for good conduct and signs of repentance; in order to make a living, she traveled from town to town at the head of a cheap theatre troupe, vending her so-called confessions of past sins.

He thought he could not be far wrong in his surmise. And it was enough to look at her face to know how she felt about her present life. He wished he didn't know. Her present condition, as he saw it in his mind, became too vivid for his own comfort. Her cheerlessness and her loneliness began to pervade his own being. He did not know what offenses she had committed, and he had no feelings about them one way or the other. But what depressed him was the thought that at the time she was engaged in wrongdoing, her condition could hardly have been less enviable than it was now. For then there must at least have been some sense of life in her, a fullness of spirit that gave her some kind of pleasure. What did she have now instead? Going from town to town, offering her shame for sale. Of course, "confession" or not, what she was doing was in fact acting on the stage. She performed for audiences who had come to be entertained. But at the same time she had to satisfy their need for vicarious participation in crimes committed in "real life," acted out by the criminal in person. What a degrading life it must be, Kensaku thought, to have to feign repentance on the stage day after day for the pleasure of strangers. And he wondered if such degradation was not in some measure forced on all who had done something very wrong and had repented.

Omasa was a big woman with a strong, masculine face. When young, she must have cut an impressive figure.

And so as he thought of Eihana, he could not help remembering that woman he had seen in Kyoto. It was oppressive enough to think of Eihana as she must be now—her lot was pitiable enough; but how much more hopeless and dark Omasa's life seemed to be than Eihana's. If true salvation was beyond Eihana, then surely she would rather live as she did now than live the degrading, sham existence of the mock penitent. Yes, Kensaku thought, it would be in Eihana's nature to continue to flaunt her sins and never give in; and perhaps that's the way one ought to be.

Deciding he hadn't the courage to arrange a meeting with Eihana, he went to his desk and began writing her story.

He came across Yamamoto some time later, and he told him that Eihana was back in Tokyo. "Yes, I thought so," said Yamamoto. "My wife and I went peony-viewing the other day, and when we were waiting for the boat at Ryōgoku, I thought I saw her standing at the end of an alley. She was looking at us."

Kensaku was certain that the woman had been Eihana, for she lived in that alley. He asked Yamamoto, "Do you have any inclination to see her?"

"I shouldn't mind seeing her, I suppose." There was no enthusiasm in Yamamoto's voice.

13

Kensaku once more began to decline, both in spirit and body. The weather was bad; and on days when the humid south wind blew mercilessly, he would feel quite ill. His way of life again became disorderly.

In trying to write about Eihana he was forced to think about women in relation to sin. He asked himself why it was that women were so relentlessly pursued by their own past sins while men were not. Not many days before he had taken a walk through the neighborhood where Eihana had lived as a girl. He passed by the bookstore that her former lover's father owned, and saw the young man sitting in front with a baby on his knee. It was strange to see this man younger than himself already a father. He sat there lazily with the baby, gazing at the passing scene with vacuous contentment. No one would have guessed that here was a fellow who had once been involved in a scandal. But surely even over such a man a cloud must occasionally pass, carrying disquieting memories of the past. Would he not remember now and then his child that was killed? Perhaps, but Kensaku thought that the past had almost been erased from this man's memory, that little of the old pain was still remembered. Then why was Eihana's present life so inextricably bound to her past, why was it so clearly an unbroken extension of that one affair? Perhaps it was not necessarily because she was a woman. There must be many men who, having committed one crime, were thrown willy-nilly into a life of desperate abandon. But there was no denying that women on the whole were more prone to be plunged into a life of despair. They were more blind to the threats of fate and thus were its easiest victims. But if this were so, then there was all the more reason to treat them with greater generosity. If it was all right to forgive children because they were children, why could not women in their misfortune be forgiven because they were women? Instead, they were subjected to particularly severe reprisals; worse than that, the public was disappointed if ever they escaped payment for their sins. Guilty women destroyed themselves, and everyone stood aside, thinking the self-destruction perfectly proper. It was strange, Kensaku thought, that women in particular should be accorded such treatment.

He was then forced to admit to himself that his mother was perhaps more fortunate than many other women might have been under similar circumstances. What might her fate have been if she had been surrounded by ignorant men? She might not have survived at all. Luckily her father in Shiba and her husband were both intelligent men. For that alone, he told himself, he ought to be grateful to his father in Hongō. But the admonition to himself was without emotional conviction.

He tried writing about Eihana from his own point of view; quickly it became evident that the story would be too bare told that way, and he decided to tell it from her point of view, giving his imagination free rein. He toyed with the idea of having her meet Omasa the Viper. He wondered, too, if he should not introduce another such character whom he had seen recently on the popular stage, a woman by the name of Hanai Oume. She had killed a man—he was a box maker—and, like Omasa, had become a professional penitent. He had found her act both pathetic and distasteful, and had come away feeling more sympathetic than ever toward the defiantly unpenitent.

He liked his story less and less as it developed. It seemed to him to become particularly contrived after the heroine's journey to Hokkaidō. Besides, he found telling a story from a woman's point of view, which he had never attempted before, far more difficult than he had imagined.

Spiritually and physically he began to feel exhausted; and together with the exhaustion came loneliness. That time in Onomichi when he received the letter from Nobuyuki telling him about his birth, he had been almost overwhelmed by shock and depression; but then at least he had had something to fight against; there had been in him the tension that came from the will to survive an immediate threat. Now his soul was like the wooden foundation of a house that rots slowly as the damp from the ground seeps deeper and deeper into it.

His loneliness was something he could not reason away. He tried to pull himself together by turning his mind to the goal he had set for himself, which was to play some part in the making of mankind's happiness, to leave some mark on the path of human progress, and so realize the life of the artist. But his mind seemed incapable of pulling itself out of the mire of depression. "Blessed are the poor in spirit"— so said the Christians. If the words "poor in spirit" were meant to describe his condition, then the saying was a very cruel one. That his condition could in any way be described as "blessed" was inconceivable to him. If a Christian minister had at that moment appeared and said to him, "Blessed are the poor in spirit," Kensaku would have hit him. It seemed to him that nothing was more abject than this poverty of the spirit. And "poverty" was the word that aptly described his state: "loneliness," "sorrow," "pain"—such words seemed to him inadequate. What greater misery was there, he wondered, than to be so destitute, to feel that one's spirit had no resources left?

This sense of destitution—it was as much a physiological phenomenon as anything else—had already been present in him when he went to Onomichi. He had had temporary relief from it when the truth about his birth was divulged to him. The shock had acted as a stimulant. But in the end the effect of the sudden discovery about himself was to aggravate his condition and make him even more vulnerable than before to attacks of depression.

Nobuyuki visited him from time to time. Kensaku felt a growing fondness for him, and came to look forward to his visits. He particularly enjoyed listening to his Zen stories. The story of how Chu-chih would hold up a single finger to show the essence of Zen, of Nan-ch'uan and the cat he put to the sword, of Shih-kung and the arrow, of how Te-shan achieved *satori* at Lung-t'an's place, and those stories about Po-chang, Kuei-shan, Huang-po, Mu-chou, Lin-chi, P'u-hua —all these appealed deeply to his susceptible mind. And each time he heard the words, "Thus in an instant was there enlightenment," he would feel like crying. Once, on hearing the story of Te-shan and the bowl, he did burst into tears. It was not only the story's content that so moved his destitute spirit, but its artistry.

Seeing Kensaku's emotional response to these stories, Nobuyuki would sometimes suggest gently that he come to Kamakura. But

Kensaku was never tempted. He had nothing against Zen; but it distressed him to imagine himself sitting humbly at the feet of some smug Zen priest. If ever he reached the point of wanting to go to a temple, he thought, he would much rather go to Mt. Kōya or Mt. Hiei.

When he had written about forty manuscript sheets he found that he could go no further with the story. How could anyone in his condition hope to articulate successfully on paper, to make real to the reader whatever was on his mind?

Several weeks of restless inactivity and loneliness had passed. It was a nasty day, with a hot, humid wind blowing. He ate his lunch, then feeling heavy and sluggish, immediately lay down in the morning room and read without much interest a few pages of a translation of a European novel. Oei sat near him, sewing. He turned to her and said, "By the way, when would be a good day to let Yoshi go to see the South Seas Exhibition?" He had received a postcard that morning from a friend named Masumoto saying that Miyamoto was fascinated by the native dancers in the exhibition and had already gone to see them several times.

"Any day is all right as far as I'm concerned. Is she going alone, or are you asking someone to take her?"

"She can go alone, don't you think?" he said, then immediately wondered if she could manage the trip by herself. He wondered, too, when she should be given her day off. Both questions threw him in a quandary. He had never liked making decisions on simple, practical matters; but of late he had become increasingly fearful of such decisions, as though once made they were bound to bring trouble. He knew that this fearfulness had no rational basis, that it was a kind of sickness, but it made no difference. "I might as well take her myself this afternoon," he said.

"But isn't your brother supposed to be coming today?"

"Perhaps he did say something of the sort the last time he was here. Or perhaps I'm just imagining he said it." He was greatly relieved that his tentative proposal to accompany Yoshi to the exhibition was not to be put to the test.

The train from Yokosuka that Nobuyuki would be on if he was coming was due to arrive at seven minutes past three. It was now three o'clock. Kensaku thought he would go out and see if he could meet his brother on his way to the house. It would be something to do. He put on a light outer kimono and picked up his pocket watch and wallet. If Nobuyuki appeared, then the rest of the day would be occupied. If he didn't, Kensaku was not sure what he would do. At least, that was what he told himself. A vague plan had actually been formulated at the back of his mind, but he did not acknowledge its presence; for if he did, he would almost certainly end up rejecting it. "I'm going out for a little while. I'll be back shortly with Nobuyuki if I see him. If I don't, I shall probably be home by dinner time."

He did not see Nobuyuki. As he walked through the Kashimadani neighborhood he heard the train that Nobuyuki would have been on roar past on its way to Tokyo. He could not see it from where he stood, but it shook the very ground under him. At Ōmori Station he discovered that he would have to wait half an hour for the next train to Shinbashi. He went outside again and caught a suburban-line streetcar going to Shinagawa.

He pulled out a small edition of Saikaku's works and began reading the last episode of *Twenty Instances of Filial Impiety*. Two or three days before, Oei had asked him which Japanese novelist he thought was "great," and he had answered, "A man named Saikaku." He had just finished reading the first two episodes of the same work, and had been thoroughly impressed. There was such relentlessness in the man, a single-mindedness that was almost obsessive. To maintain that mood of cruelty without a touch of introspection was a feat that Kensaku himself could not hope to accomplish even in a work of pure fiction. Even if he could write one made-up tale after another examining the various ways in which children could be ungrateful and disloyal toward their parents, he could not pursue the subject with such force and single-minded consistency.

That Kensaku, immersed as he was then in futile, self-punishing introspection, should so admire and envy Saikaku's audacity and detachment was not surprising. How much more bearable life would be, he thought, if he could learn to look at the world as Saikaku did.

It was true, however, that none of the stories he now read—this time he was reading them in reverse order, the last episode first—could compare with the first two.

In Shinagawa he transferred to the city line. By then he had tired of reading. He looked about at the passengers seated around him. His eyes came to rest on the man directly opposite. The thought struck him that he resembled one of those grotesque portraits by Sharaku. As it turned out, the man was not unique; for after careful scrutiny every other passenger seemed uncannily to remind Kensaku of a Sharaku face.

As the streetcar approached Satsumatsubara Junction, Kensaku momentarily felt the desire to get off and visit the house in Hongō. He had not seen Sakiko and Taeko for a long time. But he stayed on the streetcar; for the prospect of seeing his father was not inviting, and there was the possibility that Sakiko would find his visit awkward. He then thought of paying Miyamoto or Masumoto a visit. This time again he quickly changed his mind. He had the strange premonition that neither would be in; besides, given his present state of mind, there was always the danger of his doing or saying something disagreeable. Even if he did manage to behave properly, the strain of having consciously to suppress the misery within him so that it would not spill out in another's presence would be unbearable. He pictured himself, a pathetic, defeated figure leaving the scene after the ordeal, and he could not help feeling that he really had nowhere to go. Except, of course, there was that place which had been lurking at the back of his mind since he decided to come out that afternoon. There he would be under no restraint. And that was where his feet would take him. He looked at the passengers around him again. Not one of them, he was sure, looked as pathetic as he. At least, their blood flowed energetically in their veins; there was a sparkle in their eyes. But his own blood, he felt, was tepid, muddy liquid moving slowly and tiredly around his body; and his eyes were like those of a dead fish, dull and cloudy white.

14

The small woman said she was just having her hair done when she was called. Her abundant hair was lightly pulled together behind her neck with a hairpin. On the hairpin was a red stone. Showing her profile she said, "Like a Korean woman, don't you think?" It was still daylight, but the electric light hanging from the ceiling was on. The room was terribly stuffy, despite the wind that could be heard blowing outside.

The small woman talked incessantly. She seemed nervous; perhaps she was waiting for him to go.

Kensaku stood up. As he was about to leave the room, the small woman raised her hand smartly and said, "See you again!" Kensaku tentatively returned the salute, then went down the stairs. A young woman sat in the front hall. She was a pretty woman, with an air about her that pleased him.

He walked toward the streetcar stop thinking that at this rate he would be home before dark. He wondered why that woman whom he had just seen was sitting in such a public place. Presumably she was waiting to go to a customer. But why wait in the front hall? If he visited the house again, he would no doubt ask for her. And they would want to know whom he meant. What would he tell them? There were no distinguishing characteristics that he could remember. "The good-looking one who was sitting downstairs," he would say. "Was she tall or short, sir?" "Can't say." "Was she plump?" "She wasn't thin." He wouldn't get very far that way. Why not go back and try to find her now? He would regret it later if he didn't. If he met her on the street on his way back there, all he had to say was that he had left something behind. He turned around and walked back to the house.

He stood in the doorway and spoke to the maid. "The woman I saw sitting there, was she waiting to go to a customer?"

The maid understood immediately. "The customer has another woman with him now. The one you want will soon be going up to take her place. But she won't be long, so come in."

"Let her come to me first."

The maid grimaced. "As I said, she won't be long."

He went in, and as he passed the room beside the front hall he saw the woman standing behind the half-open door. She had heard the conversation obviously. He pretended not to see her and went up the stairs. Once in the room he decided to try again to get the woman immediately. He called the maid and said to her, "Let the fellow have someone else." He kept his voice low, for the man was in the next room.

"I'm sorry, I can't do that. He asked for her specifically. I'm afraid he saw her when he came in."

"It's a damn nuisance," he said, then fell into ill-tempered silence. For no good reason he had decided that the woman he wanted was not like the others. She was quiet, virtuous, and not vulgar—a sort of lady, in other words.

He heard the first woman leave the next room. Then he heard the one he wanted going in. He felt he could not sit still. He called the maid again. Before he could say anything, she said soothingly, "She just went in. It won't be long now."

"Bring me something to write with."

He had to do something to keep his mind off what was happening in the next room. When the maid had brought him a brush and an inkstone, he got out a sheet of paper he had with him and laid it out on the tea table. He dipped the brush in the ink, took a deep breath and proceeded to write: "The Bodhisattva Kannon looks upon all sentient beings with compassion/ And the blessings that accrue for them are as limitless as the ocean." He wrote no more; for the thought occurred to him that it was sacrilegious to write such words in so disreputable a place.

The woman came in smiling. She looked pleasant enough, but she was certainly not the woman he thought he had seen. She sat down not quite opposite him and gave a slight bow. "Thank you for calling me," she said, looking at him. There was nothing at all ladylike in her deportment. She was just an ordinary prostitute.

"How long have you been in this business?"

"For about two months." She sounded defensive.

"How old are you—twenty?"

"No, nineteen."

"Really?"

"Yes, really." She seemed to be affecting a Kyoto accent.

He pulled her toward him and made her sit on his lap. She was absolutely docile. Wearily she rested her head on his shoulder and closed her eyes.

"Would you like to go on a trip with me?" he asked.

"Where?"

"Somewhere far away."

"All right."

"I'm not joking, you know."

"Nor am I," she mumbled. She was about to fall asleep.

"Hey!" he said, shaking her by the shoulder.

"Right!" she answered loudly, sticking her plump, white chin out in front of his nose.

"You obviously think I'm fooling. You're too stupid to see that I'm serious."

"Yes, I'm stupid." She sat up and gazed down at his face.

Her manner became a little more earnest, and she began to talk about herself. She had been a prostitute for six months, not two. She had a mother, but her elder sister and brother-in-law were taking care of her, so all she had to do was send her sister a little money every month.

"What does your brother-in-law do?"

She thought for a while, then said, "He has a soybean shop," and burst out laughing. Kensaku did not know whether to believe her or not.

Seventy yen was all she owed her employer, she said. If Kensaku were to pay that modest debt, she would be free to go anywhere. For some reason she persisted in affecting a Kyoto accent. Whether it was this affectation, the purpose of which was obscure, or sheer illiteracy that led her to mispronounce words, Kensaku was not sure.

"Do you like Kyoto?" he asked, and was greeted with an enthusiastic response.

He left shortly thereafter, having made no firm promises, and went immediately home.

The next day, as evening approached, he again became restless. Oei was already cooking the dinner, but unable to sit still and wait even for that he rushed outside. That day, too, Nobuyuki had failed to come. Kensaku was sure he had gone straight to the house in Hongō, deliberately avoiding him. And though he tried to tell himself it was his twisted mind that gave him such ideas, he could not help feeling hurt and insulted. He had always been inclined to suspect others of harboring ill will toward him. Earlier, it had not been so difficult to dismiss his own suspicions as mere figments of his perverted imagination. But since the discovery about his birth he had begun to ask if the others had not always known about it, and seeing some ugly spirit standing behind him had not always wanted to look away. And had he not dimly sensed their aversion and in retaliation displayed his own mistrust of them?

It seemed to him these days that everyone who came near him was a potential source of humiliation for him. Why, he could not say. He simply felt that way about everyone. And the only path of escape he could think of was to uproot himself entirely from his present surroundings. Like a man with a dual personality he would beget a new identity. He would become someone who did not know this man Tokitō Kensaku, someone who did not remember who he had been before the transformation. How easy life would be then!

He would find a world where the very air he breathed was different. He would live at the foot of some great mountain, among peasants who knew nothing. And if he could live apart even from them, all the better. His wife would be an ordinary, loyal woman with an ugly, pockmarked face. The woman he had met the day before would be far too pretty for the role of a recluse's wife. Yet if she were someone tormented by a sinful past she would make an ideal partner. The two of them would live out their lives in somber humility, acknowledging and accepting each other's misery. The scorn or pity of others would not touch them in their remote hiding place. If some laughed at them it would not matter, for they would not hear the laughter. They would in time cease to exist in other people's minds, as others would cease to exist in theirs. How good it would be to live and eventually die in that condition—forgotten, unknown, untouched by the outer world!

When he got off the train at Shinbashi Station he went to a telephone booth to call Masumoto. "I came across Miyamoto," Masumoto had written in his postcard to Kensaku, "two days ago in front of Mitsukoshi, and he told me you had moved out of the city. I want to call on you at your new house, so let me know what day would be best." It was Kensaku's intention now to see if Masumoto was at home, and if he was, to pay him a visit. But as he waited for the operator to answer he began to wonder if he really did want to see Masumoto. No, he decided, and quickly put the receiver down.

The night stalls were about to open for business on one side of Ginza. Staying on the other side of the street he walked toward Kyō-bashi. He held his body erect and kept his mouth tightly closed. He must tread the ground firmly, he told himself, and not shuffle along. He must look straight ahead with the eyes of a calm and controlled man and not look about him nervously as he was wont to do. He wanted to be like a man striding alone through the wilderness in the twilight, unmindful of the crying pines and the whispering grass. (Had Nobuyuki said the image was to be found in a poem by Han-shan?) He wanted to capture the spirit of such a man—even here on Ginza. And he did not altogether fail to do so. In his present frame of mind he needed desperately to cling to some such ideal.

If he remembered rightly there were two or three bookstores on this side of Nihonbashi that specialized in Chinese classics. He would buy a copy of Han-shan's poems.

He saw coming toward him a friend whom he had not seen for some time. He was Kensaku's senior by about five years. He had a young woman with him who presumably was his wife. It was then that Kensaku admitted to himself that only a few moments before he had seen another friend of his—this one was younger than Ken-saku—walking on the other side of the street with a nicely built young woman who also had an unmistakably wifely air about her.

The friend was only a few feet away when he at last saw Kensaku. The two men stopped to exchange greetings. The friend then said, "Our home is in Gazenbō. We're always at home in the evenings, so come and see us."

Kensaku had no intention of visiting them. But the fact that he could not remember where exactly Gazenbō was troubled him inor-dinately. He must have known its location once; how then could he have forgotten it? Was it near Mamiana? "I should know," he said, "but where is Gan. . ." He stopped, thoroughly flustered for instead of *ga* he had said *gan*. He asked at random, "Is it at the bottom of Imoaraizaka?"

"It's nowhere near Imoaraizaka," said the friend. His wife, stand-ing behind him, whispered something to him. He nodded. "Look, she suggests we give you our telephone number. It's Shiba 4736."

"I'll never remember it."

"It's simple. Three and seven make ten, so do four and six. Remember, we're always in in the evenings."

As they parted the friend's wife bowed politely. Kensaku thought he had seen her somewhere before, but could not remember where or when.

The encounter had unsettled him considerably. He walked on, telling himself he had to learn to be more controlled. He came to a secondhand bookstore with a sign outside that said, "Matsuyama Bookstore." It had obviously been done by a professional calligrapher. The first thing that caught his eye as he went in was a Chinese calligraphy manual, *Yen Chen-ch'ing's One Thousand Characters*. He picked it up and opened it. It was not a particularly good edition. He went slowly down the aisle, carefully perusing the shelves on either side of him. They were full of books whose titles seemed to him vaguely familiar, yet on second thought not at all familiar. There was one with a title card stuck in it that suggested that it might be some sort of collection of Ikkyū's essays. But when he opened the book he found that it was a popular novel by the early nineteenth-century writer, Ryūkatei Tanekazu.

"Have you a copy of Han-shan's poems?" he asked the owner.

"Not just now, I'm afraid."

"What about *Sayings from the Zen School*?"

"We haven't got that either."

Maruzen Bookstore had just closed, and the clerks were coming out of the side door. In the display window were bookcases tastelessly decorated with "Egyptian" designs.

He came to a bookstore called Aoki Suzandō. He had thought there was another bookstore between this and Maruzen called Kobayashi Suzandō, but either he had walked past it without seeing it or it had shut down. He bought a small collection of Li Po's poems. About ten years before he had bought a copy of exactly the same edition of Li Po at the same shop, but like so many other things it had disappeared.

The fish market was close by. Though he was not hungry, he decided that if he was going to have dinner this would be as good a place as any to have it. He went into a side street to find a likely restaurant. A *sushi* maker whom he knew—he was notoriously lazy—had his stall out for a change. Kensaku walked past pretending not to see him and hoping he was not the sort to rush out and challenge a fickle former patron. There was a tempura restaurant a few yards farther, and Kensaku managed to reach it without mishap.

As he came out of the restaurant he wondered if the *sushi* man might not be lurking behind some corner, waiting to waylay him and give him a good thrashing. It was an idiotic apprehension, of course, but it did Kensaku no good to tell himself this.

He crossed two bridges, then turned right. He wanted to look again at a platinum watch he had seen the day before in a watchmaker's window. The price tag had said a hundred and ninety yen. He had made up his mind that if he still liked the looks of it he would buy it. It was expensive, but if he lived thriftily for the next three months he could afford it. But as he looked at it again it seemed not half so tempting as it had the day before. This saddened him. Five years ago he would never have been satisfied until he had bought whatever it was that struck his fancy—even, say, a ukiyo print. But of late he had become more and more unable to feel such attachment to anything. Something would strike him as novel one day, then the next day it would already seem stale and uninteresting. With a sense of loss he continued to stare at the watch. Ah well, he said to himself, I've saved a hundred and ninety yen.

It suddenly occurred to him that if he stood in front of the shop-window much longer someone inside might begin to suspect him of being a prospective burglar. Blushing, he walked away.

He reached the house he had visited the day before. Samisen music and rowdy voices greeted him as he went in. To the maid who led him to the room upstairs he said, "Please call the woman I met yesterday." He sat down and opened the book of Li Po's poems, but before he began reading it he realized that his instruction to the maid was rather vague. After all, he had seen two women the day before, and she might call the wrong one. He clapped his hands, and a different maid appeared. "Tell the other maid I meant the one that came later." To his relief he was informed that the right woman was being called. But supposing she's not in, he thought uneasily.

The book began with two biographical prefaces. In his idealistic frame of mind Kensaku could not but find Li Po's life extremely appealing as described in these. As he read about the poet getting drunk with his companions in the marketplace, he thought how little the great man would have cared about the terrible noise coming from the room downstairs. He would have remained untouched in the world of his making, paying no heed to all that took place outside it. Had not another poet—was it Tu Fu?—described Li Po lying on the floor in a wineshop and saying, "I have enough money in my purse to pay for all the wine I need"? No doubt about it, for Li Po wine was food for the spirit. Yet surely there must have been times when it gave him more misery than joy, for had it not eventually caused his death? Kensaku, who never did like to drink, could not envy Li Po his penchant for wine, however much inspiration it might have brought him. . . . But why had the woman not yet appeared?

When at last she came into the room, Kensaku was struck by how much less attractive she was than he had remembered her. True, when she smiled and showed her slightly crooked corner teeth she was strangely seductive; but in repose her face was distressingly ordinary. Feeling somewhat betrayed, he made no reference to the trip. She, too, kept silent about it, seemingly without conscious effort.

Yet when he reached out and held her round, heavy breast he was filled with an indefinable sense of comfort and satisfaction. It was as though he had touched something very precious. He let it rest on the palm of his hand, then shook it a little so that he could feel the full weight of it. There were no words to express the pleasure he experienced then. He continued to shake it gently, saying merely, "What riches!" It was for him somehow a symbol of all that was precious to him, of whatever it was that promised to fill the emptiness inside him.

PART III

1

His hope that the move to Ōmori might revive his spirit had proved totally vain. His life there had provided hardly a moment of relief from the oppressive misery that enveloped him. He had then come to Kyoto on a whim about a month ago, and now at last his new surroundings seemed to be having some beneficial effect on his state of mind.

The ancient land with its ancient temples and works of art led him gently back to ancient times, inviting a response from him that he had not thought possible. To escape from the present—how badly he had needed that. Yet Kyoto offered him more than a mere means of escape; for he had had little opportunity before of coming into contact with ancient things, and to live among them as he now did was, he thought, a worthy experience for its own sake. With the fleeting happiness and quiet gratitude of a man recovering from a long illness, he walked about Kyoto day after day looking at temples.

He was supposed to be searching for a house to rent; but each time he went out ostensibly on a house-hunting expedition, he would end up visiting yet another temple. Kyoto was so full of temples worth looking at.

This day, too, he came out of his inn in the cool of the morning to look for a house in the Saga area. He followed a light-colored dirt road that had become dry and dusty from days of sunshine, and stopped to see Shakadō, then yet two more temples, Nison'in and Giōji. He returned to his inn in Higashisanpongi at about noon without having looked at one house. He was satisfied, however, that he had not wasted the morning; for he had seen a fine portrait of Abbot Hōnen at Nison'in.

He idled away the rest of the afternoon in his small, hot room.

Before sunset the landlady came in to tell him that his bath was ready. By the time he had come out of the bath and sat down to dinner, there was a cool breeze blowing from across the river.

After dinner he sat on the narrow verandah, fanning himself. Immediately below him was a small, swift-flowing stream; beyond this, on the wide road recently constructed along the bank of the Kamogawa, were men and women laborers busily sorting out the pebbles that they had gathered from the river. And then there was the river itself, dotted here and there with clumps of reeds. The bank opposite looked very hot, for it was still receiving the full brunt of the western sun. Running alongside that bank was a road lined with houses, some with chimneys. Beyond stood the hills of Daimonji and Higashiyama, bathed in brilliant sunlight; to their left was Yoshidayama, and on this side of them was Kurodani. Standing above them all was the peak of Hiei. As he gazed at the panorama, Kensaku wished that autumn would come soon. Nanzenji, Nyakuōji, Hōnen'in—how pleasant it would be, he thought longingly, to visit those temples on a brisk autumn morning.

Lighting a cigarette he stepped down to the garden and walked over the plank laid across the little stream. He could feel around his legs under the kimono the warm, clammy vapor rising from the sunbaked grass. Neighborhood children clad only in jerkins, their faces covered with dirt and sweat, were still rushing about chasing grasshoppers. He walked at a leisurely pace toward Kōjin Bridge, the river on one side of him and the backs of a row of houses on the other. In these, most of which were inns of one kind or another, people could be seen eating and drinking under the electric light.

In one of them, Kensaku had noted some days before, lived an oldish man who was obviously an invalid, for besides a woman in her fifties—his wife, presumably—he had seen a young nurse in attendance. His guess was that the old man had come from the provinces and rented rooms in this neighborhood because of its proximity to the university hospital. As he now passed by the house, he saw on the verandah an unfamiliar young woman, well-built and very pretty, bent over a small cooking stove with an earthen pot on it. She was fanning the fire, and perhaps from the exertion, her plump cheeks were flushed. She was a pleasing and wholesome sight, and he was immediately drawn to her. Her beauty was not so extraordinary, yet what he felt then was somehow more exquisite, more disturbing, than anything he felt before on seeing some attractive woman in

passing. Like an adolescent with awakening passions he quickly looked away, made almost breathless by the acute happiness that came
over him.

When he reached the bridge he turned around and began to walk
back toward his inn. This time he stayed close to the river so that he
could look at her again from a safe distance. She was now standing
on the verandah, engaged in animated conversation with the older
woman who stood below her on the ground, on this side of the small
stream. As he watched, the two of them threw their heads back and
laughed. Only the young woman's laughter, pure and joyful, reached
his ears. It was so infectious, Kensaku found himself wanting to smile
in response. The laughter ended and the older woman sauntered toward the river, holding an open fan. She had the relaxed look of someone who had just had a bath. The young woman took the lid off the
pot and went inside.

She had the sleeves of her kimono—much too good for housework
—tucked up with a cord. He surmised that she had come just for the
day to help the older woman. She was clearly unused to housework;
for in the way she did her chores there was the childish enthusiasm
of a novice.

As he passed the house the young woman came out on the verandah again. He felt himself going a little stiff when he imagined he
was being stared at, but otherwise he managed to stay relatively calm
this time.

The unsettling yet pleasurable sensation remained with him after
he got back to the inn. That it was more than a passing fancy, he was
sure. But what was it all about, he asked himself, and what was he to
do about it?

He had to go past the house again, for she would surely not be there
on the following day. He went to the front hall himself to fetch his
clogs, then went out once more over the stream to the grassy bank,
busy with people who had come out to cool themselves. He walked
toward the house, more hesitantly this time.

She was sitting on the verandah with the older woman, enjoying
the cool evening air. Behind them in the room a mosquito net had
been put up under the electric light. They were looking toward the
river, away from the light, while he had to look straight into it, so

that he could not see their faces very well. She must have just come out of the bath. She wore an ill-fitting, cotton kimono so stiff with starch that it stuck out around the shoulders. The clumsiness of her attire was rather engaging, he thought. The two women fanned themselves as they talked quietly and intimately.

When he reached Kōjin Bridge, he crossed it and walked back along the opposite bank. He could see in the distance across the river the two women sitting side by side. They looked like silhouettes on a paper lantern.

He boarded a Higashiyama-bound streetcar at the foot of Maruta Bridge. It was crowded, for it was the time of evening when the citizens of Kyoto came out of their houses to visit their favorite cool spots. He got off by the stone steps of Gion, having had to stand all the way.

He felt unusually composed; and as he realized that even in the crowded streetcar he had deported himself with unself-conscious dignity, a feeling of gentle, innocent happiness came over him. That his impression of the woman's beauty should have permeated his being even to the point of affecting his deportment was proof, he thought, that it was more than a whimsical attraction. The love of that noble knight, Don Quixote, now came to mind. He had read the novel when living in Ōmori, and at the time he had not given much thought to Don Quixote's love. But now, when he thought of his own condition, he realized that it was meant to be more than a mere tool of comedy. Of course he did not wish to compare the woman he had seen today to Dulcinea. But did not Don Quixote's love, as it grew and became purified in his heart, make him even more noble, even more brave? It was not comical at all, Kensaku thought, feeling for the moment a strange sense of identification with the knight.

He was so absorbed in his newly found sense of dignity and contentment that he concerned himself not at all with the question of where his infatuation might lead him. He made his way through the crowded streets of the Shinkyōgoku quarter, unaffected by the bustle around him. By way of Teramachi he proceeded directly to Marutamachi and from there back to the inn.

Now he began to wonder what he should do next. Of one thing he was certain: he would not allow this precious feeling to die, to become yet another fleeting, soon forgotten moment in his life. But how was he to try to effect a meeting with her? The fact that they lived in the same row of houses could hardly provide him with an excuse to approach her unintroduced. Passively waiting for some fortunate accident to bring them together was out of the question, for they were both temporary residents in that neighborhood. Also unlikely was the prospect of his venturing under some clever pretext to manipulate his way into the house where she was staying. What was he to do then? No doubt about it, he told himself impatiently, he could be exceedingly unenterprising in such situations. He remembered that an old friend of his in a similar predicament had driven his car up to the front of the young lady's house, tampered with the engine, then gone to the house and, pretending that the car had broken down, asked if he might leave it where it was for the night. The following day he had gone back with his manservant to get the car, called on the family to thank them, and in this way had made himself known to her. But what could Kensaku do that was equally effective, short of throwing a fainting fit before her very eyes?

He decided to go out and try to catch a glimpse of her again. When he reached the house he found that the storm doors had not yet been closed, but a green cloth cover had been put over the light above the mosquito net, and there seemed to be no one about. Had they all gone into town, he wondered disappointedly, or had she gone home, escorted to the station or wherever by the old couple? And as he walked back to the inn he could not help thinking that even if she was indeed single, she could still be already spoken for. The thought made him feel terribly helpless and forlorn.

2

The sun was already above Daimonji when he awoke the next morning. He washed his face, and while the maid tidied his room he went outside to the path by the river. A cool breeze was blowing, and the grass under his feet was still wet with dew. He felt very conspicuous walking along the path in full daylight. He must be brave, he exhorted himself as he approached the house, he must not be dissuaded by considerations of propriety. In all likelihood she would not be there any more, he thought; but if she was, that would indeed be a good omen.

A man in his forties came toward him, accompanied by a neatly dressed, pretty little girl. It must be their custom, Kensaku thought, to come out for a walk every morning while it was still cool, for he had seen them a couple of times before at about that hour. He looked at their innocent, happy faces, so comfortable and relaxed, and was momentarily touched by envy.

The young woman had not left after all. As he caught sight of her standing on the verandah he was so unnerved that it took all the courage he could muster to continue walking. She stood holding a broom, a hand towel wrapped around her hair in the manner of a serving girl. She had stopped sweeping as the little girl with the man went by, and was gazing after her, obviously charmed by the pretty sight. She had not noticed Kensaku approaching, therefore, and he was given the opportunity to have a really good look at her. Alas, she was not as beautiful as she had seemed the day before. Don't be so fickle, he chided himself, don't be so quick to feel cheated. She must in the meantime have sensed she was being stared at, for her expression suddenly changed, and blushing prettily she retreated into the house. He was no less embarrassed, but at least he was in sufficient control of himself to note that even when caught off guard she carried herself exceedingly well. She's no fool, he thought with satisfaction.

He decided that rather than spend the rest of the morning house-hunting he would go to the museum. It would be cool there, and the exhibits would surely have been changed since he went there soon after arriving in Kyoto. After breakfast he left the inn again and got on a streetcar.

The museum was even quieter than usual. For all he knew, he might have been the only visitor there. Such quiet he had not expected, and he began to find it unsettling. A uniformed guard, his hands behind his back and his eyes riveted to the points of his shoes, walked toward him, looking utterly bored. He walked heavily and deliberately, as though mesmerized by the hard sound of his own footsteps reverberating in the cavernous hall. The sound served only to make the place seem even more boring, even more empty. Even the scroll paintings seemed to Kensaku to be staring back at him, the interloper, in ill-tempered silence. He went around quickly, daring to stop only for a brief moment before each painting. It was when he came to Josetsu's "Gourd and Catfish," with which he had always felt a sense of affinity, that he was at last able to stand and gaze in comfort. It was like meeting an old friend amidst a host of strangers.

More at ease now, he began to find several pictures that invited a response from him. A pine done by an artist of the southern school, a tiger by Lu Chi, large matching scrolls of a hawk and a golden pheasant—these he particularly liked among the Chinese paintings. "Three Patriarchs of the Ritsu Sect," owned by Senyūji, he thought nowhere near as good as the portrait he had seen the day before in Nison'in. Nevertheless, he was much impressed by the painter's handling of the priests' robes flowing over the chairs.

Inanimate things, even if they were not works of art, seemed to demand from him more than a mere passive response; they could affect him in a deeply personal way, arousing in him feelings that ranged from active dislike or an awareness of being rejected, to love and mutual acceptance. So on this day at the museum he had begun by being an unwanted intruder in alien surroundings, and then a mood of enthusiasm, of active participation, had gradually taken hold of him.

Of the sculptures he saw, one in particular drew his attention: it was the imagined likeness of the Bodhisattva Miroku. He had gone all the way to Uzumasa to see it four or five days before, only to discover that Kōryūji had lent it to the museum. It had not been in the temple for quite some time, he was told. Somehow he must have missed it when he was last at the museum.

He began to feel tired and in need of a change of scene. He went outside, and from Nishiōtani he walked across Toribeyama to the falls of Otowa in Kiyomizu. At the teashop there he found a bench close to the water and immediately ordered a cool drink. It was a pleasure to be able to sit down and rest his tired body, and watch the young people of Kyoto, all so colorfully dressed by Tokyo standards, strolling about in the temple grounds.

Remembering that he had heard about a couple of new houses for rent being constructed in the grounds of Kōdaiji, he decided he would now go and look at them. They turned out to be two-storied, semidetached houses, conveniently located and by no means unattractive. He was tempted to take one of them; but too tired to set about looking for the landlord, he walked to Yasaka Shrine and from there toward his inn by way of Shijōdōri. Just on the other side of Shijō Bridge there was a cheap-looking restaurant which, for all its modesty, had a terrace overlooking the river. He went in, and thinking that since there was hardly any breeze that day the terrace would provide little respite from the heat, he chose a table far from the edge, in as shady a spot as possible. What he wanted most of all was a cool drink. He sat sideways on the chair, his head turned toward the back of the terrace, hoping to catch the attention of one of the waitresses. But it was a busy time of day, and quick service seemed out of the question.

Two or three tables away there was a man busily eating with a knife and fork. He raised his knife, and with food still in his mouth called out in a deep voice to a waitress as she rushed by, "Hey, I want some stew! *Stew*, understand?" It was Takai.

Kensaku picked up his straw hat, walked over to his friend's table, and tapped him lightly on the shoulder. "Hullo," he said. Takai turned around quickly, stared for an instant, then jumped up. "Well, well!"

"What a nice surprise," Kensaku said.

"Isn't it!" There was sincere pleasure in Takai's face.

They had not seen each other for two years. These two, with several other friends, had tried to start a magazine. Takai, a European-style painter, was to have designed it, and to have contributed poems besides. Unfortunately there was insufficient financial backing for the venture, and they had had to postpone publication. In the meantime Takai had had a nervous breakdown, caused mostly by a bad stomach, and had gone to a hydropathic sanitarium in Kobe, where he stayed for almost a year. Kensaku had heard that the treatment was successful and that Takai had then gone back to his home somewhere in Tajima.

"Are you living here now?" Kensaku asked.

"No, I'm staying in Nara. I've been there since spring. I'm afraid I didn't bother to tell any of my friends in Tokyo that I'd moved. How about you—when did you come here?"

Kensaku said that he was thinking of settling down in Kyoto. Why not Nara, Takai suggested. "I wouldn't mind Nara," Kensaku said, "but right now I think I'd rather stay in Kyoto." He began to think that Takai might be the very person he might talk to about his recent experience.

Later, at his inn in Higashisanpongi, Kensaku described to his friend in some detail his feelings about the woman he had seen the day before. Takai was clearly surprised to see Kensaku behaving so much like a lovesick twenty-year-old. "You really are serious, aren't you?" he said.

"Yes. I'm convinced that what I feel is genuine. The trouble is, I simply don't know where I'm to go from here. I know from past experience that if I sit back and do nothing she will eventually become a dim memory. But I don't want to let that happen."

"Be positive, then, and do something about it. Find out who she is, then ask someone to act as go-between."

"How simple you make it sound."

"There's no other way. Ask someone to go to them on your behalf."

"I suppose you're right."

"I'd like to help in any way I can, but they're hardly likely to put much trust in a Bohemian like me."

"I'd be so happy if you would speak to them for me."

"Really? Do you really think I would be of use?" He seemed pleased. He thought for a while, then said, "Do you think there might be a room to let in that house? If I stayed there, I could find out at least what sort of people they were. What do you think of the idea?"

Kensaku agreed readily. But immediately his enthusiasm was dampened by the fear lest the overture, after having been successful up to a certain point, should suddenly be spurned. He was aware of the indignity of such fear, he knew only too well how abject it was to expect rejection as though it were a matter of course, but the awareness only increased his misery. I must overcome this fear, he told himself, I must try to have more faith.

"Do you think she'll be there now?" asked Takai.

"I've no idea," Kensaku answered as lightly as possible, smiling. "Shall we go and see?"

"No, I had better go alone."

Kensaku explained carefully where the house was. Takai, nodding, stepped down to the garden. Kensaku was much amused as he watched Takai walk along the path by the river with affected nonchalance, his head held still while presumably his eyes busily searched for the house. But the amusement was quickly replaced by the sobering thought that if with Takai's help he should succeed in establishing some kind of contact with her, he would have to be prepared to tell her family all about his birth. He would have to know right from the start whether or not they would regard it as a serious obstacle.

Takai came back shaking his head and grinning foolishly. "I couldn't find it," he said.

"What a dimwit," Kensaku said, laughing. "How could you miss it? All right, we'll go together."

"But I walked at least a hundred yards, and I saw no one that looked remotely like her."

"She's obviously not in the house, then. Let's go and see anyway."

Kensaku had his clogs brought to the garden, put his hat on, and walked out into the hot sun.

"See that house there with the Korean blinds? That's the one."

"Yes, I see."

"And she's there," Kensaku said, taking care not to look in her direction.

"Where?"

"Right there, can't you see? She's sitting." This time his eyes were gazing at Mt. Hiei.

Takai, whose pace had slackened while he was trying to locate her, said from behind, "Yes, I see her now. Do you think we could recognize the house from the front?"

"Let's see," Kensaku said, and turning around counted the number of houses that stood between it and a conspicuous three-storied one. "It's four houses down from that big one."

At the foot of the bridge they left the path and entered the main street. Kensaku was somewhat nonplussed by his own cheerful mood. That a mere glimpse of the young woman should have so affected him struck him as comical; but this in no way lessened his happiness. And if all went well, he thought, a completely new life, a life that he had never known before, would open up for him. Everything before had truly been shrouded in darkness; and in that darkness, dreadful worms had bred and multiplied. Perhaps now it may all be brought out into the light and cleansed by the sun. The worms would die, the sores would heal; and at last a new life, a life that he wanted, would begin.

He turned to Takai. "Can you really leave Nara so easily?"

"Certainly."

"But aren't you painting something there?"

"Yes, but I'll finish what I'm doing in two or three days. Besides, there are lots of places here that I'd like to paint, so don't worry about me."

They walked beside the mud wall of a temple, turned left and were on Higashisanpongi. Just a few yards down the narrow street was the three-storied house. One, two, three, four—now they were in front of her house. "You'll be going back to the inn, I suppose?" said Takai.

"What do you mean?" exclaimed Kensaku in disbelief. "You're not intending to go in?"

"It's never wise to put such things off," said Takai carelessly. Kensaku was overcome with uneasiness. "It'll be all right," said Takai, dismissing Kensaku with a nod. "I'll see you later." He opened the outer gate and marched down the stone-paved path toward the house.

On his way back to the inn Kensaku remembered a story he had once heard about a certain shabbily attired student who, on seeing a strikingly beautiful girl go past in a rickshaw in Ueno Park, had followed her to her house, presented himself to her father and asked if he might marry her. The proposal was accepted on the spot. Kensaku heard the story from a teacher of Japanese literature who knew the university student, and was inclined to believe that it was true. He had laughed at the time the story was told him, but even as he laughed he had felt distaste for the intrepid young man. The very whimsicality of the act bespoke insincerity, he thought. Besides, he never did like people who did conspicuously odd things, nor, for that matter, those who found such people charming. But, he reassured himself, Takai was a far cry from that university student; he would never stoop to such tricks.

Back at the inn he went to the bathroom and began rubbing himself down with cold water. Takai opened the door and came in. He said with a chagrined smile, "I'm afraid I was turned down. Perhaps they were telling the truth, perhaps not, but they said there was no room available."

Kensaku was not particularly dismayed. "They were probably telling the truth. We can ask the landlady here to find out."

"That's an idea. Why didn't we think of that before?"

The two went back to Kensaku's room. When the landlady appeared with the tea, Takai immediately asked her, "That house down the street—Tōsanrō, I think it's called—do you know it?"

"Yes," she said, pouring the tea.

"Do they take in boarders?"

"I believe so. I'm told that people who are outpatients at the university or the city hospital often stay there."

"Well, I just went in there to see if they had a room."

"I see."

"I was told they didn't. What I can't tell is whether they were telling the truth or whether they turned me down because they don't take in strangers off the street, so to speak."

"I'll find out for you. I used to know the people who owned the place before quite well, but it changed hands a couple of years ago, and I haven't seen very much of the new people. But we share the same caterer, so I'll ask him to speak to them."

She left, then came back with a letter in her hand. "I had completely forgotten about this," she said, giving it to Kensaku. "I'm very sorry. It came around noon."

It was a fairly heavy letter, from Nobuyuki at Kamakura. On the envelope was written the word "important."

3

"It is some time since I last wrote to you. I trust you are well. I enjoyed reading your last letter, and was happy to hear that Kyoto suited you. Have you found a house that you like? You must be looking forward to the autumn. How nice it will be then. No doubt you intend to come to Tokyo for a visit once you have settled in your new house there, but there is something Oei wants you to think about in the meantime.

"The day before yesterday I got a letter from her asking me to stop by at the house on my next trip to Tokyo. She wanted my advice on a certain matter, she said. So yesterday I went to Tokyo to see her.

"I'm sure you know that a cousin of hers, a woman by the name of Osai, has been staying with her in Ōmori. Oei doesn't like to talk much about her cousin, but one can guess that she, too, has a demimonde background. What the woman is doing now, I can't say exactly. All I know is that she is supposed to be running some sort of restaurant in Tientsin. I suspect that her 'restaurant' isn't quite like the ordinary Tokyo restaurant.

"Oei began by expressing her uneasiness over her present situation. Her original intention, she said, of staying with you until you found a nice wife and set up your own household had become confused of late because of the recent complications between you and father. She wasn't so sure any more, she said, that she ought to go on living with you. You may not like my bringing this matter up again, but I believe that Oei has a point.

"Now this cousin of hers—they hadn't seen each other for ten years, apparently—wants Oei to go back to Tientsin with her and help her run the restaurant. Of course by 'help' she means money mostly. At any rate, Oei seems rather enthusiastic about the idea. You seem happy in Kyoto and seem to want to live there, she has some money saved up—over a thousand yen, she says—and if neither you nor I have objections, she would like to go to Tientsin with Osai.

Incidentally, she has no intention of asking for money from the family in Hongō.

"Well, that's the gist of it. We can talk about it in greater detail when you come up to Tokyo. But please think about it in the meantime. I for my part will try to find out exactly what kind of person this Osai is and what kind of business she is trying to involve Oei in.

"I shall also think a little more about the question of money for Oei. I want you if possible to leave that up to me.

"When do you think you might be coming up? It would be nice if you could stop at Kamakura on the way. I look forward to seeing you soon."

In some confusion Kensaku put down the letter. Go to Tientsin and help run a restaurant—what a bizarre notion it was! Yet at the same time Kensaku could not help thinking that it was just the sort of thing Oei might wish to do. But what was this Osai woman up to anyway? Suppose she was a crook about to defraud a gullible cousin?

All that aside, it was a letter that saddened him deeply. True, he had no idea what the relationship between him and Oei would or should be in the future. But was this the way they had to part from each other, as though after all these years they were in the end nothing but strangers? Did the parting have to be so blatantly matter-of-fact? He looked for an answer that would give him solace; but there was none.

The landlady came in with the news that Tōsanrō was indeed full. "But the old invalid gentleman who has the front room will be leaving in about three weeks," she said to Takai. "You can have that room then, they tell me."

"That won't do, I'm afraid," Takai said. "Thank you anyway."

When the landlady left, Kensaku said, "But it was just as well we asked her to find out. We now know at least that the old gentleman will be gone in three weeks."

"You're quite right. What you have to do is to find someone suitable to act as go-between before he goes."

"I wonder if I should ask my brother to come? Something has come up at home that we have to talk about anyway. Of course I can go to Tokyo sooner than he can come here, but I'm not so sure I want to leave Kyoto right now."

"I think it would be a very good idea to have him come here. I take it he can come anytime?"

"I think he can."

"We should try to find out as quickly as possible who she is, where she's from, what her relationship is to the old gentleman, and so on."

"Do you think she's his daughter?"

"I wonder."

"Perhaps his niece?"

They laughed. Takai said, "Not exactly an observant fellow, are you?"

"I haven't been my usual self, you might say. But I'm certain she isn't his daughter."

"Look, if you want to write to your brother, go ahead. I have some shopping to do in Gojō, so I'll go out for a bit."

As soon as he was alone Kensaku began writing his letter to Nobuyuki. A short, businesslike letter would do, he told himself, since he would be seeing Nobuyuki soon. But as he wrote about Oei and about the young woman, he found himself being far more wordy than he had intended. Tired and stiff from having sat in one position for so long, he pulled himself up laboriously and left the room to give the letter to someone to post. The western sun had managed to filter through the latticework in the front hall, warming the floorboards of the perpetually dark corridor.

A little while later he had a hot bath, then sat down on the verandah with a fan in his hand, exactly as he had done the day before. He looked out toward Kōjin Bridge and saw Takai coming back. He walked quickly, wearing an innocent expression on his face. As he passed the back of Tōsanrō he turned his head toward it—rather boldly, Kensaku thought.

"I had a good look at her," he said with a bright smile as he came over the plank into the garden.

"I don't doubt it, judging by the way you were staring."

"You know, she looks just like one of those beauties on the 'Feather Screen.'"

Kensaku thought the comparison rather apt, and was very pleased by it. "Oh, do you think so?" he said, blushing a little.

While Takai had his bath Kensaku strolled out to the path. He did not venture far this time, and was content with an occasional glimpse of her figure moving about in the distance.

That night the two friends went to a cinema in Shinkyōgoku and saw an amusingly modernized German version of *A Midsummer Night's Dream*. It was quite late when they got back to Kensaku's inn in Higashisanpongi.

4

The morning of the third day after that was made cool by the unseasonable rain that began soon after dawn. Kensaku, who was accustomed to being awakened early by the bright sunlight outside, was for a change allowed to doze comfortably until late that morning. It was Nobuyuki who woke him up. The first thing he said was, "I haven't had breakfast yet. Can I have some here?"

Kensaku, having slept relatively well, was able to get up with some semblance of friendliness. He was not always so good-natured when getting out of bed.

They ate in silence, gazing toward the river that was almost hidden by the veil of rain. Nobuyuki finally broke the silence. "I told Oei about you, and she was terribly pleased. She kept on saying how she hoped it would work out all right. I feel as she does, of course, and I want to help as much as I can. But let's talk about Oei first. I really can't tell whether or not she ought to be encouraged to go into this business. I realize that her background being what it is, she would probably be more comfortable working with someone like her cousin than doing something more ordinary and respectable. That doesn't mean that she really knows what she's getting herself into, of course, but I can hardly reject her plan out of hand when I have no alternative to suggest. Besides, there's the possibility that it will turn out to be just the right thing for her. She's been completely persuaded by Osai, you know, and is very enthusiastic. If we object, no doubt she'll give up the idea, but she'll be terribly disappointed. So what I suggest is this: let her do what she wants, and if the venture proves a failure, we'll help her out later. I'm talking about money again, of course, but what I mean is that you or I can hold in trust for her the money she'll get from Hongō and whatever you yourself want to give her, and in the meantime she can use her own savings for this business."

"What will she be doing exactly?"

"Well, it's nothing I can approve of. This Osai woman, as I told you, runs a restaurant in Tientsin, and apparently also has so-called resident geisha in her employ. It's a double business, you might say. One can guess that she defines 'geisha' rather loosely. Well, she finds that she can't run both sides of the establishment very well all by herself. So she wants Oei to go over there and be in charge of the geisha. They'll still be in the same house, but financially the restaurant and the geisha business will become separate."

Kensaku thought he knew all he needed to know. "She could hardly have found a more disreputable occupation, could she?"

"No, she couldn't. But say she wants to open a tobacconist's shop or a knickknack shop in Tokyo—there'll be the rent to begin with, then she'll have to furnish the place properly, and before you know it, she won't have any money left to lay in the stock."

"I hardly know what to say when you put it so realistically. But surely there's something a little nicer that she can do?"

"You've got to realize that Oei is after all originally from the demimonde. That's where she's had her experience, and that's where she instinctively feels she'll be most comfortable. If we knew Osai better I might have suggested giving Oei all the money that was due her, but since we really don't know that Osai can be trusted, we ought, I think, to put something aside for Oei just in case things go wrong."

"I don't know what to say. I'd obviously prefer to see Oei get into some other kind of business, but I don't know what that might be. As a matter of fact, I'd be quite happy if she were to decide there was no immediate need to set herself up in business and were to stay with me for the next two or three years. You may think me sentimental, but I can't help thinking there's something awfully wrong about our having to part like this."

"I see."

"You said in your letter that she was concerned about father's attitude. But that would cease to be a problem if I were to get married."

"Perhaps. But if you're going to part in two or three years' time anyway, you might as well do so now. There are times when conditions are just right for doing something. This is the opportune time for Oei to go. If she doesn't, she may find that conditions are not so favorable next time."

Kensaku thought he knew what Nobuyuki meant by "conditions." Amused, yet irritated, by his brother's obliqueness, he decided to be blunt. "Oh," he said, "you're talking about money from Hongō, are you?"

Nobuyuki was unexpectedly solemn. "Yes, among other things. As I suggested in my letter, you had better leave everything to me. Try not to interfere. The trouble with you is that you get terribly touchy whenever money is mentioned. The first thing you do is to show contempt for it. It's an obsession, this attitude of yours toward money. I suppose it's better than being greedy, but it's not very intelligent."

"You're talking nonsense."

"All right. The question is, do you agree with my suggestion or don't you?"

"You mean, has Oei my blessings in her proposed venture?"

"Quite."

"Hardly. But having no better alternative to suggest, I suppose I shall have to give my consent—a grudging consent, mind you."

"It's settled, then. Just remember that if she finds herself in trouble, she can come to us for help."

"When does she want to leave Japan?"

"As soon as she knows it's all right for her to go, I gather. She wants to leave with Osai if she can, and Osai is leaving very soon. We should let Oei know immediately that she has our consent. Let's send her a telegram sometime today." Nobuyuki paused, then seeing that Kensaku was not about to say anything, went on: "That's that, then. Now tell me about yourself. I don't suppose there's much more you can tell me than what you told me in your letter. Is she still here in Kyoto?"

"I think so, though of course I can't be sure. You must understand that I can't keep a constant check on her whereabouts."

"I don't suppose Takai has been able to help much?"

"No."

"Well, there's one thing I thought we might do. Did you ever meet Yamazaki? He was on the baseball team in college."

"No."

"He was the same year as me. He was a pre-medical student, so we didn't take the same courses, but we were in the same dormitory and became quite good friends. Anyway, I think he is on the staff of the university hospital here. I've no idea what department he's in, but I thought he might know someone who could be helpful."

Kensaku nodded uncertainly, not because he had doubts about Yamazaki, but because he could not afford to allow himself to be optimistic. To protect himself against any possible disappointment—that had become his habitual concern.

"And if that doesn't work out," Nobuyuki continued, "then we'll ask Ishimoto." What he had in mind was that Ishimoto's family had been Kyoto aristocrats before the Restoration, and that he was therefore bound to have useful connections in the area.

"But by that time she'll have gone home," Kensaku said.

"Perhaps, but why should her going home be a disadvantage necessarily? After all, we might have even better contacts in her home province. Incidently, what are we going to do today? Had you any plans?"

"No."

"Shall we call on Yamazaki, then? Or shall we forget about it today, and go out and have a good meal somewhere?"

"Either would be all right with me."

"I suppose we ought to try to speak to Yamazaki as soon as possible?"

"I'll leave that up to you."

"In that case let's try to see Yamazaki today. We can have dinner together afterward."

"All right, let's do that," Kensaku said.

5

The preliminary stages of the marriage discussion proceeded with remarkable smoothness, for it had luckily turned out that the senior doctor under whom Yamazaki worked was looking after the old gentleman, and almost immediately Nobuyuki and Kensaku had been able to find out who the young woman was.

She was the old gentleman's niece, and belonged to a family of substance in Tsuruga. She had come to Kyoto to help look after her uncle and to do some shopping.

Another chance circumstance that proved fortunate for Kensaku was that the man—a certain Mr. S—who recommended the old gentleman to Yamazaki's senior came from a family that had once been retained by the Ishimotos. This fact became known to Kensaku and Nobuyuki when Yamazaki happened to mention the man's name in Kensaku's room as the landlady was pouring the tea. "Is that the Mr. S who is on the city council?" she had said. "If so, then his family used to be retainers of the Ishimotos."

Nobuyuki had immediately gone back to Tokyo to enlist Ishimoto's help. It was extremely gratifying to Kensaku to know that his brother was so genuinely concerned for his welfare. It was less than a year ago, Kensaku now remembered with wry amusement, that he had asked Ishimoto to stop hovering over him like a nervous grandmother and offering to help find a wife for him. "Not so touchy any more, are you?" he could imagine Ishimoto saying when they met. Ah well, he thought, Ishimoto was a friend, and he had every right to say something of the sort. He would be pleased, as Nobuyuki was, that Kensaku should so unexpectedly soon have found someone to be serious about. And though it was only through chance that he was being asked to take part in the discussions, he would be pleased nonetheless that Kensaku and Nobuyuki had come to him. Kensaku could not but be thankful that it was Ishimoto, and not some other man, whom chance had thrown into the affair.

Perhaps I'm not so unfortunate, Kensaku thought. I have often acted like a spoiled child, wanting to do only what I felt like doing; yet there are those who have forgiven me, who have offered me love. And this love is more important than the hurts I have received because of my birth.

He continued to visit temples. And often he left the inn and returned to it by means of the path along the river bank. He continued his house-hunting too. In a place called Kitanobō, by Nanzenji Temple, he found a charming cottage with a thatched roof, standing by itself, that he liked much more than those he had looked at in the grounds of Kōdaiji. It was an ideal temporary residence for a bachelor. For a married couple, it would be a little too small; but Kensaku was not about to tempt fate by looking for a house that would be more appropriate for a married couple. Besides, he was much drawn to this cottage which had so clearly been built by someone who wanted to live in it. He decided to rent it.

After a few days Ishimoto arrived. Kensaku was grateful that he refrained from making pointed jokes. Their meeting was marred, however, by an unfortunate misunderstanding which occurred when Ishimoto said, "Naturally I intend to find out all I can about them, but we on our part must be prepared to tell all."

"Yes, of course," said Kensaku, wondering what Ishimoto meant. Presumably he meant his birth; but could Ishimoto possibly know all about it, when he himself had found out the truth only recently? Uncertainly he said to Ishimoto, "I take it you're referring to my birth?" By this question he had intended only to make sure that this was what Ishimoto meant; for it was indeed his wish that the matter be brought out into the open from the start. But, alas, the question was completely misinterpreted by Ishimoto, who took it as an expression of Kensaku's reluctance to have the unpleasant secret divulged. He made a face, then proceeded to lecture to Kensaku on the advisability of candor.

Kensaku, though wounded by the misunderstanding, refrained from making any attempt to correct it. No matter what he might have said, it would have sounded defensive and unconvincing. And so he sat still, hiding his irritation, and listened to the long lecture until it was over. He would talk to Nobuyuki later, he told himself, and have him clear up the misunderstanding.

This minor piece of unpleasantness might have been avoided if Kensaku had talked openly about the subject to Nobuyuki earlier. But hating to appear too obsessed by it, he had allowed himself half-consciously to ignore it. Perhaps he was not wrong; for supposing he had mentioned it, Nobuyuki might well have thought, "Oh God, it's so like Kensaku to bring *that* up again."

Back in Tokyo, before Ishimoto's departure for Kyoto, when he, Nobuyuki and Oei met in the house at Ōmori to discuss the prospective marriage negotiations, Oei had insisted, for simple and obvious reasons, that no mention should be made of Kensaku's birth. Ishimoto, on the other hand, had argued that it would be wrong not to be candid about it from the start. Indeed, he had said, he would have no part in the negotiations if he could not be allowed to mention it. Of course he was right, and Kensaku would have agreed with him had he been present. Unfortunately, Ishimoto had come away from the meeting wondering why Kensaku had not said anything about it to Nobuyuki; otherwise, Ishimoto would presumably not have been so quick to misinterpret Kensaku's innocent question.

Happily, Kensaku was able to prevent himself from brooding over Ishimoto's unfair assumption; and the matter was allowed to rest there.

Ishimoto had taken a room at an inn he knew well in Fuyachō. Saying he had arranged to meet Mr. S there at two that afternoon, he left after a while.

It occurred to Kensaku that one way of telling the other party about himself was to write an autobiographical story. But the project came to a stop after he had written the preface entitled "The Hero's Reminiscences." He decided not to show them even this short piece, so afraid was he of seeming to be inviting their sentimental pity. Later he learned that Ishimoto in the meantime had shown the other party his letter to Nobuyuki from Onomichi, in which he had talked about his birth, having first inked out those passages referring to Oei.

Kensaku believed it his duty to tell them all about his earlier feelings toward Oei, but try as he might, he could not bring himself to do so. Why, he was not sure. That to do so would be tantamount to exposing that beautiful person to something shoddy, that it would be an insult to her dignity, was possibly the reason. Ishimoto for his part showed no inclination to talk about Oei, and so in the end Kensaku merely resolved to confess fully at some fitting time in the future.

The sun was about to set when Kensaku came back to the inn by way of the path. He had that afternoon visited a couple of bookstores in the neighborhood. A man was waiting for him with a note from Ishimoto. "If you are free this evening," it said, "come to my place and meet Mr. S. The bearer of this note will bring you in his rickshaw."

Kensaku went immediately to Ishimoto's inn. Mr. S. had not yet arrived. "I haven't been able to find out much about her," Ishimoto said. "But I have some general information about the family." The old gentleman had been a member of the National Assembly in the early years of the century, and through their being in the same party he and Mr. S had come to know each other. The young woman was the daughter of his sister, and had graduated from the girls' school in Tsuruga two years before. As she was now of marriageable age, she had come up to Kyoto to pick up a new wardrobe. That was about all Ishimoto had to tell.

Nothing particularly serious would be discussed that evening, he added. Mr. S simply thought it would be nice if he could take the two of them out to dinner.

Mr. S turned out to be a skinny man in his fifties, going rather bald. To hide the baldness he had grown his soft, sparse hair long on one side of his head near the ear and then had stretched the pathetic strands over the top to the other side. Ishimoto's given name being Michitaka, the gentleman kept addressing him as "Master Michi."

He was going to take them, he said, to a restaurant that specialized in snapping turtle meat. They went outside and caught a streetcar going in the direction of Kitano. The restaurant was at the end of a cul-de-sac bordered on one side by the mud wall of a temple. A small lantern, protected by wire netting, hung under the low eaves in the front. The entryway inside had an earth floor, and the front room which one crossed to get to the stairs had a floor of darkly glowing wood that must have been several centuries old. The stairs, too, glowed with age. It wouldn't be at all surprising, Kensaku thought, if someone dressed like the hero of a play by Chikamatsu were to suddenly come down these stairs. The steps near the top had the appropriate wormholes. They were a bit showy, but Kensaku decided the effect wasn't too bad.

The turtle meat was delicious. Kensaku remembered being told by an acquaintance who lived in a mansion in Kitano that a man from this restaurant used to come to the pond in his grounds to catch toads. But that was a long time ago, Kensaku reassured himself, and went on eating.

The three men talked little about the prospective marriage. Most of the talking was done by Ishimoto and Mr. S, who seemed still to think of their relationship as that of lord and retainer. It was not an easy social situation; for Mr. S could hardly change his deferential style of speech whenever he addressed Kensaku, and Kensaku in turn was forced to reply with equal humility, for he could hardly treat Mr. S as an inferior and accept the elaborate deference with Ishimoto's equanimity. For Kensaku, then, it became clearly easier to say nothing than to have to mumble mouthfuls of honorifics. Ishimoto made several valiant but futile attempts to bring Kensaku into the conversation, such as: "So you've found a house you like. That means you'll be settling down in Kyoto, eh?"

After dinner Kensaku and Ishimoto parted from Mr. S and took a walk around Maruyama.

"I have business to attend to in Tokyo the day after tomorrow," Ishimoto said, "so I'll be going on the night train tomorrow. I'll come back to Kyoto after about a week—which day exactly I'll know when I hear from S. There is nothing you can do in the meantime, so feel free to go back to Tokyo anytime you like." He waited, then went on. "I've left the matter entirely in S's hands. He seems to think it's likely to proceed smoothly, but I don't want you to be too optimistic, just in case it doesn't."

Kensaku said suddenly, "I'll go back to Tokyo tomorrow too. I'll catch the morning express."

"Let's go together, then."

"All right."

Shortly thereafter they said good-night and walked back to their respective inns.

6

Kensaku left Ishimoto at Yokohama to change trains. It was already evening when he got off at Ōmori Station. Carrying a small bag he walked down the familiar road toward his house.

Oei rushed out to the front hall to greet him. Before saying anything else she expressed her pleasure at the recent happy turn of events. Though made uncomfortable by her certainty, he was nonetheless gratified that she should be so happy for him.

The Osai woman was not in, having gone to Tokyo for the day. Oei and Kensaku sat down to dinner together for the first time in some weeks.

"What is she like anyway?" Oei asked.

"Do you mean what does she look like?"

"Yes. Think of someone we know that looks like her."

"I can't think of anyone right away. But Takai thought she resembled one of those beauties on the 'Feather Screen.' "

He went upstairs to fetch a book on Oriental art. There was one, he knew, that contained a reproduction of the screen. He brought it down and opened it in front of Oei, only to find that the reproduction was of just one panel of the screen, one that depicted a lady bearing little resemblance to the young woman in Kyoto. "No, she looks a lot better than this," he said.

"Really! She must be very beautiful."

They continued in this vein for some time, neither wanting to change the subject and begin talking about Oei's future. But it could not be avoided forever, and at last Oei said, "I was so relieved to know that both you and Nobuyuki approved."

Kensaku was at a loss for a suitable reply; for though it was not untrue to say that he had approved, it was not entirely true either. Yes, he had given his consent, but he had given it with obvious reluctance. There was so much more that he had wanted to say to Nobuyuki at the time. Nobuyuki must have known this, he must have known with what reluctance Kensaku had agreed. It was disingenuous of him, then, not to have communicated any of this to Oei.

"I don't know what Nobuyuki told you," Kensaku said, "but the truth is I'm not very enthusiastic. I approved only because I couldn't disapprove. Actually, I hate the idea." There was surprise on Oei's face. "Supposing I do get married," Kensaku went on, "that doesn't mean I'll want you to go away immediately. It would be nice if you could stay on for two or three more years and help take care of the house."

"Really? Of course, leaving you now will be very painful for me. But, as I keep telling myself, we'll have to part sometime anyway. Then there's your father in Hongō. I suppose I shouldn't say this, but you know, I'm rather scared of him. I always have been, but recently I've become more scared of him than ever. I stopped going to Hongō after that trouble you had with him over me, but I always have the feeling that he's thinking awful things about me."

"That's all in your imagination. I think there's something the matter with you these days. Are you feeling all right?"

"Perhaps you're right. Yes, it's possible I haven't been well lately."

"I'm sure that's what it is. After all, there's no earthly reason why you should be afraid of him. He can't possibly blame you for the trouble that's arisen between him and me. You were an innocent bystander, that's all."

"It's not that simple. He has never liked me, you know."

"All right, but why worry about it? Much more important is your health. If you aren't feeling well, see a doctor at once. Anyway, you should have thought more carefully before deciding to do something so drastic as going away to Tientsin."

Oei clearly had not expected such opposition from Kensaku at this late date. She had been led to believe, she said in a complaining tone, that he approved; otherwise she would not have told Osai that she would go with her; he should know that Osai was in Tokyo right now, making all the arrangements and doing the shopping for the two of them.

Kensaku had not intended to express himself quite so bluntly, and now he was a little sorry. Why exactly he had not made his feelings known to her more tentatively, whether it was for her sake or for his own that he was being so difficult, he was not sure. But he did know that like a spoiled child he was refusing to accept the fact that Oei could disappear from his life with such simplicity. Why wasn't she more reluctant to leave him, he couldn't help thinking, how could she accept so readily their impending separation? He had been more reasonable about her back in Kyoto; but now that he sat face to face with her, he could not control his childish resentment.

I must not be so resentful, he told himself, I must act like an adult. And in an effort to atone for his ungracious behavior, he embarked on an inept conciliatory speech.

The Osai woman returned in a rickshaw, carrying a large bundle. She was a tall, skinny woman with a sharp face, rather older than Kensaku had imagined. Kensaku took an instant dislike to her.

"So this is Kensaku," she said to Oei, then turned to him and bowed skittishly like a young coquette. "I'm Osai. How do you do." She brought her face close to his and gazed at him with unabashed familiarity, all the while grinning broadly. The crow's feet around her eyes were very noticeable, and her gums were not a nice color. Kensaku cringed, feeling all the more threatened by her evident goodwill. He had not thought that she could be this common.

He was first appalled, then irritated, by Oei's readiness to associate with such a woman. Had she no sense of discrimination? No, he thought disappointedly, she hadn't.

Osai brought out of her bundle several brightly colored kimonos. They were secondhand obviously, for they all had a slightly soiled look about them. She would stand up from time to time, and putting a kimono up against her chest would explain to Oei its particular qualities.

Kensaku was clearly out of place here; besides, he was tired. He bid the two women good-night and went upstairs to his room, taking the art book with him. Sprawled out in his bed he leafed through the book. What gave him particular pleasure were the reproductions of ancient works of art. He had seen some of them in the original in Kyoto recently, but this night the reproductions had a certain appeal for him. In this way, he thought with gentle contentment, a world that he had not known before was opening up for him.

But as he lay thus in his bed thinking of marriage and the new life it would bring, he remembered Oei downstairs. The two women were talking in lowered voices, presumably about their joint venture. What would Oei's new life be like, he wondered; what happiness lay in store for her? Was it right for him to let her go off like this, all on her own?

It was nice to be back in his own bed. He turned the light off and sank into a deep, peaceful sleep.

By the time he woke up the next morning Osai had already left for Tokyo again. One could recruit women from a distance anytime, Oei explained, but when it came to clothes for them, one had to stock up a whole year's supply in Japan. But why Osai was doing all the buying of clothes—this surely belonged to Oei's side of the business— was not made clear to Kensaku.

Thinking that there was nothing he could now do or say to dissuade Oei, he went upstairs to do some packing himself. The books that he had borrowed he put aside, and the rest he put into several trunks.

In the afternoon he went to Ishimoto's house in Ushigome. Ishimoto was not in. Had Kensaku telephoned beforehand, he would have had occasion to remember Ishimoto's saying in Kyoto that he had business to attend to that day. Not particularly disappointed— he had had nothing important in mind to say to his friend—Kensaku walked toward Ginza.

He didn't want to have to see Osai again so soon. He guessed that she knew he had once proposed to Oei; and no doubt the information would have given her all kinds of ideas. Indeed, Kensaku thought he could guess even the sort of things she would be saying about him to Oei behind his back.

Partly to avoid Osai's company, then, and partly from a desire to hear Tokyo speech at its liveliest—it would be a pleasant change after all those weeks in Kyoto—he waited till evening and then went to a vaudeville theatre to listen to a raconteur. It was quite late when he returned to Ōmori.

Oei and Osai were still up, talking under the electric light in the morning room. Osai was too preoccupied with whatever she was saying to pay much attention to Kensaku. Without so much as giving him a glance she poured some tea into a cup, pushed it toward him, and went on talking to Oei. "And like a fool I didn't know that since that spring they had been very thick," she said. She rubbed her emaciated thumb and little finger together in front of Oei's nose, and added with a coarse sneer, "Like this, if you see what I mean?" In embarrassment Oei looked down, saying nothing. "How do you think I felt? There was my patron, carrying on with my younger sister behind my back. He was bad enough, but that bitch, she was living on what I earned, don't you know? So I chased her with a kitchen knife—just to scare her, mind you."

Kensaku didn't think he wanted to hear much more. He was about to put his teacup down and get up when Oei, noticing his discomfort, raised her eyes and said, "Would you like some cake?" "No, thanks," he said, and again prepared to leave.

Osai, realizing that she had made a faux pas, put on a bright smile. "It wasn't a nice story, I'm sorry."

"Was Mr. Ishimoto in?" Oei asked.

"No, he wasn't," said Kensaku, pulling himself nearer to the brazier. "Actually, he told me back in Kyoto that he would be busy today, but I completely forgot. So I went to hear a raconteur."

"So you like things like that, do you, Kensaku?" said Osai. "So do I. But over there, we don't get good performers often. I once put up a couple at my place, the husband was a raconteur—I forget his name—and the wife was a lute player. She called herself Asahishijō. She had a fine voice. Lu Yuan-hung had inscribed something on the lute for her, I remember." She had put her hands up against her forehead, her elbows resting, on the table. Thus shielded from the bright light above, her face looked a lot younger. The wrinkles had disappeared, and the dryness of the skin was no longer noticeable. She appeared at that moment quite attractive to Kensaku—as she knew very well she would. He looked at her thoughtfully, forced to concede that once she might have been beautiful.

Osai left for Gifu the next morning, having arranged to meet Oei in Kyoto and from there journey to Tientsin together. Gifu was her home, and apparently she had a few things to take care of there. "Don't worry about Oei," she said as she left the house with Oei and the maid who were seeing her off. The remark elicited no response from Kensaku.

In the afternoon Kensaku went to Kamakura to see Nobuyuki. He was in bed with a cold, his throat wrapped in a compress. Beside the bed sat Ishimoto. "I haven't heard yet," he said as soon as he saw Kensaku. The comment was quite unnecessary, for it had never occurred to Kensaku that Ishimoto would be hearing from Kyoto so soon. The two talked briefly about the prospective marriage, while Nobuyuki tried unsuccessfully to take an interest in the conversation. Kensaku looked at him, and saw that his eyes were dull with fever. "Have someone come over from Hongō. Shall I telephone them when I get back to Tokyo?"

"No, I'll be all right. I'll just have to let it take its course. In two or three days I'll be much better, so long as I stay in bed like this."

"But you really should have someone here with you, someone who could work an inhaler for you all the time. You'd recover more quickly that way."

"Perhaps so."

"You don't have an inhaler, I take it?"

"No. I suppose I should at least have that. Could you go out and get me one?"

Kensaku immediately went into town and bought the apparatus. When he returned he found Nobuyuki dozing fitfully and Ishimoto reading a thick book, bound in the Western style, on Zen. His expression made it clear that he would have preferred a book on some other subject.

Kensaku got the inhaler ready and brought it near Nobuyuki's face. When he was about to start it the landlady came in. Accepting gratefully her offer to stay and keep the inhaler going, Kensaku explained how it worked, then left with Ishimoto.

On the platform at the station they met a doctor of Ishimoto's acquaintance, also waiting to go back to Tokyo. Ishimoto mentioned Nobuyuki, and the doctor said since he was coming to Kamakura again the next day, he would be glad to look in on him.

Over the scene that sped past the train window night was about to fall. Kensaku sat huddled in the corner by the window, overcome by sadness as he thought of Oei's impending departure. The sadness was not only for himself, but for Oei too; and it was made more poignant by the dusk outside.

7

Knowing that they would soon be parting from each other, Kensaku tried to stay at home with Oei as much as possible. This took some effort, and he quickly began to feel constrained and bored. Never before had he felt so awkward in Oei's company; never had he had so little to talk to her about.

But Oei was too busy to be bored. She was absorbed in her last-minute womanly duties, seeing to it that every piece of Kensaku's clothing was clean and without a loose stitch.

One morning Kensaku woke up earlier than usual. Feeling strangely nervous he dressed immediately and left the house without waiting for his breakfast. At the railroad station he found that there would be a long wait for the next regular train for Tokyo. Anxious to be off, he decided to go instead by the electric line, which would take him to Shinagawa Station.

As he sat on the train thinking of nothing in particular, he suddenly remembered that he had had a dream that morning just before daybreak. It was this dream, he now realized, that was the cause of his nervousness. He tried to recall it, but much of it remained vague. What was most clear was that it had made him uncomfortable.

The dream began, he thought, with his visiting T, who had recently returned from the South Seas. Inside a large, crude building that looked like a gymnasium were many cages of the sort traveling circuses put their beasts in. In one of them he saw dozens of tiny baboons, no larger than squirrels, sitting huddled together on perches. His initial fascination soon turned into acute discomfort. "I have to go, good-bye," he said to T, as he hastily withdrew. He found himself in front of the huge, old-fashioned gate of the Ueno Museum. He was surrounded by a ring of detectives, converging on him from a distance. He couldn't see them, but he knew they were there. He had somehow committed a treasonable offense.

From behind the gate he took a peek outside. Could it be Sunday, he wondered, for soldiers ambled past in little, scattered groups. He said to one of them, "Would you be interested in deserting?" The soldier complied with alacrity. Behind the gate they exchanged clothes. "This will do nicely," he said to himself. "And I've done the soldier a favor too." Leaving the soldier, now turned civilian, to go his own way, Kensaku walked nonchalantly toward a quiet-looking place in the park. The path narrowed, and on either side was a high embankment. A man dressed like a stationmaster came toward him, and as they were about to pass each other, pounced on him. He had seen through Kensaku's disguise. No wonder, for when Kensaku examined himself carefully, he saw that his appearance was anything but military. The collar, unhooked, hung limply around his neck; the trousers, obviously belonging to someone much larger, clung despairingly and precariously to his hips. In short he looked ghastly. Terrified by the arrest though he was, he could not help smiling at his own appalling ineptitude. Such, then, was the gist of his dream.

It was just as well, he thought, that he remembered he had had such a dream. If he had not identified the source of his uneasiness, the entire day might have been ruined.

He had not come out with the express intention of calling on Ishimoto, but that was what he did, hoping that perhaps by now there would have been some communication from Kyoto.

The master had just got out of bed, the maid said, and led him to a cane chair on the verandah. It was a nice, still morning, with a touch of autumn in the air. The light of the sun, still very low in the sky, filtered into the mossy Japanese garden. In a cage hanging from the eaves above was a Java sparrow, singing busily. Its song had a low, crackling sound to it, yet was full and without harshness.

"How do you do," said Ishimoto's older daughter as she came up to him with some newspapers folded lengthwise. She was about six. She was followed by her younger sister, a fat little child of about two. She toddled toward him, holding out her father's morning mail. "Me too," she said, handing the letters to him. "Thank you," said Kensaku, and patted her on the head. The older girl ran out of the room, leaving her sister to toddle after her as best she could.

Kensaku put the newspapers on his lap, then reached forward to put the letters on the table. The top one was rather fat, and was addressed to "The Honorable Viscount Ishimoto Michitaka." Something about it suggested to Kensaku that it was from Mr. S.

Ishimoto appeared, his hair dampened with water and neatly combed. Kensaku pointed at the letter on top of the pile and said, "Might that be from Mr. S?" Ishimoto picked it up and looked at it. "Yes, it is." He pulled the letter out and began reading it. After what seemed to Kensaku an inordinately long time, Ishimoto rolled the letter up and handed it to him. "It's a good letter," he said.

It was indeed a good letter. The young woman, Mr. S wrote, had besides her mother a brother considerably older than herself; Mr. N, the old gentleman, would talk the matter over carefully with them and reply in due course. What affected Kensaku particularly was Mr. N's reply, as reported by Mr. S, when informed of the unusual circumstances of Kensaku's birth: "Whether that is bad or not depends on the kind of person he is; if he himself has not allowed it to affect him adversely, then it is of no significance to me."

Mr. S. ended the letter with a request for a photograph of Kensaku and a copy of something he had written.

"For an old man, this Mr. N seems unusually enlightened," said Ishimoto. Kensaku said nothing, but inside he was terribly moved. With great effort he fought back the tears that threatened to fill his eyes.

While they were having breakfast a man came to see Ishimoto on a matter of business. Kensaku decided that this was an opportune time for him to go. Ishimoto saw him to the front hall, and said he would send Mr. S's letter immediately to Nobuyuki.

Without intending to, Kensaku walked quickly. The pace was perhaps in keeping with his buoyant frame of mind. Could he venture to assess his chances at seven in ten? Yes, he could, he told himself with a confidence he had not felt in a long time; indeed, he would be doing himself an injustice if he were less optimistic.

The young woman seemed at that moment very close; his image of her was life-size, not the distant figure that she had become since his return to Tokyo. And very soon he was seeing fragmented domestic scenes, in which she acted out her role as his wife. For the time being, then, his concern for Oei and her future retreated to the back of his mind.

When he became conscious of his surroundings again, he noticed that it was turning into a windy day. He walked toward Ginza, thinking that he would look for a farewell present for Oei. A watch was what he had tentatively in mind, with some suitable inscription engraved on the back. After going into several shops he finally found a watch he liked, with a nice old-fashioned shape to it. But he decided to forego the inscription, having failed to think of anything appropriate to say. He had come out with little money on him, so he arranged to have the watch delivered to him.

By noon he was back in Ōmori. When he told Oei about the letter from Mr. S, she was very moved.

That afternoon Kensaku wrote a letter to his friend Takai in Nara and told him all that had happened since they were last together in Kyoto. He then wrote a letter of thanks to Mr. S, and with it he sent a photograph of himself and a couple of magazines containing short pieces by him. That these pieces were to be read for highly pragmatic purposes with little heed paid to whatever artistic merit they might have did not please Kensaku. On the other hand, they were not things that he would have been happy to exhibit as examples of his craft as a writer either. They were, he now felt as he looked at them again, pretty shabby efforts.

Within a week he received a reply from Mr. S. It would be most convenient, he wrote, if Kensaku could come to Kyoto in two or three days' time. Mr. N was obviously anxious to meet Kensaku before returning to Tsuruga, and had repeatedly asked when Kensaku would be in Kyoto again. Mr. N was due to leave very soon; of course Mr. S would not presume to press Kensaku to do so, but if he could possibly find the time to make the trip, it would be extremely convenient.

Miss Naoko (that was the name of the young woman) had left Kyoto yesterday. It had been arranged that her elder brother would send a photograph of her directly to Kensaku.

Kensaku showed the letter to Oei. "What am I to do?" he asked in consternation.

"Of course you must go."

"But I feel I'm being summoned for an interview with some prospective employer!" He had been dubious about the dignity of having to present examples of his writing for their inspection; but this touched his pride even more.

"You were going there anyway ten days or so from now, weren't you? This is hardly the time for you to start worrying about your dignity. After all, Mr. S, like Mr. Ishimoto, is only trying to help you."

"You're right, I suppose," said Kensaku, making up his mind to go. "But will you be all right without me?"

Oei laughed. "What are you talking about? You were absolutely useless when we moved to this house, remember? I'll get more done without you hanging about the house."

Kensaku laughed too. "All right, then, I'll go. I don't want to be in your way, after all."

Oei, pleased that Kensaku was in so agreeable a frame of mind, said, "Yes, a terrible nuisance, that's what you are."

Their landlord had lowered the monthly rent on the understanding that they would stay in the house for at least a year. Now that they were leaving before they had been there for a year, they owed the landlord some compensation. It had been Kensaku's custom to send the maid over to him with the rent every month, but this time he went to his house in Sannō himself. And from there, after having concluded his business with the landlord, he telephoned Ishimoto to tell him that he would be leaving for Kyoto the next morning.

8

Mr. S was on the platform at Kyoto Station to meet him. "Leaving tomorrow" was all Kensaku had said in the telegram he sent him the day before, so that Mr. S's presence on the platform was both unexpected and gratifying. It soothed his wounded pride, and made him feel even a little ashamed of his prickliness.

He would call on Kensaku the next morning, Mr. S said, and take him to meet the old gentleman. Kensaku had brought with him packages containing some things that he valued, such as fragile ceramic pieces, so he took leave of Mr. S at the station and went straight to the inn at Higashisanpongi in a rickshaw.

Mr. S appeared the next morning at the appointed hour. Tōsanrō, where Mr. N was staying, was only a short walk away from Kensaku's inn.

The maid went inside with Mr. S's card; then the old gentleman's wife, whom Kensaku had seen from the path by the river, came out to the front hall, dressed rather more formally than usual. "Please come in," she said, and led them down a narrow, dark corridor. "It's a shabby place, I'm afraid."

Mr. N sat upright, his back turned toward the river. He was wearing a light jacket over his kimono. Seeing the old gentleman dressed thus, Kensaku became a little self-conscious about his own attire, which was as usual informal.

"How do you do," said Mr. N in a voice that was surprisingly clear and resonant for a man so slight. "I hear that you have decided to settle down in Kyoto for a while."

"Yes," said Kensaku. As he was not about to say any more, Mr. S adroitly added a remark or two on his behalf.

And so went the conversation, with little help from Kensaku. But he was far from feeling as awkward as he must have appeared to the other two. He had come expecting to be closely scrutinized by Mr. N, and was much gratified to find that the old gentleman, presumably out of courtesy, seemed in fact to be trying his best not to look at him. He had been immediately put at ease, then, however uncomfortable he might have seemed.

A simple meal was served, and instead of the maid Mrs. N herself poured the saké. But no one drank much. The conversation never touched on what was uppermost in Kensaku's mind. There was some mention of Dr. Yamazaki, followed by a discussion of the fishing industry in Tsuruga.

In the old days, the old gentleman said, the fish caught around there was mostly salted and put away in storehouses. When, just before the Restoration, the Mito rebels under Takeda Kōunsai came to Tsuruga—they wanted to reach Kyoto, and since the Tōkaidō was closed to them, they had come by the northern route—they were promptly arrested and locked up in these storehouses. After some days in these dark, damp prisons caked with salt, the rebels got itchy sores all over their bodies. He couldn't bear to look at the poor fellows, the old gentleman said. He then pointed to the shelves in the alcove behind Kensaku and said to his wife, "Bring me that pouch, if you will."

"Excuse me," said Mrs. N as she walked past Kensaku to the alcove. The old gentleman waited silently until the pouch was put in front of him. It was an old pouch, of purple wool that had faded very nicely—just the sort of thing that people in the old days used to put all their small valuables in. He pulled out of it a pair of glasses, a wallet, some matches, a pocket knife, a compass, and sundry other items. Among these was a small carving—a *netsuke*—which he showed his guests. "It belonged to one of them, a samurai from the Iwaki Sōma domain by the name of Sasaki Jūzō. He said I had been kind to him, and gave it to me."

"Is that so?" said Mr. S as he picked it up. He glanced at it quickly and handed it to Kensaku. It was a little too light, too fine-grained to have been made out of buffalo horn. On it were carved, in the style of the painter Ōkyo, five puppies bunched together.

"I used to talk to him whenever I could. A good man, he was. But the cold was too much for him, and he died eventually, as did all the rest of them, poor fellows."

Kensaku remembered the dream he had had about a week before. In it he, too, had committed some kind of offense against the state. True, the dream in retrospect had some charm to it, but he had woken up with an obscure, lingering sense of dread. And he imagined himself in one of those damp, salt-caked storehouses, his body covered with sores, having to watch his companions succumb one by one to the cold. Their suffering became almost too real for him then.

The rebels had first gone to Fukui, seeking protection. The domainal authorities, embarrassed by their presence and uncertain as to how they should be handled, had encouraged them to go to Tsuruga, which was just outside the domainal boundary, and then had had them arrested there. The rebels had been led to believe that Tsuruga would be safer for them. But, Mr. N said, one had to understand how very uncertain everything was in those days; no one knew which way the wind would blow; and the authorities were only trying to avoid being blamed later either for having protected the rebels or for having arrested them inside the domain.

To Kensaku's relief no one brought up the subject of marriage that day. When Mr. S got up to leave, Mr. N looked at Kensaku and said, "You live so near, there's no reason why you should go too." Pleased by the old gentleman's friendliness, by his evident sincerity, Kensaku decided to remain.

Mr. N had other stories to tell about the days just before the Restoration. One of them was about a band of rogues who had gone around collecting great sums of money in the name of the Imperialist cause. The fraud was discovered and they were all arrested. When asked at the magistrate's court what "Reverence for the Emperor" meant, they answered that the phrase referred to some holy man who had become very popular of late.

By the time Kensaku took leave of Mr. and Mrs. N he had come to feel a great fondness for them.

The next day the old couple were busy doing their last-minute shopping and making their obligatory farewell calls. Yet they found the time to stop by at Kensaku's inn to see him briefly.

On the following day Kensaku accompanied them to the station. There he met Mr. S, Dr. Yamazaki, Mr. N's nurse, and a few others who had also come to see them off.

Now that the old couple were gone, Kensaku suddenly found himself at a loose end. It would be another week before Oei arrived, and he felt much too unsettled to look forward with equanimity to a whole week of idleness. It would be a good idea, he decided, to go away on a trip with Takai, to some place like Hashidate, or Shōdoshima, or perhaps even Ise Shrine.

The next morning Kensaku caught an early train to Nara, hoping to catch Takai before he went out. It was a sparklingly clear day. He walked from Nara Station to his friend's lodging—it was a one-room annex of a teashop—in Asajigahara. To his disappointment he discovered that Takai had left Nara three days before to go and live in his hometown. He thought of visiting Murōji Temple, but quickly decided against it. To find out what train to catch, where to get off, and how to get to the temple from the station seemed to him far too much trouble. Rather than go to Murōji, then, he chose to visit Ise

Shrine, which was the nearest of the places that interested him. On his way back to the station he stopped at the museum. He looked at nothing else in Nara.

He found the visit to Ise unexpectedly pleasant. He had heard that he would be required to bow to the "divine" white horse that was kept by the shrine, but this of course turned out to be a false rumor. The clear water of the River Isuzu, the great cedars grown to their full height—these he had heard about, but he had not imagined they would be so pleasing to the eye. He enjoyed, too, the performance that night of the Ise Dance given in Furuichi, the old pleasure quarter.

His inn was the Aburaya, long familiar to Kensaku through the kabuki stage. The guest in the room next to his, on hearing that Kensaku was planning to go and see the dance, had the sliding doors between them opened and not only suggested that he go with Kensaku, but that they have dinner together. He was quick to announce that he was a member of the Tottori Prefectural Assembly. "The assembly is in recess, you know," he said. "I thought I'd give myself a little holiday." Not knowing what it meant to be a prefectural assemblyman, Kensaku was at a loss as to how to assess the stranger's self-importance; and every time the man mentioned the assembly, Kensaku felt a twinge of guilt at his own inability to give the right response.

There were a countless number of fine hot springs where he came from, he said; and the great mountain there (Kensaku failed to catch the name) was only second to Mt. Hiei as a sacred mountain of the Tendai sect. How big it was, he said, and how beautiful the country around it.

That evening a party of seven from the inn—some guests downstairs also wanted to see the dance—were guided by a maid through the streets of the pleasure quarter to the teahouse where it was to be held.

They were shown into a formidably old-looking room with woodwork so blackened that Kensaku wondered whether it was not a subtle application of dye that was responsible, rather than the accumulation of soot or some such natural process. They were made to sit in two rows on a rug spread over the floor, their backs toward a large, deep alcove. Standing before them was a low ceremonial table with some cakes and what looked like a printed programme placed on it. Beyond were bamboo screens partially hiding the front and sides of a section of the floor which, when raised, would be the stage. It would be as deep, Kensaku guessed, as the passageway in a kabuki theatre was wide.

The man from Tottori Prefecture, who was sitting in front of Kensaku, turned around and said to him, grinning, "So you intended to come to this place all by yourself, did you? You have courage, I must say."

Now that Kensaku thought of it, it was true that he might have felt awkward waiting in this huge room all alone for a dozen or so women to perform just for him.

The first to appear were the samisen players. As they sat down and held their instruments ready—they were not quite like any of the varieties of samisen Kensaku was familiar with—the wooden clappers were sounded offstage. The bamboo screens went up, the electric lights came on, the stage with a low railing around it was raised, and from either side the dancers, eight in all, appeared. The dance was extremely simple, indeed monotonous, and performed with an extraordinary lack of self-consciousness. It lasted for about fifteen minutes. The crudeness of the dance and the unmindful dancers, the lazy tone of the strange samisen, the old-fashioned surroundings—everything pleased him; and he thought that if he had come alone, he might have enjoyed the occasion even more.

The party was then shown to another room, and there a plump, fiftyish woman tried to persuade them to stay. Untempted, they all left the teahouse and followed the maid back to the inn.

The next morning Kensaku had a rickshaw take him to the inner shrine, then to the museum, and from there to the outer shrine. There was a pond in the woods of the outer shrine, with hundreds of wild mandarin ducks on it; and perched in tight formation on a large tree branch that stuck out over the water were still more of these birds. In amusement he remembered that scene in the dream.

From Futami he went to Toba, where he spent the night. On the way back to Kyoto he got off the train at Kameyama. There was an hour and a half until the next train, and he spent that time seeing the town on a rickshaw.

Kameyama was the birthplace of his dead mother. It was a shabby town, standing on a hill. After a quick tour of its center he went to the old castle grounds, where now a shrine stood. Kensaku, who remembered Kameyama as Hiroshige had depicted it in his "Fifty-three Stations," wanted to see the big slope in full view, but he had no idea where the vantage point might be.

He had the rickshaw wait at the gateway and took a walk around the grounds. Below him was an old, secluded pond, and on the other side was a hill of about the same height as the one he stood on. He went down, then climbed the steep path on the other side. The top of the hill had been made into a sort of park. There was no one about except for a woman in her fifties, poorly dressed but with an air of gentility about her, sweeping the ground. When she saw him she stopped sweeping and looked at him directly. It was almost a stare that she was giving him, but it was not at all offensive. Something about her manner appealed to him immediately, and made him want to speak to her. She was about the same age as his mother would have been, he thought, and probably from a samurai family too. "Is this," he said as he approached her, "a part of the old castle grounds?"

"Yes, it is," she answered. "The secondary tower used to be here." She then pointed toward the shrine. "And the main keep was there."

"Did you ever know a family by the name of Saeki that lived in these parts?"

"They were samurai here before the Restoration, weren't they?"

"Yes, they were." For some reason he was blushing. "There was a woman named Oshin—did you know her?" Then expectantly and betraying a trace of excitement he added, "She would be about the same age as you."

The woman cocked her head, trying to remember. "I don't think I knew her. There's Okin, and her younger sister named Okei, but I don't remember anyone by the name of Oshin."

"She had no sisters—at least, I don't think she had any. Was there another family called Saeki?"

"I wonder. You see, the only families I know are those that remained after the Restoration, and I remember nothing about those that moved away. But do go and ask the Saekis, they should be able to tell you."

In his disappointment he was reminded of how little he knew of his mother's childhood, of how little opportunity he had had to ask her about it. When had she gone to Tokyo, and what relations had she left behind? He hadn't the slightest idea. He didn't even know what the first name of his maternal grandfather had been, despite his love and reverence for him. "Grandfather at Shiba"—that had always been sufficient for Kensaku.

The woman proceeded to direct him to 'the Saekis' house, and he listened politely, without any intention of going there. He thanked her and walked away, thinking again how little he knew, what little chance he had ever had of knowing, about his mother.

The setting sun shone on the woods on the other side, where the main keep had been. Only the sumac had turned red, and stood out prettily among all the green. "What does it matter?" he thought as he scampered down the steep, busily winding path toward the pond that seemed already cloaked in autumnal quiet. "It's better this way. I am the ancestor, everything begins with me."

9

Ishimoto was waiting for him when he returned. "It's working out very smoothly," he said.

"Really?" said Kensaku, wondering if Ishimoto had heard something concrete.

"I gather Mr. and Mrs. N got a favorable impression of you."

"I liked them very much too."

"I'm glad." Ishimoto waited, then asked, "Did they say anything about it after Mr. S had left?"

"No." Kensaku gave Ishimoto a simple description of the interview, and added that he was feeling uncharacteristically optimistic about the outcome of the proposal. "And I do thank you," he then said, "for taking the trouble to come all this way for my sake."

"It's no trouble at all."

"I really am grateful." Kensaku could not remember ever having thanked Ishimoto so openly; but he felt no awkwardness.

"Let us assume, then," said Ishimoto, "that there will be no difficulty. But how shall we carry on from here? I shouldn't imagine you could manage everything by yourself?"

"You're right, I couldn't."

"There are certain things S can handle best. At any rate, would you like to leave the entire matter in my hands? I'll always consult Nobuyuki, of course, before I do anything."

Kensaku consented readily.

"And I'll try at every stage of the negotiations to get your approval first."

"But that would be far too much trouble, surely. By the way, I suppose it will be Mr. S that they will send their preliminary answer to?"

"That's right. But don't worry about that."

What Ishimoto meant, Kensaku gathered, was that Mr. N, before he left, had said something unmistakably reassuring to Mr. S.

That night Ishimoto left for Tokyo on the express train.

The next day those of Kensaku's belongings that he himself had packed arrived from Tokyo. He sent these off to his new house, and immediately had some people go there to unpack them and at the same time clean the house.

The maid in Tokyo had been let go, and in her place another one had been found for him by his Kyoto landlady. A skinny old woman she was, with sunken eyes and cheeks. Quite like a dried sardine, he thought. Her name was Sen. She, too, was at the house to help, though Kensaku had not asked her to be there that day; and it was agreed that she would remain there from that night on.

Three days later Oei arrived. She was anxious to go to the house and see to it that it was in proper order, but Kensaku dissuaded her. "There's no need," he said. "Let's wait at least until all my things have arrived. Stop fussing over me and try to have a good time. Let's do some sightseeing, I'd enjoy that. How long can you stay in Kyoto?"

"She'll be coming here from Gifu in four or five days."

"In that case we haven't much time. Forget about the house, please, and just let yourself be entertained."

As soon as she was settled at the inn Kensaku was ready to take her out. But before leaving Oei took a package wrapped in good, heavy Japanese paper out of her suitcase and gave it to Kensaku. "It came the day before yesterday." It was a large photograph of the young woman. Kensaku looked at it and said, "Yes, this is she. But she doesn't look much like one of those 'Feather Screen' beauties, I must say."

Oei responded by comparing the subject of the photograph with Aiko. In the comparison there was the suggestion of a woman's long-harbored resentment at an old slight. Kensaku was offended by Oei's mention of Aiko; yet as he sat there in silence, remembering the unpleasantness he was subjected to at the time, he could not help becoming resentful himself.

The two went by rickshaw to Kurodani, and starting with Shinnyodō visited several other temples—Ginkakuji, Hōnen'in, Anrakuji—and finally came to his house in Kitanobō in Nanzenji. There they decided to rest a while, and sent the rickshaw away.

Oei was full of praise for the house. As she looked out from the living room, she noticed that on the cozy, pine-covered hill behind Nyakuōji were numerous red flags fluttering in the wind. "What are those?" she asked Kensaku. Sen's voice called out from the next room, "That's where they're picking mushrooms!"

The Kyoto-style kitchen, long and narrow like a back alley, fascinated Oei, and she had Sen take her through it and explain every feature of it. She had shown no such interest when taken to the famed garden of Hōnen'in.

They decided not to see Nyakuōji and Eikandō that day and to end their tour with a visit to Nanzenji nearby.

Kensaku was so eager to point out everything to Oei that his own volubility became embarrassing to him. He knew he was being childish, but he could not restrain himself. The child in him seemed always to come to the fore when he was with Oei.

Halfway up the hill behind Nanzenji they came out above the embankment of the canal. They stopped briefly to look at the incline the boats were pulled up on, then walked to a restaurant named Hyōtei.

It was dark by the time they set off for Kensaku's inn. In his small room two beds had been laid out, so close together that the sides of the two quilts overlapped. Before they left the inn that day the landlady had asked Kensaku whether Oei might want to sleep in another room, and he had answered casually that his room would do. But now that he saw the two beds together he began to wonder at his own earlier blitheness. As far as he could remember, they had not once slept in the same room in all the years of living together— except, of course, when he was a very small child. "A tight squeeze, this," he muttered with a grimace.

Oei, on the other hand, seemed not at all to share Kensaku's apprehension. She sat down tiredly in the little open space at the head of the bed and said, "It was fun seeing Kyoto. Thank you very much." Was she suggesting, Kensaku wondered, that she had seen all there was to see?

"Is this arrangement all right with you?" he asked.

"Certainly."

"You'll be going to bed immediately, I suppose?"

"How about you, Kensaku?"

"I think I'll go out for a while. Take a quick walk around town, you know."

"I didn't sleep very well in the train last night, so if you don't mind, I'll go to bed right away."

"Do, by all means."

Once in town Kensaku as usual walked straight down Teramachi, his mind still troubled by the thought of those two beds.

He returned to the inn very late. Oei was sleeping soundly under the bright electric light. At first she seemed undisturbed by Kensaku's movements, but a few minutes later, when he was in bed, she opened her eyes painfully in the glare—she looked rather ugly then—and said, "Did you just come in?" She rolled over away from him, and presumably went back to sleep.

Kensaku had always found it difficult to go to sleep with someone else in the room. He pulled down the light close to his head, and began reading a book he had just picked up at a secondhand bookstore. It was a translation of a comedy called *As You Like it*. He intended to read it until he dropped off to sleep from exhaustion.

Ever since he saw the film version of *A Midsummer Night's Dream* and enjoyed it, he had been reading such comedies avidly. Just as works of art of the ancient Orient had given him such comfort by drawing him back to another age, so now these comedies offered him an opportunity to savor, even though only momentarily, a world of freedom and lightheartedness so different from what he had known. Tragedies he now avoided like the plague.

He read about half of the comedy, then put out the light. Sleep came to him with surprising ease. But sometime during the night he found himself suddenly wide awake again. And after that he could not make himself go back to sleep. He lay there in the dark, listening to Oei breathing easily beside him.

The room seemed to get increasingly stuffy, and his head began to feel hot and heavy, almost feverish. In near-desperation he tossed about in his bed; and more than once he threw his arm out noisily toward Oei.

He must have gone to sleep again. When he woke up the next morning Oei was gazing out at the view as she sipped her morning cup of tea.

She turned around when she heard Kensaku moving in bed. "So you're awake at last."

"What time is it?"

"It must be about nine. Are you getting up?"

"I think so."

"This room is a bit too small for the two of us, isn't it?"

"I'll see to it that you get a separate room."

"I really don't mind staying in this room so long as you don't. But haven't you any work to do?"

"I'm not doing anything right now." Was Oei being perfectly innocent in remarking on the smallness of the room, Kensaku wondered, or was she mindful of something else? Not that it mattered particularly, for the thought that she might be aware of his terrible frustration last night embarrassed him not at all. He was not being shameless here; rather, he simply knew that she would forgive him, that she would be neither indignant nor contemptuous.

"There's another little room just across the corridor," he said, "so why don't you move in there?"

"All right, I'll do that. By the way, one can see from here most of the places we went to yesterday, can't one?"

After lunch they went to Arashiyama. He had intended to take her to Kinkakuji Temple after that, but she said no, she had seen enough. Besides, it was already rather late, so they went straight back to the inn.

"We'll go to Nara tomorrow," Kensaku said. "And then we can perhaps go to Osaka on the electric train." Oei would not be with him very much longer, and there were so many places that he still wanted her to see.

"Thank you very much, but you really have shown me enough," she said more than once. Whether she was thinking of her own comfort or his was not clear to him.

The tour proposed by Kensaku became an impossibility anyway, for the next morning a telegram arrived from Osai saying, "Coming through tomorrow noon, be ready." Oei, accompanied by Kensaku, spent most of that day shopping.

The next day the two went to the station earlier than necessary. Oei, handing Kensaku the money for the fare to Shimonoseki, said, "I think we'll be traveling third-class."

"Will it be just you and that person?"

"No, the children will be with us, I imagine."

"She has children?"

"Of course not," she said. There was impatience in her smile. "I don't mean real children. We just call them that. There may be one or two joining us from here, as a matter of fact."

There was a gaudily dressed woman of indeterminate age hanging about on the platform. She had slack eyelids and carried a huge male doll. With her were two other women, there presumably to see her off. Kensaku looked at her, and decided she was one of the "children."

The train came in and stopped alongside the platform. Osai and two young women stuck their heads out of one of the third-class windows. The woman with the slack eyelids was led quickly toward them by one of her companions, a woman in her fifties. Kensaku looked at them all, hating the thought of Oei becoming one of them.

With an empty feeling in his heart Kensaku stood facing the

window, a step behind the two women that had come to see the other woman off. The younger of the two was in a festive mood and talked incessantly. "I cried last year when you went off like this," she was saying, "but this time I feel really cheerful. It must be a good omen." Kensaku, listening to this chatter, was made to feel all the more fearful for Oei.

"So you think we're going to be successful, eh?" said Osai mockingly. "In that case, why don't you share some of your capital with us? Sell your six-hundred-yen private telephone and give us the proceeds. That'll do for a start."

The loud woman, thus challenged, fell into an uneasy silence. Oei stood behind Osai on the train, smiling gently and saying nothing. There was dignity in her manner, yet it made Kensaku cross; for it was with the very same attitude that she had allowed Osai to talk her into participating in this ill-advised venture. Here she was, about to set off for wintry, remote Tientsin, seemingly without any awareness of her partner's crude avarice. "You're a fool," he wanted to tell Oei to her face, "a bigger fool than this silly, chattering creature standing beside me."

The woman of the eyelids sat by the open window, leaning out. She held the older woman's hand close to her face, and from time to time would rub her cheek against it, up and down, up and down. "Look here," Osai said to her, "you'd better put this thing on the rack." The woman obediently stood up and put the large doll on the rack above. She then sat down, reached out for the other woman's hand and again began rubbing her cheek against it. It seemed most likely to Kensaku that she was a little retarded.

10

It was on an unpleasantly chilly day for autumn, dark and windy, that Kensaku at last moved into his new abode. It was not the sort of day he would have picked for moving, but Sen had come that morning to say that the rest of his belongings had arrived from Tokyo, leaving him no excuse to delay the move any longer. Once at the house he proceeded to open packages wrapped in straw matting, carry up to the attic those things he had no immediate use for, and arrange his own room. Very soon his head was covered with dust, his face and hands felt raw, he had a headache from exposure to the cold drafts, and his nose was irritated beyond bearing by the dust. In short, he felt quite awful.

Sen, though she worked hard, made matters worse for him by constantly demanding his attention.

"Please sir, what is this thing here?"

"What thing?"

"This thing I'm holding." It was his iron foot warmer, no easy thing for an old woman to carry. "A bed warmer, isn't it?"

"More or less. Will you put it away somewhere?"

"Don't you want to use it?"

"Perhaps I shall, but not now, so please put it away."

"Won't you lend it to me?" She gave a little bow and looked at him furtively, grinning slyly all the while. "You see, it gets so cold at night, I can't bear the pain in my hips."

He looked at her with displeasure, thinking what an impertinent dried sardine she was. But he could hardly say no. "All right, you can have it for the time being," he said ungraciously, knowing full well that he would be most reluctant to use anything that had once been in bed with this sardine. But there was something a little comic about the situation, he had to admit: the master had brought this heavy object all the way from Tokyo, only to have it confiscated by his sly, fishy housekeeper.

Among Kensaku's belongings that had arrived earlier was a wooden washtub inside which he had packed a large metal brazier. Informed by Sen that the bottom of the tub was about to fall off, he said to her, "Did you send it away to be repaired?"

"No, I didn't," she said in a tone that suggested Kensaku had asked a silly question.

"Why not?"

"The cooper hasn't been around yet, that's why."

"Then why didn't you take it to him?"

"You're not serious! You can't expect a woman to go around

carrying a tub that large. Mind you, I've no idea where the cooper's shop is."

"Get yourself a drum, put the tub on your head, then you can pretend you're one of those sweet vendors."

"Very funny."

The harder he tried to control his irritation, the more irritated he became. It was just as well that soon afterward he went to the local public bath; for when he returned, his irritation had somewhat abated.

That it would take a while before he and Sen learned to be comfortable with each other, Kensaku was now forced to acknowledge. She had presumably come thinking that serving a bachelor with no regular employment would be relatively undemanding. He was in her eyes a sort of overage student, which was more or less what he in fact was, and he himself was more than willing to accept a certain informality from her, and not to insist on a clearly defined master-servant relationship. But such democratic intentions notwithstanding, he found her rough ways extremely trying. All he could do now was to hope that in time she would learn to be more restrained.

"Look here," he said to her, "whenever I'm sitting at my desk I don't want to be disturbed, no matter what it is that you want to say to me."

She opened her small eyes wide. "Why not?"

"I don't think I need to give you any reasons."

"Yes, sir."

She was fairly obedient to his command. Once in a forgetful moment she walked into his room saying something, but as soon as she saw him working at his desk she quickly withdrew. "Mustn't speak, mustn't speak," she muttered, covering her mouth with her hand.

Kensaku knew little about Sen's past. She had had a daughter who, if she had lived, would have been the same age as Kensaku; after her daughter's death she had gone to live with her elder brother, but he died too; then she had been taken in by a nephew and his wife, but feeling that they regarded her as a nuisance, had decided to seek domestic employment. This much, Kensaku had heard.

She liked to sing in the kitchen. Her voice was not bad, but when under the influence of saké she was prone to get so loud that Kensaku would have to shout, "Quiet!"

But their relationship became less mutually annoying as the days went by. He began not to mind her ways so much, and she on her part showed greater willingness to respect his than he perhaps had the right to expect of someone her age. And being a Kyotoite, once she knew that the management of the household was entirely in her hands, she proved herself capable of hardheaded efficiency. Drinking and smoking were her weaknesses, and she would collect all the tobacco left in Kensaku's cigarette butts and later smoke it in her pipe.

Gradually he came to feel more and more kindly toward Sen.

There was a brief communication from Oei saying that she had arrived safely, but other than that she offered no information.

He had looked forward to that time when he would be settled in his new house, and in a relaxed, leisurely frame of mind would start visiting his favorite temples again. But strangely, the more he felt settled, the more irksome that particular pastime began to seem to him. When he did go out, it was such busy places as Shinkyōgoku that he headed for; and he would come home thoroughly exhausted from the strenuous walk. There were no friends he could visit, and on some days he would feel helplessly lonely. Even then, he was spared such moments of desperation as he had known in Ōmori or in Ono-michi. And although he did not write anything substantial, he was able to complete a slight piece or two.

One morning, while Kensaku was still asleep, Mr. S stopped by on his way to the office and handed a letter, still sealed, to Sen. Without coming into the house he left immediately.

About an hour later Kensaku read it. It was a letter of acceptance from Tsuruga. He read it over again, then said to Sen, "Did Mr. S bring this himself?"

"Yes, sir."

"Why didn't you wake me up?"

"I wanted to, but he stopped me. He said he was in a hurry to get to the office, and he would come again this evening."

Kensaku was very pleased that Mr. S should have brought the

letter himself. He had been kind to him in all sorts of ways right from the beginning; but, while feeling grateful to him, he had not once called on him to thank him properly. It was an omission, Kensaku was aware, yet he had somehow not been able to bring himself to correct it. And the fact that Mr. S for his part had not called on him had begun to worry Kensaku. Did Mr. S think him discourteous, he wondered, and was that why he hadn't called? Might he have lost interest in the proceedings, and was that why the other party was so slow in replying? Would his proposal end in failure because he had incurred Mr. S's displeasure?

His recent apprehensions, then, now instantly dispelled by the letter, made his newly found happiness all the more intense.

"It has gone well?" asked Sen.

"Yes."

She sat down in front of Kensaku and with incongruous tenderness said, "Congratulations."

"Thank you," he said, bobbing his head.

"And when will it be?"

"I'm not sure, but it will be either this year or before Winter's End next year."

"There isn't much time, then."

"By the way, when is Winter's End?

"The beginning of February, isn't it?"

In his letter Mr. N said that a friend of his son's who was on the arts faculty of a certain private university had said some very nice things about Kensaku's work, much to the gratification of the entire family. How lucky he was, Kensaku thought, that the person whose opinion they happened to solicit had good things to say about him. But what would he himself have said had he been in that young academic's place? Would he have been so generous? These were uncomfortable questions, and he hastily dismissed them.

He wrote almost identical letters to Nobuyuki, Ishimoto and Oei informing them of the latest development. He then wrote to Tatsuoka in Paris, to whom he had not written for a while.

In the afternoon he went to a cake shop called Surugaya to buy some bean cake to send to Tatsuoka. He then telephoned Mr. S's office from the shop, and asked if he might call on him at his house later that day. Four o'clock would be convenient, said Mr. S. With about two hours to kill, Kensaku decided to go to Daimaru Department Store in Shijō Takakura. He would look at the bright women's kimonos there, and dream of future happiness. A foolish indulgence, perhaps, one he would not have owned up to, but it was a need he felt very strongly then. Besides, he really did want to see the exhibit of the small airplane that had crashed recently in the parade ground of Fukakusa Barracks. Tatsuoka had once praised this monoplane— its name was Morane-Saulnier—and that very morning Kensaku had written about the crash in his letter to him. In preparation for a non-stop flight to Tokyo the pilot had taken the airplane up for a test flight with an overload of fuel. The flight had lasted only a few minutes. The dead pilot's clothes, half-burned away, charred calling cards found in his pocket, his gloves, also charred—these and other such items were neatly laid out in the display case. Kensaku had often seen the airplane, small and swift like a falcon, flying high up in the sky. The children playing in the streets would look up and shout excitedly, "There's Mr. Ogino!" With the adults, too, Ogino had been immensely popular. But he was dead now, and there were all these people milling around, staring at his charred belongings. The spectacle made Kensaku feel a little queasy.

He left the department store in good time and headed for Mr. S's house.

It was a graceful, Kyoto-style house, with a small outside gate and a paved path leading up to the front door. On either side of the path was a thick border of broad-leafed bamboos.

Mr. S solicited Kensaku's opinions regarding the betrothal gift, the time and place of the wedding and so on, but Kensaku had none to give. He would leave everything in Mr. S's and Ishimoto's hands, he said. He did want to get married as quickly as possible, but he could hardly suggest that the approximate time set by the other party—before February—was anything but reasonable.

11

Kensaku decided to go up to Tokyo for two or three days. There was no pressing need for him to do so, but he wanted to see Tokyo again; besides, it would be a nice gesture to go and see Ishimoto, who had come down twice to see him.

He got off at Kamakura, and from there he and Nobuyuki went to Tokyo together. That evening they visited Ishimoto. The three of them talked until very late, but not about the betrothal, for there was not much to be said about that any more. Ishimoto persuaded the two brothers to stay; and as they got into their beds Nobuyuki said to Kensaku, "Have you any intention of going to Hongō while you're in Tokyo?"

"I'm not particularly anxious to go there, but it's true that I'd like to see Sakiko and Taeko again."

"I told them about you just the other day, and they were very pleased."

"Where could we get together, do you think?"

"Tomorrow is Sunday, isn't it?"

"No, Saturday, I think."

"Then I'll ask them to come to Kamakura the day after tomorrow, shall I?"

"That would be nice."

"All right, I'll ask the girls tomorrow. I'm sure they'll be pleased."

The next morning they telephoned their sisters from Ishimoto's house before leaving for Kamakura. Of course they would come, the girls said excitedly; what train should they catch?

On their way to Kamakura Nobuyuki said, "Do you mean to say you didn't bring that photograph of her with you? Pretty thoughtless, I must say."

"It did cross my mind, as a matter of fact."

"Of course it's just like you to deliberate about a thing like that and then decide not to do it." Nobuyuki's tone was sharp, and the laugh that followed did little to soften the effect of the remark.

"But you saw it in my house in Ōmori," Kensaku said. "And I really didn't think I would be seeing the girls."

"That's true," Nobuyuki said, and as though to make up for his outburst nodded a few times.

They went to bed early that night. The next morning Kensaku went to the station alone to meet his sisters.

The girls stepped off the train almost immediately in front of Kensaku. They were both carrying large bundles. "Where's Nobuyuki?" said Taeko.

"He's waiting for you at the house."

"How dare he! Here we are, loaded with all these delicacies, and he can't be bothered to come and meet us!" She was bursting with energy and good cheer. How much she has grown, Kensaku thought as he looked at her.

Sending a rickshaw man ahead of them with the bundles, the three walked at a leisurely pace past Hachiman Shrine and the local school. It was a mild, sunny day, and their spirits were in keeping with it.

Kensaku talked about his house in Kyoto, what his life there was like, and so on, but made no mention of the impending marriage. The girls listened politely, thinking perhaps that Kensaku was waiting for an appropriate moment to bring up the subject. At last, unable to wait any longer, Sakiko said, "I was terribly happy to hear the news."

"Yes, yes," said Taeko. "When will it be? I suppose it will take place in Kyoto?"

"Probably."

"I want to be there then."

"Ask Nobuyuki to bring you."

"Yes, I will. But when will it be? Don't forget, I won't be able to come unless it's during the school holidays."

"It may very well take place during the holidays."

"Oh, please have it then!"

"What are you saying!" said Sakiko. "You can't expect everybody to arrange something like that to suit your convenience!"

Taeko angrily stared back at her elder sister.

Kensaku knew what Sakiko was thinking: their father would never allow Taeko to go to Kyoto, holidays or no. He, too, thought so, and now he felt a little guilty about having encouraged Taeko to look forward to the wedding. He said no more about it.

When they were near Nobuyuki's house in Nishimikado, Taeko started running, leaving the other two behind. The rickshaw man, having left the bundles at the house, was coming toward them.

Taeko was seated in the middle of the living room, bringing out the various things she and Sakiko had brought for Nobuyuki: a box of confectionery, tinned food, fresh fruit, shirts, and even underwear. She then brought out a square object wrapped in newspaper and tied securely with thick string. She put it aside ostentatiously, saying, "And this is for you, Kensaku. You may not open it here; you are to wait until you get back to Kyoto."

Nobuyuki, seated beside her, reached for the package. "Here, let me see what it is."

"Certainly not!"

"Why not? I won't tell Kensaku."

Taeko became cross. "No!"

"A wedding present, is it?"

"No, I have something else in mind for that."

"A sort of preliminary present, I suppose."

"Never you mind. It has nothing to do with you, so please leave me alone." Picking up the package she stood up, walked to the alcove and put it on the shelf.

Nobuyuki, pretending to be offended, said roughly, "Who do you think you are? If you can't show it to me, you can at least tell me what it is."

Saikiko said, "It's something Taeko made herself."

Taeko glared at her elder sister. "Don't you dare say any more!" She was becoming quite upset, and it was only when Kensaku gave his firm promise not to open the package until he was back in Kyoto that she was mollified.

Sakiko started to giggle. "Let's hope it won't be like that treasure casket in the fairy tale—full of unpleasant surprises!"

"That's so unkind," Taeko said, looking at her sister with wide-open eyes. She was about to cry.

Nobuyuki said, "It'll soon be time for lunch. I expect you girls to get it ready." But Taeko, now thoroughly put out, pretended not to hear.

In the afternoon they went to Engakuji Temple, and on their way back walked to the top of Hanzōbō Hill behind Kenchōji Temple.

Kensaku decided to accompany his sisters to Tokyo and catch the night train for Kyoto from there.

When Taeko went to the bathroom to get herself ready for the return journey, Nobuyuki mischievously picked up the package from the shelf. "What could it possibly be?" he said as he felt it.

"Now, now," Kensaku said good-humoredly, taking the package away from Nobuyuki. Sakiko stood by, grinning.

Nobuyuki went with them to the station; and in Tokyo, it was the two sisters' turn to stand on the platform and see Kensaku off.

Taeko's package contained an embroidered picture frame and a jewelry box. Kensaku smiled as he saw the box. No wonder she was so angry when Sakiko mentioned the treasure casket. Inside it was a tiny envelope. "Congratulations, Kensaku," said Taeko's note. "When Nobuyuki told us the happy news the other day, I almost cried. I rushed out and hid myself in the Western-style room, I felt so funny. It was so sudden, and I felt so happy for you. I want you to give the box to my future sister-in-law, and I want you to put a picture of her or your wedding picture in the frame. My piano teacher showed me how to make them."

On the platform in Kamakura Station when she arrived, she had been her usual buoyant, carefree self, and had not said a word about Kensaku's engagement. Who could have guessed then that she cared so much?

12

The date for the wedding was agreed upon with greater dispatch than Kensaku had expected. This was thanks to Ishimoto's and Nobuyuki's efforts; they had succeeded in persuading the other party through Mr. S that the arrangements should be as simple as possible.

There was no need for the bride to bring much with her, they had said; Kensaku after all may decide to leave Kyoto in the near future, he had no intention of moving to a large house while in Kyoto, and he would not want his house cluttered with all kinds of unnecessary things. Besides, a very simple wedding ceremony would surely suffice.

On a certain day in early December Naoko, her mother and her elder brother arrived in Kyoto from Tsuruga. The next day they and Kensaku gathered at Mr. S's house for the formal marriage interview; and in the evening they were all taken to the Minamiza Theatre by Mr. S to see the opening programme of the season.

The Naoko that he now saw was considerably different from the woman he had come to picture in his imagination. He was hard put to it to define the difference. At any rate, the woman of his imagination had been made to conform to what he, in his current condition, had found most desirable: she was like one of those women of the "Feather Screen," beautiful and elegant in a classical sort of way; and if not that, she was a high-spirited but graceful girl from one of those pleasant comedies. In effect what he had done was to create, on the basis of his first impression of her, magnified versions of what he thought he had seen. That she was not like what he had imagined, then, was not surprising. The despondent-looking young woman sitting in the same box with him was rather well-built; she had a plump face, which made the faint crow's-feet around her eyes slightly incongruous; and she wore her hair in an old-fashioned, low pompadour. Whatever her hair style might have been when he first saw her, it must have been less conspicuous and more casual.

In profile she much resembled her mother, who again was a far cry from what he had imagined Mr. N's sister would be like. She was every inch the country woman, with a large face and a short, stocky body. He was not impressed by her hair either, which had been dyed a strikingly unnatural black. Naoko's resemblance to her reminded him of a story by Maupassant called "An Unfortunate Likeness," which described a similar situation. True, he was not as disillusioned as the hero of the story; but it was a fact that she was not as beautiful as he had thought.

Later, after they were married, she told him that she had felt quite awful that evening. She had had a tiring train journey the day before, and tense from fatigue, had not been able to go to sleep. All next day she had suffered not only from a nagging headache but slight nausea. And indeed it was a rare occasion when she ever looked quite as bad as she did then.

She was not the only despondent one that evening. Kensaku, too, felt strained and tired. He had always found new acquaintances an ordeal, especially those whom he could not ignore. Naoko's elder brother was a pleasant enough man, but conscious of their lack of common interests, was apt to spring on Kensaku some sudden comment about literature which would leave Kensaku searching desperately for a suitable response. He tried to tell himself that this was only light conversation, that he could say anything he pleased, but it did no good; words came slowly, ponderously, as though his very reputation as a writer were now at stake. The brother seemed not to mind. He would look straight at Kensaku with affectionate eyes and interrupt their conversation with some such remark as, "Do forgive my awkward ways," or "You mustn't mind mother, she's getting on in years." There was such decency and goodwill in the man that Kensaku could not resist his offer of friendship. They had known each other for only a few hours, and already he had become much more than a new acquaintance to Kensaku.

On the stage they were doing a scene from Chikamatsu's *Love Suicide at Amijima*. Kensaku had seen it a number of times; besides, he was not much taken with the actor who was playing Jihei. Though a skillful performer, he was far too mechanical and predictable. But it was not just the performance on the stage that left Kensaku feeling uninvolved. This was supposed to be a festive occasion, yet here he was, unable somehow to participate in it, unable even to accept the reality of his fiancée's being the same young woman whom he had admired from a distance two months before.

Naoko, looking sad and dispirited yet with an air of concentration, watched the stage. Her forlornness touched him. But he was too preoccupied with his own wretched condition to feel more than a fleeting pity for her.

He managed with great effort to maintain an outward calm. Inwardly, however, he was struggling against the desire to rush away from the scene, which increased with every passing moment until he thought it would soon overwhelm him completely. He had of course often felt this way before; but the necessity under the present circumstances of having to be on his very best behavior made the strain all the greater. The truth was that the prospect of getting married had driven him into a life of debauchery again—just as his imaginings about Oei as his potential wife had done earlier—and as a result he had again become tense and unresilient, easily subject to moods of utter nervous exhaustion.

It was late when the performance at last concluded and they came out of the theatre. The moon, nearly full, hung high in the sky. He quickly parted from the others, and feeling like a small bird just freed from its cage, began to walk away from Yasaka Shrine toward Chion'in Temple. Solitude was all he wanted at the moment. As he approached the great gate of the temple the moon became hidden behind it, and in the darkness the gate appeared even bigger.

The evening had not been an auspicious prelude to their marriage. But, he reminded himself, he was the culprit, no one else. If he had been able to lead a more disciplined life of late, he might have behaved better. And though he had no intention of excusing himself, he was nevertheless tempted to think that once again he had been betrayed by the ugly heritage bequeathed him by his grandfather. But he must forget what had happened that evening, he told himself. What was done was done. Of much greater importance was the way he would conduct himself in the future. If he did not learn to exercise moderation, he could easily end up destroying himself. Yes, he would try to lead a better kind of life, especially after marriage. And so again he made that very same resolution he had broken repeatedly in the past.

He and Naoko were married about a week after that. One day before the marriage she, her mother, and her brother paid him a visit. It was a cloudy and cold afternoon. Sen was busy in the kitchen, so he had come out to mail a card he had just written to Nobuyuki. He was standing by the mailbox when he saw in the distance the three figures walking toward him. The mother walked a step or two behind her son and daughter. Naoko walked close to her brother, almost leaning against his large body, and was talking animatedly. She seemed so beautiful then, so full of life, that Kensaku could hardly believe it was the same person he had met the other night. He watched her, conscious of the mounting excitement inside him.

Kensaku himself was feeling very relaxed that day, so the visit was altogether a success. Sen, too, entered into the spirit of the occasion and worked hard to please her future mistress. Kensaku brought out his casket which he had not opened for a long time and showed his visitors photographs of his dead mother, his brother and sisters, Oei, and old school friends.

They decided to go out and visit Ginkakuji. On the way they stopped to look at Anrakuji and Hōnen'in. When Kensaku was explaining the history of Asoka's Tower at Hōnen'in, Naoko listened intently, rather in the manner of a schoolgirl listening to her favorite teacher.

They were near Ginkakuji when Naoko's brother suddenly said, "I'm afraid I shall have to go back to the inn. I'm not feeling well." He did look pale, and there were beads of sweat on his forehead. "Nothing serious, I'm sure," he said as the others looked at him with concern. They agreed that it was probably the heat in Kensaku's room; for Kensaku, who hated the cold, had kept a very hot fire going in his brazier that day. Fortunately there was a rickshaw nearby; and despite the brother's insistence that he would be all right by himself, the mother decided to go back with him.

Left by themselves the two silently walked up the rest of the path paved with broken tiles, and entered the gate. Just inside the gate there was a standing screen that had written on it the word "virtue." Here they waited for a guide, exchanging a few awkward remarks. They began to feel more comfortable with each other, however, as they were led through the temple by a small boy wearing formal Japanese trousers that were too short for him. For his size he had a remarkably loud voice. "And there in the garden is our famous miniature sandscape, depicting the hill of the moon standing over the silver sand rapids!" "What you see on the sliding screens to your right and left is the work of Taigadō!"

During the tour Kensaku turned to Naoko and said, "You left your bag and umbrella behind at my house, didn't you? If you're intending to go back to the inn by rickshaw after this, I'll send them along sometime this evening." Naoko looked at him a little angrily, saying nothing. "Or perhaps you'd like to stop at the house?" "Yes," she said brusquely, as if what she meant was, "What a stupid question!"

There was a drainage system that led from the back of Nanzenji Temple to the ricefields near Kurodani. The two walked along the path beside this small canal, side by side where they could, and Naoko behind Kensaku where the path was too narrow. As he walked ahead of her he would picture in his mind her neat, little feet (they were small for a woman her size) in spotless white socks following his own footsteps, firmly and determinedly yet gracefully. That such a person, or rather such pretty feet, should be following so close behind him gave him a novel sense of well-being and contentment.

A baby turtle, its neck stuck out purposefully, was crawling with tremendous effort over the pebbles laid on the bottom of the canal. Amused by the sight, the two stopped for a while to watch. Suddenly she said as they stood there, "I know nothing about literature." Kensaku squatted down, and picking up a handful of mud, threw it into the water just a few inches in front of the turtle. The turtle withdrew its neck a little and stopped, waiting for the water to clear; then it resumed its slow journey, carrying on its back a thin layer of mud.

"I'm glad," Kensaku said, still squatting.

"Well, I'm not."

"Really, I'd much prefer it if you didn't know anything about it."

"But why?"

Kensaku was not sure how exactly he should answer her question. He used to feel differently once, but more recently he had come to feel that it mattered very little whether or not his wife had any understanding of his work. Indeed, by the time he proposed to Oei, he had already started feeling this way. And had Naoko said, "I love literature," or something of the sort, he would have found it unbearable.

At any rate, Naoko seemed to think it necessary to warn Kensaku of her ignorance. There was another matter, she said, that she had to mention: she had an aunt, a divorcée, who had come to live with her mother before she was born; being childless, this aunt had showered Naoko with affection; she was now past sixty, and would miss her niece terribly; would Kensaku mind if occasionally she were to visit them in Kyoto? "My aunt begged me to ask you."

The two rested for a while in Kensaku's house. Naoko still seemed worried about her lack of literary knowledge. Examining the book-shelves in the study she said, "Tell me, which of these should I read?"

Kensaku accompanied Naoko all the way back to the inn. There they found her brother sitting up, seemingly fully recovered. "A short nap was all I needed," he said.

13

The simple wedding ceremony took place five days or so later at a restaurant called Sa'ami in Maruyama. In Kensaku's party were Nobuyuki, Ishimoto and his wife, Miyamoto who loved Kyoto, Takai who had come back to Nara, and a few others. In Naoko's party, be-sides Mr. and Mrs. N and three or four other relatives and friends, were Mr. and Mrs. S, who were the official intermediaries, Dr. Yamazaki, and Kensaku's former landlady from Higashisanpongi. "Simple" perhaps by ordinary standards, the occasion was still considerably more festive than Kensaku had ever imagined his own wedding would be, and at times he felt his own presence to be something of an incongruity. Yet all in all he felt surprisingly relaxed and cheerful, and was able to watch all the goings-on with innocent pleasure. How good it was, he thought, to be the cause of so much cheer in others.

Among the dancing girls who wore their beautiful dresses with ac-customed aplomb, Naoko in her long-sleeved formal dress looked conspicuously awkward. And her stiff, high coiffure sat very badly on her, making her seem quite provincial. He felt a little sorry for her; but his mood was such that he looked at her more with kindly amusement than with any sense of condescension.

The festivities came to an end at about eleven. As he was about to leave, Nobuyuki said to Kensaku, "I'm staying at Ishimoto's inn. I'll send Oei a telegram the first thing in the morning, so don't you worry. But it would be nice if you wrote her a letter when you felt settled." He had drunk a great deal that evening, and had become very boisterous. But there had not been the slightest unpleasantness in his rowdiness, and no one had been made at all uncomfortable by it. Nevertheless Kensaku, who had not seen Nobuyuki in such a state before and had therefore watched his antics with curiosity and amusement at first, had finally become somewhat apprehensive. If Nobuyuki has another drink, he began to think, he's going to become really unmanageable. But now he seemed incredibly in control of himself as he made his parting statement. With renewed respect and affection, Kensaku bid his brother good-night.

When Kensaku and Naoko returned to the house, Sen came out to the front hall to receive them, decked out in an old-fashioned dress with her crest on it.

Early next morning they went to Mr. S's house to offer their formal thanks. It was past Mr. S's time to leave for his office, but he was waiting for them. After that they went to see the Ishimotos at their inn, and from there they went to Tōsanrō, this time accompanied by Nobuyuki, to see Naoko's family.

The two spent the next couple of days busily meeting their social obligations—seeing some people off, accompanying others on a trip to Nara, and so on.

The house that Kensaku had rented was a small one, with an eight-mat living room, a narrow, four-mat anteroom that faced north and unusable now that there were the two of them, and a maid's room. Obviously, they had to move.

Kensaku had no work that had to be done immediately. But he was loathe to get into that post-marriage condition where one did no work for a while; he was therefore anxious to set himself up so that whenever he felt like working, he could do so comfortably. One day, then, he and Naoko went to look at a house in the grounds of Kōdaiji Temple that had interested him earlier. They discovered that the house, one of two semidetached houses, had already been promised to someone else. But two more semidetached houses, also with two stories, had since been built next to these. The one on the east side appealed to Kensaku and Naoko, and they thought they would take it.

"This isn't too good," Kensaku said, sticking his head out of a second-floor window facing south. "If someone were to look out of the same window next door, we would be staring right into each other's face."

"Absolutely," said Naoko.

The landlord's son, who had come with the key to let them into the house, said cheerfully, "We could put up a small fence on top of the lavatory roof. It would keep the afternoon sun out too."

"That would certainly be satisfactory," said Kensaku. "By the way, would you put a longer cord on the light? I'll have my desk in the corner of this room, and I'll want the light there when I'm working. I could have it done myself, if you'd rather."

"Oh no, we'll do it," the landlord's son said. Everyone seemed to be in an amicable mood.

They then went downstairs to the morning room. Kensaku saw that here, too, the electric cord hanging from the ceiling was no more than two feet long. "This won't do either," said Kensaku. "You couldn't possibly do any sewing with the light so high up, could you, Naoko?"

"Surely it stretches," she said, standing on tiptoe and trying to pull the cord down.

"No, it doesn't," said the young man. He stepped away from them and looked at them in offended silence. He knew Kensaku and Naoko were waiting for him to offer to have the cord lengthened; but for some reason, he had chosen this moment to be obstinate.

Now it was Kensaku's turn to be offended. By nature willful, he was not one to tolerate such perverse behavior from another. He thinks we're arrogant, he thought; perhaps we are, but why be so damn difficult about a small thing like that? "You wouldn't mind if we had it lengthened ourselves, would you?" he said challengingly.

"Yes, I would," the young man answered with extreme brusqueness.

"Why, if I may ask?"

"No Kyoto man would have wanted it longer."

Kensaku was speechless with anger.

"It would be ridiculous to have a long cord like that dangling from the ceiling."

"When we move out we'll have the cord shortened again. That would satisfy you, wouldn't it?"

"No, it wouldn't!" The young man's face had gone pale.

"You're an idiot! All right, then, we won't rent the house. Come on, Naoko." Without giving the young man another look Kensaku marched out of the room. Naoko, utterly confused, stood there for a moment, then bowed and said she was leaving. The young man returned her bow with great courtesy.

Outside, Naoko opened her parasol and ran after Kensaku. She was laughing. "What a short-tempered pair!"

Kensaku grinned sheepishly. "A likeable sort of fellow, wasn't he?" Now that he had calmed down, he was a trifle ashamed of his own impetuosity, and couldn't help thinking that the young man's animosity was not entirely unjustified.

"What's the point of approving of a man after quarreling with him like that?" she said. "I liked the house, and I'm sorry we can't have it."

"Well, it's too late now."

"Next time, don't say anything, take the house, and then make the changes. Of course they get annoyed if the first thing you do is tell them you want this and that done."

They decided to do no more house-hunting that day, and instead look for presents to give in return for their wedding presents. They went to Gojōzaka, where the famous potters—Rokubē, Seifū, Sōroku —had their shops, and stopped at each one to look at their wares. At Sōroku's shop they were received courteously by a man who showed them red-glazed incense burners made by the last Sōroku but one. These were there to show only, the man explained, and not for sale. He was relatively young and very modestly dressed, but Kensaku guessed that he was the present Sōroku. The first Sōroku, Kensaku had been told, had come originally from Kameyama in Ise; and the family which Kensaku's aunt on his mother's side had married into were closely related to the potter's family, so that whenever she came to Kyoto she would stay with them. For this reason, then, Kensaku was drawn to this man; yet, when he thought of his aunt, he somehow could not feel that he himself was truly her nephew.

In contrast to Sōroku's shop, which was dank and gloomy, Mokusen's shop that they next went to had a bright and lively atmosphere. The first Mokusen had once worked for the house of Sōroku, but had left to establish his own workshop. Here they found much that they liked, and were able to buy all the presents they needed. It was a pity, for Kensaku would have bought them from Sōroku, if only he had had suitable things to sell. The second Mokusen, seated in the midst of all his wares, talking to his customers as he poured the tea himself, was indeed the very picture of vigorous entrepreneurship.

Kensaku decided to buy several sauce bottles, also red-glazed, from him. Only the writing on the wooden boxes that they came in, it was explained, was the work of the first Mokusen, who was now bedridden.

The sun was about to set when they came out of the shop. A cold wind was blowing. Kensaku put up the collar of his Inverness cape and said, "I'll catch cold if we don't go somewhere to eat soon."

"I'm sure Sen will have prepared dinner for us."

"I wonder."

"Have you eaten out that often?"

"No, not really, but since we left the house rather late, she's probably assuming we won't be home for dinner."

They came down the gently sloping hill to Gojō Bridge. The bridge was being rebuilt, and alongside it a narrow temporary bridge had been put up. As they went over it Naoko said, "So that's Gojō Bridge." Kensaku nodded. "My uncle is terribly excited because he's going to get one of the old footstones from it. I think Mr. S got it for him."

"What will he do with it?"

"Put it outside his tea hut and use it as a step or something."

"Your uncle is rather keen on the tea ceremony and things like that, isn't he?"

"Yes, he is. He's not at all like my mother."

"When I met him for the first time at Tōsanrō he showed me an old wool pouch that I liked very much. He fancies such things too, does he?"

"That's a very old pouch. I remember his carrying that around with him when I was a child. Did you really like it?"

"Of course. It's a beautiful thing."

Naoko laughed. "I see that your tastes aren't very different from my uncle's. I thought as much when I saw you buying all those bottles today."

"And what kind of things does your brother like?"

"He's my mother's child too—not what you'd call a man of refined taste."

"It's better that way. Young people who cultivate elegant tastes aren't exactly admirable."

"You really approve of ignorance, don't you? You don't want people to know anything about literature, you don't want them to cultivate a taste for fine things . . ."

"Quite right," he said solemnly. "To go around cultivating a taste for so-called subtleties is not a particularly worthwhile endeavor."

"What a strange point of view," Naoko said, and broke into loud laughter. "That, too, I don't understand." Kensaku found himself laughing with her. She brought her face close to his and said, "I suppose you'd have disapproved if I had understood, wouldn't you?" She seemed to find the thought unbearably funny.

"Don't be a fool," Kensaku said, enjoying her merriment at his own pomposity.

On the other side of the bridge they caught a streetcar. They got off at Shijō, and went to an oyster boat restaurant moored beside a narrow bridge called Kikusui. Kensaku had not been to such a restaurant since his sojourn in Onomichi, and of course he could not but be reminded of his pain then; but in his present happiness the memory cast only a momentary shadow. Besides, the atmosphere of this place was totally different from that of the gloomy oyster restaurant in Onomichi, with all those warehouses standing ominously above it. In their place now were the brightly lit teahouses of Gion and the ever-gaudy Shijō Bridge, and beyond that the Minamiza Theatre. Beneath these lay the river, glittering with reflections of their brilliant lights.

About an hour later they left the restaurant. With a light spirit they walked through the teahouse district of Gion, mingling with the beautifully dressed dancing girls and their little attendants with their hair pulled back tight. As they came to the main thoroughfare on the Higashiyama side, Kensaku saw the shabby, little theatre where once he had seen Omasa the Viper coming out. "Have you ever heard of Omasa the Viper?" he asked Naoko.

"I think I remember reading a novelette about her."

"I saw her here once."

"Really? I had no idea she was still alive."

"She goes about acting out her so-called true experiences on the stage." He then described the large woman, her head shaved like a priest's, as she emerged from the theatre. How hopeless she looked, he said, how utterly joyless. He told Naoko about Eihana, too, and how that spring he had tried without success to write a story about her. "A confession ceases to be a confession once it's been made, don't you think?" he said. "When it's repeated, all the emotion that was there the first time is gone, there's no meaning left. Just imagine how empty it must feel to 'confess' day after day in front of an audience!" How much better, he went on to say, to be like Eihana, who in her pride had asked for no forgiveness for her past crimes, who had chosen to pay for them in her own defiant way. How much more abject was Omasa's life; of what use was her public contrition, or the public forgiveness, when all it brought was such emptiness as he had seen in her face?

"I wonder?" Naoko said. "You know, when I do something wrong and say nothing about it, I feel awful. I feel much better when I tell someone about it."

"But you can hardly equate your kind of wrongdoing with Omasa's or Eihana's."

"Do you really think so?" she asked seriously.

"Of course," he replied, thinking how innocent she was. "When *you* do something wrong, it's bound to be the sort of thing anyone can forgive once you own up to it. But it's not that simple with people like Omasa and Eihana. Once you've confessed, you can forget about it, and people will let you. But people don't let the likes of Omasa and Eihana off so easily. They demand that even after the confession the offender continue to be contrite. They don't like to see the offender too openly enjoying the benefits of his confession."

"But who do you mean when you say 'they'?"

"Who? Well, let's say the people who have been wronged."

"But that seems so vindictive."

"Maybe so—anyway, I suppose unless one makes a clean breast of it all, one runs the risk of feeling guilty all one's life. On the other hand, a confession can bring one a lot of trouble too, even worse trouble."

"What does one do, then?"

Kensaku, remembering his mother, suddenly was at a loss for an answer. He had pushed himself into a trap, and there was nothing he could find to say. In silence the two walked on.

As if threatened by something Naoko said, "Let's not talk about it any more." She had heard about Kensaku's mother, but it was not likely that she had associated her with the conversation. Rather, it was something she had sensed in his mood that had frightened her. She cuddled up to Kensaku. "Let's talk about something more pleasant," she said coaxingly. "Do think of something nicer to talk about. I get lost when you talk about difficult things like that."

Kensaku grinned. "You've now decided that the best way to win me over is to say you don't understand, right?"

By the time they reached their house in Kitanobō they were again in a cheerful mood.

14

About ten days later they found a newly built, two-story house that they liked very much in a place on the outskirts called Kinugasamura, and immediately moved in. It was on a cold day in January that they moved, cold even for Kyoto; and inside this new, unlived-in house with plaster just barely dry, the cold seemed intense.

An aged janitor in the employ of Mr. S's company was there to help them. This old man said to Kensaku, "Won't this place be a little lonely for the womenfolk when you're out? I'm not saying it's dangerous, but won't it be advisable to keep a dog?" Kensaku, impressed, asked him to find one for them.

That night Kensaku and Naoko brought into their bedroom all the braziers from the other rooms, and waited until the room had become thoroughly warm before they went to bed.

Kensaku chose a room upstairs for his study. He placed his desk before the north window, where the view gave him much pleasure. Immediately before him stood Mt. Kinugasa, gentle in outline and covered with pine groves. On this side of it were the woods of Kinkakuji, and behind it, only partly visible, were the highlands of Takagamine. To his left was Mt. Atago, much higher than Kinugasa; and if he leaned over his desk a little, there was Mt. Hiei to his right, its top covered with snow. He would often sit at his desk and simply stare at the view, not writing a word.

He and Naoko went out a great deal. They would walk to various temples and shrines not far from where they lived—Myōshinji in Hanazono, Kōryūji in Uzumasa, Kaiko Shrine whose deity was Hata-no-Kawakatsu, Ninnaji in Omuro, Kōetsuji in Takagamine, Daitokuji in Murasakino; and in the evenings they would go to some busy part of town—by streetcar to Shinkyōgoku if they felt like going far afield, or Senbondōri, known as "the Kyōgoku of Nishijin," if they wished to stay closer to home.

It was at about this time that an old high school friend of Kensaku's named Suematsu came to live in a boardinghouse in Okazaki. He was two years younger than Kensaku, but as boys they had lived near each other and so had become good friends. Four or five years before, Suematsu had entered a university in Kyoto, but through illness had had to return to Tokyo; and after a two-year absence from the university, had begun to return to Kyoto at half-yearly intervals to take the examinations he had missed. One evening this Suematsu came to see Kensaku with another young man who, he said, was a faithful reader of Kensaku's writings.

"Mizutani here says he likes your things and Sakaguchi's best of all," Suematsu said, much to Kensaku's discomfort. To be complimented together with Sakaguchi, of all people, did not make him exactly happy; besides, he never did know what to say when someone made favorable remarks about his work to his face.

"Mizutani is entering the university this year. He, too, is a student of the humanities. He writes poetry and things—stuff that I don't understand too well, of course."

"When I have something worth looking at," said Mizutani, "I'd like to bring it and show it to you, if you don't mind." He had a peculiarly straightforward manner about him, a little too clean-cut.

"Have you met Sakaguchi?" Kensaku asked.

"No, sir, I haven't had the pleasure."

When Naoko came in with the tea and cakes, Kensaku introduced her to Suematsu—and to Mizutani. She had changed her clothes and redone her hair in the few minutes since the visitors' arrival. With comely modesty and graciousness she poured the tea. She was every inch the model bride.

Suematsu turned to Mizutani and said, "You know Mrs. Tokitō's cousin, don't you?"

"Yes, I was at high school with Kaname, all the way through. And with Kuze."

Naoko for some reason blushed. Kensaku had never met Kaname, but knew he was Mr. N's son now attending an engineering college in Tokyo. "Who is Kuze?" he asked Naoko.

"He's a good friend of my cousin's," Naoko said quickly, almost too easily. "He goes to Dōshisha University here. He's the one that said such nice things about your work to my family, didn't you know?"

"I see."

"Kuze, too, wants very much to meet you," Mizutani said. "May I bring him?"

"By all means."

Naoko sat very close to Kensaku, almost leaning against him. Kensaku, embarrassed, tried to ignore her, but was at the same time concerned lest he should appear to be doing so too self-consciously. At an opportune moment, then, he moved away an inch or two nonchalantly as he pretended to change his sitting position.

"Does Kaname write to you at all?" Mizutani asked Naoko directly. What a familiar young man, Kensaku thought.

"No, I haven't heard from him at all," Naoko replied. She turned to Kensaku. "Isn't it terribly mean of him? He hasn't written to me once since we got married." Kensaku said nothing.

"He's apparently told Kuze that he intends to stop at Kyoto on his way home or on his way back to Tokyo," Mizutani said, "in order to observe you in your new role." He then laughed.

"How nasty!" Naoko said, blushing.

Suematsu was Kensaku's friend, yet made shy by Naoko's presence, he was not half so talkative as he usually was. But this Mizutani, who was a total stranger, showed no constraint whatsoever. His jokes, his facile remarks, were altogether inappropriate for someone his age; he was, in short, impertinent. He had a light complexion, a small, neat physique, and when he smiled, deep vertical dimples appeared on his cheeks. As for his eyes, they were somehow muddy. His kimono was blue with splashes of white; his long, student's skirt was of serge, and its cord was tied in a small, tight knot, with the long ends left dangling rakishly down the front. He and Suematsu lived in the same boardinghouse, and had only recently come to know each other. Their friendship seemed to be based on a common interest in chess, cards, billiards and other such diversions.

From the other side of the door Sen said, "Madame, will you please come here a minute?" When Naoko left the room, Suematsu, as if he had been waiting for such a chance, made a quick gesture with his hands, in imitation of someone dealing cards. He said with a grin, "Do you still play?"

"No," said Kensaku, shaking his head and smiling. At high school they and Oei had often played cards together.

"Do you have cards?"

"They should be around somewhere—the very same ones we used to play with."

"Oh, I'd like to play," Suematsu said wistfully, like a child.

"Are you keen on cards?"

"He's the keenest one in the boardinghouse," Mizutani said.

"How about your wife?" Suematsu asked Kensaku.

"I've no idea."

Letting Sen open the door for her, Naoko came in with a large cut-glass bowl filled with apple slices. Before she sat down, Kensaku looked up and said, "Do you know how to play 'flowers'?"

"Flowers?" she asked, cocking her head.

"I mean this," Kensaku said, gesturing as Suematsu had done.

"Oh, that," she said, sitting down and placing the bowl where everyone could reach it. "Yes, I know the game."

"How clever of you!" exclaimed Mizutani with eager admiration.

"Do you know where the cards and chips are?" Kensaku asked Naoko.

"Aren't they wrapped in a red cotton cloth? I think I saw them when we were moving."

"That's it."

She cocked her head again. It was a mannerism of hers. "Do you want me to find them?"

"Please do."

Soon the four were sitting under the electric light, around a cushion covered with a white cloth.

Suematsu divided up the chips, saying, "We'll multiply the points by four—everything else will be as usual."

"I don't understand," said Naoko. "It doesn't quite seem the same as the game I know."

"You know how to match them, don't you?" Kensaku said.

"Of course. There's the moon-viewing group, the flower-viewing group, then there's the boar-deer-butterfly group, and so on."

"I'm afraid that's not quite how we play."

"Really? I'll watch, then. It would be best if I stayed out."

"You'll learn soon enough, so do play," said Mizutani as he cut the cards deftly. "One of us who has to be the sleeper can help you."

"That's right," said Kensaku. "Join us, you won't find it difficult. If you'll bring me a piece of paper and something to write with, I'll write out the rules for you."

Naoko got up and left the room. Mizutani distributed the black cards. Kensaku got the crane. "I have the lead," he said, and started dealing the red cards. When Naoko returned, Mizutani said, "I'll write them out for you," and took the paper and the inkstone. He explained each point meticulously to Naoko as he wrote.

Kensaku looked at his cards briefly, then put them down. For lack of anything better to do he lit a cigarette.

"Where's Tatsuoka?" Suematsu asked. "Is he still in Paris?"

"Yes. Studying very hard, I gather."

"I'm told he's *the* Japanese authority on airplane engines."

"Is that so?" said Kensaku, very pleased. "He's already the top man, is he?"

"That's what they say. Does he write to you much?"

"Occasionally."

Having given a summary explanation of how the cards were

matched, Mizutani was now engaged in writing out some of the subtleties of point-counting.

"Enough's enough," said Suematsu impatiently.

"Wait a minute," said Mizutani. "I've finished with the first part of the explanation, and now I'm on the second part. I won't take long."

"How's Oei?" Suematsu asked Kensaku.

"She's in Tientsin right now."

Suematsu was flabbergasted. "In Tientsin! What in the world is she doing in a place like that?"

"A cousin of hers lives there. This cousin was back in Japan in the autumn of last year, and when she left, Oei went with her." Kensaku hoped Suematsu would not ask what sort of business Oei was in. He had no reason to lie about it, but somehow he did not want to mention it in front of a stranger like Mizutani.

"Is she in some sort of business there?"

"Yes, something or other she and her cousin decided to do together."

Suematsu did not pursue the matter any further. Just then Mizutani said, "Right, let's start." Kensaku immediately put his cards down to indicate he was to be the sleeper. "How many points will it cost me?" "Twenty-four," said Mizutani. After paying the fine Kensaku pulled himself close to Naoko and peered at her cards. "How are you doing?" he asked. Naoko held out her cards under his nose. "What do you think?" "Try playing them." "Is this a matching set?" she asked, painstakingly checking her cards against Mizutani's notes. The men all laughed.

Such was the way she began, a complete novice. Yet with the help of the sleeper in each deal, she somehow managed to pile up a great many points; and finally, under Mizutani's supervision, she won so many points that she emerged as the winner of the first round.

"Try playing on your own the next round," Kensaku said.

"All right, I shall," she said enthusiastically. But on her own she did so poorly that it was agreed she would again play with the sleeper's help.

She was not a good loser; and when the points were being counted at the end of a game, she was inclined to question the accuracy of the counting. "Are you sure?" she once said. "I thought I had a matching set."

"What are you talking about," Kensaku said. "That was in the last game. Don't be so greedy." Though he spoke in a jocular tone, he did think that she was being womanishly petty, that there was indeed a greedy streak in her.

Mizutani had the lead, and said he would play. Suematsu, the next to declare, and then Kensaku after him, both said they, too, would play. Willy-nilly Naoko had to be the sleeper.

"I'll buy your hand," said Kensaku, looking at Naoko. "Have you anything worthwhile?"

Naoko showed him her seven cards, neatly spread out like a fan. "I have a set," she said.

Taking a quick look at her cards he announced to the others, "Right, I have a set." Then noticing a chrysanthemum card in her hand he reached over and spread out the fan. The chrysanthemum card that had drawn his attention had a saké cup on it, which made it valueless. The cup had been covered up by the card next to it. She had hidden it on purpose, Kensaku thought.

Naoko, too, showed displeasure. "You don't think I knew about it, do you?"

"All right, but as punishment you won't be paid for your hand." Kensaku took out the useless card, shoved it into the deck of cards on the floor, and started playing. His action was quick and careless, but as he played he began to wonder about the little incident. Was it possible that the reason why he had been unable to dismiss it with some playful remark was that she had indeed tried to lie about her hand? The thought depressed him slightly; and it may have been his imagination, but the others, too, seemed suddenly to have become very quiet.

At about eleven the two visitors said they would be going. Kensaku and Naoko decided to go out with them.

"Come to our place sometime and have a game with us," said Suematsu.

"Perhaps I shall," said Kensaku without enthusiasm. He was not particularly anxious to seek recreation in the company of fellows like Mizutani.

"Yes, do come," said Mizutani. "On most days you'll find a game going on in one of the rooms."

"I'm not much of a card player, you know."

"Oh, but that isn't true! I find your style very interesting, Mr. Tokitō—it's so logical. Now, take Suematsu's style—it's what we call 'prayerful.' It has no form to it."

Kensaku turned to Suematsu. "What does he mean by 'prayerful'?"

"Oh, nothing much," Suematsu said, laughing.

"What I mean is," Mizutani said, "that Suematsu always hopes that the right card will turn up, and puts his trust in providence."

From Tsubakidera they crossed a small bridge and came to Ichijōdōri. At this late hour, with all the shops closed, this normally busy street was absolutely quiet. Naoko, her chin buried deep in a wool muffler belonging to Kensaku, walked behind him, not saying very much.

"Let's all go home, shall we?" said Suematsu.

Kensaku turned around and said to Naoko solicitously, "What would you like to do?"

"I'm all right, so please don't worry about me," she said.

"Then let's all walk as far as Daijōgun."

It was a cold night, and when no one was speaking, the harsh sound of their wooden clogs scraping the frozen ground seemed to shatter the brittle air around them.

Kensaku remembered that one spring, about ten years before, he and Suematsu had toured the five lakes of Mt. Fuji. "When it gets a little warmer," he said to his friend, "shall we go somewhere together?"

"That would be fun," said Suematsu. "I've been thinking of going to Tsukigase this spring. If you've never been there, it might be a good place for us to go. You get there from Kasagi, you know, over the pass."

"Tsukigase would be worth seeing, I'm sure," said Mizutani immediately. "I've never been there myself."

The two friends ignored him, and started reminiscing about their trip to the five lakes.

Soon they found themselves in front of the small, red-lacquered shrine of Daijōgun. Here Kensaku and Naoko said good-night to the two men, and started walking toward home. Naoko looked downcast. Guessing that she was still feeling hurt, Kensaku wished he could say something comforting to her, as much for his own sake as for hers; for his pride, too, had been hurt, as though he himself had taken part in the attempt to deceive.

An ox-drawn cart, piled high with vegetables, its wheels clattering, came toward them and went past. The ox swung its lowered head slowly and heavily from side to side, emitting clouds of vapor from its nostrils.

Unethical behavior—and cheating was unethical—Kensaku had always regarded with distaste. Why then, he wondered, did he not feel the slightest distaste or ill will toward what she had done? The tenderness that he now felt was overwhelming; through the unfortunate incident, it seemed he had become aware of a love for her that was deeper than what he had known before.

Silently he got hold of Naoko's hand, drew it toward his breast, and snuggled it under his coat. She narrowed her eyes like a coquette, and put her cheek against his shoulder. She is now absolutely a part of me, he thought, and surrendered himself to the poignancy of the moment.

15

Kensaku saw a great deal of Suematsu, partly because there was no other friend to see in Kyoto. Suematsu had at the time just become somewhat involved with a third-rate geisha of the Gion quarter, so that Kensaku had to exercise care in his choice of the time he would visit his infatuated friend. It would be awkward, after all, if he were to show up when Suematsu was about to leave for Gion. What added to the complication was Suematsu's reluctance, out of consideration for Naoko's feelings, to ask Kensaku to go to the quarter with him.

Late one evening, thinking that if Suematsu were going out he would have left already, Kensaku stopped by at his friend's boardinghouse on his way home from town. He had mistimed his visit; for Suematsu was still there but on the verge of leaving. The two friends faced each other guiltily.

"It's perfectly all right," Suematsu said, "really, it is." He sat down by the brazier as nonchalantly as he could, and began adding charcoal to the fire. But he betrayed his nervousness soon enough. "Shall I ask her to come over here?"

"No, let's go there instead," Kensaku said. "It'd be easier."

"Do you really mean that?" Suematsu said, scratching his head in embarrassment, yet visibly pleased. "Are you sure your wife won't mind?"

It was past nine o'clock when they walked out into the cold. They walked straight down the wide, quiet road past Heian Shrine toward the main thoroughfare.

"Where shall we meet her?" Suematsu asked.

"Why not where you always see her?"

Suematsu grinned. "I'd be too ashamed to take you there. The teahouse is third-rate, just as she is. Let's go to a restaurant instead."

"But what if she's already engaged for the evening? There would be no point in our being at a restaurant if she couldn't come. I've just eaten, and so, I presume, have you."

"Yes, that's true, but she's not likely to be engaged. She's not in such great demand, you know."

They got off the streetcar by the stone steps outside Gion, and went into a nearby bar. There Suematsu telephoned to find out if the geisha were free. "Yes, I see," Kensaku heard him saying. "Goodnight, then." He put the receiver back noisily and returned to the table looking ill-tempered. "True, they get only sixty yen a month out of me, and I mustn't expect too much, but it's annoying all the same." He turned to the waitress and ordered a strong drink.

"Wasn't she there?"

"She's gone to the theatre in Osaka, they say, and won't be back tonight. Of course they're lying." He was so openly upset, Kensaku began to pity him. No doubt, he thought, Suematsu is imagining her cavorting with some other patron; and judging by his irate expression, what he imagined was all too vivid.

The telephone rang, and a waitress went to answer it. "If it's for me," Suematsu called out shrilly, "tell them I'm not here!"

The call was indeed for him. "But I can't say that," the waitress said, covering the mouthpiece with her hand. "The lady knows you're here."

"Tell her I refuse to leave my table, then."

It was the madam of the teahouse, and she was obviously being persistent. At last Suematsu relented and went to the telephone. After some arguing back and forth Suematsu agreed to go to the teahouse. "It's a shabby establishment, understand," he said as he sat down. "At any rate, since my woman won't be there, there's no reason to hurry. We'll stay here a bit." He ordered another drink, determined to calm himself down. Besides, he was not about to be bullied into hurrying by a mere teahouse madam. "Are you sure you want to go?" he asked Kensaku. "It's turning out to be a pretty dull evening for you, I'm afraid."

"Not at all, "Kensaku said casually, wishing there was some way to console Suematsu. But it was true that, for the time being at least, the two friends' respective moods were too far apart for either to offer the other much in the way of companionship. And Kensaku for his part would catch himself from time to time thinking of Naoko in that isolated house in Kinugasamura waiting forlornly for her husband to return; he would then quickly assume a bland expression, hoping that he had not given Suematsu reason to suspect that his mind was elsewhere.

"I know another teahouse in Hanamikōji," Suematsu said. "That's where we should have gone in the first place."

As they left the bar and made their way to the teahouse, Suematsu still fretted about its being such a shabby establishment. He was decidedly a little drunk.

At the teahouse he refused to be shown to a room. He would rather go to a restaurant he knew in Kōdaiji, he told the madam; and since it was past ten, he had her telephone to warn them of their coming. The two then left the madam, who was to join them later at the restaurant with appropriate reinforcements.

The second floor of a small wing at the rear of the garden was lit up in readiness for them. There the two men waited. After about twenty minutes they heard the busy sound of several women coming through the garden in their wooden clogs. Then the door opened, and the madam, led by the maid, rushed in noisily with two geisha in tow.

Suematsu, still in an aggrieved mood, immediately began making himself extremely unpleasant to the madam. The two young geisha tried to distract him by teasing him about his paramour, but to no avail. Ignoring their chatter, he continued to taunt the madam.

"Ah well," he said at last, "who am I to complain—I'm only a sixty-yen patron." And he did seem to wilt for a moment, as though overcome by the indignity of his own jealous infatuation for such a woman.

The madam was now sick of this party which she herself had insisted on having. Unable to maintain her professional composure any longer, she suggested that they all leave the restaurant.

Kensaku wanted to return to Naoko as quickly as possible. He knew she would be worrying, for he had never gone home after midnight since they were married. But to go away by himself now, he felt, would appear rude.

They stepped out into the quiet night, and cut across the grounds of Yasui Shrine. The short, not unattractive geisha with the kinky hair was teasing Suematsu about something; and without interrupting her teasing she found Kensaku's hand in the dark and held it. Kensaku led her hand into the pocket of his Inverness cape. He could now feel her shoulder against his arm. Not many nights before he had walked home like this with Naoko. And despite the geisha's proximity, he continued to think only of Naoko sitting up and waiting for him to return. The geisha soon became aware of his unresponsiveness; and as though by mutual agreement, they let go of each other's hand.

The madam pleaded with Suematsu to stay the night at her tea-house, but he would not listen. Just put the two geisha up for the night, he told her, and came out with Kensaku.

Neither of them suggested going home. Such nights were always difficult to end. Had Kensaku felt free to do so he would have put a stop to their wandering happily enough, but he knew from his own past experience how loathe Suematsu would be to end it then and there.

"It'll be all right so long as I get home by two," Kensaku said.

"Can we go to the teahouse in Hanamikōji?" asked Suematsu hesitantly.

"All right."

"By the way, don't expect me to come to your house for a while. I'm afraid your wife will disapprove of me."

They were in a dark alley. Suematsu stopped, faced the wall and began urinating. Just then a young man wearing a felt hat low over his eyes walked past him. "Forgive me," Suematsu said solemnly. The young man walked on, ignoring the apology. "Idiot!" shouted Suematsu. "How dare you not answer when someone speaks to you!" And as soon as he had finished urinating, he began running after the young man, his long body swaying like a reed. Kensaku stood in the middle of the narrow alley, his arms stretched out, and blocked his friend. The young man quickly disappeared around the corner.

"Let me have a good fight, please," said Suematsu, his breath reeking of alcohol.

"Do as you please, but I want no part of it."

"All right, but I'm going to knock him down. Where the hell did he go?" Suematsu shook himself free of Kensaku's hold and rushed out into the main street. But of course the young man was nowhere to be seen.

The teahouse in Hanamikōji was newly built, and had little in the way of atmosphere; but it was presumably a better-class establishment than the other one. The madam was a large woman, looking remarkably like a respectable housewife. "It's been a long time," she said as she bowed.

"Would you call a geisha for me?" Suematsu asked.

"Surely."

Kensaku said, "But not for me. I'll be leaving in a minute."

The madam looked questioningly at Suematsu, as if to say, "Does he mean it?"

Suematsu said unhappily, "If only we didn't have to worry about your wife." He really did seem to want Kensaku to stay.

Kensaku had had too much experience of the demimonde to demand chastity of himself. It was merely that by staying he would in fact be insulting his wife in Suematsu's presence. And to insult her was finally to insult himself. His desire to leave, then, was a selfish one, motivated by considerations which had little to do with his conscience. Before long he was being carried in a rickshaw through the cold, windy streets toward Kinugasamura, which seemed to him then very far away.

When he got off the rickshaw in front of Tsubakidera it was past two o'clock. From there he ran a hundred yards or so down the path that led to his house, and came to a sudden stop a few feet from the gate. Perhaps because he was breathing heavily, he coughed. Naoko must have heard him, for through the glass door of the maid's room he saw her running out of the morning room. Her voice reached him, dimly as if from a distance, as she called out, "Sen, the master is back!"

Without waiting for the gate to be opened he jumped over the low and still straggly hawthorn hedge. Naoko rushed out of the kitchen door to greet him. "I'm so glad!" she said, holding his hand under the cape tight.

"You should have gone to bed," Kensaku said.

In the morning room she tood before him and nervously started unbuttoning and unhooking his cape. "I thought you had fainted in the street or something . . ."

Sen shouted from the adjacent room, "Madame can be pretty silly sometimes!"

"It's not silly at all!" Naoko shouted back. She then said to Kensaku, "Sen kept on telling me not to be silly, but I couldn't help worrying. Anyway, it's wonderful that you're back."

"But did you really think I'd fainted?" Kensaku asked, laughing.

"Yes, I did."

Sen was laughing. "Madame was going out to look for you at about one o'clock. So I said to her, where will you look for him?"

"Don't bother to get me any tea," Kensaku said. "Let's all go to bed." He quickly changed into his night clothes and went into the bedroom. Naoko was still strangely excited as she folded and put away his clothes, and kept on laughing and saying, "I'm so glad."

Kensaku, lying in bed and with his head turned toward her, told her about that evening. But in her excitement, she did not even pretend to hear a word he said.

16

Their uneventful life together in Kinugasamura was extremely peaceful and happy. Yet sometimes, when he was reminded that indolence necessarily accompanied the peace and happiness, he would feel vaguely dejected and begin fretting about his work. He had not been able to do anything substantial for a long time—not even the piece he had promised to give to Nobuyuki's friend.

He continued to see much of Suematsu. Knowing that Kensaku disliked Mizutani, Suematsu made some effort to come alone to the house; but almost every other time he brought Mizutani with him. The reason was simple: it was better to play cards with four than with three players.

One evening, during a game, Kensaku picked up his hand and thought he had a set. But later, when he saw the saké cup on the chrysanthemum card, he realized he had made exactly the same error that Naoko had made. The coincidence both amused and pleased him. It was as though someone had deliberately arranged it so that he might know that Naoko had indeed made an innocent mistake. He had never thought to condemn her for what he imagined she had done; he was nevertheless happy to know that she had not cheated. He wanted to tell her about his discovery, but too ashamed of his own suspiciousness, he could not bring himself to do so.

February and March passed, and with the coming of April all of Kyoto, like the flowering trees, burst into activity. The people flocked to Gion to view the cherries by night, or to Saga to view them by day; and later, when the double cherries began to bloom, to Omuro. When such annual festivities as the dance of the Gion geisha, the procession of the Shimabara geisha, and the mime of Mibu were over, and the lines of red lanterns in the streets of Gion were no more to be seen, it was already May. By the time the fresh foliage on Higashi-yama had become more beautiful than the flowers, and the red-tinged leaves of the camphor trees had begun to show in gently outlined clumps behind the pagodas of Yasaka and Kiyomizu, even the citizenry of Kyoto seemed ready for a rest.

Certainly Kensaku and Naoko had had a surfeit of gaiety in celebration of the coming of spring. And it was at about this time that he learned of her pregnancy.

June and July were tolerable enough, but by August the notorious Kyoto heat had become quite intense, and in her condition Naoko was particularly affected by it. Signs of fatigue were detectable even in her plump cheeks; and occasionally Kensaku would find her sitting forlornly in the room, seemingly too tired to do anything. It was a relief to Kensaku, then, that at this time Naoko's aged aunt should have decided to come to stay with them for a while. Large-bodied, her craggy face covered with deep wrinkles, she was a somewhat frightening woman to look at. But she turned out to be an unusually open sort of person, who began behaving with utter ease as soon as she stepped into their house. Toward Kensaku she was kind but firm, and all in all treated him as though he were a child. She was like a true aunt to him, he soon began to think, and found himself being increasingly drawn to her.

When the heat became unbearable, it occurred to Kensaku that they might go to some hot spring resort up in the mountains for two or three weeks. Having never gone to such a place in his life, he was enchanted by the prospect of doing so in the company of Naoko and this likeable old lady.

Excitedly he communicated his idea to the two women. "I wonder," said Naoko's aunt. "A train journey may not be good for her."

"Surely it would still be all right?"

"No, you're wrong. This heat won't hurt her—after all, it's not so terrible—but riding on a train might. Besides, constant bathing in that hot water might make the baby inside grow too fast."

And so in the face of this opposition Kensaku had to drop his well-intentioned plan. In the meantime, however, Naoko had begun to show more liveliness in her demeanor, and the three of them passed their time together pleasantly enough. Occasionally they played cards, albeit simple, old-fashioned games. After a sojourn of about a month Naoko's aunt went home.

With the coming of September Naoko's condition showed much

improvement. Often, late at night, when Kensaku came downstairs from his study, he would find Naoko with her big belly sitting under the electric light, sewing baby clothes.

"Isn't it pretty," she once said as he came into the room, pointing at a red padded vest she had just finished. She had devised a make-shift coat hanger for it by tying a string around the middle of a ruler, then hanging it on a pull on the chest of drawers. The distance be-tween the outstretched sleeves of the vest and the floor was about what the height of a baby would be.

"Yes, it's very pretty," Kensaku answered, experiencing a new and joyous sensation as he imagined the tiny, living thing standing in the room. It had its back turned toward him. It had plump little buttocks—it was plump all over—and its head barely showed above the high, tucked collar of the vest.

"Do you want a boy," he asked, "or a girl? Which really would you prefer?" He was of course asking himself the same question.

"Whichever it turns out to be," was her reply. She put a thread through the eye of the needle, then ran the thread through her hair a time or two. Her manner was very calm and assured. "That, after all, is a matter for the gods to decide."

Kensaku laughed. "Why, you sound just like your aunt!" No doubt, Naoko had heard her aunt saying precisely that.

Other baby clothes arrived, sewn by Naoko's mother. And from her aunt came a large number of diapers, made out of old cotton, limp and faded from numerous washings. Naoko, who had expected to find more baby clothes in the parcel, was much embarrassed. "What does she think she's doing, sending me these shabby things!"

"You're being ungrateful," said Sen. "You can never have too many diapers. Besides, these are better than the ones made out of new cloth, which would be much rougher on the baby's skin."

Kensaku said, "I suppose these were made out of an old summer kimono of yours?" He imagined Naoko as a young girl wearing such large-patterned and coarse clothes, and was touched.

"Yes, and that's why I'm ashamed. I hate to think that I had to wear my clothes until they got this shabby, even if I was a simple country girl." She was clearly upset. "My aunt should have had more sense."

"It was very thoughtful of your aunt," Sen said. She was smiling, but her smile was not altogether friendly.

The baby was due, they were told, in late October or early November. The delivery would be at home, they decided; but if by any chance it was early and coincided with the harvest, and for this reason Naoko's mother could not come, then it would be at the hospital. Either way, Naoko's aunt would be present.

One sunny and pleasant morning Kensaku and Naoko went out for a walk. They cut across the fields behind their house and walked almost as far as the temple. When they returned, they found Nobuyuki waiting for them by the gate. He was smoking a cigarette; and though still in his Western clothes, he had taken his shoes off and put on a pair of their garden clogs.

"Hullo," he said to Kensaku, giving him a quick nod. He then turned to Naoko. "As well as ever, I trust?"

"When did you come to Kyoto?" Kensaku asked. "This morning?"

"Yes. Something suddenly came up that I thought we ought to talk about."

Kensaku led the way through the gate and into the house. Nobuyuki looked around the living room and said, "It's a nice house, this." He picked up the cushion Sen had put out and put it down nearer the verandah. "It concerns Oei, as a matter of fact," he said as he sat down. "Can you spare three hundred yen or so?"

"Yes, I can."

"Very good. We'll send her the money right away, shall we?"

"Is she in some sort of difficulty?" Kensaku understood why Oei would now want to go to Nobuyuki for help and not him, but he felt a little slighted nonetheless.

"It turned out that Osai—that's her name, isn't it?—had no interest whatsoever in Oei's welfare. You were quite right about that woman. Anyway, Oei left Tientsin in June—she didn't tell you that, I gather—and lived in Mukden for a while, then moved to Dairen. She's there now."

"What's she doing there?"

"Nothing. She lives in rooms above a seal maker's shop, and has some young girl from the neighborhood coming in daily to help her with the chores. She says she was managing all right until burglars broke in about a fortnight ago and took just about everything she owned."

"When did she tell you all this?"

"In a letter I got from her the day before yesterday."

Unable to contain himself any longer Kensaku cried out, "What an idiot she is! Why didn't she come home at once?"

"I feel as you do. But she apparently owes the seal maker some money, and besides, she hasn't any money for the fare. I thought three hundred yen would probably cover her debt and the fare, but unfortunately, I haven't a penny right now. I could have borrowed from father, but I really didn't want to tell him about Oei. Of course, I haven't come all this way just to discuss Oei's plight with you. The rectory of our temple is in need of repair, and I'm going around trying to collect money for it." Nobuyuki then mentioned a certain abbot in Kyoto. "Is it true that he's a painter?" he asked.

"I suppose so. All I can tell you is that I've seen his things for sale at the Shirokiya Department Store."

"I'm told they fetch very high prices. Anyway, our rector thought he might give us a half dozen or so of his things in lieu of a cash contribution, and asked me to go and see him. That's another reason why I decided to come down so suddenly."

"I trust Oei has no other worries besides money?"

"Well, she did say she had the ague. By that I suppose she meant malaria. I never realized you could get malaria in that part of the world."

"I should imagine you could get it anywhere. But it's not a particularly dangerous disease, is it?"

"She says it's not all that serious. Oh yes, she did say that it was the indirect cause of the burglary. She had taken her medicine at the wrong time, as a result had had a very bad attack of the fever, and was lying in bed exhausted and in a near-delirious state when she saw two Chinese coming in through the window. It was night, but she had left it open, you see, because of the heat. In the corner of the room were three trunks containing those kimonos for the geisha that she collected in Tokyo, and these the burglars took away. She was obviously hoping to start up another business, you know, with the kimonos as her capital. So she watched the two men carrying her trunks out of the window, thinking they must be burglars. But she was too exhausted to do or say anything, and simply fell asleep."

"Well, one misfortune leads to another, as they say," Kensaku said lightly. With the realization that he would soon be seeing Oei again, his mood had suddenly become quite cheerful. "But if she comes back immediately, her misfortunes will have been a blessing in disguise."

"Perhaps so," said Nobuyuki, grinning back at Kensaku.

Kensaku had never approved of Oei's going to China. If she had not known this in the beginning, it was because Nobuyuki, in reporting his thoughts to her, had not been entirely candid. He felt quite smug now, and if Oei had appeared at that very moment, his first words of welcome would have been, "See, what did I tell you?"

The next day Nobuyuki, having finished his business in Kyoto, left for Osaka where also he was to see some potential donors. He then returned to Kinugasamura to spend another night with Kensaku and Naoko.

"How about a contribution from you two," he said the following morning, pulling a notebook out of his imposing briefcase. The pages, Kensaku noticed, were of stout, high-quality Japanese paper; it was bound with what looked like cloth from a priest's surplice.

Kensaku picked it up and looked at the entries. "Two hundred yen, two hundred and fifty yen, thirty yen, ten yen, five hundred yen—I say, people are generous. And I see here an entry for one hundred and fifty yen under your name. Am I correct?"

"Yes, yes, but I haven't given it yet, you understand. I couldn't, you know."

"Do you mean to say you can put your name down for an amount like that and not have to pay up?"

Nobuyuki laughed. "Hardly. Of course I shall give them the money sometime."

Naoko said, "Forgive me, but will a little sum be acceptable?"

"Yes, indeed. Two yen, three yen, it doesn't matter how little."

"Really? In that case, I'll contribute five yen."

"That's very nice of you," Nobuyuki said. "Will you please write your name down in the book?"

Naoko stood up and went to fetch the ink box lying on top of the chest of drawers. As she sat down, she said to Kensaku, "And you?"

"Your contribution will be enough," Kensaku answered. "I'm entirely in favor of maintaining temples, but I'm against the idea of my contributing toward their support. That's the job of the government. They ought to be more responsible about such things."

"Aren't you being a little inconsistent?" said Naoko.

"Not at all. But all right, if the amount doesn't matter, put me down for ten yen."

Kensaku's handwriting was atrocious; and when he wrote with a brush, even he was appalled by the result. Naoko's handwriting was very much better, so that he had got into the habit of asking her to write whenever the brush was required.

"Thank you very much," Nobuyuki said, and when the ink had dried, put away the notebook in his briefcase.

In the evening Kensaku and Naoko took Nobuyuki for a walk around Teramachi and Shinkyōgoku, then later accompanied him to Shichijō Station, where he caught the train to Kamakura.

17

On a certain day in late October Kensaku, Suematsu, Mizutani, and a friend of Mizutani's named Kuze went to Kurama to see the fire festival. At sunset they walked northward from the edge of Kyoto along a road that went gradually uphill. They had walked perhaps eight miles when they saw a red glow in one of the mountain valleys, still far from where they were. They could see, too, a veil of smoke hanging over the valley and its environs. The mountain air, scented with moss, became chillier as they proceeded; and Kensaku began to wonder how it was that a nighttime festival should ever have come to be held in such a remote place. There were others on the road— men, women, and children—all carrying lanterns. Occasionally an automobile would pass them, sending shafts of bright light into the woods and mountainsides ahead. From the mountains night herons flew toward them, uttering their sharp cries. Then, as they approached Kurama, they became aware of the smell of smoke lingering in the air.

In front of every house along the street a small wood fire was burning. Each fire was surrounded on three sides by large tree roots and logs the size of a grown man. Because the street was narrow, the fires in front of the houses looked like a continuous line of flickering flames right down the middle of it. They were an eerie sight, like cave fires in ancient times.

The street led into a fairly open area on one side of which was a flight of wide stone steps. On top of the steps was a great red-lacquered gate. In this open area, surrounded by enthralled spectators, were young men carrying huge torches made of brushwood tied together with wisteria vine. They wore loincloths, leggings and straw sandals, and skimpy protective coverings on their shoulders and the backs of their hands. "*Chōsa, yōsa!*" they shouted to each other as they moved, or danced, heavily yet skillfully under the weight. Some would pretend to totter, bringing the torches dangerously close to the spectators, and some would go under the eaves of the houses, then come away before any damage was done. When the flame got weaker, or the shoulder too painful, one young man would suddenly let his torch, which was an armful in girth, fall to the ground. A vine band would snap, the brushwood open up, and the flame revive. The young man, wiping the sweat off his face and breathing deeply, would then bend down, and with the aid of someone standing by, pick it up and place it on his other shoulder.

The torch carriers now left the open area and went into the street on the other side. Here there was no line of fires. "*Chōsa, yōsa!*" cried the young men to one another as they staggered back and forth in the narrow space. Children, carrying appropriately smaller torches, mingled with the young men and imitated their stagger. There was a thin mist of smoke everywhere in the town; and the mountain air, so chilly earlier, had become pleasantly warm.

It was a moving experience for Kensaku to watch this fire festival under the clear, star-filled autumn sky. Behind the single row of low-roofed houses ran a deep mountain torrent; and all around him were high mountains, whose stillness in the night seemed to mute even the noises of the festival. Kensaku had never seen such a festival as this; all he had seen before were those raucous affairs in the city. Here, all the participants seemed so serious. There was not a drunk to be seen, despite the fact that it was an all-male festival, and the only ones who raised their voices were the young men crying, "*Chōsa, yōsa!*"

In the middle of a small, fast-flowing brook under the eaves a young man sat chanting some wordy prayer, his eyes closed, his hands placed together before him. The pure, icy-looking water dashed against his chest and swirled past him. By the brook, waiting for him to come out, were a girl holding a strangely dim lantern with a crest on it and a woman holding out with both hands a plain-colored, hemp kimono. At last the prayer was over. As the man stood up and stepped into the clogs lying on the ground beside him, the woman silently draped the kimono over his wet body. Without waiting for the girl to precede him with the lantern, the man shuffled into the dark, earth-floored entrance hall of a nearby house. Kensaku and his companions learned that he was one of the men who would carry the portable shrine down the hill.

Soon afterward these men gathered together at the foot of the stone steps in the open area. On either side of the steps stood a thick bamboo pole, and stretched between the poles was a rope. The rule was that until this rope had been severed by fire from the torches, no one could go up the steps. But it was more than twenty feet from the ground, and even when the torches were held upright the flames by no means went near it. A great number of torches were gathered under the rope, and their flames, like a great bonfire, lighted the upturned faces of the expectant crowd.

At last the rope caught fire, then split in two, scattering sparks through the air. Immediately a man brandishing a naked sword rushed up the steps. With a roar the crowd ran up after him. Stretched across the open gate was another rope, placed lower than the first, a little above a man's height. The man ran under this, holding up his sword. The rope cut easily, allowing the crowd to go through the gate and run farther up the hill toward the inner shrine.

Kensaku turned to Suematsu and said, "Shall we go home now?"

"Let's wait and see the dance of the fires around the portable shrine."

At the first stop of the procession of the portable shrine, men carrying even larger torches than those already seen—each required four or five men to carry it—were to dance around the shrine to the festival music.

"We have a pretty good idea of what that's going to be like," said Kensaku. "Don't forget, we're going to the recital tomorrow, and we've got to get some sleep before then."

Suematsu looked at his watch. "It is two-thirty already, I must admit."

"If we leave now," Mizutani said, "we'll be in Kyoto by dawn."

"I suppose we should leave," Suematsu said, still not convinced. "They say it's very exciting when they carry the shrine down the hill. It's so steep, the men can't check the momentum, and they start running faster and faster. They have a large rope tied to the back of the shrine, and the women act as brake by holding on to it. It's the only time women take any part in the festival."

"Let's go anyway," said Mizutani. "Can you imagine what it would be like having to walk back eight miles in the sun?"

Suematsu at last relented. The fires in the lower part of the town, which Kensaku had thought were like flickering cave fires, were now burning vigorously. And when the four men came out of the town, away from the fires, they suddenly felt the chill of the mountain air. From time to time they would turn around to look at the valley, which glowed red in the surrounding darkness. The walking was easier going downhill, and the road seemed shorter. But they were tired, and they said less and less to each other as they walked.

The first to break the silence was Suematsu. "I can't keep my eyes open!"

"Here, I'll hold on to you," said Mizutani, putting his arm around Suematsu, "so go to sleep as you walk."

Mizutani had said it would be dawn by the time they reached Kyoto, and he was right; for just as they entered the city, the sky behind Mt. Hiei began to light up. At the streetcar terminal they were able to sit down and rest their tired bodies. In a short while the first streetcar of the day arrived. They all got on, and at Marutamachi Kensaku alone got off, to change to a streetcar going to Kitano.

He was in Kinugasamura at last, walking toward his house in the soft morning sun of autumn. "The master is back!" he heard Sen shouting excitedly. She rushed out of the kitchen, a big grin on her face. "The baby has arrived, yes indeed."

Kensaku, his heart pounding unreasonably, rushed into the room that they had assigned for the delivery. Conscious of the smell of creosol or some such disinfectant, he looked at Naoko lying in the middle of the room. She lay on her back, her forehead drained of color and her hair lying loosely around the pillow; she was in a deep sleep. The baby slept in a small bed which had been laid separately beside Naoko's. But it was Naoko, and not the baby, that engaged Kensaku's attention. He looked at the young nurse, who bowed silently, and asked her in a low voice, "How was it?"

"It was a comfortable delivery."

"I'm glad, I'm very glad."

Sen, seated by the door, said, "It's a boy."

"Is that so?" Kensaku said.

In relief he looked over the low screen that had been placed at the head of the baby's bed, but the face was hidden under a piece of gauze. "What time was he born?"

"Twenty minutes past one," replied the nurse.

"The mistress wanted you to know at once," Sen said, "and we sent a rickshaw man off to find you. I don't suppose you saw him?"

"No, I didn't. Let's go to the morning room and talk there. We mustn't wake them."

On the previous evening, just as Kensaku left the house, the newspaper boy had come in to deliver the evening paper. According to Sen, what then happened was that this boy, too lazy to hand the paper to Naoko who was still in the front hall after having seen Kensaku off, had thrown it to her. It fell on the stone step below the raised floor. Naoko reached down to pick it up, when suddenly she felt a strange pain in her womb. Later, when the pain returned, she realized what it meant, and had Sen telephone the midwife, the doctor, and Mr. S. She then had her evening bath (she was about to do so when the pain returned), put on her delivery clothes, and waited.

When Sen had finished her story Kensaku said, "That was impressive." He did indeed admire Naoko for her surprising control and presence of mind at such a time.

"Mrs. S came at once with her maid. They left shortly before you returned."

"I see. Is the baby healthy?"

"He's a magnificent baby."

Kensaku wanted to ask more questions about the baby. "Will you ask the nurse to come in?"

The nurse appeared on the verandah and sat down, spreading out the starched panels of her long, white skirt around her.

"Please come into the room," Kensaku said. "Wasn't the baby born much sooner than expected?"

"No, not really. It's true that the pregnancy was a little shorter than normal—it was two hundred and fifty days—but I don't think he's exactly a premature baby."

"I see. And there's no cause for me to worry about either of them?"

"None at all."

"Thank you very much," he said, bowing. But as he did so, he could not help feeling that thanking her was not enough, that he owed his thanks to something else too, though exactly what, he didn't know. The nurse went back to the delivery room.

He was about to change his clothes and go to the bathroom to wash when the nurse appeared again to say that Naoko was awake.

Naoko lay on her back, her head still, only her eyes expressing her expectancy as he came in from the verandah. He looked at her pale, tired face, and thought how beautiful she was.

He sat down beside her pillow. "Well, how are you?" he said, wishing he could have sounded less offhand.

Naoko merely smiled contentedly, then with great effort brought out her pale hand with the veins showing and opened it in invitation. Kensaku held it tightly and said, "Was it painful?"

Naoko shook her head slightly, her eyes fixed on his.

"Really? I'm so glad." Her brave denial touched him deeply, and he wanted to reach out and stroke her head. He tried to free his hand, but she would not let go. He changed his sitting position, and with his other hand that had been resting on the floor began stroking her head.

In a voice that was low from exhaustion she asked, "What's he like? Is he a nice baby?"

"I haven't had a good look at him yet."

"Is he asleep?"

"Yes. Haven't you yourself seen him properly yet?"

She shook her head. The nurse said, "Would you like to see him?" Without waiting for an answer she pushed the screen aside, took the gauze off the baby's face, and rather roughly—or so Kensaku thought—pulled his bed closer to Naoko's.

He had a red and uncannily hairy face; his head came to a point, and this point was covered with lank, black hair that looked as though it had been pasted on; and his closed eyelids were swollen. He was altogether a dismaying sight, like no baby Kensaku could remember ever having seen.

Kensaku giggled. "It's just as well he's a boy, eh? Couldn't have a face like that on a girl."

The nurse clearly disapproved of his remarks. "All babies at first look like this, sir."

The baby's lips, which looked so delicate that Kensaku wouldn't have dared touch them lest the skin peeled off, twitched nervously. Then he opened his mouth wide, creased his face, and began to wail.

Naoko turned her head toward him, reached out and pressed her fingers on his quilt-covered shoulder. The look in her eyes as she gazed at him was extraordinarily gentle, extraordinarily motherly.

Kensaku, for his part, did not in the least feel like a father. "Are you sure he's going to look all right?"

"His face is swollen now," the nurse said, "but when the swelling goes down, he'll be a fine-looking baby."

"Really? I'm relieved to hear that. It would be terrible if he were to grow up looking like that." Reassured and more cheerful now, he added jocularly, "There is a comic mask in the Nara Museum that looks just like him."

Neither Naoko nor the nurse smiled; but Sen, who was setting the table in the next room, laughed. "What an awful thing to say, sir!"

"I don't suppose telegrams have been sent out yet to the various people?"

"No," said Naoko.

"I had better do that right away, then," Kensaku said, and went up to his study.

18

All went well. Occasionally Kensaku would go into Naoko's room to have a look at the sleeping baby, motivated more by curiosity than by fatherly concern. That this baby was of his own flesh was something he could not yet feel with any sense of reality. And he never even tried to pick him up, afraid that he would somehow hurt him if he did. But Naoko had completely become a mother. He would watch her as she nursed the baby in her bed, thinking how confident she seemed. Sometimes the sight of the baby sucking away contentedly, his nose almost buried in the soft flesh, would strike him as beautiful; and sometimes it unsettled him, for the baby would resemble some strange, rapacious creature about to devour Naoko's white breast. If he had not so rarely seen a newly born baby before, he would have been less uncertain.

No one came from Tsuruga. Naoko's mother could not come until later, and her aunt, who would normally have rushed to Naoko's bedside, was suffering from an attack of her chronic neuralgia. But Naoko seemed not at all distressed by their absence.

The so-called ceremony of the seventh day drew near, and they had to name their baby by then. A name that appealed to them both was difficult to find; and eventually they settled for Naonori, which was a combination of the first characters of their own names, "nori" being another reading for "ken" of Kensaku. A rather resounding name for a baby, they agreed disconsolately. "But," Kensaku argued, "he won't be a baby forever."

The first week went by exceedingly smoothly. Then on the eighth night, when everyone had gone to bed, the baby started crying incessantly. He would stop briefly when Naoko put her nipple in his mouth, then start crying again. They examined his navel to see if it was giving him pain, but it seemed quite normal. Thinking that perhaps he was being bitten by a bug, they changed all his clothes, but that made no difference. Puzzled and now thoroughly uneasy, they took his temperature. It was a little higher than it should be.

"What do you think?" Kensaku said. "Should we ask Dr. K to come?"

Naoko said worriedly, "Yes, perhaps we should."

But in a little while the crying became weaker and weaker, until at last it ceased entirely, and the baby fell into a deep, seemingly untroubled sleep. With a sigh of relief Kensaku said, "What was the matter with him?"

Naoko did not answer the question; instead she merely said, "Thank goodness it's over."

"There are babies who habitually cry at night," Sen said, then began to urge them to stick on the ceiling a picture of the devil saying his prayers. "That might help, you know."

The baby continued to sleep. Making as little noise as possible, everyone went back to bed.

Kensaku lay in his bed in the study, unable to go back to sleep. He was sure that Naoko, too, would be awake, especially since in her present condition she would have had several naps during the day. But he dared not go downstairs to her, for fear he might wake the baby.

In an attempt to settle down he was reading something light when the clock in the morning room started to strike. It was midnight, and before the loud striking was over the baby was awake and crying again. He could hear Naoko and the nurse talking.

When he went downstairs he found Naoko sitting up in her bed with the baby in her arms. The crying was desperate.

Naoko looked up at Kensaku and said angrily, "Can't you do something about that clock? It woke the baby."

"I'll go and stop it."

"Please do," she said, vainly offering her breast to the baby. "And I'd rather you never started it again. We have no need of it."

When he returned from the morning room he said, "Let's at least have some local doctor come and look at him. Dr. K lives so far away, and it's very late. Besides, the baby is likely to stop crying soon."

"All right."

"I'll go out right away and find a doctor, then."

He went out by the back door. It was pitch-dark outside, and windless. He had seen a house on Onmaedōri, less than half a mile away, with a sign on it saying simply, "Doctor." With latticed door and windows, it had looked more like a shopkeeper's house than a doctor's. Running part of the way he reached it quickly. He banged on the door two or three times, and a woman's voice answered, "What do you want?"

"Can the doctor come to my house?"

"Where do you live?"

"In Kinugasa Park, very near here. Our baby isn't well, and we want the doctor to come and look at him."

"Please wait a minute," the woman said, still behind the closed door, and went away. She came back promptly and asked, "What's your name?"

"Tokitō."

"What?"

"To-ki-tō."

"Tokitō?"

"That's right."

Muttering the name to herself the woman retreated inside again. This time she was away an inordinately long time. His patience exhausted, Kensaku shouted, "Please hurry!" There was no answer.

At last the woman returned and opened the door. She was a shabby-looking woman, skinny and tall, dressed in her night clothes. "Sorry to have kept you waiting."

Inside the house the doctor was in the process of getting dressed. No less seedy than the woman, but small, he sported a poor excuse of a goatee. He was perhaps a little older than Kensaku. As he finished trying his sash he said, "What appears to be wrong with the baby?"

"We don't know. He simply won't stop crying."

For some reason the doctor was now all bustle. He came hurrying out of his room, saying, "Sorry to have kept you waiting."

"It is I who must apologize for troubling you at this late hour."

"Not at all. Lead the way, sir. I shall follow you."

He was being singularly accommodating, Kensaku thought, suspecting that he was a little drunk. He was certainly not one to inspire confidence, and Kensaku began to regret not having called Dr. K, however inconvenient it might have been for him. On the way the seedy doctor asked Kensaku when the baby was born, whether Naoko had ever had beriberi; and when he had finished with such professional questions, he became more personal: when had Kensaku come to Kyoto, what had brought him there, and so on. Kensaku, loathe to talk to this inquisitive man, walked on ahead. Panting, the short-legged doctor trotted after him.

The doctor's diagnosis, alas, was exceedingly ambiguous. He examined the baby's soiled diaper, and pronounced that he was suffering from some kind of indigestion. No matter how much he cried, he said, Naoko was not to give him any more milk; and with that he was gone.

The baby cried all night—or so it seemed to everyone in the house. There were indeed moments when he would go to sleep from sheer exhaustion, but when the others were about to doze off in the blissful silence, he would be awake again, crying. They thought the morning would never come.

When finally the sky began to lighten Kensaku went out again. The family whose telephone he had been in the habit of using were still asleep, so he ran to Kitano, and from there called Dr. K's house and asked if the doctor would come to their home before he went to the hospital.

An hour later Dr. K arrived. A biggish man with a thick, graying mustache, he exuded quiet competence, and was a marked contrast to his seedy colleague of the night before. Cutting short the customary greetings he went straight to the baby's side and began asking them questions about his condition. The baby was then asleep in Naoko's bed, having just finished feeding; but when the doctor put his hand on his forehead he immediately began to cry. The doctor withdrew his hand, and watched the baby. He in turn was watched by Naoko, lying silently and expectantly beside the baby.

"Let me look at his body at any rate," the doctor said.

The nurse closed the door, then picked up the baby and put him down on his tiny bed. "That will do," said the doctor as the nurse opened up the front of the baby's multilayered clothing. He pulled himself close to the bed, then examined closely the baby's chest and stomach, his neck and even his legs. He tapped him a few times, then undoing the bandage around the navel put his large, old man's hand on the lower abdomen and pushed. The baby's crying became more like a scream. "Let me look at his back now." The nurse pulled down the baby's clothes from his shoulders, and with some effort freed his little arms, bent rigid with the strain of crying, from the sleeves. She then laid him on his side, with his naked back turned toward the doctor. His fists clenched, his elbows held tight again his sides, his knees drawn up, his stomach heaving, the baby cried with all his might. Helplessly Kensaku looked at Naoko, who lay still, her eyes filled with an anger that he found strangely endearing.

The doctor was looking closely at a red spot, about the size of a thumbprint, an inch above the baby's buttocks. Still crouching, he looked up at Kensaku.

"I now know what the problem is."

"What is it?"

"Erysipelas."

Naoko closed her eyes, then suddenly covering her face with her hands turned away on her side.

"But it hasn't spread," the doctor said, "and if we attend to it at once I'm sure we can stop it." The nurse said nothing as she dressed the baby. The doctor went out to the verandah to wash his hands. "We'll have to get a few things from the hospital. Is there a telephone nearby?"

"Our landlord has one," Kensaku said. "Would you like me to go and call the hospital?"

"You could, but I think I'd better call them myself."

Kensaku took the doctor to the landlord's house. There the doctor instructed the hospital to send over the necessary injection, ichthyol, oiled paper, alcohol, and other items that occurred to him as he spoke on the telephone. He turned to Kensaku and asked, "Do you happen to have any mercury chloride in your house?"

"Probably not."

"And some mercury chloride, then. Send somebody over—it doesn't matter who—right away. Tell him to come on a bicycle. Kinugasa Park—understand?"

The two men went back to the house and waited upstairs for the things to arrive from the hospital. The baby continued to cry endlessly downstairs.

Overcoming his dread of what he might be told, Kensaku finally said, "What do you think?"

"It would have been easier if the baby had been a year old. But the infection is still at an early stage, and we may be able to do something about it."

Even for adults, the doctor explained, erysipelas was a rather serious disease, and with an infant, it was very much a matter of whether or not his constitution could withstand for long the struggle against the infection. He must therefore get his nourishment, and what had to be avoided at all costs was the stopping of the mother's milk. It would be good if Naoko could be put in a part of the house where she could not hear the baby crying. "I don't particularly like the idea of your wife's being moved about so soon after the delivery, but I'm afraid that her milk will soon stop if she has to go on listening to that crying. Of course being separated from the baby isn't going to prevent her from worrying, but her state of mind will depend to a great extent on how you yourself handle the situation. You must be extremely tactful, and do everything you can to reassure her that the baby is in good hands and doing well. Otherwise her milk will undoubtedly stop."

"I understand," said Kensaku, but with little conviction. He believed neither that Naoko could be appeased nor that the baby's infection could be checked; nor, indeed, that the doctor himself had any real hope. Dejectedly he asked, "But isn't erysipelas in an infant normally thought to be fatal?"

"No, that is not so. I grant that it's a very serious disease. And if it turns into cellulitis and pyemia, then there's nothing we can do. But I'll do what I can to prevent it from getting to that point."

Kensaku lowered his head a little and said nothing. "You see," the doctor said, "the purpose of the injection is to anticipate the spreading of the infection, and by injecting certain strategic places one hopes to contain it. If that works, then it might turn out to be not too serious."

"The baby's incessant crying—does it mean that he's in pain?"

"I'm afraid so."

"Is there no way of lessening his pain?"

"That would be difficult."

The man from the hospital arrived. Kneeling on one knee on the verandah, the doctor disinfected his syringe. "Please put a solution of this mercury chloride in a basin," he said to the nurse. "And you, too, must wash your hands in it afterward."

After he had given the injection he began to rub the ichthyol, left in its thick state, on the baby's body, moving gradually from the periphery to the center. As he did so he explained the technique to the nurse. The baby continued to cry.

"I just told your husband," he said to Naoko as he washed his hands in the disinfectant, "that unless the baby is fully nourished, he'll succumb to the infection. So please try to relax as much as possible so that your milk won't stop. It's very important. Remember, we were lucky to be able to start our treatment so soon, and even though the infection may spread a little, I'm convinced that we'll be able to stop it. Do you understand me?"

Naoko nodded several times like a child. Kensaku said, "And we're going to move your bed into the morning room. You come to this room only when the baby needs to be fed, all right?"

"Yes," she said almost in a whisper, then burst out crying.

The doctor left soon afterward.

"You must keep a firm grip on yourself," Kensaku said. "What good will worrying do? There's nothing you can do for the baby, except to see that he gets enough milk from you. So try to be as relaxed as you can, and stop worrying."

Naoko turned her swollen eyes toward Kensaku and glared at him. "That's quite an order you're giving me."

"Maybe so," said Kensaku sharply, losing control of himself, "but it would be most unfortunate if you didn't do as I asked."

Silently Naoko lowered her eyes. Kensaku was of course irritable, not having had any sleep the night before. But he was filled with anger too, anger at this misfortune that had suddenly befallen them. "I'm not a fool you know," he said. "I'm perfectly aware that to tell a mother not to worry over her sick baby is unreasonable. I say what I say because it has to be said. Do you want your milk to stop?"

"Please, don't say any more. I know the situation as well as you do. You see, we had a neighbor whose child died from erysipelas. How can I not think of that? But I promise, I'll try not to worry,

I'll try to forget he's ill. And I'm sorry I spoke to you as I did. It's not easy for you either."

"That's all right. But tell me, when was it that your neighbor's child died?"

"Four or five years ago."

"Oh, well, the injection that Dr. K used today wasn't available then. You know, there's been a lot of progress in medicine in the last few years. And don't forget what Dr. K said—thanks to the early diagnosis, the baby will most likely be all right. Just keep on remembering that."

"I will."

"And we are fortunate, don't you think, in having a nurse as good as Miss Hayashi?"

"Yes, we are. I know she'll take good care of our baby."

Hearing someone come into the house, Kensaku went out to the front hall. The baby was asleep at the time, and the nurse had got there before him. By the doorway stood the local doctor, already wilting before the harsh, unforgiving nurse. Even the night before she had made quite clear by her manner that she had little respect for him, but now she was being openly antagonistic. What the baby had, she was saying, was erysipelas, not indigestion, and to have kept him away from his mother's milk was the worst possible thing they could have done.

The little doctor's eyes darted about as though in search of a hole he might sink into. "Oh, really, really—I'm awfully sorry to hear that." He then turned to Kensaku and said embarrassedly, "I had a call to make near here, so I thought I'd drop in and ask how the baby was doing."

Kensaku felt sorry for the doctor. Besides, he might be useful in the future when some elementary medical care was needed. "Since you're here, perhaps you wouldn't mind coming in to look at the baby?"

"No, no, Dr. K's diagnosis needs no confirmation from me. Well, I must be going. I hope the baby will get better soon." So saying the little doctor scurried out of the house.

19

His brow puckered, his tiny lips quivering, the baby continued to cry almost without cease. Kensaku and Naoko were pierced to the heart by the crying; and even when it stopped, it continued to echo in their ears. When sometimes Kensaku was walking outside, well beyond earshot of the cry, he would suddenly hear it. Sometimes, inside the house, when the cry seemed to become even more desperate than ever, Kensaku would find himself saying aloud, "Oh, what are we to do, what are we to do!" There was nothing they could do.

Gradually the crying got weaker and weaker, until it became inaudible and only the face cried. For the poor baby, the inability to cry aloud meant that he had been deprived of one of two means of expressing his agony; but for the others, the silence was a reprieve.

Fortunately, Naoko's milk did not stop; and despite his suffering, the baby had a surprisingly good appetite. On this, then, they rested their hope. But before two weeks had passed, the baby developed cellulitis.

Naoko's mother, who had in the meantime come to stay with them, kept on insisting that the willow tree by the back door had been planted in a very unlucky position—"the willow at the demon's gate," she called it—and that it should be put elsewhere. Kensaku was at first not inclined to give in too easily to such superstition, but was finally persuaded.

What had been worrying him more was the fact that on the evening of the very day his child was born, he had kept his appointment with Suematsu and Mizutani to attend a recital being held at the Young Men's Hall in Sanjō, and there had heard Schubert's "Erlkönig." Had he known that this piece was being performed, he would probably not have gone. And as he listened to the song about the child who was taken by the demon of death on a stormy night, he could not help thinking what an inauspicious thing it was for him to hear on the day of his child's birth.

It was the main item on the program, and was sung by a young contralto. Kensaku listened to the music at first with indifference, then with an increasing sense of animosity and repugnance. It was all too obvious, he thought, much too cheap. The only aspect of the performance that elicited any response from him was the literary content. Why not, then, he asked himself, read the original work and leave it at that? All Schubert had done was to exaggerate and make more crude what was already a little too'theatrical as literature. Surely, music had a nobler mission than that?

And so even Goethe's work did not impress him. He did not think it a serious treatment of death; rather, it seemed to him like a drawn-out rendering of a clever notion. Goethe must have been relatively young when he wrote it, Kensaku decided; he simply could not respect it as he could, say, Maeterlinck's "La Morte de Tintagiles."

They were in Teramachi, on their way home, when Mizutani said with emotion, "What a marvellous piece 'Erlkönig' is!"

"Yes, it is," said Suematsu. He could not play any music, but he was fond of it and knew a great deal about it. To Kensaku who was silent he said, "I think that it's the best thing Schubert wrote."

Kensaku gave no reply. He didn't know enough about music to want to express openly unqualified opinions about it. Surreptitiously he pulled out the crumpled program from the pocket of his Inverness cape, and let it drop to the ground—rather in the manner of someone trying to shake off a curse.

Since that night he had tried not to think about the recital. It was not worth worrying about, he told himself; besides, what good would it do to worry about it anyway? Of course he never mentioned it to Naoko. And if his child had not become so desperately ill, he would never have started wondering again if hearing "Erlkönig" that night had not been a bad omen.

Fearing contagion, they were all careful to disinfect their hands in the solution of mercury chloride. One beautiful morning Kensaku and his mother-in-law were having breakfast in the morning room. It was nursing time, and Naoko had just left them to go to the baby's room by way of the verandah. She walked quietly, trailing the skirt of her night kimono along the wooden floor.

"No, Bell, no!" Kensaku heard her cry out.

"What's the matter?"

"Please come here, Bell is trying to drink the disinfectant."

Kensaku stepped off the verandah, put on his clogs, and went into the garden. There he found Bell, the puppy that the old janitor had found for them, running about happily.

"He was about to drink that," Naoko said, pointing to the basin lying on the stone step by the verandah. It had been put there to be emptied out and refilled.

"He wouldn't do a silly thing like that," Kensaku said. "He was just sniffing at it, I'm sure."

"But he really was about to drink it, I thought. It would kill him if he did."

The puppy was not theirs any more. When it was learned that Naoko was pregnant they had given him away, together with the kennel, to a neighbor living two houses away. It would not be a good thing, they had been persuaded, to have a puppy and a baby in the same house. He had continued to come to their house to play, however, and seemed to think he had two homes.

Miss Hayashi appeared. Without a word, and looking cross, she picked up the basin and marched away toward the kitchen.

Kensaku had come to place great trust in this strong-willed and possibly short-tempered nurse. She was utterly unyielding in her concern for the baby's welfare, and there were times when Kensaku would marvel at her tenacity, and wonder how much longer she could possibly continue to demand so much of herself. Mostly for her sake, then, Kensaku had decided to employ another nurse. But Miss Hayashi was far from grateful. Disapproving of the new nurse's handling of the baby, she worked as hard as ever, never resting even when her colleague was supposed to be in charge. And when the new nurse had had to go home with a cold, she had immediately come to Kensaku and said, "If it was for my sake that you hired her, then please don't ask her back. Of course it would be a different matter if you thought I wasn't doing enough."

But it would be a terrible thing for the baby, Kensaku had said, if Miss Hayashi were to collapse from exhaustion; she would be irreplaceable. Never fear, had been her reply, she would never collapse.

Under the present circumstances, what was required of Naoko

was that she should be the provider of milk and nothing more; so that only at nursing time was she allowed to be with the baby. But, Kensaku could not help feeling, even a baby so young must need a mother's love; and it was this need, he was convinced, that no nurse other than Miss Hayashi could ever satisfy. At any rate, he was grateful to her because what she gave to the baby was much more than the care of a competent nurse.

The baby's condition became more and more hopeless. His entire back was now red and swollen, filled with pulsating pus. Surgery now being the only recourse, Dr. K brought a surgeon from the same hospital with him. It was a chancy operation, the surgeon said, and he refused to make any promises. Kensaku was aware that without the operation, the baby was doomed; and he thought he knew, too, that even if the baby were to survive the operation, his chances of recovery later would be very poor, far less than even. Could he dare to hope, Kensaku wondered, that the baby had as much as one chance in ten?

Kensaku sat beside Dr. K, helping him prepare the saline injection. But he was not going to stay to watch the operation. He was too frightened. "Would you mind if I left?"

"Not at all," said Dr. K.

Kensaku went outside into the garden. The young surgeon in his white gown was on the verandah, energetically scrubbing his hands with brush and soap. When he had gone into the baby's room, Kensaku, too, went back into the house to join Naoko. "Aren't you going to stay with him?" she asked sharply.

Kensaku grimaced and shook his head. "I just couldn't."

"Poor baby, you've deserted him."

"Dr. K said it would be all right for me to leave."

"I don't care what he said, we can't leave our baby all alone without any of his kin beside him. Mother, will you please go?"

"Yes," her mother said, and left.

Kensaku went out into the garden again, and hung about outside the baby's room. He heard low voices behind the closed door, and the occasional sound of something or other being moved. The baby was utterly silent, having lost his voice long ago. A new fear assailed Kensaku: might the baby be already dead? Unable to stay still, he paced up and down the garden. Bell, in a frolicsome mood, kept jumping at his ankles.

The door slid open, and Miss Hayashi looked out. Her tension made her seem more stern than ever. Seeing Kensaku she said to him, "He needs milk, so please tell madame," and promptly withdrew. He's come through, thought Kensaku as he hurried to Naoko's room.

"Quickly, Naoko, he needs milk."

"Is he all right?"

"Yes."

Naoko rushed out of the room. A moment later, Kensaku espied Miss Hayashi walking quickly toward the bathroom with a basin under her arm. It was filled with blood-stained cotton and gauze, and she carried it as unobtrusively as she could.

By the time Kensaku went into the baby's room it had been completely tidied up. Naoko sat beside Dr. K, holding back her tears as she watched him administer oxygen to the baby.

Without looking up Dr. K said, "There was an enormous amount of pus." Kensaku said nothing. "Thanks to the injection and the oxygen, he managed to pull through. He did very well, I must say."

Kensaku sat down and relieved the doctor of the inhaler. The baby was in a deep, exhausted sleep, his brow puckered in a grimace. His cheeks were sunken, making the head above look unusually large. His was truly an old man's face. Suddenly, with his eyes still shut, he opened his mouth wide. His face was now a mass of wrinkles. He was trying to cry, to express his pain, but the sound he made was so feeble, it could hardly be called crying. As he looked at him, Kensaku could not make himself believe that there was any hope at all. What was strange was that this baby, barely alive, was still able to respond when Naoko brought her nipple to his mouth. He moved his head quickly, put his lips around the nipple, and began to suck. But for all his will to live, the effort did not last long; and very soon, before he had had enough, he was asleep again.

After the operation it was the surgeon, and not Dr. K, who came to their house every day to attend to the baby. And always, when he took the day-old bandage off, it was soaked with blood and pus. The wound was no bigger than the open palm of an adult's hand, but it covered nearly all of the baby's back. Eventually parts of his back-bone began to show here and there. To Kensaku, it was incredible that the child should still be alive. At times he would stop breathing altogether. They would immediately give him a camphor injection and oxygen, and he would revive. He was to be given a prescribed amount of oxygen daily as a matter of course, but sometimes, when such instances of emergency occurred too frequently, they would run out of their oxygen supply and have to send a rickshaw man to the hospital in the middle of the night to get more. The uneasiness at such times, as they waited for the man to return with the oxygen, was unbearable. Night was always the worst time for them, whether or not such emergencies occurred. And it was with immense relief that they would see the sky lighten and hear the first chatter of the sparrows. They would watch the gentle light of the early morning sun gradually approach the verandah, grateful that yet another night had passed.

There was always the smell of camphor and oxygen in the baby's room; and no matter where they went, the smell stayed with them.

Though he was without hope, Kensaku still awaited eagerly the surgeon's daily visit and his prognosis. Once, as they drank Indian tea upstairs in Kensaku's study, the surgeon said: "I can hardly believe that he's still alive. You know, when I looked at him yesterday, I didn't think he would last much longer, so I told the people at the hospital to get in touch with me at once if they heard from you, and I was ready to rush over here at a moment's notice today." He was being blunt, but Kensaku was too disheartened himself to be offended. He had already asked himself why, if the baby was sure to die, he should be made to suffer any longer. Later, as he watched the baby struggling to stay alive, he had regretted his own presumptuous thought. But once again, as the surgeon so bluntly confirmed his own hopelessness, he could not help wondering why they had to let the baby suffer such misery. The pity that Kensaku felt was more than he could bear. He said to the surgeon, "Must you keep alive at all costs someone who is about to die, someone for whom living only means immense pain?"

"The Germans and the French think quite differently about that. In France, if the person's family wish it, and responsible doctors agree, the person can be given something that will put him to sleep permanently. But in Germany, that's not allowed. There, it's the doctor's duty to fight for the patient's life to the very last moment."

"What about Japan?"

"Oh, it's more or less like Germany. By that, I don't mean necessarily that we share their conviction. But you see, modern medical practice here was based on the German model. Anyway, there are grounds for holding either point of view."

"If we could be certain that doctors are never wrong about a patient's condition, I surely would support the French point of view."

"Perhaps, but after all, we are talking about thousands of doctors and thousands of patients."

The following day, one month after he had become ill, the baby died. It was as though he had been born merely to suffer.

The funeral service, and all the necessary arrangements preceding and following it, were made with a minimum of fuss by Mr. S, to whom they had had to turn again for help. Not sure that they would remain in Kyoto long, Kensaku and Naoko decided against a burial; for if they were to leave, who would look after the grave? There was a temple in Hanazono called Reiun'in, where the Ishimoto family had their burial ground; in this temple, then, they left the urn containing the baby's bones.

It was Naoko who was most affected by the baby's death. Moreover, having moved about so soon after the delivery, she was very slow to recover physically. Perhaps, Kensaku thought, a trip would do them both good. He had never seen her home in Tsuruga. They could go there, see Naoko's aunt who was still in bed with neuralgia, then make a round of the spas in that area—Yamanaka, Yamashiro, Awazu, Katayamazu.

Unfortunately Naoko's health would not permit such a trip. Her heart, it turned out, had been a little affected by her ordeal; and her face began to swell, especially around her eyes, so that she almost looked like a different person. All in all, the doctor said, she was unfit for any kind of journey, let alone a tour of remote spas.

Every day now, she spent much of her time visiting the hospital. Kensaku sought to immerse himself in his work, which had lain discarded too long. But he felt so weighed down by a sense of fatigue

—it was like a heavy chain wrapped around him—that he was incapable of such immersion. Like a man suffering from cerebral anemia, he saw and felt everything as though through a veil of unreality. He would sit vacantly for hours before his desk, smoking one cigarette after another.

What thoughts occupied his mind were gloomy and obsessive. If fate was to treat him thus, baring its teeth at him at every turn, then so be it; he would simply have to learn never to trust it. True, others had lost their children too; and to die of erysipelas after many days of pain was a fate not reserved for his child alone; yet why must he be betrayed now, when after years of journeying down the dark road, he had thought that the waiting and seeking had not been in vain, that the dawn had at last come? Why must the birth of his first child have brought him such pain, when it should have brought only joy? He tried to tell himself that these were vain thoughts, the products of a twisted, self-pitying mind. But he could not in the end escape the conviction that he was the victim of some evil force bent on hurting him.

As Reiun'in was not far from Kinugasamura, Kensaku walked there often to offer his prayers.

PART IV

1

The winter that saw the death of his first child passed, and he greeted the coming of spring with a mood totally different from his mood of the spring before. The dance of the Gion geisha, the viewing of the double cherries—these he had enjoyed without reserve the year before, but this spring these festivities seemed to him to have an undercurrent always of a certain sadness.

He anticipated having several children in the future. But the thought that that baby would never return, however many children he may have, always brought a new feeling of sorrow. Perhaps when the next child was born, the memory and the sorrow would gradually fade away; but until then, he could not stop thinking of him.

The misfortune would not have so deeply affected him had it not occurred just when he had thought that a new life lay ahead of him, that his dark fate that had inexplicably tormented him for years had finally let him free. To remind himself that no one could guard against erysipelas, that it was a misfortune that befell his child by accident, was not enough to induce a sense of resignation in him, as it might have done in another man. For what was accident, he would ask himself, if not an act of arbitrary mischief? He would then hastily tell himself again that it was abject of him to think thus; and he did indeed despise himself for indulging in such self-pity. But always the suspicions returned to haunt him.

Naoko often cried for her dead child. Kensaku, whenever he saw her in this tearful state, wanted to look away, and made a point of not showing any sympathy. Once she said accusingly, "You don't care, do you?"

"What's the point of moping always?"

"I know that, and I try not to cry in front of other people. But we mustn't forget poor Naonori just because he's gone."

"All right, all right, go ahead and cry. But don't expect me to do likewise. It really doesn't do any good, you know." Naoko was silent.

Kensaku then said, "It's Oei I'm more concerned about right now. She hasn't written to me for months, and considering what we were to each other, I can hardly leave her entirely in Nobuyuki's hands. I'm thinking of going to Korea to see her." Naoko gave a slight nod, still saying nothing. Kensaku waited a little before speaking again. "Why don't you go home to Tsuruga while I'm away?"

"I don't want to. It would be like running back home to cry on their shoulders."

"What's wrong with that?"

"I don't want to, that's all. I don't mind your seeing me cry, but I will not let them think I'm asking for their sympathy."

"Why not? Look, I'll take you there, and then leave for Korea."

"Thank you, but no. You won't be gone for more than two weeks or so, and I'll be perfectly all right with Sen here. If I get too lonely, then I may decide to go."

"I wish you would. It'll be a miserable trip for me if I have to worry about you all the time."

But having announced his intention to go to Korea, he showed no inclination to depart immediately. He had once gone to Itsukushima from Onomichi, and that was the farthest west he had ever been. Seoul, then, seemed unimaginably remote to him, and to journey there a fearful undertaking. Even so, he would have been more decisive had there been any reason to think that there was some urgency in Oei's situation.

It was true that after Naoko's entry into Kensaku's life, his feelings toward Oei had undergone a certain change. But this was a woman who had taken care of him as a boy, this was a woman to whom he had once proposed (however unhealthy his state of mind then seemed to him now), and he could not but chide himself for being so slow to go to her, even if there was no urgency; indeed, he could not but be ashamed of his own heartlessness.

One day a registered letter arrived from Nobuyuki, in which was enclosed a letter to him from Oei. Owing to an unpleasant incident, it said, she had recently left the police inspector's house, and was now living at the above address. She could not believe her own idiocy. Here she was, at her age, still unable to manage her life properly. She was truly ashamed to write to Nobuyuki for help once again, but she had no one else to turn to. Osai, whom she had relied on to give assistance if it was ever needed, had turned out to be not the woman she had thought her to be. She was sorry, but she had no choice but to beg Nobuyuki's indulgence.

She could not give all the details in the letter, she said. They weren't fit to be told anyway. All that she now wanted was to come home to Japan as quickly as possible.

Such was the gist of her letter. She was asking for enough money, in short, to pay the bill for her room and the fare. As he read her letter he was inclined not to dismiss too readily what Nobuyuki said in his covering letter: after the burglary in Dairen she had been sent money and told to return at once; yet she had chosen to go to Seoul, and was now asking for money again; something odd was going on. Perhaps, Kensaku was forced to think, she had picked up those slovenly, colonial ways, and found herself some disreputable male companion, and under his evil tutelage was now trying to squeeze money out of the two brothers.

Remembering the woman he had lived with, Kensaku found such speculation distasteful. But no matter how unbalanced he might once have been, he had found her seductive, and others no doubt still would. Also, there was her past to consider. Distasteful or not, his suspicions were not so outlandish. And why would she not give details in her letter? Did not her reticence suggest some kind of sexual involvement gone awry?

Anyway, it was Nobuyuki's opinion that Oei had to be fetched. The bank was already closed that day, so Kensaku decided to leave on the westbound express train the following night. To Oei in Seoul and to Nobuyuki in Kamakura he sent off telegrams informing them of his decision.

2

Though it could hardly be said that the failure of Oei's business venture in Tientsin was due to Osai's dishonesty, there was no doubt that Osai's behavior toward Oei, whom she had after all pressed into joining her, was a little inconsiderate and irresponsible. It was not malicious perhaps, but it was certainly not kind. Later, even Osai must have felt somewhat guilty, for after Oei had gone to Dairen she wrote her several times suggesting that she return to Tientsin. But Oei had ceased to trust Osai. She could believe that Osai was for the moment being sincere; but what she could not have any faith in was the constancy of Osai's goodwill. Each time she received an invitation from Osai, then, she declined as tactfully as she could.

One suggestion of Osai's did tempt Oei, but this, too, she finally declined. Osai had an acquaintance by the name of Masuda, who ran a "hotel" in a small city about fifty miles to the north of Mukden. Oei had heard of the woman, for she had a formidable reputation as a businesswoman—a match for any man, it was said. According to Osai, Masuda had recently quarreled with the head of the local geisha exchange, and was determined to set up her own exchange. She had written to Osai, asking if she knew of anyone who might come and assist her in her new business. Would Oei, Osai asked in her letter, be interested?

This was clearly an ideal opportunity for Oei. Equipped only with enough clothes for four or five geisha, she needed the backing of some such larger enterprise to enable her to get back into business. Osai no doubt expected Oei to jump at the chance.

She was sorry to have to seem ungrateful, Oei wrote back to Osai, but possibly because of her recent illness she lacked the audacity to go to so remote a place. Had it been Dairen or Seoul she would have accepted the offer with alacrity. Incidentally, she added, there seemed little in the way of business opportunities in Dairen, and she was thinking of leaving for Seoul. Seoul seemed so much closer to Japan, besides. If Osai heard of any possibilities there, would she please let her know?

A reply soon arrived from Osai, saying that she knew a police inspector in Seoul by the name of Nomura. He would be glad, she was sure, to take care of Oei. If and when Oei decided to go to Seoul, she must let her know, and she would write to Nomura.

Oei wrote back immediately, asking Osai to write to Nomura. But she was at the time suffering from the tertian ague and barely keeping it under control with quinine, so that a long journey was out of the question for the time being. And it was while she was waiting to get well enough to leave Dairen for Seoul that she was robbed of her only remaining capital, the kimonos for the geisha that she had packed in trunks in anticipation of the coming journey.

Of course she was made despondent by the burglary. At the same time, however, she felt enormous relief; for now there was nothing she could do but return to Japan. And when the money for the fare arrived from Nobuyuki, it was her intention to return to Japan directly. But she hated long sea journeys. Besides, this was probably her last chance to see a little more of the continent. She would return to Japan, she decided, by way of Korea.

By October her ague had improved considerably. She went to Korea as she had planned, and on reaching Seoul called on Nomura, the police inspector. "But why go back to Japan when you have no idea what you'll do there?" was his comment. "Stay here in Seoul and start up a business."

Why Nomura made such a suggestion, Kensaku could not quite guess from Oei's account. He did try to seduce—or more accurately, rape—Oei later, so it was possible he had ulterior motives right from the start. Or possibly he was being casually kind and helpful then, and it was only afterward, when she had lived in his house for a while, that he came to desire her. At any rate, Oei was persuaded to stay at his house.

"I paid for my food," Oei told Kensaku. "But I was aware that that wasn't really enough, so I did their shopping and that sort of thing for them whenever I could. They had a five-year-old daughter—her name was Kyōko—who became quite attached to me. 'Auntie, auntie,' she would call me and follow me around. I became attached to her too, and I used to take her with me when I did my errands, and buy her sweets and toys. Then one day, when his wife was out, Nomura came in and began making suggestions. When I said no, he tried to use force, and I shoved him hard. Just as he fell to the floor, Kyōko came in. She had no idea what was going on— all she knew was that I was hurting her father. 'You beast!' she said, bursting into tears, and picked up a long ruler and started beating me with it. She was really quite violent, you know. I felt so hurt, I wanted to cry. I thought we had been so close, but her father was much closer to her, I suppose. I was after all a stranger to her. I was angry, I was sad, I wanted to laugh—I felt all mixed up. But one thing was brought home to me, and that was how nice it is to have a child. Perhaps I wouldn't have felt that so strongly if I had had one of my own."

After the incident she had felt that she was too old to tell anyone about such an indignity; besides, Nomura's wife had been kind to her; so the next day she left their house quietly.

Oei's experiences seemed so remote from Kensaku's own recent life that he listened to her story with a feeling of increasing discomfort. Even in his profligate period he had always found himself depressed by the atmosphere of the demimonde after only half a day in it, itching to escape into a brighter, freer atmosphere. Such was the way he felt now. As Oei told her story, he thought constantly of his house in Kyoto and Naoko.

He was nevertheless pleased to know that Oei had not become a "loose woman" in the colonies. She was as always a good person, whose fault was only that she was too easily swayed by circumstances of the moment. If anyone was to blame, it was he; he should never have let her go off on her own like that.

He had left for Onomichi, he remembered, despite Oei's objections; and when after several months of absence he had returned to Tokyo in a state of exhaustion, she had said how thin he had become, that he was not to go to such remote places alone ever again.

He wanted to say the same sort of thing to Oei; and in his own fashion he did. "You're a silly woman," he told her. "You don't know yourself at all, that's your trouble. To imagine that you could start a business like that on your own was an incongruous notion in the first place."

Having said that, Kensaku had no clear idea as to what Oei's plan for the future should be. If he had not once proposed to her, he would have asked her then and there, without hesitation, to come and live with him and Naoko. But under the circumstances, he would have to sound out Naoko first. If she showed no reluctance, then he would be very happy to have Oei live with them. But if Naoko seemed at all inclined to take his past feeling for Oei into consideration, he would have to think of some other solution. At all costs, he wanted to avoid unpleasantness at home.

He did not wander about much while in Korea. Aside from taking an overnight trip from Kaesong to P'yongyang, he limited himself to modest outings such as to a nunnery in Ch'ongnyang-ni with Oei to sample their vegetarian cuisine. They did this on a fine, cloudless day. On the way there they came upon a Korean family having a picnic by a mountain spring. An old man with a white beard was talking, and the others sat around him, listening attentively. He seemed to be telling a story. The two onlookers gazed at this scene, which was probably the enactment of an age-old custom, with pleasure and longing.

On another day Kensaku went to the top of Nam-san, and much taken with the view from there of another mountain, Pukhan-san, repeated the trip later. He visited Kyongbok Palace and Ch'angdok Palace, and in the evenings strolled down Chong-no looking at the shops. He saw a fine toilet table with mother-of-pearl inlay that he thought he might buy for Naoko, but decided that for an imperfect piece—it had a crack in it—it was too expensive. Instead he bought her a lovely letter box inlaid with horn. This, too, was not of recent make, and had acquired the pleasing unobtrusiveness of age.

On the train to P'yongyang he met a Japanese student of Koryo pottery who was touring the sites of the old kilns. He talked interestingly not only about his specialty but about Korea in general. He seemed mature for his age—he was no older than Kensaku—and his opinions about the Japanese administration, for instance, struck Kensaku as worth heeding.

He told a story about a certain young Korean who had been designated "insubordinate" by the Japanese authorities. By name Min Togwon and a member of the landed gentry, he was before his fall rich and a person of consequence in his district. One day he was approached by a Japanese official who informed him that they were planning to build a railroad through the district. Would Min Togwon undertake single-handedly to buy up the necessary land for them? Min Togwon agreed to do so.

The matter was to be kept absolutely secret, mostly to enable him to acquire the land cheaply. Mortgaging his entire landholdings and raising what money he could from those of his kinsmen who had any to spare, he proceeded to buy up one piece of property after another. Very soon the secret was out.

He was now a hated man, a puppet of the Japanese. To those who attacked him he simply replied that he was pro-Japanese in principle.

But when the Japanese authorities finally announced their plans for the railroad, he was shocked to learn that they intended to build it not along the stretch of land he had amasssed, but almost ten miles away. Presumably it had not been the Japanese official's intention to put Min Togwon in such a predicament, but the change in plans occurred after Min Togwon had already bought up a lot of land, and he must have decided that it would be too awkward to inform him of it.

It was a terrible blow to Min Togwon. Penniless, hated by his kinsmen, derided by his neighbors—"Serves the traitor right," they said—he was now a total outcast. With no one to turn to but the Japanese authorities, he pleaded with the viceroy's office to accept some of the responsibility for his present predicament. True, he said to them, he ought not to have been so naively trusting of the Japanese administration as to agree to undertake the disastrous venture, but surely he was entitled to some kind of compensation; surely they were not content to see him destroyed before their very eyes. But no one in the office would listen to him. When he asked that they at least bring out the official who had first negotiated with him, they replied merely that he had gone back to Japan. Perhaps they were lying, perhaps they were not. At any rate, there was not the slightest show of sympathy for him. And as his indignation at their injustice grew, so did their indifference. Indeed, it was suggested that should he become more openly indignant, he might very well be viewed as an "insubordinate Korean." There was no choice left for Min, then, but to withdraw.

A couple of years later, Min became in fact an "insubordinate Korean." He was bent on having his revenge on the Japanese, whatever form that revenge might take. He was not the man to think of independence for his nation. He did not think it possible; nor was he capable of committing himself to such an ideal in any case. All he wanted was to avenge himself on those who had taken everything from him. He had become a hopeless, desperate man, for whom the only end was to satisfy his craving for revenge; and he came to associate himself indiscriminately with all kinds of destructive activities.

"He was caught, you know," said Kensaku's companion. "The last I heard of him, he was due to be executed. I met him four or five years ago when I was looking for kiln sites, and he offered to help me locate some. He was such a quiet fellow, you'd never have imagined that he would end up like that."

3

Ten days after he had left Japan, Kensaku returned with Oei. The long train journey to Kyoto took place during the day, and was hot and uncomfortable. "I think I may come and meet you on your way back to Kyoto," Naoko had said. So in the hope of being met by her before they reached Kyoto—say, in Osaka—Kensaku had sent her a telegram from Shimonoseki. As they neared Osaka, he stepped off the train every time it stopped—at Kobe Station, at Sannomiya Station—just in case she was on the platform looking for them. At Osaka he stuck his head out of the window before the train had even entered the station; and as it drew alongside the bustling platform, he felt that at last he had come home.

He looked for Naoko in the crowd, but she was not there. Feeling somewhat let down, he began to regret not having told her clearly that he would like to be met before they reached Kyoto.

Oei sat sideways on the seat, her legs folded under her in the Japanese fashion. She was dozing fitfully. She had been away from Japan for a year and a half—and what an eventful year and a half it had been—yet she showed little emotion. She's too exhausted to feel much, Kensaku thought, she's emotionally all dried up.

"Can't you find her?" she asked wearily, straightening herself up. Then, just as wearily, she brought out of her sleeve pocket a package of Shikishima. She had stopped smoking before her departure for the continent, but while there had started again.

Though Kensaku had been away for only ten days, he was very conscious of having come home. He looked at the faces of the people that had come on at Osaka, and he felt as if he knew them all. Naoko was sure to be at Kyoto Station. He pictured her smiling as she saw him, and wished the train would go faster.

They finally reached Kyoto some minutes after nine o'clock. He immediately saw Naoko standing a step or two behind the waiting crowd. With her was Mizutani. Kensaku raised his hand.

Mizutani pushed his way through the crowd, then trotted alongside the train which had not yet come to a stop, all the while trying to reach through the open window for the small bag that Kensaku was holding. Suematsu's presence on such an occasion Kensaku would have accepted without a thought; but why, he wondered uneasily, had Mizutani come? He hardly knew the fellow. There was something unnatural and unpleasant about his being there.

"Call a porter, would you?" he said to Mizutani as he and Oei handed over to him various small pieces of luggage through the window.

"There's no need," said Mizutani, "I can manage it all."

Naoko approached the window, smiling a little hesitantly. "Welcome home," she said, bowing first to Kensaku and then to Oei.

Kensaku said to Naoko, "Will you please get a porter for us?"

"No, no, Mrs. Tokitō, there's no need."

"What are you talking about?" said Kensaku, irritated by Mizutani's enthusiasm. "Do you really think you can carry all this?" There were three large suitcases in addition to all the smaller bags and packages.

Mizutani scratched his head in belated embarrassment. "I'll find one for you," he said, and hurried away.

Having made sure that they had left nothing behind, Kensaku followed Oei off the train. "This is Naoko," he said simply. "How do you do," said Oei politely, and the two women exchanged bows.

Mizutani returned with a porter in tow. "Please go ahead," he said, "we'll take care of the luggage."

"I'll carry one of the packages myself." Kensaku picked up the package containing a few pieces of Koryo pottery and several Yi dynasty jars.

"I'll take good care of it, so please let me have it," Mizutani said, and pulled it out of Kensaku's hands. He was only being his usual self, but he seemed particularly offensive to Kensaku that day.

Kensaku and the two women waited for Mizutani and the porter just outside the ticket gate. "Why is Mizutani here?" Kensaku asked Naoko.

"He happened to be at the house today. By the way, my cousin Kaname came to Kyoto recently, and stayed at the house for about three nights. On one of those nights Mr. Mizutani and Mr. Kuze came over and we played cards all night."

"When was that?"

"Oh, four or five days ago."

"When did your cousin go home? And didn't Suematsu come to the house at all?"

"No, I didn't see Mr. Suematsu at all. My cousin left three days ago."

"Did he go back to Tsuruga?"

"No, he said something about going to Kyushu to look at a steel mill."

"Yahata, I suppose."

"That's right."

There was nothing particularly untoward about Naoko's cousin coming to stay at their house. But he had come during Kensaku's absence, and not only had stayed three nights but had invited his cronies over and played cards with them all night. Kensaku could not ignore the man's effrontery; and as he looked at Naoko, he wondered why she had permitted it.

He had been away for only ten days; but it was the first time he and Naoko had been separated since their marriage. Thinking that she would not be able to bear the loneliness, he had pressed her to go to Tsuruga; and all the time he was in Korea, he had felt guilty about his protracted stay there. He had wanted to come home as quickly as possible, he had so much looked forward to seeing Naoko again. Their meeting at the station, however, had somehow been a disappointment to him. There was from the start something in Naoko's manner that was not exactly right; and his displeasure at seeing Mizutani seemed to have made her behave even more unnaturally.

For him, then, it was not altogether a happy homecoming.

The porter appeared, followed by Mizutani carrying the package. Smiling brightly at Kensaku, Mizutani said, "You have some checked luggage too, haven't you? Let's have the porter collect it."

Kensaku, not deigning to reply, turned to the porter. "I suppose you deliver within the city?"

"Yes, sir."

"I live in Kinugasamura. Can my things be delivered there?"

"That's outside the city limits, so it will be a bit slow."

"I see. In that case, we'll take it with us." Still ignoring the ingratiating, chattering Mizutani, Kensaku handed over his check to the porter.

Kensaku ordered four rickshaws, one of them for the luggage. Mizutani, who had at last begun to show some sign of being subdued by Kensaku's ill-tempered treatment of him, was still able to say as they were about to leave him, "Suematsu and I will call on you in two or three days' time."

"Never mind that, just tell Suematsu I'll drop in to see him tomorrow."

"Very well, sir. The classes end for both of us at noon tomorrow, so we'll be waiting for you."

Kensaku barely managed to keep his temper. "Tell him I want to go out with him and talk to him about something."

One streetcar after another passed them as they proceeded northward along Karasumarudōri. When they passed a large temple, Kensaku, who was on the last rickshaw, shouted to Oei who was at the head of the procession, "That's Higashihonganji!" The old man who was pulling Oei's rickshaw saw fit to take over as guide and launched into some long explanation. And again, as they passed Rokkakudō, he slowed down to a snail's pace and began another speech.

Kensaku said to Naoko who was immediately in front of him, "It's dark, thank goodness. Just imagine this rickshaw procession crawling along this street in broad daylight!" He was trying to tell Naoko that he was not in a bad temper any more.

Naoko said something, but Kensaku could not hear. She seemed so dispirited, he began to feel sorry for her. "I should have put Mizutani in charge of the luggage, and we could all have gone home on the streetcar!" This blatantly insincere remark, too, was intended to cheer her.

It was about eleven when they reached Kinugasamura. Sen, the dried sardine, rushed out to the front hall, as excited as a pet dog. That her welcome should have been so much less guarded than Naoko's seemed incongruous to Kensaku. Naoko needed comforting, he decided; she needed to be reassured that he really did not mind her having played cards with those fellows; it would be cruel not to make it clear to her that he was not annoyed any more.

The rooms had been swept spotlessly clean, and a hot bath was ready for them. When she had had her cup of tea in the living room, Oei got up to have a look at the rest of the downstairs. "What a nice house you have," she said.

"Where is Oei to sleep?" Kensaku asked Naoko.

"I wasn't sure, so I had her bed laid out in your study. I thought that would do for tonight anyway."

Kensaku nodded, then turned to Oei. "Do go to bed early tonight. You must be very tired. And please have your bath before we do."

"No, you have it first, Kensaku."

"No, I'm about to unpack all the pottery, and I'll be filthy afterward. So tonight at least, please go first."

Kensaku unpacked the bowls and jars, wrapped in straw, in the front hall. "Some of this Koryo pottery looks a bit fake to me."

Naoko picked up a decagonal Yi dynasty jar colored with cinnabar. "What a lovely piece."

"I brought you a rather nice horn-inlaid box. But if you want that too, you can have it."

"I'd love to have it." She held it up to the light with both hands and gazed at it. "Why does it feel so sticky?"

"Perhaps they put oil on it."

"When Oei comes out, can I have my bath with you?"

"By all means."

"I'm going to wash this in the bathroom."

"Do you really want to? You'll probably wash all that fine patina off, you know."

"Never mind. It's much too dirty as it is. I'm going to scrub it clean with brush and soap. It's mine now, and it's no longer an antique."

Kensaku thought she was beginning to sound like her old self.

They took all the pieces into the living room, and arranged them in the alcove. "My jar is the best of the lot, isn't it?" she said.

"Well, of the Yi dynasty things, it may be the best."

"Don't start regretting that you gave it to me. You won't get it back."

From another package Kensaku got out the box he had bought for her. She was pleased with it, but seemed not at all sure she liked the way the horn inlay was beginning to come off here and there.

"I should have bought you something new," he said. "You like things to be pretty and shiny."

"You're a snob."

"But it's true."

"My taste is improving gradually, you must admit."

When Naoko had finished her toilet after their bath, he asked her what they should do with Oei. She would like to have her stay, was her answer. Kensaku was not sure for what reasons she had given this answer. He was certainly not about to assume that she really meant what she said. He was nevertheless pleased that she had not been openly negative.

"It was very good of you to say that," he said.

"Why? We simply have no right to think of any other solution, that's all."

"You're right, of course. She brought me up, after all. But you know, she comes from a background that's quite different from yours, and it's possible that the two of you will find yourselves thinking differently about all kinds of things. Looking after her doesn't necessarily mean that we have to have her living in this house. We can rent a small house for her nearby."

"That'll be much too complicated."

"All right, so long as you're agreeable, we'll keep her here. I just thought that if you didn't want her here, setting her up in another house might be a good solution."

"It'll be fun having her around to talk to."

Since neither of them was particularly opinionated or temperamental, Kensaku decided, they would probably get along quite well with each other. And one of the nice things about Oei was her capacity to put the past behind her and accommodate herself to the present.

Kensaku thought it strange that Naoko so far had said nothing voluntarily about what she had done during his absence. Had his brief display of ill temper at the station put such a constraint on her? Perhaps out of consideration for her feelings he ought not to bring up the subject, and simply accept her uncommunicativeness as an indication of remorse. But would not such restraint on his part in fact create unnecessary awkwardness between them? Would it not be best if he were to invite her to talk openly about what had happened, provided, of course, he could do so without any suggestion of threat? And then perhaps he could tell her gently to be more careful in the future. Having thus made up his mind, he sought some way of introducing the subject inoffensively; but it was difficult to find the right opening, especially in the wake of the agreeable discussion of Oei's situation. Gradually the conversation became more and more strained.

Finally Kensaku said, "When is Kaname going to graduate?"

"Either he has graduated already or will graduate this year—I don't remember which he said. I think he went to Yahata as a student observer, but I suspect that's where he'll be employed later anyway."

"Is he stopping here again on his way back?"

"I'm not sure. I hardly talked to him all the time he was here. On his first day here he went out immediately after arriving, and then the next evening there was that card game with Mr. Kuze and Mr. Mizutani. The game went on all night and all next day, until nine or ten in the evening. We played over thirty complete year-cycles. They were talking about finishing fifty, but I couldn't go on so I left the game then."

"And did Kaname leave the day after that?"

"Yes, he left without saying anything while I was still in bed. Wasn't that rude of him? It was hardly what you might call a friendly visit."

"It's obvious he came to our house to play cards. No doubt at Mizutani's suggestion."

"I'm sure you're right."

"The whole thing must have been planned beforehand. They were taking advantage of my absence. Why couldn't they have played in Mizutani's place anyway? Why did they have to use our house?" Kensaku was becoming increasingly critical. Naoko said nothing. "In matters like that Suematsu is almost neurotically conscientious. But Mizutani is a different kettle of fish."

"But my cousin, too, is to blame."

Kensaku was about to blurt out, "It's you I blame most," but restrained himself in time.

"I won't let it happen again," Naoko said. "You're right, my cousin was being very thoughtless. He should never have behaved like that in our house while you were away. He may be my cousin, but he had no right to be so rude."

"Yes, do tell him not to do that sort of thing again. I've never met him, so I have no idea what sort of person he is. But if you're that close to your cousin, I should think you could be quite frank with him." Again Naoko made no reply. "And that fellow Mizutani really annoys me. What did he think he was doing, coming to meet me at the station and rushing around like a damn devoted houseboy. I suppose even that clown felt guilty about the way he'd behaved in my absence, and was trying somehow to make up for it." Naoko was still silent. "He must have asked Suematsu to come with him to the station, but I know Suematsu wouldn't want to make such a fuss over someone who had been away for only ten days. He has taste." Kensaku was now so angry, he couldn't check himself. "Suematsu knows I can't stand Mizutani. That may be why he didn't come to the station." He paused briefly, then went on. "I'm going to tell Mizutani not to come to this house again. I don't say he's really bad. He's just unbearably small and cheap. All I have to do is look at his face, and immediately I become irritated. And whenever I'm off my guard and unwittingly laugh at his jokes or something, I hate myself afterward. It's stupid to associate with fellows like that. What I can't understand is why a fastidious chap like Suematsu associates with him. But Suematsu aside, I'd have serious doubts about anyone who goes around with fellows like that." Kensaku realized that he was now indirectly attacking Kaname, but he was in no mood to be reticent.

"I should have known better," Naoko said. "I'll never let anything like that happen again, so do forgive me."

"I can't say that I like what you did, but I'm not attacking you. It's those fellows that make me angry."

"It was my fault. They were simply taking advantage of my stupidity. I should have been more firm."

"No, that's not so."

"I'll tell my cousin never to come here again—yes, that would be the best thing to do."

"Don't be an idiot. What would your uncle think if you did a thing like that?"

"My uncle has nothing to do with it."

Kensaku thought of that dignified old man, Mr. N, who had never been anything but kind to him, and felt a twinge of guilt at his own intolerant attitude toward the man's only son, who was after all still a student and had committed what was at worst a harmless indiscretion. One of his own great weaknesses, Kensaku was aware, was his tendency not to control his initial disapproval of someone, and to allow it to develop into an irrational dislike that was out of all proportion to the cause. It was not merely guilt toward Mr. N that he felt after his outburst, then, but a certain uneasiness over his own state of mind. Kaname's behavior, he reminded himself, was really not worth getting so angry about. If he had kept silent, his resentment would have remained moderate and under control. It was a bad habit of his to be carried away by the momentum of his own rhetoric. Only a short while before he had succeeded in persuading Naoko that he was no longer in a bad mood, yet here he was now, haranguing her. Once having cheered her up, why could he then not have let well enough alone? Why had he to be so mean?

Once more, he looked for ways to bring her back to her normal self. "But never mind," he said. "I tend to let little things bother me—you know, things that other people take in their stride. I always get over them eventually, but it takes a long time. I have to let them slowly work their way out of my system, so to speak. You see, it was my seeing Mizutani at the station that started it all. As soon as I saw him, I felt something was wrong. And you must admit I wasn't altogether mistaken. But never mind, so long as you understand how I feel, so long as you promise to be careful from now on, no more need be said. Don't give it another thought."

They went to bed a little while later. Outwardly at least, harmony had been restored; yet a certain restraint had developed again between them which could not be easily overcome. Naoko was clearly despondent. And though Kensaku knew that he ought to go to her bed and hold her in his arms, he could not do so for fear of seeming theatrical. She did not cry, nor was she in a sulk; but she lay on her back, utterly still, with the coverlet pulled right up to her eyes. There was something almost menacing in the air, beyond Kensaku's power to dispel; and it prevented him, for all his solacing words, from bringing his body to hers.

Kensaku could not bear the thought of spending the night thus. He would have preferred it if something violent had happened, for then it would have cleared the air. He was tired, but he was loathe to desert Naoko in her present condition and try to go to sleep. He could not have gone to sleep anyway. He reached out and sought her hand, but she did not respond. Hurt by her unresponsiveness, he said sharply, "Are you angry about something?"

"No."

"Then why are you looking so miserable?"

4

An unpleasant thought suddenly occurred to him, which he instinctively tried to dismiss. It had had its effect on him nevertheless. Controlling the agitation that he felt mounting within him, he said with forced calm, "Why don't you say outright what you're thinking? You don't think I'm still reproaching you, do you?"

"Of course not."

"I really don't mean to reproach you, but quite honestly, I can't help feeling there's something very wrong. There's been something between us ever since I saw you at the station. It's all very vague, I'm sorry, and I wish I could be more precise, but there's something wrong, I know. You may think I'm still bothered about Kaname and Mizutani, but they have nothing to do with it. Perhaps they're not entirely irrelevant, but what I'm talking about is you and me. Somehow we seem to have lost touch with each other, and that's what I'm talking about. What has happened? It's never been like this with us before." Naoko was silent. Kensaku moved over to the side of his bed. "We don't want to be heard upstairs. Come here so that we can talk more quietly."

Wearily Naoko got out of her bed and sat down beside Kensaku. Her face was so gloomy and expressionless it was ugly. She looked away from him toward the alcove, but she was not seeing the pottery and the box there that had pleased her earlier. "Don't sit there like that, come and lie down," Kensaku said, but she would not move.

For a while neither said anything. Kensaku's mind felt like that of a man with fever, heavy and tired, yet animated. It was a very still night. They were surrounded by the silence of a world gone to sleep. Only they, it seemed to Kensaku, were kept wide awake by the invisible little spirits of calamity who danced maliciously in the heavy air of their room.

"Can't you say something? We can hardly go to sleep in this state. Or are you determined to stay silent?" He paused, then tried again. "Try to be open with me, will you? True, what you have to tell me may make me angry, but my being angry may at least clear the air. How can we hope to settle anything by saying nothing?" Still there was no response from Naoko. "I don't think either of us could stand this kind of strain for very long. If only I had some notion of what it was that I was trying to force you to say! If you have nothing to tell me, just say so, and I'll be satisfied. What's so difficult about that? Just say there's nothing you have to tell me. Or is there something? Well, is there? Tell me, is there something?"

Naoko suddenly shut her eyes tight and hung down her head. She held her breath, then covering her crinkled face with her hands, threw her head down on her knees and started to cry violently. Kensaku felt his face going cold. He stood up and stared down in fear at her quaking shoulders. For a moment he lost awareness; then, as he regained it, as he awakened from the terrible dream, he asked himself the question: how am I to interpret this outburst? And he knew clearly then that whatever it was, something quite awful had happened to them.

5

There was an incident that occurred when Naoko and Kaname were still children that lent a not entirely innocent character to their relationship. It was no more than a game that they once played, a game which expressed merely childish curiosity and dimly understood desires. Yet it held lewd implications which neither ever forgot afterward, and which later excited in Naoko a certain romantic longing whenever she remembered Kaname.

It was early spring, when the snow had not yet disappeared from the ground. Kaname, who had first gone home from school, was sent to Naoko's house by his father to fetch her mother. Naoko was at the time playing house with a neighborhood girl, a little younger than herself, on the sunlit verandah. She was so enjoying the game that when her mother suggested she go with her, she refused and kept playing with her friend.

Naoko assumed that Kaname had gone back with her mother; but a few minutes later he came into the garden through the side gate and joined the two girls. Packing a metal basin with snow and pretending that it was rice in a cooking pot, the three played quite amicably until their hands became numb and the verandah was covered with water from melted snow. They then went inside and warmed themselves at a footwarmer under a coverlet. "Why don't you go home?" Kaname said to Naoko's playmate repeatedly, but she refused to leave.

Kaname now wanted to play a new game. It was called, he told them, "the turtle and the snapping turtle." Would Naoko fetch something like an inkstone? Obediently Naoko went and found one. It was a round slab made of Akama stone. This was to be hidden in the garden, Kaname explained, and Naoko's friend, in the role of a young girl, was to go and look for it. When she had found it she was to call out from the other side of the door, "Mama, I've found the turtle." Naoko was then to say, "But that's not a turtle, that's a snapping turtle." And just as she had finished saying this, Kaname was to shout, "A snapping turtle!" The two girls had no idea what the game was all about, but were willing enough to play it.

Kaname and Naoko lay under the coverlet while her friend searched outside for the inkstone Kaname had hidden. And when the little girl announced from the other side of the door that she had found it, Kaname leapt in the air shouting, "A snapping turtle!" He clapped his hands, stamped his feet on the coverlet, turned somersaults, and otherwise made a wild spectacle of himself.

He had been taught the game by a manservant, and was not unaware of its lewd implications. Naoko of course was utterly puzzled by it. But when they were lying in each other's arms under the coverlet while her friend was outside, she had experienced a sensation that was new to her, a sensation that put her almost in a trance. The three children repeated the game a number of times. It was finally interrupted by the return of Naoko's elder brother from school. Naoko and Kaname jumped up, guilty and frightened, as he walked into the room. And for reasons not clear to Naoko then, she was too ashamed to look at her brother.

Never again did Kaname and Naoko indulge in such play. But of all her childhood memories of him, the memory of that game remained the most vivid in her mind.

And so it was with some uneasiness that she received her cousin when he appeared unannounced at their house after Kensaku's departure for Korea. But such uneasiness was indecent, she told herself, and resolved to treat him in a bright, cousinly manner. And when on the following day Mizutani and Kuze came and the card game began, she was so relieved there were others in the house that she joined the game, giving no thought to the propriety of such conduct on her part. Morning came, and still they played on. Exhausted and unable to sit up any longer, she asked Sen to take care of the guests, then retired to the small room at the back of the house and promptly fell asleep.

When she woke up, it was already dark. As she passed the living room on her way to the bathroom, through the opening between the sliding doors she saw the three men, their eyes sunken and their faces grimy, still seated around the cushion. They seemed easily amused, and laughed or giggled at the slightest provocation. Even Kuze, who was normally not particularly flippant, seemed now to be possessed of an unending supply of witticisms.

When she had finished her toilet she went into the kitchen and helped Sen prepare dinner.

Even while eating the three men could talk only about the game. It would be fun, one of them said, if they could complete fifty year-cycles; that would be some kind of a record.

After dinner they immediately started playing again. Naoko played with them. The three men had had no sleep whatsoever since the day before, and whenever one of them had to play dummy, he would lie down and promptly fall asleep. Kaname suffered from extreme stiffness around his neck and shoulders, and complained constantly about it.

At about ten they stopped at last. The men had a bath together, and even then they had enough energy left in them to splash about rowdily. Kuze and Mizutani left soon afterward.

Kaname lay down in the middle of the living room, using a folded cushion as pillow. Naoko pressed him several times to go upstairs and go to bed. "Yes, yes, I'll go up in a minute," he would say, but showed little inclination to get up. Resignedly Naoko put a wadded kimono over him, sat down beside him and began to read. Not many minutes had passed when Kaname stood up abruptly, and saying, "Good-night," went upstairs.

Naoko, wide awake, continued to read. Then she thought she heard Kaname's voice. She got up, went to the foot of the stairs and called out. He said something incomprehensible in a sleepy voice. She went to the top of the stairs to see what it was he wanted.

"My shoulders are terribly stiff," he said. "Could you possibly call in a masseur?"

"The only one I can think of lives rather far from here. Besides, it's past midnight." Kaname looked disappointed. "And Sen has just gone to bed," she added. "It would be a pity to wake her up."

"All right, then, no masseur."

"Is it really bad?"

"Yes, it is. It's a stinging pain, and even my head feels funny. I couldn't possibly go to sleep in this state."

"Would you like me to massage you?"

"No, thank you."

"I'm pretty good at it, you know."

Naoko went into the room and sat down beside him. She began to massage his neck and shoulders, but the stiffness was such that she could hardly hope, with her limited strength, to alleviate it much.

"Is it doing any good?"

"Perhaps."

"It's pretty useless, isn't it?"

"Perhaps."

"Make up your mind," she said, laughing. "Try to go to sleep while I'm massaging you. As soon as you wake up in the morning, I'll have the masseur come."

Naoko continued the massage for a while. Kaname lay still with his eyes closed. She was not sure whether he had fallen asleep or not; if he had not, it would be rude to stop massaging and leave.

Kaname suddenly rolled over toward her and grabbed her hand. Taken aback, Naoko tried to pull away. Kaname, his eyes still shut, put his free arm around her neck and pulled her toward him. "What are you doing!" she said in a shocked whisper.

"I won't do anything bad, really I won't," he said, and forced her to lie down.

Nearly beside herself with shock and anger she tried to free herself, but he kept her down with his entire body, saying, "Really, I won't do anything bad. It's my head, it feels funny."

The struggle continued for a time. Then Naoko felt herself drained of all power to resist. Indeed, she soon lost even the capacity to think.

Later she came down the stairs quietly, desperately afraid that Sen would know. She got into bed, and lay awake for hours.

Next morning, when she awakened, Kaname was no longer in the house. He had left Kyoto.

6

On the following day Kensaku was on Ichijōdōri, headed east. He walked quickly. The south wind was warm and humid, and his skin felt clammy. Partly because of the weather, partly because he had not slept, his head felt heavy and dull. Yet his senses seemed acutely receptive, and his overall state could not be described as despondent. He was too stimulated to brood, to engage in sustained thought; only fragmented perceptions, memories, and questions would run across his mind like little revolving wheels.

"I do not want to condemn her," he said to himself, repeating what he had said to Naoko the night before. "I want to forgive, not because it's virtuous to forgive, but because I know that if I can't forget what she did, the unhappy incident can only cause more unhappiness. I have no choice but to learn to forgive her." A moment later, however, he could not avoid adding, "And so I shall be the only fool in the entire affair, the only loser."

It was his habit whenever he went to Suematsu's lodgings to catch a streetcar at Shimonomori. But when he got near there he found a festival in progress at Kitano Shrine. Reluctant to push his way through the great crowd, he went around to the back of the Hall of Martial Arts with the intention of going to the Kitano terminal. But this route, too, was packed with people. Everywhere, even in the riding ground, there were stalls selling sweets, balloons, toys, ice cream. Peepshows, showing picture-story versions of popular romances, had been set up too, mostly in the open area by the gateway. Such old favorites from the Edo period as "Oshichi the Grocer's Daughter," he noted, had been replaced by more recent romances, such as "The Gold Demon" and "The Cuckoo." But the faces on the pictures were still as exaggerated and vulgar as ever, and the colors, done in distemper, as lurid.

He entered the pleasure quarter of Kamishichiken, intending to catch a streetcar on Senbondōri.

"I shouldn't mind if we were both to forget the incident, if in time we were able to live as though it had never happened; but supposing I were to remember, and she alone were to forget, or at least appear to have forgotten, could I accept that? Could I bear to watch her carefree face?" His reply to his own question was that he probably could; but it was a reply given without confidence. More fearful was the prospect of their both pretending to each other that they had forgotten, when indeed they still remembered.

He looked at the houses with the hanging lanterns on either side of him, and wondered whether he would start visiting such places again.

Kensaku had the feeling that he was in a peculiarly irresponsible mood that day. He would therefore say nothing to Suematsu about the matter, he resolved; otherwise he was sure to say all kinds of indiscreet things he would regret later.

"Damn," he said, realizing that he had forgotten to bring the present he got for Suematsu in Korea. He took his hat off and wiped the sweat from his brow.

He got on the streetcar at Senbon. It was a terminal in those days, and he had no trouble finding a seat. It was like evening outside, sunless and gray; in the streetcar it was darker still, and the air was so stuffy that very soon Kensaku began to feel nausea. Unable to bear it any longer, he hurriedly got off at the Karasumaru corner of the palace and went to the rickshaw stand.

Suematsu was coming down the stairs just as Kensaku entered the boardinghouse.

"Hullo," said Suematsu. "Come up, won't you?"

"No, let's go out somewhere."

"Come up to my room for a minute. I have something to show you."

"Show it to me another time," said Kensaku, anxious to avoid Mizutani.

Suematsu looked nonplussed. "All right, let me change my clothes at least."

"I'll wait for you in front of the zoo. And don't bring anyone else."

Suematsu burst out laughing. "I see. Well, I'm sorry to disappoint you, but he isn't in right now. I'll be with you in a minute."

Higashiyama loomed before Kensaku as he came out of the alley, its outline made vague by the dull weather. Scudding over it were numerous little clouds, all of them the color of diluted black ink. It was a limp sort of day, very dreary.

A lone young man crouched low on a racing bicycle was circling the sports field in the park. He wore a red shirt and a pair of shorts. His shoulders swayed to the right and left, his head bobbed up and down as he pedaled against the wind. When he came around and the wind was behind him, his movements became visibly more relaxed, and the bicycle went much faster. Kensaku stood on the side of the road and watched this spectacle until Suematsu appeared.

"I wish you could have looked at it," said Suematsu as they started walking. "I'm told it's a flower basin of the Fujiwara period. I picked it up in a dirty secondhand shop in Matsubara a couple of days ago. If I bring it over sometime, will you look at it and tell me what you think of it?"

"But I know nothing about such things."

At the streetcar stop they sat down on a bench in the open area to wait for a streetcar from Ōtsu.

"There's nothing wrong with wanting to keep a worthless fellow at a distance," Suematsu said suddenly, "but your trouble, Tokitō, is that you allow your dislike of someone to become a kind of obsession."

"I realize that. You see, what happens is that in the process of trying to avoid someone because I don't like him, I come to hate him. It's a terrible habit, I know. I always begin by liking or disliking someone immediately, and if I like a person, I assume he's good, and if I dislike him, I assume he's bad. But you know, I'm hardly ever wrong in my judgment."

"That's simply because you choose to think you've been right."

"No, I really don't make many mistakes about people. It's not only people either; I'm usually right in my discernment of a particular situation too. When I sense something is wrong, I usually find later that there was good cause for me to feel that way." As he said this, Kensaku remembered how peculiarly prophetic his distaste and apprehension at seeing Mizutani at the station had been. His intuition had certainly not betrayed him there.

"No doubt there are times when you're right," Suematsu said.

"But I must say that your trust in the infallibility of your own intuitions can be a bore to the rest of us. In fact, it's quite frightening sometimes. Can't you just occasionally be more rational about people?"

"But of course I can."

"In matters involving your feelings, you really are a tyrant. You're a terrible egotist, you know. True, you're not a calculating person, and I suppose that's a good thing. But you can be very thoughtless." Suematsu paused, then spoke again. "Let me put it another way. Perhaps you yourself aren't tyrannical; rather, it's as though a little tyrant is living inside you somewhere. I suppose it's possible that the real victim is therefore you."

"You can say that about anyone," Kensaku replied. "I'm not the only one like that." He was nevertheless forced to think that his struggle in the past had indeed been with something inside him, not outside.

"All right," Suematsu said, "let's say that in your case, the tyrant within is unusually active."

Kensaku had always allowed his emotions to tyrannize over him; but he had not before thought to describe his own condition quite in these words. Now, as he remembered the various incidents in his life, he had again to grant that more often than not he had been wrestling with himself, that his enemy had been a creature residing within him. "You stay out of it, don't interfere," he had said to Naoko the night before. "I'll find a way out of this mess." All he was saying, he now realized, was that their problem was entirely his to solve. What a strange thing to have said to her, he thought. He said to Suematsu, "It's true. If I am going to spend the rest of my life fighting with this thing that's inside me, what was the point of my having been born?"

Suematsu gave him a consoling look. "Perhaps it isn't so bad, if at the end of it all there's peace of mind waiting."

There was still no sign of a streetcar coming from Ōtsu.

Kensaku was gazing vacantly up at Higashiyama when suddenly he noticed a weird black thing weaving its way through the clouds, against the wind. Something akin to dread gripped him for a moment, then the realization dawned on him that he was looking at an airplane. The wind had drowned out the sound of the engine; he had not expected to see an airplane flying in such weather; and because of the clouds, it had looked like a flying shadow.

It flew past with difficulty over the Warrior's Tomb; then gradually it lost altitude, and barely missing the roofs of Chion'in, disappeared behind the temple. "I'm sure it crashed," Kensaku said. "In Maruyama, I think. Shall we go and see?"

They had both read in the newspapers that the army was going to attempt their first flight from Tokyo to Osaka that day; but it had not occurred to either of them that the attempt would still be made in such weather.

They stood up and started walking quickly toward Awataguchi.

7

From Maruyama the two men walked past Kōdaiji toward Kiyomizu. Nowhere did they hear any talk of the airplane. So vague had been the apparition, so uncertain was Kensaku about the state of his own mind, that had he not read about the flight in the morning paper, he might have decided that he had suffered an hallucination. Feeling a terrible hollowness inside, he talked endlessly to his companion as they walked in search of the airplane. He had earlier resolved to say nothing about the night before to Suematsu; but he had little confidence in the authority of that resolution. And as he chattered he kept on asking himself, should he or should he not tell him about it?

For a time in Onomichi, after hearing about the circumstances of his birth, he had found himself more or less in the same state of mind. Then, however, he had felt that he had in him somewhere the strength to fight against the shock of his discovery; and he had not been wrong. Now, for whatever reason, that residue of strength seemed to be nowhere in him. I mustn't give in, he told himself, but in vain. There was no firm foothold anywhere within reach, it seemed, and he was sinking deeper and deeper in the quagmire. It made no sense, he thought sadly, to be so much more helpless after his marriage than he had been before.

The two climbed the stone steps of Ninenzaka, and went into the teashop on top. Seeing a rattan chair on the verandah, Kensaku made straight for it and collapsed into it. He was so exhausted, so bereft of all vitality, that he could not keep his eyes open. Perhaps I'm ill, he thought, already half-asleep.

Suematsu's voice calling to him from the room brought him back to awareness. "The tea's here. Do you want to have it there? What's the matter with you, anyway?"

"I haven't been sleeping well. And it's this weather." Limply Kensaku pulled himself out of the chair, then getting down on his knees almost crawled toward the cushion in the middle of the room.

"I would guess from that performance that you were an extremely tired man," said Suematsu.

"There's something I want to talk to you about. It's been weighing on my mind. What makes it worse is that I feel I shouldn't talk to you about it." Nonplussed, Suematsu said nothing. "Keeping it to myself is proving a terrible strain. It has to do with my present state of mind." All the while Kensaku tried to restrain himself; for he still knew that if he said anything about Naoko, he would be sorry later.

"With your state of mind?"

"That's right. I feel exactly like this weather we're having—nasty."

"Why?"

"I'll tell you sometime. But I don't want to today."

"All right."

"Not to change the subject, but how are you getting on with your third-rate geisha?"

Suematsu, unprepared for the question, could only smile uncomfortably. Then he said with a laugh, "Oh, so-so. The affair isn't exactly over, but it's lukewarm at best."

The affair was at its peak, Kensaku remembered, when he himself had just got married. It seemed then to be causing Suematsu a lot of annoyance. Kensaku, too engrossed in his own new life with Naoko, had not bothered at the time to inquire too deeply into it. And since then, apart from an occasional report from Mizutani on its uncertain progress—there seemed to be several ups and downs—he had heard little about it. He did know that the geisha had been as casual as Suematsu had been passionate; he knew what lonely torment Suematsu used to go through whenever the fickle woman went off with some other lover, and how useless were his jealous rages.

"But you're still carrying on with her, then?"

"That's right."

"Doesn't it upset you?"

"Not really, not any more. I suppose I don't feel so strongly about her as I used to. You might say that I've stopped looking for things in her that aren't there. As a matter of fact, we get along much better with each other now. I've stopped wondering what she does when I'm not with her. What would be the point? Do you remember that night at the restaurant when I behaved so badly?" Kensaku nodded. Suematsu was grinning. "Well, I've stopped creating such scenes in public. By the way, is that the way you're feeling now?"

Kensaku pondered, then said, "Perhaps it's not very different."

Suematsu looked at Kensaku thoughtfully. "I don't know the details of course, but isn't it true that in matters of this kind the devil is usually of one's own making? My impression is that seven, eight times out of ten, one's suspicions are ungrounded."

"No, I'm not imagining anything. The incident itself is closed and the facts are clear. My trouble is that I know I must accept what has happened, and yet I can't. That's all. Perhaps it's a matter of time. I may just have to wait for this mess inside me to clear up. At any rate, it's very painful for me right now." Suematsu remained silent. "If I try too hard to rid myself of this pain, this conflict inside me, we may very well end up living a life of lies. Perhaps the only right thing to do is to regard what I feel now as inevitable and let it run its course. I'm sorry if I seem to be indulging in a lot of abstractions."

"I have a pretty good idea of what you're talking about, I think. Does it involve Mizutani?"

"No, not directly. I might as well be blunt about it. Naoko has a cousin who's a friend of Mizutani's. She slept with him." There was nothing Suematsu could say. "But she didn't have any intention of doing so, and I really can't hate her for it. All I ask of her is that she doesn't make the same mistake again. I can't believe she ever will. And I do think I have truly forgiven her. After all, she's hardly to blame for what happened. The fact is, then, everything is over and done with. But you see, I somehow can't accept the fact for what it is. There are cobwebs in my head, and I can't get rid of them."

"As you yourself said, perhaps the best thing to do is to wait and let everything run its course. It's probably the most natural thing to do, anyway."

"I have no other choice, it would seem."

"It's easier said than done, I know, but try not to brood too much. As you say, the incident took place, it was brought out into the open, and there's nothing more you can do about it. Don't go on brooding about it—it would be stupid to let it cost you both more than it should."

"I understand that. But what makes sense objectively and what the person who is directly involved feels are two different things."

"Of course. But you've got to will yourself to make things better, otherwise it will be terrible for Naoko. For you right now it's a deeply emotional problem, but you owe it to yourself to transcend your emotions. What a fine thing it would be if you could. You do have the advantage, you see, of knowing everything there is to know about what happened. You haven't been kept in the dark about anything, and that places a certain responsibility on you."

"What you say is absolutely true, but I'm the last person in the world to be able to do as you suggest. Besides, I can't help thinking that since something has happened to us as man and wife that never happened before, something that we probably assumed would never happen, we have to find a new kind of relationship. It may be an extreme way of putting it, but I mean the kind of relationship that won't be shaken by a recurrence of the same sort of thing. I suppose that by saying this, I'm merely showing that I really haven't taken in what you've been telling me."

"Well, I can't say that you're being entirely unreasonable . . ."

"There's the saying, 'black clouds cover the sky, yet still no rain'— I feel just like that. It's an awful feeling."

"I'm sure it is. But you must look at the whole incident as a kind of test, and make sure you survive it. Do try to be prudent."

"Yes, thank you, I will. It would be idiotic, I know, to allow misfortune after misfortune to pile up on us through sheer negligence on my part."

"It would be different if you didn't know what happened, and you had to grope in a fog of uncertainties and suspicions."

"I understand that. Thank you for listening. I feel much better now that I've talked to you about it."

"What's Naoko doing?"

"When I left the house she was in bed. She had a headache, she said."

"You should go back to her right away."

It occurred to Kensaku then that he might ask Suematsu to come home with him and comfort Naoko. But quickly he dismissed the distasteful notion. Suematsu was not the sort to look kindly on such a suggestion, anyway.

Outside a boy selling extras ran past, ringing his bell loudly.

As Kensaku and Suematsu came out of the teashop they found an extra lying on the ground by the door. Suematsu picked it up and said, "So there was a forced landing after all. In Fukakusa, it says." But the other plane—two had taken off from Tokyo—had reached Osaka safely. The two friends began walking toward the streetcar stop at Higashiyama-Matsubara, down a gently sloping hill.

8

The days passed peacefully in Kinugasamura. At least, surprisingly little happened to disturb the surface calm. Naoko and Oei got along well with each other, as Kensaku had expected; and the relationship between Kensaku and Naoko was not bad. But—how should one put this?—while a new, morbid kind of physical attraction drew them together, there came between them an emptiness that prevented a union of their entire beings. Indeed, the stronger this morbid desire was at any given time, the greater was their sense of emptiness afterward.

That the seduction of his wife by another should so affect the nature of his desire shamed Kensaku. And in order to recall his earlier love for Naoko, he sought to find passion even in his morbidity, passion that would perhaps fill the emptiness. There were times when he even tried to persuade Naoko to describe in detail her own seduction scene.

It was not long afterward that Kensaku learned Naoko was pregnant. There was no need for Kensaku to start counting back the days, for the child had clearly been conceived before he went to Korea. But what oppressed Kensaku was the thought that now, with the pregnancy, their future together had been decided.

Often Kensaku's despondency was such that he would want to rush into Oei's arms like a child. But of course he could hardly do that. And when instead he sought solace from Naoko, he would suddenly find himself confronted by a steel wall, rudely awakened from his dream of comfort found.

Summer passed, and at last it was autumn; but Kensaku's psychological condition still remained poor. His physical health, undermined by long neglect and irregular habits, was now equally bad. He would tell himself he must pull himself together, he must mend his ways, but it was difficult to reshape his disorganized, undisciplined style of life. He had indeed become unpredictable. One moment he would be sitting at the dinner table limp, silent, and despondent, then suddenly in a paroxysm of rage he would throw all the bowls and saucers at the stone step below the verandah, smashing them to pieces. Once with a pair of sewing scissors he slit the back of the dress Naoko was wearing from the collar almost to the waist. These were only momentary outbursts as far as Kensaku was concerned, but Naoko, seeing them as expressions of his continuing rage at her one mistake, would bear them in silence. Alas, her quiet acceptance of her guilt only made him more angry, more barbarous.

Oei had for years been aware of Kensaku's hot temper. But she had rarely seen such extreme manifestations of it, and she seemed puzzled as to why in the last year or two he had become so prone to these outbursts.

One day a letter from Nobuyuki arrived saying that he would like to visit him soon. Kensaku wrote back promptly, expressing his pleasure; but when later he discovered that Oei had been in touch with Nobuyuki, he wrote another letter withdrawing his invitation. He was immediately sorry that he had done such a thing to his brother, and wondered whether he should not himself go to Tokyo to see him. But he had not the energy to undertake the long train journey; besides, he really did not want to see his brother, for he knew that if he did, he would tell him everything.

Suematsu tried several times to persuade Kensaku to go on a trip with him. "How about the San'in area?" he would say hopefully, producing yet another guidebook. "Now, that's a place I'd like to see." Kensaku appreciated his goodwill, but he could do nothing about his own obstinacy at such times; and always, his inner response was to vow to solve his own problems by himself.

It was high time, he came to feel, that he started visiting ancient temples and shrines again, seeing ancient works of art. It was late autumn now, a particularly beautiful time. And slowly, as he began to go on pilgrimages—sometimes he would be away for several days visiting such places as Kōyasan and Murōji —his state of mind improved.

Autumn passed, and Naoko's time drew near. More in control of himself, especially now that there was danger of hurting the unborn child, Kensaku was hardly ever violent to his wife.

The baby should arrive, the doctor said, in the first week of the new year at the latest. Remembering that Naoko's last delivery had been hastened by that incident in the front hall, Kensaku admonished her repeatedly to be more careful this time. He found Oei's presence reassuring; and having seen to it that everything that could be done to ensure a safe delivery had been done, he was able to avoid undue anxiety.

But when the new year had come and gone, and ten days had passed after that, he began to worry. He approached the doctor and suggested that perhaps Naoko should have the baby in the hospital, and stay there for a month afterward. No, said the doctor, there was no need; there were enough people in the house to take good care of her. And when Naoko, too, showed no enthusiasm for the idea, Kensaku had no choice but to give it up.

Then this chilling thought occurred to Kensaku: what if the doctor had miscalculated by a month, and the child were to be born some time in February—what if he then counted back the months and discovered that the child had been conceived while he had been absent?

The fear was ungrounded. One day in late January he went to see the mansion of the daimyo Katagiri Sekishū in Yamato-Koizumi. After that he walked to Hōryūji. When he returned to his house that night, the baby had been born. It was a girl. The delivery was far more difficult than the last, he was told, because she was so well developed. He looked at the round face of his new baby daughter, and gave a deep sigh of relief. He would take the second character of "Hōryūji" and name her Takako; for it was at about the time he was in that temple that she was born.

9

Every year without fail, during that season when spring turns into summer, Kensaku would become a near-invalid, so enervated was he by the heavy dampness. At the same time his nervousness would increase, and his irritability would reach such a point that often he would surrender himself to it completely.

One morning he, Oei, and Naoko with the baby set out for Shichijō Station. They had arranged previously with Suematsu to go to Takarazuka for a day's outing, and they were to meet him at the station. They would catch the nine o'clock train, and be in Takarazuka in time for lunch. It was an unusually pleasant morning, and Kensaku was in a peaceful mood. True, he had become quite irritated as he waited by the gate of his house for Naoko to come out—she was being very slow—but he had somehow managed to control himself.

Suematsu was waiting for them at the station. As he and Kensaku were busily talking to each other, the ticket gate opened to let the passengers through. It was then that Kensaku noticed that the women had disappeared. "Have they gone to the toilet?" he muttered;

then more angrily, "Why couldn't they wait until they got on the train? The idiots!"

The two men were about to go to the toilet to find them when they saw Oei coming hurriedly toward them. "Please give me our tickets," she said to Kensaku.

"What in the world are you doing? The gate's already open, can't you see?"

"Please go ahead. We're changing the baby's diaper."

"But why do it now? All right, you and Suematsu go ahead, and we'll catch up." Bad-temperedly he handed Suematsu two tickets, then hurried toward the toilet.

"Don't forget, it's a pay toilet!" called Oei from behind.

He met Naoko just as she was coming out of the toilet, holding the baby precariously with one arm while trying to extract her purse from under the sash with her free hand.

"Hurry up!" said Kensaku. "What do you think you're doing, changing diapers at a time like this!"

"But she was uncomfortable, and she was crying."

"Then let her cry. Everyone else is now boarding, didn't you know? Give her to me, I'll carry her." He almost grabbed the baby away from Naoko, then half ran toward the gate. On the platform on the other side guards were blowing their whistles loudly to signify the train's imminent departure.

"The other person is immediately behind me," said Kensaku to the guard at the gate as he handed him the two tickets. He turned around and saw Naoko coming toward him in what he could only describe as a "sliding trot," all the while trying to put away the soiled diaper in her cloth wrapper.

Not caring what an onlooker might think of his behavior, he shouted, "Damn it, hurry up!" Then saying to himself, "Who the hell cares," he ran up the stairs of the bridge two steps at a time. But even he was more careful when going down the stairs on the other side.

The train began to move slowly. Holding the baby tightly under one arm he got on. "Be careful!" shouted a guard as Naoko ran alongside the train toward the doorway where Kensaku was standing. The train was moving no faster than a man walking.

"Idiot!" shouted Kensaku. "Go home!"

"But I can get on! If you take hold of my hand, I can get on without any trouble!" She had to run faster now to keep up with the train. She looked at Kensaku with pleading eyes.

"It's too dangerous! Just go home!"

"But the baby needs my milk!"

"Never mind! Go home, I said!"

Naoko, refusing to give up, got hold of the handrail. Half-dragged along by the train, she at last managed to get one foot on the step, then pulled herself up. Just at that moment Kensaku's free hand shot out, as in a reflex action, and hit Naoko's chest. She fell backward on the platform, rolled over with the momentum, then lay still, once more face up. Suematsu, who had been watching from the coach ahead, jumped off and came running toward her. "I'll get off at the next station!" Kensaku shouted to Suematsu, who gave a slight nod as he ran past.

Far away, two or three guards were lifting Naoko up gently. "What in the world happened?" said a shocked voice behind Kensaku. It was Oei. "I pushed her off," said Kensaku. Oei was speechless. "I told her it was too dangerous to try to get on, but she wouldn't listen." With great effort he controlled himself as he added, "Let's get off at the next station."

"But how could you do such a thing, Kensaku?"

"I don't know myself, I don't know why I did it." He could still see the strange look in Naoko's eyes as she fell off the train. It was unbearable. Oh God, he thought, I've done something irreparable.

At the next station Kensaku was called to the telephone as soon as he and Oei came off the train. It was Suematsu. "She seems to have a slight concussion," he said. "Otherwise she seems all right. The doctor should be here any minute. No serious injury, anyway, from what we can tell."

"The next train going back will be here in fifteen minutes," Kensaku said. "We'll be on it. And where are you all now?"

"In the stationmaster's office."

Oei, standing beside Kensaku, asked, "How is she?"

"She wasn't injured, apparently," Kensaku said as he put back the receiver.

"Thank goodness. What a shock it was."

On the Kyoto-bound train Kensaku asked himself again why he had done such a thing. He could find no answer, except that he had had some sort of fit. That he had done Naoko no serious physical injury was fortunate. But he dared not contemplate what his action had done to their future relationship.

Oei said, "Kensaku, is there something Naoko did that has annoyed you? You seem to have changed so much." Kensaku gave no reply. "You always have been irritable, but you seem to have become much, much worse lately."

"That's because of the erratic life I've been leading. Naoko has nothing to do with it. I've got to pull myself together, that's all."

"I can't help wondering if it isn't my being in the house that has caused difficulty between you two."

"Absolutely not."

"Well, it's true that Naoko and I get along very well together, and I have told myself that I can't be the cause of your trouble. But, you know, having an outsider in the house does often make things difficult."

"Don't worry about that, really. Naoko doesn't think of you as an outsider at all."

"Yes, I know that, and I'm very grateful. But I can't help having doubts when I see you behaving as you have lately."

"It's the weather. I'm always like this at this time of year."

"Perhaps. But you've got to be kinder to poor Naoko. Besides, it's not only her that you should think of. Supposing her milk stops because of what you did to her today—what will become of the baby?"

The mention of the baby left Kensaku at a loss for an answer.

With vacant faces Suematsu and Naoko sat in the stationmaster's office, Naoko rigidly on a chair too high for her, rather like a woman criminal about to be interrogated.

Suematsu stood up and said, "The doctor hasn't come yet."

Naoko looked up for a second, then cast her eyes down again. When Oei went up to her, she burst out crying. She took the baby from Oei, and still crying, began to nurse her. "What a shock it was," said Oei. "Still, what a good thing you weren't badly hurt. How's your head? Did you cool it with water or something?"

Naoko said nothing. What could she have said, when she had been so badly hurt inside?

"I do wish passengers wouldn't do it," said the stationmaster. "There's no need to try so desperately to get on that train when there's another one only forty minutes later. It doesn't make sense to risk one's life for the sake of forty minutes. Anyway, I'm glad madame wasn't hurt."

Kensaku bowed and said, "I'm very sorry for the inconvenience we caused."

"The doctor who's on our part-time staff was unfortunately out when we telephoned. They said he would be back soon, so we left a message asking him to come here immediately. But perhaps we should have called another doctor. Shall we do that?"

Kensaku turned to Suematsu. "What do you think?"

"Well, she seems a little quiet. It would be best, I think, if we were to take her to a doctor ourselves, instead of waiting here."

"That's what we'll do then," Kensaku said to the stationmaster. "Thank you all the same. We've given you a lot of trouble, I'm afraid."

Suematsu left to order the rickshaws. Kensaku went to Naoko's side, thinking he would say something. He searched for the right words, but it was no use. He lacked the strength to find them; besides, Naoko had made herself so unapproachable that no words would have reached her. Finally he said, "Can you walk?" Naoko, without looking up, nodded. "How's your head?" This time she gave no sign of having heard.

Suematsu came into the office and said, "The rickshaws will be here soon."

Kensaku lifted the baby from Naoko's arms. The baby, in the midst of feeding, screamed with anger. Ignoring the noise Kensaku again thanked the stationmaster and his deputy, and left the office ahead of everyone else.

10

Though Naoko had indeed escaped serious injury, she had hit her hip quite badly in the fall, and was confined to bed for a couple of days.

Kensaku wanted to have a good talk with her, but she obstinately refused to give him an opening.

She seemed convinced that his action was related to the Kaname affair. But as far as he was concerned, he had acted on sheer, uncontrollable impulse; he had been overcome momentarily by a fit of irritation; he had certainly had no time to think about Kaname.

"How much longer are you going to stay this obstinate?" he asked her at last. "If you are really angry with me, if you feel that to go on living with a fellow like me would be too dangerous, then please tell me so."

"No, I don't think for a moment that living with you is dangerous. What's so hard for me is that though you said you had forgiven me for what I did, you really haven't forgiven me at all. I don't believe that one can have 'fits' like that. I don't believe you can do a thing like that to me just because I have annoying ways. I asked Oei about it, and she told me she had never seen you behave quite so irrationally before. She said that you had become very strange of late, that you were a different person. What can I think, except that you really can't find it in yourself to forgive me? And if you have managed to forgive me at all, it's only because you think it would be stupid to make yourself more unhappy by hating me. You've said so yourself, don't forget, more than once. What comfort is there for me in that, to know that you want to forgive me because it's to your advantage to do so? That's not forgiving me at all, really, and it never will be. I'd much rather be hated outright by you. And if you couldn't stop hating me, then that would be that. But you might eventually grow tired of hating me and learn to forgive me truly. How happy I'd be then. But the way things are now, I don't know where I stand. I was terribly pleased when you said you weren't going to hate me, you weren't going to brood about it, since hating and brooding did no one any good. But you can't expect me to go on believing what you said when you do something like what you did the other day. I can't help thinking that deep inside, you do resent me. And if I'm right, what hope have I that you'll ever forgive me?"

"What are you proposing to do about it, then?"

"I'm not proposing to do anything. All I want is to find some way of being forgiven."

"Do you want to go home?"

"Why do you say such things? Why should I want to go home?"

"I just asked, since you seem to have little hope for the future of our marriage. At any rate, I'm very glad that you've been so frank. You've been so obstinate and aloof lately, I simply haven't been able to talk to you."

"I understand. But tell me, what do you think of what I've just been saying?"

"It makes a lot of sense. But I really can't believe that I resent you secretly. You ask me to forgive you after I've had my fill of hating you, but how can I make myself hate you when I don't want to?"

Naoko looked accusingly into Kensaku's eyes. "It's just like you to say that."

Perhaps, Kensaku began to think, she was not entirely wrong, perhaps he ought to re-examine himself. "Anyway, it's not fair to assume that what I did the other day had anything to do with that business. It's the way we're living right now that's the real problem. Perhaps that business did have something to do with our present troubles, but you mustn't assume that it still is responsible for everything that goes wrong, when the real cause is the way we live."

"Yes, it may be that my thinking has become warped. But there's one thing that's been very much on my mind these last few days. Do you remember that story you told me about Omasa the Viper, or have you forgotten? Do you remember the things that you said then?"

"What did I say?"

"Oh, that a confession once made lost all meaning afterward, that you much preferred someone who refused to confess, who defiantly suffered alone, to someone who imagined that once having confessed, he was forgiven. You mentioned some woman ballad singer, I remember, or was she a geisha?"

"Eihana, you mean?"

"That's right. You said all sorts of other things too at the time. And now they've come back to haunt me. You know, you can sound very magnanimous, but you aren't at all actually. As a matter of fact, I remember that even when you were telling me about those women, I was frightened by something in you that struck me as unrelenting."

Kensaku became angrier and angrier as he listened to Naoko. "All right, that's enough. I suppose what you say is true to a certain extent. But what you have to understand is that, for me, everything is my problem, mine alone, to solve. As you say, my feelings aren't as magnanimous as my ideas. But when they become so, then all my problems will be solved. It's an egotistic way of looking at things, but given my nature, it may also be the most practical for me. You don't have a place in it, I know, but all I can do is to try to get there in my own way. That's the way I've always been. Anyway, we shall have to try to live a little differently. Perhaps we ought to separate temporarily."

Naoko stared past him, deep in thought. For a time neither said anything.

Now feeling more gentle toward his wife, Kensaku said, " 'Separate' sounds a little ominous. I want merely to go away to some mountain for half a year, and live quietly by myself. A doctor may say I'm suffering from a nervous breakdown. But even if I am, I don't want to go to a doctor for help. I said half a year, but perhaps three months will do. Just tell yourself I've gone on a little trip."

"Are you sure it'll be nothing I can blame myself for?"

"Of course."

"Do you really mean that?" she asked. And when he reassured her, she said, "In that case, all right."

"We'll both benefit from it, physically and psychologically. Just imagine how marvellous it would be if we could then start a new life together. We will, I promise."

"All right."

"Do you understand me?"

"Yes."

"There need not be any negative meaning in our being apart for a while. Do you understand?"

"Yes, I do."

That evening Kensaku told Oei of his plan to go away for a few months. She was adamantly opposed to it. She had seen how useless the trip to Onomichi had been, she said; this trip would do him no good whatsoever; no matter how unsatisfactory his and Naoko's life together might have become, it was most unlikely that they would find new happiness after such a separation.

Kensaku found it hard to explain his position to her. "You must first of all try to see that my reasons for going away this time are not the same. I went to Onomichi to force myself to get some work done; I found that it was too difficult, and I failed. But this time, work is not my primary concern. I'm going in order to find spiritual well-being, you might say, and to recover my physical strength. It really isn't a 'separation.' I'm not going to set up house somewhere else or anything like that. It would be appropriate if you could just think of it as a trip I'm taking for the sake of my health."

"Where are you thinking of going?"

"Daisen in Hōki. Last year I met a prefectural assemblyman from Tottori who couldn't stop boasting about the mountain. It's a holy place of the Tendai sect, and I understand I can stay at one of the temples. It may not be as bad as it sounds. In fact, staying at a temple may be just what I need right now."

11

Kensaku could hardly pretend that this journey he had resolved to undertake was no different from his other trips; and because it was different, he found leaving strangely awkward.

"It really doesn't matter what time I leave," he said to Naoko as nonchalantly as he could on the day of his departure. "I couldn't hope to get there in one day anyway."

He looked at the timetable. "There's a train going to Tottori at

3:16. If I miss that, I can catch the one going to Kinosaki at 5:32."

"Whenever you need tinned food and that sort of thing, let me know, and I'll have Meijiya send it to you."

"I'm going to try my best to live on whatever I'm given there. If I am reminded too often of big-city comforts, I may find myself wanting to come home too soon. So don't write too often either. Let's promise to write to each other only when we have to, shall we?"

"All right. But do write when you find that you want to, please. I hope you will want to."

"Of course I will when I want to. You're not being unreasonable, of course, but you mustn't make me feel that you're waiting to hear from me all the time. That'll make me nervous."

"All right, then, forget what I just said."

"Just worry about our baby, don't worry about me at all. So long as I know the baby is fine, I'll be able to relax." He grinned and added, "I can concentrate on attaining Buddhahood."

Naoko laughed. "Why, you sound as though you've already left us mortals!"

"That's right. And the departed shall return as Buddha."

"What an inauspicious thing to say just before leaving."

"It's not at all inauspicious. 'The attaining of Buddhahood in this very life' as they say. I shall become a Buddha as I am, and return to you with a halo around my head. Anyway, don't worry about me, all right? And please make sure nothing happens to our baby."

"Be a good wet nurse, you mean?"

"A wet nurse, a mother, I don't care which, so long as you can for the time being forget that you're a wife. Pretend that you're a widow, if you like."

"Why do you like saying such inauspicious things?"

"A premonition perhaps," he said lightly.

"What a thing to say!"

Kensaku grinned. He was indeed leaving in a frame of mind akin to that of a man about to take holy orders, but he could hardly tell Naoko so. It was just as well, he thought, that the conversation had ended on this flippant note. He could now begin to get ready for his departure with good grace. He would catch the Tottori train at

Hanazono Station. "You don't have to see me off," he said. "I want to leave as simply as possible."

Just then Oei appeared with the tea. "I'm leaving at three," Kensaku told her. He then turned to Naoko again and said, "Will you tell Sen to call a rickshaw? I want it here at three."

"Couldn't we leave together a little earlier, and walk to Myōshinji, say?"

"It's too hot to walk."

Naoko, looking a little disgruntled, went out to the kitchen to speak to Sen.

Oei prepared the green tea carefully. "Don't come back looking as you did last time," she said, "all skin and bones."

"Don't worry. I'll survive very nicely, you'll see. I'll be a different man when I come back."

"Don't forget to write now and then."

"As I just said to Naoko, please assume that I won't write; then if you don't hear from me, you'll know that I'm well."

"At least, it won't be so lonely this time, since there'll be the three of us."

"There'll be four of you, counting the baby."

"That's right, I'd forgotten. As a matter of fact, she'll be the equal of two."

"I haven't written to Nobuyuki to tell him, so will you, please? Tell him as casually as possible, and don't say anything unnecessary."

Oei nodded. Kensaku, sipping his tea, looked at the clock. It was a little past two.

Naoko came in with the baby in her arms. Awakened from her sleep, the baby seemed dazzled by the light and in ill humor. "See how well she's behaving," Naoko said. "She's not going to cry before you leave."

"What a scowl," Kensaku said laughing, and poked her fat cheek with his finger. "Try to look a little more cheerful, will you?" The tiny head bobbed up and down loosely, without control. "If anything happens, get a doctor from the hospital. Don't ever call a local doctor as we did when poor Naonori was ill."

"No, we won't. But we won't let her get ill in the first place."

Oei said as she poured tea into Naoko's cup, "There isn't much to worry about while she's having only milk, but next summer, when she starts eating all sorts of things, you'll have to be very careful."

Kensaku went to the bathroom and washed himself down with cold water. Not long after he had changed his clothes the rickshaw arrived. With his large suitcase propped up between his legs, and facing the hot sun that was now in the west, he proceeded alone to Hanazono Station.

The view of the River Hozu from Ranzan to Kameoka was beautiful. And the deep pools were more than beautiful, they seemed so cool and inviting. Above the mountains that rose sheer from the river stood Atago, its peak barely showing. He had always seen it from the east, he thought, and now, so soon, he was seeing it from the west. For a moment his house in Kinugasamura rose before his mind's eye, very distant and very small.

Ayabe, Fukuchiyama, then Wadayama. At last the summer sun went down. As the train left Toyooka, Kensaku watched for the famous Genbu cave, but it was a dark night, and all he could see were a few lights shining on the other side of the wide river.

He got off at Kinosaki as he had planned, and put up at an inn called Mikiya. What he saw of the town as the rickshaw carried him to the inn seemed to him to be pleasingly characteristic of a mountain spa. Through its middle ran a shallow stream that reminded him of the River Takase in Kyoto. On either side of it stood a row of two- or three-storied inns, all with closely latticed windows. Yet for all its resort-town atmosphere, it had a remarkably simple and clean look about it. As they turned into a narrow street from near a bathhouse called Ichinoyu, Kensaku saw a row of shops specializing in articles made of mulberry wood, in straw work, in Izushi pottery, and so on. The straw work, with the straw split and then pasted together, looked particularly beautiful under the electric light.

At the inn Kensaku first wanted a bath before he had his dinner. He went across the street to a bathhouse that called itself Goshonoyu—presumably because some imperial personage had once visited it—and there soaked himself in the hot spring water. The bathtub, framed in marble, was very deep, and the water reached his chest even when he stood in it. As he breathed in the fragrant vapor that filled the room, he could feel the tension gradually leave him.

He could not immediately put on his cotton kimono when he came out into the dressing room, so covered in sweat was his body. Repeated wiping with a towel did no good, so he sat down in front of the electric fan, and picking up a little book entitled *A Guide to the San'in Area*, leafed through it until the sweating stopped.

In the book was a description of Daijōji, popularly known as Ōkyo's Temple. It was in a place called Kasumi, it said, three stations away from Kinosaki. He might go there the following day, he thought, and see what the paintings were like. Not that Ōkyo, or the entire Maruyama school for that matter, had ever aroused much interest in him. Indeed, what he had seen of the master's paintings—of cavorting puppies, chickens, bamboo and the like—had impressed him not at all. But Ōkyo was a name he had heard since childhood; besides, he might never come to this part of the country again.

Either Kinosaki was a hot place generally, or it was a particularly hot night; at any rate, the heat prevented Kensaku from having a good sleep. It was probably a better place to come to in the spring or the autumn, he thought, or even in the winter.

It was about six when he woke up the next morning. He wandered out blearily into the turf-covered garden of the inn, his head heavy from lack of sleep. On the side of the mountain that rose immediately before him was a pine tree with a dead branch on it; and on this branch were perched three or four black kites, crying by turns. In the garden was a pond filled with water drawn from a stream outside, and there a half dozen herons stood, their necks pulled in. Looking at this scene, Kensaku felt as though he was still asleep and dreaming.

At about ten he caught a train for Kasumi; then from the station there he went to Ōkyo's Temple by rickshaw.

When Ōkyo was still a student—so the story went—the rector of his temple gave him fifteen pieces of silver to enable him to go to Edo to study. Years later, when the temple now standing was being built, Ōkyo remembered the priest's kindness and returned with his disciples to paint all the sliding doors.

Ōkyo had painted the sliding doors of the study bay and the anteroom, and those facing the altar. Kensaku particularly liked the black-and-white landscape in the study bay, which struck him as remarkably unaffected and true. In the anteroom were two paintings, one of the Chinese general, Kuo Tzu-i, and the other of a pine and a peacock.

Goshun's depiction of the four farming seasons was gentle and harmonious. Rosetsu's monkeys, on the other hand, showed an abandon typical of him; and the last two of the eight panels all too plainly betrayed both in composition and brushwork the artist's loss of interest. What an amusing contrast, Kensaku thought, as he pictured the drunken Rosetsu working beside his more restrained colleague.

A copy—reputed to be by Ōkyo and uncompleted—of the Zen master Ch'an-yueh's painting of the sixteen sages was exhibited on the second floor of the rectory.

Near it was a pair of eagles by Shen Nan-p'in. Perched on a small rock sticking out above the waves was the female eagle, its wings spread out, legs bent, back lowered, neck thrust out. It looked up at the male eagle standing on top of a large rock above. The male eagle stood straight, and stared back fiercely at the female below. Kensaku was intrigued by the bluntness with which the artist had expressed the female eagle's instinct to mate; and no less interesting to him was the male's overbearing posture.

He turned to the acolyte who stood behind him and said, "Anything else to see?"

"You've seen all the paintings, I think. But on the roof there's a dragon that is supposed to have been carved by Left-hand Jingorō."

Downstairs the two put on clogs and came out of the rectory. It was now cloudy outside. They went around to the left of the main building. A few feet up the hill from the top of the stone steps was a small open area, and from there they viewed the large dragon in the gable above. No doubt a realistic rendering, Kensaku thought with amusement. "Life-size, isn't it?" he said grinning; but the acolyte seemed not to understand. On Kensaku's upturned face a large drop of rain fell. "It's beginning to rain," he said, and as they walked back to the rectory, he could not resist another joke: "Brought on by the angry dragon, eh?"

12

That night Kensaku stopped in Tottori. The people at the inn pressed him to see the local sights. In the nearby beach, they said, which was seventeen miles long and over two miles wide, there were two hollows, named "the large cone" and "the small cone"; and then there was a small lake by the beach called Tanegaike. But the thought of being dragged around for miles over bumpy terrain on a rickshaw did not appeal to him. He bought postcards instead. The young maid who served him dinner recounted to him some of the local legends, such as the legend of the squire of Koyama and the legend of Tanegaike.

In Tanegaike there dwelt a young woman by the name of Otane, who had turned herself into a large serpent. Once she chased a Tottori samurai to the gate of his house. The samurai, rushing in, shut the gate in her face. In indignation Otane peeled three scales off her body and stuck them on the gate before going away. Until very recently, the maid said in all solemnity, these scales had been passed down in the samurai's family from generation to generation.

Kensaku went to bed worrying about the next day's weather. If it rained, he would have to spend another night at an inn somewhere. Of course he might quite enjoy staying at another spa—the one by Lake Tōgō, say—but he did want to reach Daisen as quickly as possible and begin a life of quiet on that cool mountain.

He was awakened in the middle of the night by the sound of a heavy shower. At this rate it might clear up by morning, he told himself, and went back to sleep.

The next morning indeed turned out to be so clear that he now became apprehensive about the impending journey in the burning sun. He did not look forward either to having to go through dozens of tunnels again as he had done the day before.

On the train he opened the "Imperial Library" edition of *Lives of Eminent Priests* that he had bought in town the previous evening, and read a little of the chapter on Gansan. He soon tired of it, however; putting the book down, he gazed out of the window. They were passing Lake Koyama. It was a fine view. According to the legend as told to him by the maid, it had once been ricefields belonging to the squire; but in punishment for his having called back the sun at the end of a rice-planting day, his land had been turned overnight into a lake. Covering a large, flat area stretching between low hills, the lake did look very appropriately like fields covered by floodwater—at least it could to anyone who had heard the legend. Lafcadio Hearn, Kensaku remembered, had described many of the legends of this area. Might he have written about the squire of Koyama, he wondered, and wished he had brought some Hearn with him.

Unlike Koyama, Tōgō was a lake with no charm or character to it. Perhaps it also had a legend associated with it; but Kensaku doubted that it did, for he was inclined to believe that every place that had a popular legend associated with it had something about it that appealed to the imagination.

As they passed Agei, Akasaki, Mikuriya, Kensaku continued to gaze out of the window without tiring of the scene. The vitality of midsummer, or something like that, began to communicate itself to him, reviving in him a rare sense of well-being.

The rice, grown thick and over two feet high, seemed to sway in the heat of the sun, though the day was windless. It's the color of burning green, he thought excitedly.

The color of the rice really was luxuriant. And so affected was he by the sight of the stalks rippling and jostling, indeed dancing in the brilliant sunlight, that he thought he could hear their joyous song. As though for the first time, he was made aware that such a world as this existed. There are people, he thought, that live like wild cats in a cave, forever snarling at each other; and then there is this life. For him that day, the harsh light of the sun was not at all unkind.

He got off the train at a lonely station called Daisen. The rickshaw man who came in answer to his call said that Daisen itself was fifteen miles away. The rickshaw could negotiate only seven miles of that; one had to walk the rest.

"What do I do with my suitcase, then?" Kensaku asked. "Do I hire a packhorse?"

"Oh, no, I'll carry it myself," said the rickshaw man, picking up the suitcase and weighing it. He was a skinny man, somewhere in his fifties.

"It's pretty heavy, you know. It has books in it."

The man picked up the suitcase again. "It's not that heavy," he said, grinning.

"Have you eaten?" Kensaku asked.

"Have you, sir?"

"I had a box lunch on the train."

"In that case, you can feed me something at a teashop on the way."

The prospect of being on the road together for fifteen miles, it seemed to Kensaku, had already established a spirit of camaraderie between them. As Kensaku got in the rickshaw the man said, "We have a lot of the day left, but it's going to be a pretty stiff climb after we've done the first half."

Kensaku looked at the handsome outline of Daisen in the distance, and thought how strange it somehow was that he should be going to that mountain in the scorching heat with this rickshaw man. "I suppose it's much cooler up there?"

"Of course. In the old days, all the ice we used to get down here came from that mountain. In the winter we used to pile up the snow up there, then cut it up into pieces in the summer and bring them down. That was our ice. When I was young, I was one of the fellows who made their living doing that."

In the narrow street a crowd of children were noisily playing a game that might have been "prisoner's base." They were so absorbed in it that they would not move aside for the rickshaw. Picking up a thin piece of bamboo which happened to be lying on the ground, the old rickshaw man began tapping lightly the heads of those children nearest to him. "Doddery old fool!" shouted the children as they grudgingly stepped aside. "Idiot!" Ignoring their insults and still grinning, he continued to tap whatever child's head came within reach.

They came out into a street that was about fifty yards wide. The houses that lined either side had low eaves, and this made the street seem even wider and lighter. In front of half the houses on one side of it were bamboo poles laid across three-legged stands; hanging from these poles were countless numbers of long strips of some white stuff. They were gourd shavings, the rickshaw man told Kensaku.

"But aren't they very broad for gourd shavings?"

"That's because they aren't dry yet."

"Are they a local specialty?"

"Not really."

Conversing with Kensaku in this pleasant, easy fashion, the old man pulled the rickshaw at a varied pace, sometimes jogging, sometimes walking. There was a farmhouse at the end of the road, seven miles out of town. Here the old man left his rickshaw; then strapping Kensaku's suitcase to his back, he proceeded to go up a steep, narrow path that led off the road. Kensaku tucked up the skirt of his hemp kimono, and went up after him.

Spread out before them at the top was a large, open field, skirting the foot of the mountain. Kensaku stood there for a time appreciating the view. Until recently, the rickshaw man said, the army used it as a grazing ground for their horses; did Kensaku know that Daisen was famous for its horses?

Unhurriedly, the two made their way up the narrow path across the gently sloping field.

13

Wild flowers bloomed in abundance all around them. There were gentian, wild pinks, agueweed, yarrow, mountain iris, scabious, burnet, and various members of the chrysanthemum family whose names Kensaku did not know. Cows and horses grazing in the field would look up and stare at them as they went past. There were large pine trees here and there, and on their upper branches the cicadas were crying with all their might. The air was clear, and already they could feel the mountain coolness; yet because of the effort of climbing, they were warm. And when the distant sea behind them became visible, they would occasionally stop to rest.

"Just one more lap to go," the rickshaw man said.

"The suitcase is heavier than you expected, isn't it?"

"Yes, it is. Very heavy, in fact. What did you say you had in here—books?"

"If it's too much for you, we'll take a few of them out at the tea-shop, and you can bring them up to me the next time you come this way."

"Don't worry. Give me a good meal at the teashop at the fork, and I'll be as good as new."

"Do you drink?"

"Not very much."

"Have a drink there. It'll make you feel better."

"All right, you can buy me a cup of sweet saké. How about you?"

"No, I won't have any. I haven't much resistance to drink."

"But I'm sure you drink a little. Have a cup with me, and we'll both have a nap for an hour or so afterward."

"I don't know about a nap, but let's have a good rest there anyway."

"It's no more than a quarter of a mile from here. It used to be called 'the lone house at the fork,' and there isn't another house for miles around. A notorious old man lived there years ago, and he used to rob travelers."

"When was that?"

"Oh, when I was a young man. He broke into a temple in Daisen —Renjōin, it was—armed with a bamboo spear. He was caught, and I saw him being tortured outside the teashop. They gave him 'the shrimp treatment,' you know. That's when you make a fellow sit on the ground on his knees, tie his legs up, then push his head down forward as far as it'll go. I happened to pass the place—I was carrying ice down the mountain—when they were giving the old man this treatment. It was a terrible sight. Screaming and writhing he was, tossing his long, white hair about like a madman, and they kept screwing him down lower and lower. He really was like a shrimp, all bent up. It's a terrible torture, don't you think?"

The rickshaw man then described in some detail the attempted burglary of the temple. As the masked burglar was threatening the rector with his spear, an acolyte who had a lot of sense rushed to the big temple bell and began striking it wildly. Only in cases of fire or some such mishap was the bell to be struck that way; and in response all the other temples nearby began sounding their bells similarly. This was in the middle of the night, and the sound of the bells echoed through the forests and the valleys, shattering the stillness. The moon was out, bright and low in the sky. A priest coming out of one of the temples saw in the distance an old man with dishevelled white hair running through the woods.

"There are no bamboos on the mountain," the rickshaw man said, "except for the bamboo grove in front of the 'lone house.' And when they searched it, they found a stump that fitted exactly the bamboo spear the burglar left behind. When they showed him that, even the obstinate old fellow didn't have much to say. They found out later that he had committed many other crimes too. He was eventually executed in Yonago."

The teashop was a spacious bungalow with a low roof. There was a large rain tub under the eaves, filled to the brim with water. In front of it stood a woman of about sixty, washing a salted salmon.

"What a hot day," the rickshaw man said, unstrapping the suitcase and putting it down on the bench by the entrance.

The large bungalow was divided in the middle by an unfloored passageway; to the left were the proprietor's living quarters, and to the right was the room used to serve customers. In the middle of this room sat a white-haired old man of nearly eighty, with his knees drawn up and his arms hugging them. Before him in the distance lay the field at the foot of the mountain, and beyond, the inlet, then Yomigahama Point and Mihonoseki. Even the outer sea was within view. He sat still, gazing at this scene, apparently unaware of the arrival of the two customers.

"A meal and a cup of saké for the rickshaw man," said Kensaku to the old woman. "And I think I shall have some cider and cookies."

"Grandpa, grandpa," called the old woman, keeping her wet hands away from her clothes. "My hands smell, so please serve this gentleman some cider and cookies."

Silently the old man stood up. He was tall, and reminded Kensaku of an old mountain tree shorn of its leaves by a storm. "Cookies and what?" he said.

"It's all right, grandpa," said the rickshaw man, going toward the kitchen at the end of the passageway. "You get the cookies and I'll get the cider." He then called out from the back, "The bottles on this side are the cool ones, right?"

The old man fetched a glass plate from the cupboard, then put on it a handful of coarse cookies which he extracted from an old petrol can. He walked up to Kensaku, and put the plate down in front of him. "Welcome," he said with a quick bob of the head, then went back to his place in the middle of the room.

"Will you eat this?" asked the old woman of the rickshaw man as she cut up the salmon.

"I'd like that very much," the rickshaw man replied, wiping the sweat off his chest.

Kensaku, fanning himself and sipping the cider, gazed at the distant scene from behind the old man. He then looked at the back of the still head covered with a two-inch growth of white hair, and was much intrigued by the contrast between this serene old man and the other, lawless old man who had also lived in the house. He must have gazed at the same scene countless times before; yet here he was, still gazing at it without apparent boredom. What could he be thinking about? Surely not about the future; and in all probability not about the present either. Might he then be recalling the various incidents of his long life, incidents that took place long, long ago? No, Kensaku thought, he's probably forgotten them. Rather, he was like an ancient tree in the mountains, he was like a moss-covered rock that had been placed there in front of the view. If he was thinking at all, he was thinking as an old tree or a rock would think. He seemed so tranquil, Kensaku envied him.

Piled up in several layers against the wall to the left of the old man were straw sacks filled with rice. For some time Kensaku had been hearing scuffling sounds behind these sacks; and now suddenly a kitten appeared on top of them. Its ears pointing forward, the kitten was looking intently into the gap that it had just emerged from. Its body was still, but its tail moved busily, as though it had a life of its own. Then a fat paw reached out from the gap, and tapped at the kitten playfully.

The rickshaw man approached Kensaku holding a cup of sweet

saké that the old woman had just poured for him. "Why don't you have a cup too?" he said.

"I've never tasted sweet saké, and I don't think I should try it now."

"I haven't touched this cup, so why don't you take a sip from it?"

"Thanks, but I really don't think I shall."

"All right. It's the best thing to drink in the summer, I think." The rickshaw man took a few sips of the coarse saké as he walked back to his table.

"Were the kittens born here?" Kensaku asked.

Acting as intermediary the rickshaw man repeated the question for the old woman's benefit. "Were those kittens born here?"

"That's right. We were given the mother last year, and she had those two kittens."

"That was pretty quick, wasn't it? Do you have a male cat too?"

"No, we don't, but she must have found a mate somewhere."

"Where would she have found a mate around here? There isn't another house for miles around."

"She disappeared for over two days, so she could have gone quite a long way."

The old proprietor still sat quietly with his back turned toward them. He was like a piece of furniture that had been put there. The two kittens were playing with each other on top of the sacks. One missed its footing and fell to the floor. It got up quickly, looking stunned, then meowed pitifully. From somewhere the mother cat made her appearance, and began licking the kitten.

A man in his thirties, wearing riding breeches and gaiters, came in. "Hullo," he said, and sat down heavily and tiredly on the wooden border of the room, his legs spread apart, his hands resting on his thighs. "I went right up into the mountains looking for Yamada, but couldn't find him. Has he passed by here today, granny?"

"Who?"

"Yamada."

"No, I haven't seen him."

"I wonder if he's gone to Mikuriya."

"What's happened to the horse that broke his leg yesterday?"

"It's because of that horse that I'm looking for Yamada. Ah well,

I'll just have to shoot the horse and bury him."

"He's Yamada's horse, is he?"

"Yes."

"What a terrible loss."

"By the way, what's the fish today?"

"Salted salmon. Would you like some?"

"Salted salmon . . . I think I'll have dried squid instead. Will you grill me some?"

The old woman poured him some saké, then started grilling the squid. "I hear there were mosquitoes even up in the mountains this year."

"Really? I hadn't heard that."

"Around here, we had to start putting up mosquito nets at the beginning of the month."

The mother cat, attracted by the smell of the dried squid, hovered about, making a nuisance of herself. Each time she brought her nose close to the squid slices which were on a plate beside the old woman, she would have her head smacked. With eyes narrowed, ears pulled back, she would withdraw, but only temporarily.

Kensaku and the rickshaw man left the teashop soon afterward. They had not walked for more than half an hour when Kensaku was already thirsty again. Only a few yards more, the rickshaw man said, and they would come to a very nice stream. But all that they found when they got there was a dry, sandy bed, cracked by the sun. "There was heavy rain last night in Tottori," said Kensaku ill-temperedly. "Didn't it rain here at all?"

The rickshaw man looked at him consolingly. Less than a mile away, he said, there was the gateway to a shrine, and there they would get cold water. "Where will you be staying?" he then asked. "Renjōin, the temple I mentioned earlier, has a separate apartment. You won't have a view, but if it's vacant, you might want it. You could do a lot of studying there, I think."

"I'll make up my mind when I've seen it."

"Are you staying for long?"

"I intend to, if I like it here."

"You wouldn't want to stay after the summer was over, of course. When it gets to be autumn, you might as well go down to the hot springs below. There are lots of good spas around. There'll be no sense in staying up here. The food's so bad, you wouldn't want to stay up here for very long anyway."

"Do they stick to a vegetarian diet at the temple?"

"Oh, no, they'll give you meat. They eat anything, those folks. The priest has a wife too. Worldly, that's what he is. He spends most of his time buying and selling horses."

It was disillusioning for Kensaku to hear such things about Daisen, which was after all supposed to be second only to Mt. Hiei among the sacred places of the Tendai sect.

Beside the large gateway with its paint peeling stood an inn; and here they were given cold water at last. The temple was yet another half mile, the rickshaw man said. Then in a whisper he asked, "How would you like to stay at this inn?" Kensaku shook his head in silence. Clearly the rickshaw man was beginning to succumb under the weight of the suitcase. He would pay him more than he had promised, Kensaku decided.

He bought some cigarettes and postcards, then followed the rickshaw man out of the inn.

They left the road that led up to Daisen Shrine and went down a path to the right. At the bottom they crossed a dry riverbed full of stones. The bed continued down between forests toward the foot of the mountain at a fairly sharp incline. Upstream it came into view between sheer cliffs. No wonder the cliffs were called "Jizō's Cut," Kensaku thought, for they did look as though some deity with superhuman power had split apart a huge rock.

The two men went up a steep path on the other side of the riverbed through a dark forest. To the right stood Kongōin, and above it to the left stood Renjōin.

They went into the unfloored entryway of the rectory. "Hullo!" the rickshaw man called out. An angular-faced woman, fortyish, came out. Eyeing Kensaku and the suitcase, she said, "Do you intend to stay a while?"

Kensaku could see two men sitting by the fireplace inside. One was a youngish priest, dressed in a white summer kimono, and the other looked like a horse trader. They were talking loudly and drinking.

"Yes, I should like to," said Kensaku.

Dubiously the woman turned around and said to the priest, "What do you think?"

The priest came out to the front hall. His face was flushed with drink. "Welcome," he said, giving a bow that somehow seemed to lack all spontaneity.

"Will you be able to put me up?" asked Kensaku.

"I won't say I can't, but my predecessor, who lives in Sakamoto in Gōshū, has unfortunately fallen ill, and I've got to go there tomorrow. Besides, we're rather shorthanded at the moment. But come in anyway. If we decide we can't take care of you, we'll introduce you to another temple."

Kensaku was shown to the annex. The living room with a study bay, the anteroom, and the front hall at right angles to it were all about four and a half mats in size. The annex had been built, the priest told Kensaku, by his predecessor's predecessor as a retreat in his old age. Beneath the ceiling of the living room two long bamboo poles had been laid like rails over the crossbeams; and resting on these poles were several plain paper screens. In the winter, when the drafts got severe, these would be brought down and put up around the room to form an inner enclosure. Kensaku found this small living room a little oppressive, but when he was told he could rent all three rooms he was well enough pleased.

The rickshaw man spent the night at the temple, and departed the next morning.

14

For Kensaku, who had been thoroughly exhausted by the stress of his relationships with people in the last several years, his new life in the mountains was a sheer pleasure. In the woods a few hundred yards up from the temple was a little shrine called Amida's Chapel. He went to it often. It was in a state of utter disrepair, though it had been declared a historic monument by the authorities. Vegetation grew wild around it, and the wooden porch was rotten. Yet its neglected condition made it all the more attractive to Kensaku. He would sit on the stone steps leading up to the porch and watch the scene around him. One day there was a large dragonfly that kept flying past, back and forth, about twenty yards in front of him. It flew in a straight line four or five feet above the ground, and when it reached a certain point it would turn around and fly back, again in a straight line. Everything about the creature was beautiful: its large eyes the color of green jade, its black and yellow stripes, the strong line of its body from the tight, thin waist to the end of its tail; and in particular its remarkably decisive movements. How much more dignified were this tiny creature's movements, Kensaku thought, than those of some little men he had known—Mizutani, for example. He remembered how drawn he was to the double-scroll painting of the hawk and the golden pheasant in the Kyoto Museum two or three years ago, and thought that he had probably had the same feeling then.

Once he saw two lizards playing. They would stand up on their hind legs, jump in the air, twine themselves around each other. As he watched their nimble, joyous play, he, too, became lighthearted.

Here he discovered that wagtails were little birds that literally ran when on the ground. They were not like crows, say, that would alternately walk and hop.

Everything he saw here fascinated him. There was a little shrub growing in the woods by the chapel. In the middle of each leaf was a tiny fruit like a red bean. The leaf was like the upturned palm of a man's hand, gently proffering the precious fruit. It was, Kensaku thought, a gesture full of reverence.

As he looked back at his own past, so much of which seemed to have been wasted on worthless dealings with this person and that, he felt that a whole new world had now opened up for him.

Far above him a kite flew with proud audacity under the blue sky. How ugly was man's creation, the airplane, compared to it. Three or four years ago, when he was so absorbed in his own work, he had praised man's tenacity of purpose, man's conquest of the sky and of the sea. But since then, his attitude had changed completely. Now he wondered if nature had ever intended that man should fly like birds or go down into the sea like fish. Would not such limitless ambition lead man to some kind of misfortune? Would he not in time be severely punished for his overweening confidence in his own intelligence?

He had praised man's limitless ambition in the belief that it was an expression of his unconscious desire to save his own species somehow from the certain destruction that awaited his planet. And in those days, he had no alternative but to interpret all that he saw and heard around him—all the struggling and the scrambling—as manifestations of this unconscious will. After all, that was the only way he could understand his own dissatisfied, desperate attitude toward his work.

He felt very differently now. True, he was still tied to his work; it still was capable of upsetting him. But his present state of mind was such that if he were told that man would be destroyed together with his planet, he would gladly have accepted that fate. Though he knew nothing about Buddhism, such realms believed in by Buddhists as "nirvana" and "the realm of bliss" seemed irresistibly attractive to him.

He read a little at a time passages from *Sayings of Lin-chi*, which Nobuyuki had given him. He did not understand very well what he read, but it gave him solace all the same. *Lives of Eminent Priests*, which he had picked up in Tottori, was a rather conventional, popular work, but he could not help crying as he read the account of Eshin's visit to Kūya and the dialogue between them.

"If we reject this mundane world, and desire with all our hearts the Pure Land, then surely rebirth cannot be denied us." They were simple words, but when Kensaku read them he wanted to join E-shin in prayer.

So long as the weather was good he would spend two or three hours of the day on the steps of Amida's Chapel. In the evening he often went down to the riverbed. He would pick up a stone the size of an orange and throw it as hard as he could at a large stone some distance away. It would make a hard, clean sound as it hit the target, and if thrown just right, it would ricochet and hit another stone, and then another. When the throw was thus successful he would promptly return to the temple, unreasonably pleased. There were days, however, when success eluded him no matter how many stones he threw, and he would leave the riverbed in a state of acute exasperation.

He was generally satisfied with the living conditions in Daisen.

But one thing almost defeated him, and this was the food he was given at the temple. Though he had come prepared to eat frugally— had he not rejected Naoko's offer to send him food parcels?—he had not imagined that rice could be quite so bad anywhere. He had never been fussy about rice, but what he got at the temple even he found unbearable. Grimly and uncomplainingly he tried to eat it, which meant that he did not eat enough; and he began to suspect that he was growing weaker as a result.

The priest's wife was a nice person, and tried to take good care of Kensaku. One thing she made which Kensaku did like, and this was pickled wild asparagus. It was just as well, for she was rather proud of it.

Their married daughter, now living in Tottori, was staying there with her baby. She was a pretty girl, no more than seventeen or eighteen. She didn't make a habit of coming to his apartment, but she would often stand outside the window and talk to him. "I'm hardly more than a baby myself," she once said, laughing, "and here I am, with another baby." Kensaku guessed that she was merely repeating what someone had said to her. She seemed to do little but wander about with the baby, while her mother single-handedly did all the chores. Kensaku had no opinion of her one way or the other. It did strike him as interesting, however, that she should so often come to his window to talk. No doubt, he concluded, marriage had freed her from all fear of men. And this supposition led him to wonder if Naoko would have made that mistake if she had not been a married woman, if she had still been a virgin.

One day the priest's wife came to him with a letter she had just received. It was from a group of forty or so tourists who wanted to spend a night at the temple. "What am I to do?" she asked.

Not knowing what would be entailed in putting up such a group, the best he could do was to ask, "Can you feed them?"

"It's not impossible."

"Why don't you say yes, then? Not that I could be of any help, of course."

The woman pondered uncertainly for a while, then decided she would take on the group. "I wish Oyoshi was more helpful," she muttered as though to herself.

"But she has the baby to take care of," Kensaku said. "Why don't you get Také to help you instead?"

Také was a young roofer from one of the villages below, now engaged in replacing the shingles on the roof over the purification fountain in Daisen Shrine. It was a formidable task for one man, for not only was the roof heavily shingled, but he himself had to make the shingles from the trees that had been cut down in the nearby woods. He was given food and lodging at the temple, and that was all he would accept in return for his labors. Kensaku took a liking to this man, and he would often go to where he was working and talk to him.

Kensaku was made to write a reply to the group of tourists on the woman's behalf.

One afternoon a couple of days later, as he was sitting at his desk doing nothing in particular, the woman came running up the stone steps from the path below, crying, "They're here! They're here!"

What a momentous occasion she's making of it, he thought amusedly; surely she must have received many such groups before. But of course her husband, who would presumably have helped her, was absent, and to have to take care of so many people by herself was indeed an immense responsibility. After lunch she had gone out several times to the top of the path to see if the group was approaching. And now she had seen these tourists, all forty of them, crossing the riverbed one after the other. It must have been an extremely anxious moment for her.

With the arrival of the group the temple suddenly became noisy. Kensaku would have liked to help, but seeing that there was little he could do, he went out for a walk.

He returned to the temple at dusk. When at last dinner was ready, it was the daughter, carrying her baby, who brought it in.

"Don't bother to stay," Kensaku said. "I can serve myself."

"Oh, no, I'll serve. I have nothing better to do." She then laughed and said, "You'll have to let me sleep beside you tonight, by the way."

Kensaku was at a loss for an answer. She presumably didn't mean "beside" literally, he told himself; she must be intending to sleep in the front hall. But supposing there was a shortage of mosquito nets—which was not unlikely, considering the number of people staying at the temple that night—would she not perhaps want to come under his?

He went to bed as usual, as though he expected no intrusion. And sure enough, the daughter never appeared. This, of course, was not surprising. But he did wonder why she was inspired to make such an odd suggestion.

15

That night Kensaku had a dream.

The grounds of the shrine were packed with people. Pushed by the crowd behind him he was going up a long flight of shallow stone steps. Far away, at the top of the steps, stood the main shrine, built on a grand scale and very new. There, some kind of ceremony was taking place. He wanted to get near so that he could see it properly, but was prevented from doing so by the crowd in front of him.

A separate walk, waist-high and made of wooden planks laid over logs tied together, stretched from the top to the bottom of the steps. When the ceremony was over, the divine medium was to come down this walk.

There was sudden excitement around him. The ceremony was over. A young woman in a white ceremonial dress—she was the divine medium—appeared at the top of the walk, then quickly began her descent, followed by five or six attendants. Kensaku, who was still being pushed helplessly and slowly up the steps by the crowd, felt at that moment an overwhelming desire to break free and rush up to her.

Hurriedly yet nonchalantly, as though the murmuring crowd were not there, she came down the walk. She was Oyoshi, just returned from Tottori. Kensaku was not sure whether he had or had not known the identity of the divine medium; at any rate, her face was as always expressionless and not very intelligent, but as always beautiful. What he particularly approved of was that the adulation now being showered on her seemed not to affect her vanity. And it never occurred to him to think that there was anything untoward in her being a divine medium. Indeed, as far as he was concerned, no one could have excelled her in that role.

Oyoshi almost ran past him; as she did so, the long sleeve of her dress caressed the top of his head, and at that moment, he experienced a strange ecstasy. Yet in the midst of his ecstasy he was still able to make the detached comment: "This is why everyone in the crowd imagines she's divine."

He awakened from his dream. What an odd dream, he thought. Obviously, the crowd he dreamed about had been occasioned by the arrival that day of the group of tourists. But what was the nature of that strange ecstasy? It must have had an element of sexuality in it, he decided, though as far as he could tell, he had not been aware of its presence while dreaming. The realization made him slightly uncomfortable; for he had imagined that in his present state of mind, such things had lost their immediacy.

He went back to sleep. When he awakened the next morning he could hear the sound of raindrops coming down on the eaves. He got up and opened the storm windows. There was a thick mist outside, the color of grey. Only a little of the large cedar in front was visible, and that merely a vague, inky outline. He could smell the mist as it poured into the room. It felt cold against the skin, and pleasantly refreshing. What he had imagined to be rain was in fact the mist turned into water trickling down the thatched roof. It was very still, this misty morning in the mountains. A cock was crowing somewhere in the distance. And over in the rectory people seemed to be already up. He picked up a hand towel and a toothbrush and went outside. As he strolled about brushing his teeth, Oyoshi came out of the rectory, carrying a shovel piled high with burning charcoal. "I slept in the temple last night," she said. "It was miserable. They were all so noisy, the baby couldn't go to sleep."

"I could hear a little of the commotion, but it didn't bother me particularly."

"I came over to your apartment thinking I might spend the night there, but you were sound asleep, and I didn't want to disturb you."

This was not the Oyoshi he had dreamed about. "I dreamed about you last night," he said. "You were a divine medium."

"What in the world is that? Are there really such people?"

"Have you ever heard of that old woman—I forget her name—who started the Tenri sect? Well, you were something like her. Of course, you were much younger. It would seem that I was one of your devout followers."

"Really?" she said, drawing her neck in and giving a giggle. She was silent for a while, not quite sure what she should say next. "Také's father was a Tenri believer, you know," she said finally. "He was ruined because of that."

"I see. Is Také the only one in his family that comes here to worship, then?"

"His family were always members of the congregation here until his father's time. And when his father went bankrupt, I suppose Také got fed up with the new religion and came back to the temple."

"Mind you," Kensaku said, "he has a touch of the Tenri zealot, doing all that work on the roof for nothing."

"But he's a really admirable person, don't you think?"

"Yes, he seems so. He does work hard."

"Even in his village, he's regarded as someone special."

"He seems rather mature for his age, I must say. Not exactly frivolous, is he?"

"He's suffered a lot."

"Suffered?"

"His father was ruined when he was still a child. That was bad enough, but more recently he has had troubles of the sort he can't talk about."

"Is that so? By the way, has he been helping your mother since yesterday?"

"No. Apparently mother didn't ask him."

Later, while serving Kensaku breakfast, Oyoshi told him about Také's "troubles." Také had a wife three years older than himself, who had not yet given him a child. She was a slut, and had always had lovers—not only before but after her marriage to Také. He was her husband only in name. He was merely one of many men whom she favored with her graces. He had known what she was like when he married her; but this did not make his pain any more bearable. Others told him to leave her; and though there were times when he thought he would, he never did in the end. He was a weakling, he would tell himself. No doubt he was, but his dilemma was simply that he could not bring himself to hate her.

Unpleasant incidents occurred continually. They arose out of so-called triangles, but, alas, they were not even "triangles" that included him. What he could not bear was not so much his wife's loose ways as having to watch the endless, mean complications that she caused between her rival lovers. Yet he made no attempt to leave her.

"You won't believe the sort of things that go on in that household," Oyoshi said. "She would be entertaining one of her men in the living room, while Také would be in the kitchen, either cooking or doing the laundry. I hear that sometimes she sends him out to get saké for herself and her guest. He's been seen, you know, rushing back to the house with a bottle of saké."

"Well, he's different, I'll say that for him. If such treatment doesn't make him angry, he's either very saintly or a pervert of some kind. The latter, I should think."

He pictured in his mind the man he knew, vainly searching for some aspect of his visage or personality that suggested such abnormality. But as he thought more about it, Také's condition seemed not so appallingly strange after all. He asked Oyoshi, "What does Také himself say about the whole business?"

"He does occasionally grumble to my mother, I gather."

"I see."

"I suppose he has pretty well decided to accept his lot."

"But can he really?"

"Well, his wife has always been like that. But however resigned he may be, they live in a small place, and there's a lot of gossip. He's come away to the mountains partly to escape that, apparently."

"I can see now that he has the look of a man who's had a hard time, but I would never have imagined that his life was as you described it to me. You've seen him at work, haven't you? He's always singing, I've noticed. He looks so carefree, I've often felt quite envious."

"Oh, but there are times when he looks rather downcast."

"I'm sure you're right. But who would have guessed by looking at him that his home life was like that?"

Oyoshi burst out laughing. "Are you saying that you should be able to recognize a cuckold by just looking at his face?"

Kensaku laughed too. "You're absolutely right. But tell me, what would you say about me by just looking at my face? Would you say that something of the kind had happened to me?"

Oyoshi dismissed the question with another burst of laughter. Just then a fearful thought crossed Kensaku's mind: would Kaname, learning of Kensaku's absence, again visit his house in Kinugasa-mura? No, he hastily and firmly told himself, Naoko would never make the same mistake again. Yet in that act of reassuring himself, there was an element of wishful thinking; in his determination to trust her, there was still a vestige of doubt left somewhere in his heart.

That she would never steal—this he could believe wholeheartedly. He thought he believed too that she would never be unfaithful; but here, his belief was not firm enough to eliminate all doubt. Was it because he thought that women, being passive, were ultimately defenseless? Or was it because of his own particular circumstances that he could not rid himself of doubt? He did not know. At any rate, he tried very hard to believe in her, to convince himself that Naoko could never do such a thing again.

But what of Kaname? Perhaps he regretted what he had done. But he was a young bachelor, an easy prey to temptation. Supposing he discovered that Kensaku had gone away, might he not find the opportunity irresistible, however good his earlier intentions were, and wander back to the house for another attempt at seduction? If only Oei were more reliable in such matters, if only she had a little more sense and were more watchful by nature, if only she were less gullible. No question about it, she could be quite trying sometimes.

16

He had told Naoko not to expect any letters from him, and to assume that if he did not write, it was because he was all right. So far, then, there had been no communication between them. Naoko for her part could not have written to him, for she did not know his address. But now, after having heard Také's story from Oyoshi, he found himself suddenly wanting to write to her. The desire came from his realization that it would be cruel to let her go on remembering him as he was when he left, and that not to reassure her would only do them both harm.

He remembered her sad eyes and the way she cocked her head like a child when she said, "Are you sure your going away is not something I can blame myself for?" The memory filled him with compassion; at the same time, it made him uncomfortable. Naoko could not believe that she was completely forgiven; or, even if she could, she felt somehow that she must not allow herself to believe that she was. For what if she were to allow herself that luxury, and then were to find herself being subjected to some sudden act of vindictiveness on Kensaku's part?

It pained Kensaku to know that such was her state of mind, to know that his own incapacity for generosity had justified it. He had wanted not to brood over her mistake for the reason that to do so would only lead to further unhappiness for both of them, and that therefore it would be senseless. He knew that there was something calculating in this attitude. So did Naoko, and this was why she could not allow herself to trust him. Yet, for all his understanding of Naoko's dilemma, his response had been to think angrily: if this is the best I can do, if I can't be more generous, then why can't she try to make the most of what little I can offer? And so he had come away to Daisen, hoping to rid himself of that hardness in him, of his incapacity to be truly gentle.

As he sat down to write his letter to Naoko, he felt that the gentleness he sought in his own heart had come sooner than he had hoped. "Are you all well?" he wrote. "I trust that you are. I said I would not write, but all of a sudden I wanted to, so here's my letter. I have settled down quite nicely, and I feel I have benefited enormously from the trip. Coming here was very good for me from all points of view. I read and write something every day. So long as it doesn't rain, I take a walk in the nearby woods or go to the riverbed. Since coming to this mountain I've spent a lot of time looking at the little birds, the insects, the trees, the water, the rocks. As I observe closely all these things by myself, I find that they give rise to all kinds of feelings and thoughts that I never had before. That a world which had never existed for me before has opened itself up to me has given me a sense of joy. I don't know that I ever expressed them to you, but all those vain, persistent thoughts which cluttered my mind for years have at last begun to leave me, easily and pleasantly. When I was in Onomichi alone, I was ceaselessly tormented by these thoughts. But it's very different now. If my present condition were to become a true part of me, I would be confident that I would never be a threat to others or to myself. I have learned to take pleasure in that feeling that comes from humility. (By this I do not mean humility toward persons.) When I think about it, I realize that this happiness was what I desired, perhaps unconsciously, at the very start of the journey, and that it is not something that has come to me unexpectedly or whimsically. I am very happy that it has come to me sooner and more naturally than I would have hoped. The way I behaved toward you was inexcusable, but given what I was, I could not have behaved any better. But no amount of remorse now would help either you or me. What I want for us both is simply to find security in each other from now on. And please don't feel apprehensive any more about us. As I sit here alone in the mountains and think of home, I find that what I want to do more than anything else is to tell you not to worry. I suppose there will always be times when I'll get angry and make you unhappy, but please believe me when I say that there will be no ulterior reason for my outbursts. I like to think that I'm ready to come home, but I want to be absolutely sure that once home I'm not going to end up exactly as I was before. I want to remain here a while longer—not very long—and know that this state of mind I now enjoy has become a firm part of me before I come back to you. I want you to have no doubts about us at all, no doubts of any kind. I know that all the things that happened between us were utterly stupid. I have suffered from a certain sickness, you might say: and the sickness has to be allowed to run its course. As a matter of fact, I really believe that it has left me; so there's nothing that you need worry about.

"I sometimes think of our baby. Please be very, very careful that she doesn't catch anything. In this temple there's a baby, half a year younger than ours. They're remarkably casual in the way they take care of him. There is no doctor or pharmacist in these parts, and though it's not my business, I worry about him occasionally.

"The rice they feed me here is incredibly bad, unfit for human consumption. It's not the cooking that's at fault, but the quality of the rice itself. It's a totally new experience for me.

"If there are any letters for me, please forward them. Has Nobuyuki written? Tell Oei that this has been a very different kind of trip from the one I took to Onomichi, and that she has no need to worry. Take good care of your health. I myself am quite healthy, but because the food is so bad, I tend to eat less than I need, and I think I've lost some weight as a result. Don't send me any provisions, however."

He leaned on his desk, and gazed out of the wide-open bay window. Facing him, about twenty feet away, was a low, whitewashed mud wall. Then down the hill from it was an old stone wall covered with lichen, and beside it the path. Twenty feet down the path stood another temple, Kongōin. The mist of the morning had not yet cleared, and the large thatched roof of the temple, level with his eyes, was a mass of grey.

He felt he ought to write more; or rather, he feared that Naoko, on reading this unexpected piece of communication from him, would not quite know what to think of it. Would she not suspect that he had written it on an impulse, when perhaps he was feeling desperately lonely?

From his Western-style notebook he tore off a few pages, and writing on the margin of the first of these the note, "Here's an example of the kind of thing I write sometimes," enclosed them in the envelope with his letter. These pages contained a detailed description of a scene he had witnessed a couple of days before—a spider on the bay window trying to keep a small beetle that had got caught in the web. After a struggle the beetle had got away. It was his thought that this little exercise of his would give Naoko a glimpse of at least a fragment of his life in the mountains.

His supply of cigarettes had run out, so he decided he would go out immediately and walk to the inn beside the gateway of the shrine, on the other side of the valley. There he could also mail his letter. Having been sold too many cigarettes dampened by the mountain mist, he insisted this time at the inn that a new carton be opened. He took a pack, smoked one cigarette from it, and satisfied that it was dry enough, bought several more packs out of the carton. As he walked back to the temple, he found himself in a generally lighthearted mood. He tossed his packs of cigarettes into his room through the open bay window, then continued his walk up the path. A cedar stood just ahead of him. Its leaves, made heavy by the moisture, hung down in numerous large clusters. He walked to it and stood under it. The sun, filtering through the leaves above, made brilliant, differently shaped patches of light on the wet grass by his feet. The air around him smelled pleasantly of the mountain.

Beside the path a little way ahead stood a stone washbasin, filled with water drawn from a mountain spring. Near this was a clearing, and here Kensaku found Také busily working. The clearing was surrounded by large oak trees with widespread branches, and the sunlight that came through the leaves was gentle and beautiful. Také was cutting shingles out of a felled oak tree; those that were finished were piled up high beside him. He gave a quick bow when he saw Kensaku. "Do you need that many?" asked Kensaku.

"Certainly. I shall need three times this."

"It's a big job you've agreed to do. You've got to make all the shingles yourself before you can even begin on the roof." Kensaku sat down on a tree trunk that lay near him. "It's a pity to cut down so many of these lovely trees. I suppose some more of these around here will have to go?"

"Well, I try my best to get my wood from places where people don't go much."

"Maybe, but there aren't that many trees on this mountain to begin with. It is a pity."

"Don't worry, it's only a small roof that I'm doing after all."

The tool Také was using looked like the middle part of the blade of a samurai sword with a wooden handle put on each end. It was a tool Kensaku had seen coopers often use. Také put it down on the ground beside him, then produced from one of the pockets of his ancient, khaki-colored riding breeches a pack of cigarettes. Kensaku waited until he had lit his cigarette before asking, "Do you really cut down these huge trees yourself?"

"Oh, no. Only an experienced tree cutter could do that. He cuts them down, then brings them here."

"Yes, I'd have thought so."

"By the way, when are we going to the top of the mountain?"

"Whenever it's convenient for you," Kensaku answered. "Anytime is all right with me."

"Well, I've been asked to act as guide tomorrow night for a small group of high school students. There are four or five of them, I think. Would you like to come?"

"Yes, that would be fine."

"It might be fun going with young, carefree students, don't you think?"

"Yes, I agree."

The edge of the stone washbasin was covered with moss that had formed from the constant wetting. And along this edge were strange creatures crawling about. They were smaller than those caterpillars one saw on cherry trees, and from under their sparse hair the black skin showed through. There were thousands of them, perhaps tens of thousands, moving about in a pulsating mass. It was a terrible sight to behold. Some members of the insect world were indeed disillusioning, Kensaku thought. "Are these some kind of caterpillar?" he asked.

"There weren't any yesterday, but they appeared all of a sudden today."

"They seem somewhat unusual. Do they belong to the caterpillar family?"

"We'll leave the temple at midnight, climb at a leisurely pace, and we should be able to reach the peak in time to pay our respects to the rising sun. It would be helpful if the moon stayed out, but lately it's been disappearing rather early."

"Is that so? I suppose we'll use lanterns if there's no moon."

"If the sky is clear, the stars will give us enough light since there won't be any trees most of the way. Of course we'll take lanterns with us."

"I'm sure I'll get tired if I don't have an afternoon nap, but the trouble is, I can't sleep during the day."

"Go to bed early, then. I'll come and wake you up when we're ready to go."

"But I can't go to sleep in the early evening. I never could."

"That's very unfortunate," Také said, and began to laugh.

Také dropped the cigarette end on the ground, stepped on it, then went back to work. Kensaku walked around to Amida's Chapel as usual, and from there returned to his apartment.

His letter to Naoko, he thought, would reach her the day after next at the earliest; and if the mailman who came to collect the mail only on alternate days were not coming that day, it would take yet another day to reach her. He sat down before his desk, and opening *Lives of Eminent Priests,* began reading Gansan's life from where he had left it. He was interested to learn why so many country houses had pictures of Gansan, looking extremely fierce, stuck above their doors. He learned also that Gansan was one of the two priests commemorated at the Two Priests' Chapel in Ueno.

He heard an unfamiliar voice calling from the entrance. Thinking that the visitor had mistaken the annex for the rectory—why would anyone be calling on him?—Kensaku remained at his desk. But when the visitor announced himself again, he got up and went out to the front hall. A priest was standing by the door. He looked to be about forty; his manner, Kensaku thought, exuded a curious mixture of exaggerated courtesy and expectant intimacy. "Might I come in for a minute?" he said. Kensaku, though certain that his visitor was under some misapprehension, invited him in and showed him into the small room between the living room and the front hall. The visitor looked about him uneasily and inquisitively as he walked through the front hall and into the small room; and when he saw the pile of books in the alcove he said, "Are you engaged in some kind of research?"

"No," answered Kensaku, determined not to invite any further familiarity from this vulgar person. He was sure that if the visitor had indeed come to the right place, his errand was bound to be of a questionable nature.

"Let me state my business right away. I am the rector of a temple called Manshōji. It's in Akazaki, at the foot of this mountain. Anyway, starting tomorrow, there's going to be a ten-day course on Zen at Kongōin Temple, and I thought that if you had any interest in Zen, I might persuade you to attend."

"Are you giving the lectures?"

"Oh, no, I'm involved only because the teachers at the local primary school asked me to organize such a program. No, the lecturer is someone who studied under the master Gazan of Tenryūji. I myself don't belong to the Zen sect."

Kensaku had heard about Gazan from Nobuyuki. Perhaps, he thought, if this lecturer were a bona fide disciple of the master, he might be worth listening to. "What text will he be discoursing on?" he asked.

"I believe it will be *Sayings of Lin-chi.*"

"I happen to have that with me," Kensaku said. Then seeing the surprised look on the priest's face, he quickly added, "I have a brother who goes to a temple in Kamakura, and he gave it to me."

"In which case you, too, must know quite a lot about Zen."

"No, I don't. I don't know a thing about it."

"I can hardly believe that. At any rate, if you've been reading *Lin-chi*, then surely you would like to come."

"Will there be a catechism?"

"Yes, indeed."

Kensaku thought he remembered Nobuyuki telling him that a catechism in Zen was pointless unless the teacher really knew what he was doing. After a short silence he said, "I'll think about it and let you know later." But as he looked at the priest and imagined himself having to associate with him for ten days, what little interest he had had in the lectures quickly evaporated.

"Please don't be so formal," said the priest. "Do say you'll come. It'll be only for ten days. There'll be no one who knows much about it, they're all beginners, and all we ask is that you have some vague idea of what Zen is about. Please think of it as something not at all serious, and do come, please. I can't help feeling that your having a copy of *Sayings of Lin-chi* is some kind of happy omen."

"I'll let you know later."

"Please, do say yes."

Kensaku did not deign to reply. The priest seemed for a moment to lose his composure, then suddenly put on a solemn expression and said, "I have a favor to ask of you, as a matter of fact."

Kongōin, the temple below, had no annex, he said; which meant that only a screen door separated the master and the students, and when he gave the catechism to each student individually, the others would overhear him. If Kensaku would consent to become one of the students and lodge with the rest, the master could then use Kensaku's place for his catechisms. How convenient it would be if Kensaku could grant this favor. How fortunate that he should be a connoisseur and know what a catechism in Zen was like; otherwise it would have been much more awkward to make such a request.

Kensaku lost his temper completely. He might not have been quite so angry if he had not been gulled into taking the priest's invitation to the lectures so seriously. "If you had asked me that in the first place," he said hotly, "I would have given some thought to your request. But you tried to flatter me first. You tried to manipulate me, didn't you?" He continued to berate the priest thus for some time.

"You do me an injustice," said the priest. "I did not come with that intention. I simply wanted to recruit as many people as possible for the course, people who might be interested in learning about Zen. It was only after I came here and saw how convenient this annex would be for the teacher that I decided I would ask you if you would let us use it. I knew it was forward of me to ask, but I thought I should anyway. I did not come here with the express purpose of making such a request. Please understand that. I do not relish being thought of as some kind of cheat."

Kensaku was no longer able to contain himself. "You're a liar!" he shouted.

The priest turned pale. There was more vehemence in his tone as he said, "Why do you say that?"

"You might at least try being a little less transparent!"

In silence the two glared at each other. Then to Kensaku's amazement the priest spread out the sleeves of his robe and prostrated himself. Looking down at this spiderlike figure stretched out on the floor, Kensaku was hardly able to suppress a giggle. "I beg your forgiveness," said the priest, successfully throwing Kensaku into a state of utter confusion.

In the end Kensaku agreed that he would vacate his quarters if another place, equally quiet, were found for him. After all, he said, it was not essential that he should remain at this temple. The priest said that he was most grateful, and departed. And so Kensaku's mood of contentment of that afternoon was broken by this idiotic incident. But he was determined not to brood about it.

17

That evening Oyoshi had something extremely unpleasant to tell Kensaku. Také's wife and a lover had been badly wounded by another of her lovers, and she was in a critical condition. Také was at this moment rushing down the mountain to get to her. "I feel so sorry for him," Oyoshi said. "She's such a dreadful woman, yet he doesn't hate her at all. He cried when he heard the news, apparently, and kept on saying he knew something like this was bound to happen."

"It's not a nice story, is it?"

"The one that stabbed her is someone who knew her before Také's time, and the one that got stabbed with her is an old friend of Také's. He came up here with him once, I'm told."

"This wife of his, is she likely to recover?"

"Someone was saying that she probably would be dead by the time Také got there."

"What good would she be to anybody if she did recover?" said Kensaku disgustedly.

"But that's not the way Také feels."

What a strange way to be, Kensaku thought; but perhaps it was because Také was so strange that he wasn't himself dragged into the whirlpool. "I saw him this afternoon, you know. He promised to take me up the mountain tomorrow night."

"So mother told me. But they've already found someone else to be your guide."

What an irony, what a disillusionment, Kensaku thought, to come all the way to this supposedly sacred place and be told such a story. But how fortunate that Také should have been in the mountain when the ugly incident took place, and that he himself should have escaped injury. That morning, when Oyoshi told him Také's story, he had wondered whether Také was not a little perverted; but now, he wondered whether Také's forbearance did not simply come from his total understanding of what his wife was. Perhaps through knowing completely his wife's nature and all of the bad traits she had always exhibited, he had been able to ignore his own feelings and forgive her. In all likelihood the bloody incident was taking place below just as Také and he were having that pleasant conversation. Despite all his detachment, Také must now be a defeated man. If it was true that he felt no hatred toward his wife, then he probably was grieving terribly.

What his mother and Naoko had done was more a mistake made in helplessness than an act of infidelity. Yet how much of a curse on others it had been allowed to become, how much of his own life had been haunted by it. Of course Také must have suffered, he must be suffering now. Yet he had somehow managed to rise above his misfortune. Perhaps if one couldn't be like Také, then one was destined to take part in some such desperate play as was enacted that day in the village below. What might have happened to himself, Kensaku wondered, what kind of a person might he have been, if he had not had his work to turn to, if he had not had the sense of his own identity? "What a frightening business," he said aloud.

"Isn't it?" said Oyoshi, unaware of Kensaku's meaning. "But I simply can't understand his wife. Why does she behave like that?"

"Také himself is a mystery too, don't you think? Don't you find it odd that he can't hate her?"

The next day was a clear, sunny day, just right for hiking. But the depression of the day before had not yet left Kensaku entirely, and the prospect of going out on a hike with a group of strangers held little attraction for him. He decided he would not go that night.

That afternoon he went to Amida's Chapel, and sat on the steps for about an hour. When as a child he missed his mother, he would often go alone to her grave. These visits to Amida's Chapel somehow offered him the same kind of solace. Hardly anyone ever came there, and in the place of people there were always numerous little birds, dragonflies, bees, ants, and lizards to occupy his attention. Sometimes he could hear turtledoves cooing on trees nearby.

On his way back he stopped at a deserted temple named Fujimon' in. The great thatched roof high above was almost buried by the even taller cedars surrounding it. It must have been deserted for some time, for here and there boards had been pulled off the closed storm doors. Keeping his clogs on, he went inside. Facing him was a large altar, without the customary statue or accouterments. On either side of the altar was something that looked like a doorless cupboard, about six feet wide; and on the shelves were dozens of dust-covered memorial tablets, some still standing and some fallen on their sides. They were large, impressive tablets of black lacquer with gold lettering, capped with what looked very much like the curved gables of Momoyama-period buildings. They were presumably memorials to all the past rectors and great patrons, and it was not pleasant to see them in such disarray. Either squirrels or field mice were responsible, Kensaku decided.

In the long, unfloored section of the dark rectory was the scullery, and here Kensaku found a huge tub, about the size of one floor mat, for storing water. It was partly inside the house and partly outside. Water from a spring flowed steadily into it through a pipe, and was spilling over the sides. The bottom of the tub was covered with mountain sand carried there by the water. The summer sun, which not even the cedars could hide, shot shimmering, green shafts of light through the water onto the sandy bottom. In this temple, where everything else seemed dead and forgotten, here was one place graced with beauty and life. He went to the other side of the rectory to look at the study bay. It was in a state of utter neglect, its surroundings far wilder than he had expected. Although he had known that it was a lonely place in the middle of the woods, that there was not a soul living within a half mile of it, he had come there thinking that if it looked habitable enough, he might move in. But clearly it was not fit for habitation.

Oyoshi, with the baby in her arms, was standing on top of the stone steps when he returned. "Did that person come again while I was out?" asked Kensaku. He was referring to the priest.

"No, he didn't." Her tone suggested she didn't care much for the priest. "He knows very well you won't find a place as convenient as this."

"Well, it's just as well he didn't come again. I went to have a look at Fujimon'in, but it's a real wilderness out there."

Oyoshi shook her head and said, "You couldn't possibly think of living there—absolutely not."

The baby was avidly sucking his fist. It was a peculiarly shaped fist, Kensaku thought, remarkably straight along the top. As Kensaku approached them the baby pulled it away from his mouth and stuck it out toward him. It was very wet. Making loud gurgling sounds and squirming excitedly in his mother's arms, he leaned precariously forward, as though he wanted Kensaku to hold him. Kensaku laughed and said as he walked away, "He had a taste of my condensed milk the other day, and he wants more. No, you can't have any."

18

Two or three days passed, and still there was no news of Také. The priest did not appear again either. Once Kensaku heard the Zen cry of admonition, "*Katsu!*", coming from the temple below. The teacher was presumably discussing its significance. Kensaku had thought that he might go and listen to him discourse on *Lin-chi*, but since the priest made no attempt to contact him again, he decided not to bother.

The weather stayed good, and he continued to take his solitary walks in the woods. He missed Také rather. They were not particularly close, but it used to be pleasant to stop and have a chat with him. His going seemed to have left a gap in Kensaku's daily life. The pile of shingles lay in the clearing; those unpleasant caterpillarlike creatures had disappeared from the stone basin, and in their place a wagtail was hopping about on it.

Kensaku was not exactly postponing his hike to the top of the mountain until Také got back, but it was true that Také's going had dampened his enthusiasm for it; and if he had not been afraid that the fine weather might suddenly break and be followed by days of rain, he might have put it off indefinitely.

Deciding, then, that he should not tarry any longer, he went to the priest's wife one afternoon and asked her to find a guide for him. "I don't care if no one comes with me," he said. "If possible, I should like to go tomorrow night."

"All right. It does seem a little extravagant to hire a guide just for one person, but I agree, it would be a pity if the weather were suddenly to get bad. Let me find out if there's anyone available for tomorrow night, then. You never know, you may find that there will be others to keep you company."

"Thank you very much."

Just then the young mailman, wearing gaiters and straw sandals, came into the unfloored entryway of the rectory where the two were standing. Wiping the sweat off his brow he walked over to the edge of the front hall and sat down heavily. He brought out a bundle of mail tied together with string, leafed through it and pulled out a couple of letters. "There," he said, and put them down beside him.

"Thank you," said the priest's wife. "It must be hard to have to walk so much on a hot day like this. Would you like some tea, or would you prefer water?"

"Water, please."

"Shall I put some sugar in it?"

"That would be very good."

Kensaku had watched the bundle as the mailman leafed through it in the hope that he would catch a glimpse of Naoko's handwriting. But of course there was no reason why she should have been able to write so soon. "Then please find me a guide for tomorrow night," he called out to the priest's wife as she left to go to the kitchen. "Don't worry if I'm the only one."

He was about to withdraw to the annex when the mailman said, "Wait a minute, I just remembered," and began searching through his pockets. "Ah, here it is." He produced a badly crinkled telegram. "You are Mr. Tokitō, aren't you?"

Kensaku stood still, rigid with fright. He felt the blood drain from his face; he could hear his heart thumping. Naoko is dead, he thought, she's committed suicide; they couldn't let me know before because they didn't know where I was.

"From your family, is it?" asked the priest's wife as she returned with a glass of water on a tray. The very casualness of her tone made Kensaku even more frightened.

"Letter received," said the telegram. "Not worried any more. Letter follows. Naoko." He thanked the mailman and walked back to the annex, unaware that as he did so he was folding the telegram over and over into a tiny square.

His own shock when he saw the telegram in the mailman's hand now amused him. There were several reasons why he had reacted that way: one, of course, was that he had not expected it at all; another was that in these last few days, he had had several thoughts which he wished very much he had expressed in his letter to Naoko, thoughts which she would have liked to know; and another was that the recent unpleasant incident involving Také's wife had so impressed itself on his mind that on seeing the telegram, he had immediately associated one with the other. But whatever the reason, he had to smile at the idiocy of his reaction. Suddenly cheerful now, he read the telegram again and again, thinking, "Everything is all right."

That night he pushed the bedding under the mosquito net to one side, and lying on the floor beside it, began writing a long overdue letter to Nobuyuki. He tried to describe in detail his present state of mind. But because those thoughts that had for so long dominated his life before were so fanciful, the change that had occurred in his way of thinking since his coming to the mountain, when described exactly as he had experienced it, seemed equally fanciful and vain. He simply didn't know how to write about such matters, he decided; much better, then, to write a simple, reassuring letter to his brother, who presumably would have heard from Oei and Naoko about his departure from Kyoto and who might be worried about him. He folded the five or six pages that he had already written, put these away in his briefcase, and began anew.

The door opened, and the priest's wife looked in. "Are you already asleep?" She then went on to tell him that a guide would be taking a party up to the top the following night, and he could join them. Would he be ready by midnight?

"Thank you very much," Kensaku said. "In that case, I'll stay in bed as late as I can tomorrow morning, so please see to it that no one opens my doors. I'm incapable of taking naps during the day, so the only thing I can do is to try to get extra sleep in the morning."

"I understand." She remained seated by the door. "By the way," she said, lowering her voice, "I'm told Také's wife died."

"Is that so? And what about the man that was with her?"

"He may live, they say."

"What about Také?"

"Well, everybody is very worried that his wife's killer may now be waiting to kill him."

"Kill Také? Why in the world would the man want to kill him? Haven't they caught him yet?"

"No, they haven't. He's hiding somewhere in the mountains."

Kensaku was a little disgusted. "Why do the people in the village imagine that the man would want to hurt Také? He hasn't done anything. It's an idiotic notion."

"But the man is more or less crazy, don't you see? I agree with them —I think Také should be very careful."

"Yes, yes, but I'm sure he'll be all right."

"I suppose so. He's such a harmless soul—but you never know."

Kensaku was close to losing his temper. Také has suffered enough, he wanted to say; what sense was there in anything if someone were allowed to hurt him again?

The next morning he woke up as usual at seven o'clock. It was, after all, unrealistic of him to have thought that he might break his habit and sleep late. And the night before he had not been able to fall asleep easily. It was already late when he had finished his letter to Nobuyuki; then he had had to listen to the distressing story about Také; and in bed he had stayed awake thinking not only about Také but about Naoko too, wondering, among other things, what effect his letter might have had on her. A cock had begun to crow somewhere far away; taken aback, he had consulted his watch and discovered it was already two o'clock.

He had had hardly more than four hours of sleep, therefore. He closed his eyes again, hoping that he might force himself to sleep a little more. But he managed only to doze fitfully, and at ten he resignedly dragged himself out of bed. He felt dull and heavy all over. At this rate, he thought, the hike would prove quite an ordeal. The only consolation was the thought that being so tired, he might not find it so difficult to take an afternoon nap.

19

The hiking party that Kensaku was to join consisted of employees of an Osaka company, who had stopped to see the mountain on their way back from the Grand Shrine of Izumo. Kensaku was not suffering from lack of sleep any more, having succeeded in getting a two-to three-hour nap that afternoon; but the sea bream he had had for lunch must have been bad, for in the early evening he began to suffer from a severe attack of diarrhea. It was debilitating to say the least, and he wondered whether or not he should still go up the mountain that night. A double dose of some herb medicine he had brought with him seemed to have its effect, however, and he resolved to go after all.

At midnight the party left the temple. The guide, an older man of nearly fifty, led the way carrying a lantern. The men from the Osaka company were all young, and, determined to make the most of their one-week holiday, were even more jolly than their age might have warranted. To a man they wore Western-style suits and rubber-soled canvas shoes, souvenir towels around their necks, and carried rough-hewn pilgrim's staffs. "Hey, uncle, take good care of our half-gallon bottle!" shouted one in the rear to the guide in a broad Osaka accent. "Don't forget, we intend to let you have some!"

"You've said that before!" the guide shouted back. "If you're that worried, carry the bottle yourself!"

"Why should I, idiot! You're going to drink it too!"

The cheerfulness of everyone in the party made Kensaku all the more apprehensive about his own physical condition. What added to his burden was his fear of making a fool of himself in front of all these fellows. It was stupid of him, he realized, but he was their age after all, he was the only one from Tokyo, and he could not but feel competitive. "Have you been here long?" asked the man walking beside him. Aware that Kensaku was the only stranger in their midst, he seemed to be trying his best to be friendly.

"I've been here a fortnight," answered Kensaku.

"How can you stand it? We'd go mad after two days here."

The fat man in front of them turned around and laughed loudly. "What do you mean, two days! Who do you think you're fooling? You were homesick on our first night away from Osaka." He then said to Kensaku, "He just got married, you understand, to a most attractive young lady."

"You clown!" Kensaku's companion said, thumping his fat friend's back to cover his confusion.

When they had gone up a thousand yards or so beyond the clearing where Také used to work, there were no trees any more, and the side of the mountain was covered instead with coarse grass. The sky was clear and dotted with numerous stars as though it was already autumn. They came upon a rectangular guidepost, weathered by the elements and standing at a slight angle. Here the real climb was to begin. The party rearranged itself in single file, and chanting the prayer, "Begone all the senses, let the spirits guide us to the clear sky above," began to march manfully up a narrow path that was as bumpy as the bottom of a mountain stream. From either side the tall, coarse grass reached out over the path, almost overwhelming it. There were four men in front of Kensaku, two men behind; he had no choice but to keep pace with them, and soon he began to tire. He had set out intending to reach the top no matter how hard the climb might prove, but he was not sure any more. After an hour they were fairly high up; at least Kensaku thought so, judging from the way the night around him looked and felt. At last the party agreed to stop for a rest.

What reserve of strength Kensaku had had when they began the climb was now completely exhausted. He could not, he was certain, keep up with the rest of the party any farther. "I'm not feeling well," he said to the guide. "I'll go back from here. It'll be light in about two hours, so I'll just sit and rest until then."

"I'm sorry to hear that. Is it something serious?"

Kensaku told the guide that he was just feeling weak from an attack of diarrhea earlier that day, and that he would be perfectly all right by himself.

"But are you sure? I don't like leaving you alone here."

"There's no need for you to worry, really. Do go on without me."

"Are you sure you couldn't manage it?" said the friendly young man. "Look here, uncle, do we still have a long way to go?"

"Farther than we've already come."

"I can go down without much trouble," said Kensaku, "but I really don't think I can go up. Don't worry, I'll be all right here."

There were murmurs of encouragement and sympathy from all, and Kensaku tried to respond to each one with appropriate cheer, tiresome though it was to do so. At last they decided to go without him. Very quietly, presumably out of consideration for him, they disappeared into the dark. Kensaku put on the sweater he had brought with him, tied the cloth wrapper that he had carried the sweater in around his neck, and left the path; then finding a suitable resting place in the grass, he sat down with the mountain at his back. As he sat there, breathing deeply through his nose, his eyes closed, he realized that there was a certain pleasurable quality in his tiredness. He heard twice, or perhaps three times, his erstwhile companions chanting somewhere far above, "Begone all the senses, let the spirits guide us to the clear sky above!" Then there was silence, and he was quite alone under the wide sky. A chilly wind blew, making no sound and barely disturbing the heads of the wild grass around him.

He felt his exhaustion turn into a strange state of rapture. He could feel his mind and his body both gradually merging into this great nature that surrounded him. It was not nature that was visible to the eyes; rather, it was like a limitless body of air that wrapped itself around him, this tiny creature no larger than a poppy seed. To be gently drawn into it, and there be restored, was a pleasure beyond the power of words to describe. The sensation was a little like that of the moment when, tired and without a single worry, one was about to fall into a deep sleep. Indeed, a part of him already was in a state hardly distinguishable from sleep. He had experienced this feeling of being absorbed by nature before; but this was the first time that it was accompanied by such rapture. In previous instances, the feeling perhaps had been more that of being sucked in by nature than that of merging into it; and though there had been some pleasure attached to it, he had at the same time always tried instinctively to resist it, and on finding such resistance difficult, he had felt a distinct uneasiness. But this time, he had not the slightest will to resist; and contentedly, without a trace of the old uneasiness, he accepted nature's embrace.

It was so still a night, even the night birds were silent. If there were lights in the villages below, they were quite hidden by the mist that lay over the rooftops. And all that he could see above him were the stars and the outline of the mountains, curved like the back of some huge beast. He felt as if he had just taken a step on the road to eternity. Death held no threat for him. If this means dying, he thought, I can die without regret. But to him then, this journey to eternity did not seem the same as death.

He must have slept for some time as he sat there, his elbows resting on his knees. When he opened his eyes again, the green around him had begun to show in the light of early dawn. The stars, though fewer now, were still there. The sky was soft blue—the color of kindness, he thought. The mist below had dispersed, and there were lights here and there in the villages at the foot of the mountain. He could see lights in Yonago too, and in Sakaiminato that lay on Yomigahama Point. The big light that went on and off was surely from the lighthouse at Mihonoseki. The bay, as still as a lake, remained in the shadow of the mountain, but the sea outside had already taken on a greyish hue.

All aspects of the scene changed rapidly with dawn's hurried progress. When he turned around, he saw the mountaintop outlined against a swelling mass of orange light that became more and more intense; then the orange began to fade, and suddenly everything around him became clearer. The wild grass grew shorter here than it did down below; and in its midst were large wild asparagus, standing singly and far apart from each other, their flowers dotting the landscape near and far. There were yarrow, burnet, day lilies, and scabious, all blooming among the grass. A little bird flew out, chattering, and like a pebble tossed in the air drew a sharp arc and dropped back into the grass.

As the mountain range jutting into the water on the other side of the bay began to take on color, the outline of the white lighthouse in the straits became more clearly etched. The sun now reached Daikonjima Island, stretched out like a huge stingray across the bay. The lights in the distant villages went out, and from some of the chimneys smoke began to rise. But there was no sign of activity yet in the villages immediately below, which lay still and dark in the shadow of Daisen. Kensaku then saw for the first time the sharply delineated outline of this shadow in the distance as it retreated from the bay and crept toward him over land, allowing the town of Yonago to emerge in the light. It was like a great dragnet being pulled in; or it was like the caressing shadow of a passing cloud. And so Kensaku watched with emotion this rare sight—the shadow of the proud mountain, the greatest in central Japan, etched boldly across the land.

20

It was about ten in the morning when he finally reached the temple. He was so exhausted, he wondered how he had managed not to collapse on the way. Oyoshi was in the front hall with the baby, whom she had let loose to play about on the wooden floor. On seeing Kensaku she was so taken aback by the way he looked that instead of greeting him, she turned around and called out, "Mother! Mother!"

The priest's wife was no less appalled. She immediately put him to bed and took his temperature. It was just over a hundred and two. When she took it again a little while later, it had reached a hundred and four. She put an ice bag on his head, then dispatched a messenger to the village at the foot of the mountain to fetch a doctor; and partly because Kensaku in his delirium had called for Naoko several times, she had the messenger take a telegram with him.

The doctor arrived a little after eight o'clock that night. Until then, Oyoshi and her mother had gone outside a great many times to see if he was coming; and after sunset, when as usual a deathly quiet fell with the darkness, the two women had become very cross, as if this particular night were to blame for the absence of human life outside. They were both kind people; but their agitation was owing also to their fear of having a dead man on their hands. So anxious were they to have the doctor—or, for that matter, a man—to relieve them of at least a part of their burden that when the messenger appeared on the path carrying a lantern and a doctor's bag, followed by the small, aged doctor himself wearing gaiters and straw sandals, their joy was enormous.

Oyoshi rushed to Kensaku's bedside, leaving her mother to receive the doctor; she sat down by his pillow, so close that her face touched the mosquito net, and said excitedly, "The doctor's here! Did you hear me? The doctor's here!" All Kensaku did in reply was to open his eyes a little. But when the doctor came in and began asking him questions about his illness, he was able to answer with surprising clarity, though in a weak voice. Perhaps because the priest's wife was sitting there, the doctor was not as positive as he might have been about the cause, which clearly was the sea bream. It had traveled about fifteen miles in the heat of the summer, having been grilled first; then at the temple it had been grilled again. After giving him a quick general examination, the doctor began gently pressing Kensaku's abdomen. "Does it hurt here?" he would ask as he applied the pressure. "And what about here?" When he had finished with the probing, he gave his diagnosis: it was acute intestinal catarrh, aggravated by Kensaku's stopping the diarrhea with herb medicine. But the fever should go down, he thought, when Kensaku's bowels had been cleared out with castor oil and an enema. The doctor had come prepared with these things, having been told about Kensaku's diarrhea by the messenger.

The enema had little effect. The castor oil, however, should work in two or three hours, the doctor said. He would remain in the annex until then, and examine the feces. The priest's wife, now that she knew the doctor would be there for some time, left for the rectory to prepare some food and drink for him.

The doctor sat down cross-legged in the small room next to where Kensaku lay and took a sip of the tea now gone cold. "What does he do?" he asked Oyoshi.

"He's a literary man."

"I'd say he was from the east, judging by his accent."

"He's from Kyoto."

"From Kyoto? Really?"

Kensaku listened to the conversation, which seemed to him to have nothing to do with himself.

"How is he?" Oyoshi asked, lowering her voice.

"He'll be all right," the doctor answered, also in an undertone.

Half-awake, Kensaku was having a dream. In it his two legs had detached themselves from his torso and were walking about the room, making a terrible nuisance of themselves. Not only were they visually distracting, but the noise they made—thud, thud, thud, thud —as they paced quickly and determinedly around him was excruciatingly loud. He hated them, and tried desperately to will them to go far away. Since it was all a dream—he knew that it was—he thought he could indeed do this. But they would not leave him. By "far away" he meant the mist, the black mist, and it was into this that he tried to drive away the legs. After tremendous effort on his part they would finally retreat toward the mist, becoming smaller and smaller. Behind the black mist was total darkness. If the legs could be driven into this core of darkness, they would then disappear completely. Using his very last reserve of strength he would make one more mighty effort to be rid of them once and for all, but when only one short step away from the darkness they would suddenly fly back into the room, like a rubber string that had been stretched to the limit and then had snapped. And once again the legs would pace around him noisily—thud, thud, thud, thud. No matter how often he tried to drive them away they would invariably return, refusing to give his eyes or his ears any rest.

After that he was mostly unconscious. Surprisingly clear moments would come to him occasionally, but these were only brief intermissions. He no longer suffered. If he felt anything at all, it was that his mind and body were being purged.

The old doctor left early the next morning, and at about noon his assistant, not very young either, arrived, bringing with him a supply of saline injection and the like. By then Kensaku's fever had gone down. But what he evacuated from his bowels was like thin gruel; his hands and feet were extremely cold; and his heart had so weakened that his pulse was hardly detectable. It was as severe as a case of intestinal catarrh in an adult could be, the doctor said; and he began to wonder if Kensaku did not have cholera. First he gave Kensaku an injection of digitalis, then proceeded to give him a saline injection. The solution was pumped into him through a thick needle stuck deep into the thigh. The flesh around the needle began to swell abominably; and the pain was such that it brought tears to Kensaku's eyes.

Not long after this, Naoko arrived. But the priest's wife, aware of Kensaku's anxiety to see her, refused to let her go near him, fearful lest his sudden relief on seeing her should have an adverse effect on his precariously weakened condition. The doctor agreed with her. Kensaku's pulse would become more steady when his body had had time to absorb the saline solution, he said; so would Naoko wait until then? Naoko was appalled. She had come imagining all kinds of unhappy possibilities; but at the same time she had hoped that his illness would prove to be not so serious after all, and had even pictured to herself Kensaku smiling and saying to her as she arrived, "The telegram scared you, didn't it?" That he could be so ill, she had not imagined even in her most pessimistic moments.

She was easily enough persuaded to postpone her meeting with Kensaku; for she was very afraid that she herself was in no fit state to see him. The sheer physical strain of walking eight miles up the hills under the hot summer sun, and now the shock on hearing the news about her husband, had left her with little confidence in her own capacity to withstand the ordeal of seeing him in his present condition. Supposing he had changed drastically in appearance, and she were to break down as soon as she saw him?

She was herself a very sorry sight. Her face was pale and drawn from lack of sleep, and covered with a mixture of soot from the night train and sweat. The priest's wife, making sure that her voice did not carry to the next room, pressed Naoko to have a bath, but she would not get up.

"Do have a bath and change into more comfortable clothes," the priest's wife said again.

"I'll just wash my face, then. Thank you anyway."

In the bathroom Naoko washed quickly, then in front of the small mirror combed the loose hair back into the bun. Just as she was about to step out of the bathroom she saw the doctor and the priest's wife sitting on opposite sides of the fireplace in the rectory, talking in an undertone. They stopped abruptly when they heard her coming out.

"Will you please come here for a minute?" said the doctor. Frightened, Naoko went into the room and sat down. "His pulse is much better now," the doctor said. "He's asleep, but I suggest you see him when he wakes up. You must try not to excite him, of course."

"Is his condition very serious?"

"I can't say with any certainty. It is without doubt intestinal catarrh. With children and adults in poor health, it could be very serious, but normally it's not such a frightening thing to get. I don't think you have much reason to worry. I was talking to madame here about this, but there's a good man I know—he's the head doctor of a hospital in Yonago—and I was wondering if you would like him to come and have a look at your husband."

"Yes, please," Naoko said quickly. "Please ask him as soon as possible. My husband has an elder brother living in Kamakura, and he's got to be told if it's really serious."

"Oh, no, I don't think your husband's condition has reached that point. Let's send for the doctor right away, then, either by telephone or by telegram. Of course, he couldn't possibly get here today, but he should be here by tomorrow afternoon."

"And could you arrange to have a nurse come too?"

Oyoshi came in. She looked around at all three and said in a surprised tone, "He knows, he knows madame's here."

"Really?" said the doctor, cocking his head somewhat ostentatiously to show disbelief. "He's dreaming, I'm sure."

"Not at all. He even knows that mother kept madame from seeing him."

Naoko, already half-standing, looked at the doctor expectantly. He responded by asking Oyoshi, "And does he want madame to go to him?"

"Yes, sir, he does."

The doctor picked up a piece of charcoal with the tongs to light a cigarette. He inhaled deeply once, then said, "All right, but please don't excite him by crying or anything like that." Naoko gave a little bow, then went away toward the annex with Oyoshi.

"What do you think?" the priest's wife asked the doctor when they had gone, her brow creased in consternation. It was a question she must already have asked him several times.

"Well, I don't know what my senior said, but I certainly can't give a definite answer. For a while I thought it might be cholera, but I don't think so any more. I'm inclined to think that if we keep his belly and bottom warm, and give him digitalis, he'll be all right so long as no complications develop."

"My husband isn't here, as you know, and I'd hate to have anything awkward happen during his absence."

"Well, his wife is here now, so surely you don't have to feel too apprehensive."

"True enough, but he does look very bad."

"His heart is terribly weak, I admit, and to be honest, I don't know what his chances are."

"Yes, he does look bad," she said, and gave a deep, theatrical sigh. The doctor smoked his cigarette in silence.

Naoko went into Kensaku's room trying desperately to hide the fear that she felt, but it showed in her wide-open eyes and in her tensely controlled face. Kensaku lay still on his back, only his eyes following Naoko as she came in. She looked at his ashen face, his sunken eyes and cheeks, at his body that seemed so small under the cover, and felt a deep pain in her breast. Silently she sat down beside his pillow and bowed. In a hoarse, almost inaudible voice he said, "Did you come alone?" Naoko nodded. He said again, "Did you not bring our baby?"

"I left her at home."

With effort he proffered his open hand, placing it in her lap. She held it tight with both hers. It was strangely cold and dry.

Without saying anything Kensaku looked at her. His gaze was like a caress. She thought she had never seen such gentleness, such love, in anyone's eyes before. She was about to say, "Everything is all right now," but she refrained, for in the presence of such contentment and quiet, the words seemed hollow.

"I gather your letter arrived yesterday," he said, "but I had a fever, and they wouldn't show it to me."

Afraid that she would cry if she tried to say anything, she merely nodded. Kensaku continued to gaze at her.

After a while he said, "You know, I feel very good right now."

Naoko at that moment lost control and said violently, "I don't want you to say that." Then more softly she added, "The doctor says there's nothing to worry about."

Kensaku seemed too tired to say any more. His hand still in hers, he closed his eyes. She had never seen him look so tranquil. Perhaps, she thought, he is not going to live through this. But the thought somehow did not sadden her very much. As she sat there looking at him, she felt herself becoming an inseparable part of him; and she kept on thinking, "Whether he lives or not, I shall never leave him, I shall go wherever he goes."

NEIGHBORHOOD TOKYO
Theodore C. Bestor

A glimpse into the everyday lives, commerce, and relationships of some two thousand neighborhood residents living in the heart of Tokyo.

THE BOOK OF TEA
Kazuko Okakura
Foreword and Afterword by Soshitsu Sen XV

A new presentation of the seminal text on the meaning and practice of tea—illustrated with eight historic photographs.

GEISHA, GANGSTER, NEIGHBOR, NUN
Scenes from Japanese Lives
Donald Richie

A collection of highly personal portraits of Japanese men and women—some famous, some obscure—from Mishima and Kawabata to a sushi apprentice and a bar madame.

WOMANSWORD
What Japanese Words Say About Women
Kittredge Cherry

From "cockroach husband" to "daughter-in-a-box"—a mix of provocative and entertaining Japanese words that collectively tell the story of Japanese women.

THE THIRD CENTURY
America's Resurgence in the Asian Era
Joel Kotkin and Yoriko Kishimoto
"Truly powerful public ideas."—*Boston Globe*
Available only in Japan.

THE ANATOMY OF DEPENDENCE
The Key Analysis of Japanese Behavior
Takeo Doi / Translated by John Bester
"Offers profound insights."—*Ezra Vogel*